ROAD TO RIBBLEHEAD

PART ONE

CHAPTER ONE

Beth squatted down and let her pee mix into the muddy water of the puddle beneath her. The rest of the family waited as the fine drizzle continued and the clouds came even lower. It was like cold steam smearing over the five year old's face and hands as hunger tightened her ribs.

'Hurry up' said Maggie her mother.

It was always the same, trying to hurry but getting nowhere.

The young girl pulled up her filthy underwear and rearranged her rough skirt and coat. Beth wanted to cry but knew it would make no difference.

'I'm coming.'

A gorse bush emerged from behind a grey stone wall like rigid hair, spikes sticking into the mist. It was another ghost. There were too many. Beth waited, listening, scared of the wet silence.

Her father was looking along what could be seen of the rutted road. His headache from lack of food and anxiety was becoming uncontrollable.

Clare licked her lips tasting more Yorkshire rain. Her feet were bleeding but at least the blood kept her toes warmer than usual. She had hummed every tune she knew over and over again along the way and now her throat and stomach were sore. Arms felt heavy. Legs were numb, wet hair plastered over her white face. At the moment she hated her sister. Things changed in moments. Moods shifted all over the place, but Beth was playing for sympathy and it irritated her.

'We're still on the road,' Ethan remarked as they started walking again. Stupidly Beth reached out for her sister's hand but it was pulled sharply away.

'Where?' she muttered, 'Where are we?'

'Where we were before,' Clare answered spitefully.

She did not want to think of all the days and nights trudging from one miserable place to another. It had been walking and walking, sleeping under hedgerows or in some farmer's barn. It had seemed ages since they had eaten anything. People had stared as the Granger family had hobbled by. Ethan would not have them begging.

'Never. Not my children.'

Pride was making them suffer and Maggie knew it. She wondered whether this was the plan that would at last destroy them. He led and they followed but not without argument, defiance, not without blazing rows, accusing him of sacrificing his own children for the sake of his stupid pride. He could not be wrong. It would be the end of them if he had made a mistake this time.

'Can't anymore, can't.'

'Beth, come on!'

'I can't....I'm.....I'm too tired. I can't.'

'You can!' bellowed Clare with her last residue of effort as her sister suddenly was wrapped in thick, swirling mist and disappeared from view.

'This is the road,' Ethan repeated.

Maggie had been terrified the whole journey that the family would become ill. They could not afford doctors or even wise old women who expected half a crown before they would give the benefit of their wisdom. There was no money. Illness would finish it for all of them. Nightly prayers were for the Lord to keep her girls safe.

'Can't be far. Can't be.'

Ethan's voice was an attempt to sound easy on the ear so as not to expose his worry.

'Beth!'

'Beth!' Maggie repeated Clare's call.

Suddenly she was there as the mist momentarily shifted away.

'No!'

'What do you mean, no?'

'I'm fed up,' announced Beth as she stopped and threw down her knapsack.

Maggie caught up with Ethan saying, 'They've had enough.'

He turned his head but kept on walking.

'I said they've had enough.'

'So what do we do then?' he asked harshly.

'Stop! Ethan, stop!'

Angrily he spun round, 'So we just stop, give up? Is that what we do? Here on this God forsaken road! It's not far I tell you.'

'It doesn't matter where it is,' she said back.

He came to a halt, tossed his bag off his shoulder and looked at her.

'It's alright you two,' Clare tried before turning on her sister, 'Look what you've done.'

Beth's bottom lip stuck out, 'Not my fault.'

'Never is.'

'I'm hungry is what I am.'

'You silly sod,' muttered Clare.

'And you.'

They stopped then to listen to the adults, Clare bending to tie up the laces of what was left of her boots.

'We can't bloody go back now.'

'There's no need for such language.'

'Course there bloody is when we're so close. They said seven miles; well we must have done at least three or four by now.'

Again shifts of the mist passed between them, wet and clinging to their skin.

'They said we'd pass a pub.'

'The Hill Inn.'

'Well we haven't.'

'Might have done. How do we know when it's as thick as this? We can't see owt.'

Maggie felt the whole journey had been a disaster. One poster in a shop window advertising jobs up north had been the start of it. The day Ethan had seen it he was ready for packing up and leaving straightaway. So they had followed never realising how far he would take them. A few times they had managed to get a lift on a friendly farmer's cart, one full of offal that had made them feel sick and stink even worse. The rest of it had been a daily slog, through strange towns and villages, rain, hail and now thick cloud. They were suffering too much. She knew the girls were at the end of their tether. All that followed would be sheer cruelty.

Ethan had gone into a moody silence, looking at his wife and then his daughters as they stood close together. He was a stranger to them now, even an enemy. He hated the responsibility and yet knew the decision he had made had to be carried through.

He was tall with a lean figure and in his early thirties, strong looking with a grim expression on his dark, weathered face. He had been educated to the age of thirteen, had married at twenty and had never done any work other than that which required raw muscle. It was all he was used to, the digging and carrying, the hammering and drilling. All he ever used his brain for was to force himself through each mindless day. Hopelessly he rebelled against a life that had conditioned him to be nothing but a labourer.

He looked around only to see momentary movements in the mist exposing a stone wall across the mudded road and part of a hillside before the cloud heaved over and everything was gone.

'We'll rest up,' he finally announced.

'And then what?'

He made no reply as he squatted down and waited.

'I'm knackered Mam,' said Clare as she held onto her mother's sleeve.

Maggie had her arm round Beth who seemed ready to fall. They were soaked through, moisture soaking their young faces, cheek bones jutting out, eyes bigger than usual, signs of their daily starvation that was grinding them all down. Time was in suspension. Time had meant movement but that had ceased. They could go no further. Maggie had decided. He would have to go on by himself and find some way of coming back and collecting them.

They all shifted slightly at the sound of cart wheels and horse hooves emerging from the bleak silence.

Ethan stood up unsure of which direction the cart was coming from.

Maggie put her hand first on Beth's forehead and then Clare's to feel for any fever. Worryingly their skin was cold and damp. Before they had time to shift off the road two horses pushed suddenly through the mist as their driver shouted at them, standing up on his cart to pull on the reins.

'Hells bells! Wo there! Wo!' the driver called, dragging back the reins as hard as he could until the horses finally came to a jerking halt, 'I could have run the lot of yer over!' he shouted at them.

Ethan looked up feeling embarrassed. The driver seated so far above them put him on edge.

'Have we passed the Hill Inn?' Maggie asked.

The driver was dressed in a black cape and tight fitting gabardine hat. He looked at her critically.

'Is that you speaking missus?'

'Yes, I asked a question,' said Maggie, not to be beaten.

'And is this yer man like?'

Ethan's anger increased but still he made no response.

Maggie hated it when her husband remained silent like this.

The two girls stared up at the driver, his coat gleaming with the moisture from the mist gradually shifting back up the hillside.

'Depends which way yer were coming from,' the driver finally answered.

'Going to Ribblehead,' Ethan eventually replied.

'Oh, up to there is it? I could have given yer a lift if I was going that way. No luck for yer.'

'It doesn't matter, we'll manage,' said Maggie strongly, defying the tone of this man.

'You sound funny mister,' Clare said.

'Hssh you,' her mother chided.

Beth's attention was held by the huge horses and the noise of their breath coming from their nostrils like a new wind.

Nothing was said. The horses shifted nervously, their driver sitting back down.

Ethan despised the man. There was no warmth in his voice. It sounded derisive.

Maggie wanted him to speak up, to ask the driver how far it was to go.

'I don't envy yer like.'

Ethan muttered, 'We don't really mind what you think.'

'No need to tek it like that.'

'Like what?'

'Miserable like.'

'Miserable day,' Ethan said.

'That it is.'

'Affects folks' moods.'

'Can do.'

'But not you.'

'I tek it as it comes,' answered the driver, flicking the reins to have them tight, 'All as I'm saying is that it ain't a picnic up at them works. Just saying it as I see it. Hell I'm up there twice or thrice a day. And I can't complain. Two more years they reckon before the line reaches Ribblehead and that is a lot of business. Carry owt and nowt up to there, wood, iron, coal, this and that, even had me horses part o the lot that pulled up the first steam engine. Forty horses pulling that day. Nobody had ever seen the like. So,' he added, 'they're still wanting more, like yersell, yes like you.'

'Like what?'

'You'll be looking for work then are yer? Is that what yer doing and the Missus to be drudging after those you'll be sharing wi?'

'Might be.'

'Suit yersell.'

'That's what I'll do.'

'How far?' Maggie asked as the girls held tight hold of her.

'Not more than three miles from here Missus.'

'And where is here? Where are we?'

'This here valley is the emptiest of the Dales. Three farms, a few sheep and that's yer lot, that is until some bloody bright spark minded to build a railway line right across it. Bloody madness if yer ask me.'

Nobody made any response to this.

'Anyroads I better be going. Got to collect a load of wood from the station before night fall. I might pass yer on the way back.'

'What are your horses called mister?' Clare wanted to know.

'First you tell us what you'd call em.'

The girl froze with this unexpected request.

'Don't know,' she mumbled.

'What about Carrot and Big Tom? How does them names sound?'

'Is Carrot this one?' Clare asked as she pointed to the nearest horse.

'There you are yer see. You did know all along. Right, I'm off. Hope yer get there alright.'

'And we hope it's better than you've made it out to be,' Ethan had to respond.

'You'll find out soon enough. Get on yer!' the driver called.

The Grangers stood to the side of the road to let the horses and cart past, watching them disappear into the mist.

'Stupid sod of a man,' Ethan muttered angrily.

'Three miles he said,' Maggie responded to her husband's dismal anger.

'Can we get a horse?' asked Beth as she let go of her mother's arm and took up her knapsack.

There was no answer to this as the rest of them picked up their bags and started along the roadway that was covered in mud and loose stones.

'You weren't exactly polite to the man.'

The two girls were already a few yards behind arguing about what their horse would be called if they ever got one.

'He was full of it, sounding off.'

'This is his route, it's his job.'

'So what?'

'So he knew more than we did, that's all.'

'And we're ashamed of that I suppose.'

'I thought you'd be relieved.'

'Why?'

'Because we're almost there.'

'I'm not having you looking after a load of other men, drudging as he called it.'

'If that's how it's got to be, we've no choice. '

'Lodgers.'

'That's what the driver said.'

'Bloody hell Maggie.'

'Nothing pleases you anymore,' she muttered in frustration.

Suddenly Clare was calling.

They both turned to see Beth sprawled out on the road.

'For God's sake!' shouted Ethan as Maggie rushed back.

'I…….I don't feel…..so good Mam. I feel…….feel sick,' Beth muttered as her mother turned her over and started wiping her face. Clare stood looking down joined by her father.

'What's wrong with her?'

Maggie jerked up saying, 'The lass is all in. She's had nowt to eat since yesterday morning. How do you expect her to feel?'

'I've had nowt as well,' Clare wanted to add.

'I'll carry her, give her here.'

'Oh just let her be a minute.'

'The quicker we get there the better, I'll tek her.'

'Just leave her,' Maggie repeated in an empty voice, 'You go on ahead of us and……'

'No,' interrupted Ethan, 'We've got this far together and we can do the last three miles together.'

'She can't. Beth can't.'

'Then like I said I'll carry her.'

'You're carrying enough already.'

He felt defeated. When it came to the children Maggie was always stronger.

He wiped the moisture from his face, sorted the straps of his bag before leaning down to lift Beth into his arms.

'At least there's one thing I can bloody do, I can carry me own daughter.'

'Listen to yourself,' responded Maggie as she picked up her own bag and then helped Clare on with hers.

For the last miles the Granger family walked in silence. Gradually they began to hear the sounds of the works up ahead. It was impossible to tell what time of day it was until at last the low cloud began dispersing with the first wind up the valley. The near hillside was a mess of broken stone and coarse, brown grass. A few hawthorn bushes seemed to be growing out of solid rock. The valley itself was a wide stretch of marshy land with a few isolated farm buildings on the lower slopes of the further hillside. Several times they had to get off the road to let more carts past, their drivers nodding to them as they went by in the opposite direction. Now they could hear the sounds of machinery dominated by a regular banging sound like metal striking metal.

'Thank God,' said Ethan.

'Come on Clare, hold my hand,' added Maggie as the road rose a little and they could see the first signs of habitation, the first signs of Ribblehead.

CHAPTER TWO

As the Granger family were approaching the works James Tranton sat back in his chair, rubbing his forehead in agitation. Outside the mist was pressing against the small window pane in his bedroom. This was the room where he slept and used as his study. His desk was near the window and one wall was covered in bookshelves. The narrow single bed had a tartan blanket cover. Bare floorboards meant that his every movement could be heard downstairs. The rest of the house had a kitchen down four stone steps from a narrow hallway, a parlour, two bedrooms on the next level including his own and finally an attic below the roof where Lizzie Twizleton the maid slept.

He pushed his chair backwards balancing on two legs. All he could see through his window were dribbles of moisture running down the glass.

'James!' came the call from downstairs, 'Tea!'

He stood up, looked at himself in his wall mirror, took a deep breath and held himself still, his body and face becoming rigid. It was his attempt to drive out all unwanted thoughts. In the society of other people he had to be clear of all such nonsense, all the tricks the mind could play, all the pictures his imagination could produce. He would be cleansed. It was his duty. Being the Methodist missionary for the whole area meant he had a reputation to maintain.

He left his room and started descending the dark, narrow staircase. The routine was to take a cup of tea with Jane his cousin at eleven o clock every morning when he was at home. As he ate his breakfast at six o clock every morning he felt tea at eleven necessary before a light lunch at two and dinner at six thirty.

'I'm supposed to be seeing the Austwicks this afternoon,' Jane announced as he entered the parlour, 'They were going to pick me up at two but now the weather is so awful I'm not sure if they will.'

'I'm sure they'll manage,' James answered as he seated himself over the other side of the low tea table.

'I hope you're right.'

'The Austwicks keep their promises.'

Jane glanced at him. Even though she had been staying in the house since early July she still had no sense of what her cousin really thought about her. She needed some kind of definition from him, some kind of security. She shivered with the coldness in the room. James did not allow a fire to be lit in the parlour until the beginning of November and now she was permanently cold.

She poured out the tea. Everything for James had to be careful and precise, so much so he made her nervous.

Most of the furniture in the parlour had come with the house, the two armchairs beside the empty fireplace, the worn carpet, glass fronted cupboard in the corner and thick, dark red curtains over the window that overlooked the front lawn which today was lost in the mist. His prize possession was the upright piano that had been given him by a wealthy Methodist family.

'Do you like the Austwicks James?'

He glanced at her and frowned, his chin jutting out as though the question had given offence.

'Why do you ask?'

'Because I'm not sure if you do.'

'Jane,' he began, 'I don't dislike anybody. It's not my place to dislike people.'

'That's not the same thing I'm afraid.'

'Well it is to me,' he said sternly.

'It's.....it's too circumspect.'

'As human relations tend to be Jane.'

'Unless effort is put in to make them work, surely James.'

'That is always the case.'

Jane heard his voice changing. He was forcing her to agree with him but she would not.

'Anyway I like them and I like their house,' she continued while holding both hands round her cup for warmth.

James made no response to this. He felt it was a pity that his cousin did not have more serious things to think about.

Jane was small and very thin with a long neck and brown curls. Her blue eyes were large and she had an attractive smile, something she had rarely used since coming to the house. She was familiar with the busy streets of Sheffield where her parents had run a draper's business. Up here her only friendship was with the elderly Austwicks who she had met at Horton's summer fair. Other than that there was her sewing, her reading and regular walks over the hills when the weather would allow it.

Returning to the subject of the Austwicks he said, 'I suppose you mean their house in comparison with this humble abode.'

'I never meant that James, not at all.'

'So long as you remember that this house is only rented.'

'But your occupancy is not under any kind of threat, surely?'

'Certainly not. The mission has leased it for the next three years with a proviso for extra years if needed.'

'I'm glad to hear it,' Jane responded in as light a tone as possible.

'And I'm glad you're glad.'

She set down her cup and saucer and said, 'You know how much I appreciate your giving me a home here. You have been so good to me since my parents died.'

'Not at all. Anybody would have done what I did.'

'I was homeless James.'

'I'm sure others in the family would have helped.'

'Only by asking you.'

'Well I agreed. That's all that matters.'

It was necessary to remind him of his generosity.

She waited while he ate a piece of bread and butter and then asked, 'Why hasn't it got a name, the house?'

'I suppose nobody thought it was necessary.'

'Such a shame.'

'I don't see why everything has to have a label, a name.'

'But you know what I mean.'

'So what would you call it?'

'The house in the clouds,' she joked.

'Today I would agree with you.'

At that point Lizzie knocked and popped her head round the door.

'I was just seeing if you were finished,' she announced in her broad Yorkshire accent.

'We'll ring,' said Jane, 'when we're ready.

'Right,' Lizzie muttered in a doubtful tone.

'So off you go.'

'I'm going,' said the girl, clattering the door behind her.

Jane turned quickly to her cousin looking for any change in his expression. Momentarily it was there, his face paler, his eyes half shut and lips pressed together.

She waited and then asked, 'And what are you doing this afternoon?'

James refocused, his mouth opening as he tried to register what Jane had asked.

'Doing?'

'Yes, this afternoon.'

'I'm going up to Ribblehead, to the works. They're still taking on more men and I need to talk to Richard Stockton about having a proper missionary hall. I need a base up there, somewhere the people can come and be part of the mission indoors now the autumn weather is getting worse. Of course I prefer outdoor services but not on days like this.'

'You need somewhere for over the winter.'

He seemed pleased at her response, nervously trying to smile as he set his hands on the edge of the table. They were such white hands with long, bony fingers. He had jet black hair and was short in height but was as thin as his cousin. Always he wore a black jacket and breeches and was never seen outside without his wide brimmed hat and his Bible.

'And if the Austwicks do not come what will you do?'

This question worried her, unsure whether it was a trap to give him the opportunity for another lecture.

'I have some sewing to finish and if the weather clears I might go for a walk.'

'No Jane.'

'Yes James. I need some fresh air.'

'Not unescorted.'

'I have no idea what you think is going to happen to me.'

His face tightened as he answered, 'You know exactly my concerns. Sometimes it seems you want to ignore my advice on purpose.'

'James that's nonsense,' she exclaimed.

'Is it?'

'I like taking walks by myself. You're the same, you enjoy solitary walks.'

'For me it's different.'

'Why?'

'Jane stop this,' he said strongly, his hands stretched out on the table.

Quickly she started gathering up the tea things.

'Lizzie can do that.'

'I know.'

'So leave it.'

'Anything else?' she suddenly asked defiantly.

His back was now ramrod straight as he looked at her.

'Jane I don't want to argue with you.'

'So accept what I want, please James.'

'Of course I can't. Even though there are not many years between us I think of myself as your guardian. I take that role gladly, but it means you have to listen to what I say, not to be dictatorial in any way, but to keep you safe, safe Jane because even here in such a remote part of the country as this is there are still threats to your wellbeing. As you know there are over a thousand people in the settlements at Ribblehead and that number is increasing by the day. We don't know them. They are strangers to us. And what do some of them like doing? Tramping over the hills looking for mischief, looking to poach, to go drinking and so much else and we do not know them so you must trust my words. They are for your benefit Jane. You have to believe that.'

'I do, however.....'

'Well then.'

'But it still doesn't mean I have to agree with everything you say. I'm not trying to be awkward. You know that James, but at my age I don't see why I can't have certain freedoms.'

'To go wandering over the hills when I do not know where you are. Anything could happen.'

'To you it seems there is nothing but evil everywhere.'

'That's nonsense!' he said strongly.

'That you don't trust other people.'

'Not if I don't know them, no I don't.'

'And yet you preach to them.'

'That is my job to do that, my mission.'

'And to keep me always in this house when you know I hate to be held in like that, to have to wander from one room to the other. I've even started to have chats with Lizzie to pass the time.'

'You should be letting her get on with her work.'

'I do, of course I do.''

'Well she can clear the tea things now we're finished.'

Miserably Jane did not move.

'Are you not finished?'

'Eating yes, expressing my opinions, no.'

He sighed and sat back, clasping his hands in his lap and waited for her to continue.

The tension was there. Always she asked herself how much she could risk by defying him.

'Anyway it's not going to clear,' she complained.

'And you should wait to see if the Austwicks arrive.'

'Of course.'

'Right,' he said quickly as he stood pushing back his chair, 'I'm going upstairs for half an hour and then I'll saddle Bess.'

'And I'll have Lizzie clear these things.'

Again she looked for his reaction but this time his face showed no response as he nodded to her before leaving the room.

After closing the door of his bedroom he stood listening to Jane and Lizzie's voices downstairs followed a few moments later by the sounds of the tea things being washed in the kitchen's stone sink. Slowly he sank to his knees, resting his elbows on the bed before gripping his hands together in prayer, his body bending with the effort and urgency of his words.

'Oh God help me be strong, help me have confidence in my work. Oh Lord give me the strength to resist all temptation, to resist all unhealthy thoughts and desires. I am being tested. The devil lingers in the shadows of my needs and I am weak and frail without you oh Lord, without the strength you give me, without the certainty of faith. The Lord gives and the Lord takes away. I am a missionary of the Lord and I ask for your help in these hours of doubt. Am I worthy oh Lord? Am I up to the task you have given me? I must overcome. I must be pure in thought and deed. Please oh Lord, please oh Lord.'

CHAPTER THREE

It was nicknamed the Contractors' Hotel this wooden hut on wheels that had been pulled to the site by a traction engine in 1869 to house the surveyors and engineers through the first winter. These men had been the first to survey a route from Settle along the spine of the Pennines to Carlisle.

On this miserable afternoon there were two men in the hut hunched over maps and diagrams set out on a long trestle table.

'It's too slow. We're behind again.'

Andrew Murray was expressing his growing concerns to Richard Stockton, chief engineer and manager of this section of the new railway line.

'It's the weather. It's this damned place. No wonder we're always losing men.'

'They're the best paid in the country. They can even bring their women and children with them, what more do they want?'

'They want everything Andrew, everything.'

An oil lamp hung above their heads. The light from the two small windows hardly made a difference. Both of them were in their work suits, waistcoat and mudded boots. Their features were tired. Both had beards and thick mops of hair. Murray was the taller of the two, Stockton broader with darker hair.

'We can't force them to stay,' Richard remarked as he took up his pipe from the table and stuck it between his teeth.

'Look what so many of them did in the summer, just downed tools and went off to help with the haymaking. We should have sacked the lot of them.'

'And what good would that have done?'

'Taught them all a lesson. We can always replace them quickly enough.'

'They're not children Andrew.'

'Well they damned well act like it sometimes.'

'The men have learnt the one lesson they need. They know that without them there is no railway line. They're not stupid. Most of them have been around long enough to know the score. They're experienced.'

Murray tried to hide his frustration. He could never agree about this with his chief engineer. The workers needed to be squeezed into the required shape, to be held to account and that was all there was to it.

'It's that bloody Tom Myres. If anyone is an agitator it's him.'

'He thinks he's read his Karl Marx.'

'He needs a damn good dose of the Bible, that's what he needs. Why can't we just get rid of him?'

'He's still a good worker.'

'Who should have been thrown off the site months ago.'

Richard paused, tapping his pipe stem against the back of his hand. He was tired of the same old arguments. Andrew was a good engineer but he had no idea how to keep the workforce motivated. To him everything was a battle. With the men he was too brusque, too forceful and that was why he was so unpopular, not that it mattered to Andrew, in fact he probably relished being the one the men detested.

'You know why Myres is still here,' he said wearily.

'Whatever you do it's a risk.'

'Yes, that's what it would be, a risk, something we have no time for at the moment. Another dispute would destroy our timetable altogether. Then we'd never catch up. Do you really think the sacking of one man is worth that?'

Without thinking Andrew answered, 'Yes I do. I certainly do. While he's still around there will continue to be trouble.'

'Times have changed.'

'So they can change back Richard.'

'Impossible Andrew I'm afraid.'

'It is if we don't try to make the men see sense.'

'It's this Union movement that has got them agitated. Now they are led to believe that nothing can touch them.'

'Next they'll want to take over the whole thing.'

'Well that would be the logical conclusion, especially to the likes of a Tom Myres,' Richard explained.

'And you say you've come across him before.'

'Must be ten years ago. He certainly was no leader in those days. He was as miserable as the rest of them working that Plymouth shipyard extension. The whole experience was dreadful and not one I would want to repeat. It's ironical really,' Richard Stockton added.

'What is?'

'The fact that it's the Unions themselves that will destroy the likes of Myres. He stands no chance.'

Murray's face showed puzzlement as he rested with both hands onto the table top.

'Myres is an extremist. He wants the revolution. He wants the workers in power and the end of the capitalists. But what do the Unions want? They're looking for gradual improvement, gradual. Compromise is not a dirty word to a Union representative. They're realists. They know what they can get out of the bosses and what they can't. They're the future of industrial relations in this country, not stupid idealists like Myres.'

'I hope you're right.'

Richard smiled and patted his colleague on the shoulder saying, 'So do I Andrew, so do I. Only time will tell and unfortunately that's what we haven't got up here.'

'So what's Mr Armsworth saying about the holdups?'

'He'll be here next week,' Richard said of one of the company directors.

'He's worried, isn't he?'

'I'm not sure. According to what I've heard the advertising campaign in the Midlands and down South has gone better than expected.'

Richard sat on one of the hard backed chairs positioned around the long table. He gave one of the plans a cursory look thinking how his young engineer was always so earnest, so dedicated. Richard recognised the same trait in himself but one that was a little softer. He knew Andrew thought he should delegate more than he did, should give him more responsibilities.

'So what do you think?' he unexpectedly asked.

He turned to him, staring as he waited for a reply.

Andrew looked away, suddenly uncertain as he walked over to give a cursory glance out of the hut's window at the thick mist that swirled around the work site.

'Think,' he repeated, 'about what?'

'What we are doing here.'

The young engineer turned in irritation. He knew this conversation was going nowhere. In fact it was becoming a waste of time.

'I'm not sure whether to take such a question seriously or not.'

'You can take it any way you like.'

'I'd rather leave it if you don't mind.'

'It's not a trap Andrew. It's up to you.'

'I'm not sure if it is.'

'You're my second in command and I like to know what you're thinking.'

'That there are some things on which we don't agree.'

'Well believe it or not I agree with you on that.'

Andrew stiffened slightly, his arms tensing a little as he came back to the table his features stiff and unsure.

'The winter,' he said sharply, 'I'm thinking about the winter if you must know.'

'It's not about must. It's your opinions I'm after. We should share this load Andrew if we can. I keep telling you that.'

'If you must know,' Andrew repeated, 'I was hoping when I came here to eventually have more responsibilities.'

'Such as?'

'Everything has to go through you at the moment.'

'Yes.'

'Alright we discuss things, but in the end whatever it's about it will be your decision.'

'I have to trust you more, is that it?'

'Something like that.'

Richard nodded, his face locked in concentration.

'So what would you suggest we do?'

'I take over the tunnel project.'

'Don't you think that's a little ambitious?'

'I don't see why.'

'Have you had much experience of tunnelling before you came here?'

'Not much, no.'

Richard paused, wondering how far this conversation might go unless he brought it to a halt. He was irritated now. It had gone further than he had wanted and all it would do would be to create more conflict.

'Let me think about it,' he finally said.

'Of course,' Andrew replied, his features stiffening in disappointment.

'And I will think about it Andrew.'

'I know you will. And now I'd better be off to see what calibre of new workers we are taking on today. For some reason there's a sudden rush.'

'Advertising.'

'Could be.'

Andrew went for his long gabardine hanging on the back of the door.

'And I'll check these figures again,' said Richard.

There was a momentary pause before Andrew nodded to him and left the hut.

When he had gone Richard started criticising himself at playing such a foolish game. He had wanted to see how far Andrew Murray would go and now he knew. The idea of him in charge of the tunnel at Blea Moor was impossible and he should have told him that and stopped any more thoughts on it. Now he was sure his engineer would return to the subject before long.

Outside the mist was lifting as he walked down to where the viaduct was under construction. The air was cold and full of the usual smell of steam, mud and the stench from the settlements' privies. And then there was the odour of the Dales themselves, stone and wet earth mixed in with mist and low cloud that filled his nostrils as he strode along one of the unsteady boardwalks set over the bog.

'We're down, but nowt enough Mr Stockton.'

He nodded to Davie Wilkins the foreman who gave him this information as they both looked down into the wide, rectangular hole that would eventually be filled with concrete forming the foundations for the fifth pillar that would like the rest go down nearly twenty five feet.

Above them came the banging and hammering from the network of wooden scaffolding and the shuddering release from one of the steam cranes as it hoisted a huge slab of limestone in its cradle of ropes.

'We're way behind,' the foreman added.

In the hole men were on ladders and planks trying to shore up the sides of what had already been worked on.

'Bloody land's like a sponge,' he added.

'We'll get there Davie,' Richard said.

'Oh ay, no doubts about that, it's just when like.'

'Well, keep at it,' he added before walking over to another group of workers talking with Sam Bradbury.

Taking him aside he had to shout at the geologist above the din, 'Fifth's foundations are taking some time.'

Bradbury thought about his response before answering, 'Nothing different Richard except more rain than usual isn't helping.'

'And what would help?'

'I don't think at the moment there is anything. We've got all the men we need for the work itself. It's just you leave it overnight and have no idea what state everything's going to be in by next morning.'

'That's the challenge of this place Sam, unpredictable,' Richard said easily.

'Oh I gave up predicting anything up here I think two days after we started.'

Sensible man.'

'Of course,' Bradbury laughed.

'So there's nothing you.....'

'No, I don't think so,' the geologist interrupted.

'Right then,' Richard sighed, 'I'll be getting on.'

'Oh, if you're popping in the office ask where the last shipment of drilling stakes has got to. That is something we need.'

'Drilling stakes?'

'Should have been here two days ago.'

Richard strode past the company offices as he made his way along the muddy road that ran past the brick factory with its two tall chimneys and up by the side of some of the long, whitewashed huts of Batty Green.

'Miserable day Mr Stockton!' a woman called from where she was quickly gathering in her washing as a group of children ran past him followed by a herdsman and his flock of sheep.

Richard waved and carried on up the moor side lined by the felt roofed huts. Batty Green was the biggest settlement at Ribblehead. The smaller ones had biblical names such as Jericho and Jerusalem or exotic titles like Sebastopol as well as the more mundane Surbiton or Tunnel Huts.

Finally he turned down one of the makeshift streets, trying to steady himself along the wobbly boardwalk before he noticed a man on crutches struggling towards him.

'Elijah, I was just coming to see you,' Richard greeted him.

'Well I've saved you the bother Mr Stockton.'

The worker was in his forties with a rough beard and hair hanging over his shoulders that were hunched forward as he held onto his crutches.

'And how's the leg?'

'Bloody rough, if yer don't mind me saying so.'

'So when did you last see doctor Shawcross?'

'Happen last week. Nowt that he can do, it's knackered and me with it.'

'Don't say that Elijah.'

'It's the truth Mr Stockton. If it weren't fer me brother I wouldn't be here at all.'

'Things might mend.'

'If yer believe in miracles they might, but seeing as I don't then nowt'll change.'

His voice sounded bitter and anxious. There had been a rock fall at the cutting where he had been working and Richard as with all accidents took full responsibility. He hated to see any of his men injured this way and was sure there was a lot more to be done for the safety of the workforce.

'How yer doing?' Elijah asked of the two women who went past on the other side of the mud rutted street as a boy leading three small pigs approached. There were other groups of women, some quickly gathering in their washing, others with their shawls over their heads laughing and talking away oblivious to the drizzle.

'Thee'll do nowt wi them runts Taffy lad!' Elijah shouted.

'Don't know like,' the boy responded in a broad Lancashire accent, his filthy face screwed up in doubt.

'Well thee don't know much then.'

'Is that Freddie Jones boy?' Richard asked as they watched him trudge his way to the end of the street, the three pigs hurrying in front as a cart with its milk churns approached in the other direction.

'It is and a right dozy devil he is. Couldn't rub two thoughts together if he tried.'

'Well you haven't lost your sense of humour Elijah.'

The older man looked at him with his small grey eyes but made no response.

'So your brother Joseph is......?'

'He's trying,' Elijah interrupted, 'but I know it meks him sick to have to be looking after us.'

'Oh I'm sure that's not true.'

'If yer asked him he'd say no but after a couple of pints he'd say yes.'

Richard knew that sarcasm was part of the man's bitterness. There had been too many accidents already at Ribblehead including fatalities. The safety of his men was paramount and yet nothing seemed to stop the number of workers maimed or killed. It sickened him more deeply than anyone would know. He hated the idea of navvies being just work fodder, discarded when no longer of any use like Elijah here who would never work again.

'Anyroads yer kem to see us,' Elijah said, 'but I know yer a busy man so I won't keep yer Mr Stockton.'

'You're not keeping me from anything Elijah, not at all.'

'And that's kind of yer to say so but I know it ain't the case so I'll try and turn mesell round on these bloody things and mek me way back.'

Richard watched him struggle with his crutches, a light drizzle making the journey back to his hut more difficult.

Another farmer's cart stacked with peat squelched by while the smoke from the huts' chimneys and the cold rain filled the atmosphere. The afternoon was this dense mixture from the settlement and the works as he turned at the end of the street to make his way further onto the moors.

From here he could look over the whole site. Batty Green was the makeshift town and the rest of the settlements like its surrounding villages, its streets busy with women returning from the permanent market stalls and gangs of children rushing around the place. Carts were taking bricks down to the viaduct site while others coming from Ingleton station seven miles distance came over the bridge that straddled the stream that was known locally as the Beck. Everywhere there was smoke swirling about and the constant clatter of the men digging and hammering. He started thinking about the journey he had walked as he had made his way from Settle to Carlisle, seventy two miles along the spine of the Pennines. Across the other side of Chapel le Dale he had stood that first time realising the enormity of the task he had been given, bridging across such a wide valley and then half a mile on having to tunnel for nearly a mile under the formidable Blea moor. Now he was imagining what the viaduct would look like when it was finished. It would be magnificent, like a cathedral of twenty four huge arches curving across the bog filled Dale for exactly a quarter of a mile, some of the pillars a hundred feet above the valley floor faced by huge slabs of quarried limestone, some weighing up to eight tons.

He could hear the sound of the men digging into the cutting nearby and see in the distance more carts bringing up provisions along the toll road. Ingleborough was still shrouded in a low cloud as were the more gradual slopes of Whernside. The tone of Elijah had soured his mood but now he was suddenly filled with a wave of anxiety and joy at the thought of all the work that had to be done and all the challenges to be faced. Instead of having to pay the London and North Western for the use of the Lancaster – Carlisle line The British Midland Company would have its own railway whatever the cost and he would make sure of it. Its directors had faith in him to get it done and he would not fail them.

The rain soaked his face and hands as he stood there, his long coat swirling in the growing wind. He pulled the brim of his wide hat further down, his features tight with concentration. Soon he would have to go back down but for a while he would stay here allowing his thoughts to wander into the future. The Settle Carlisle line would be the last great railway built in Britain. He had been fortunate to get such a job. He relished everyday of it, smiling to himself and slowing his breaths as he looked over at the first tramway, its small steam engine bringing down huge lumps of stone in metal trucks.

They had diverted the water of a stream bed to quarry its rock that would be worked on by the masons to face the pillars of the viaduct. All was action and business, all working towards the same purpose. Life was one of practical achievement. That was all that mattered to him.

CHAPTER FOUR

A roughly erected wooden sign read, 'WELCOME TO BATTY GREEN.'

The Grangers tramped onto the narrow stone bridge straddling the fast flowing Gill. A group of children rushed past them as women were making their way from the stream with baskets full of washing. It was the smell and the noise that overwhelmed them. The huts of the settlement were all over the hillside and there was an all pervading stench, a thick, moist stink of humans and animals mixed together and blown at them by the cold breeze. The noise was a clattering, banging, steam blasting, hammering metal and wood mixed in with the cries of the children and the chatter of the women coming from the stream. Suddenly out of nowhere had arisen this bustling, smelly, noisy place. They could see other, smaller settlements further up the hillside and on the moorland all huts exactly the same, whitewashed with felt roofs, some looking brighter than others with smoke pouring out of narrow tin chimneys. Other women were standing in the hut doorways, several of them smoking clay pipes.

Ethan kept his head down. Maggie on the other hand looked straight ahead as the two girls hobbled either side of her, all exhaustion forgotten as they entered such a new, strange setting. Here was all this filth, smoke and activity in the middle of such a bleak, miserable place. There were dull coloured hills, sweeps of moorland and outcrops of grey stone around them. They were here surrounded by such emptiness where nothing seemed to grow except charred looking heather and clumpy grass.

They approached the brick factory, smoke belching out of its two tall chimneys. After asking one of the men loading bricks into a cart where to go to see about work, Ethan was pointed in the direction of an office building between the carpenter's shop and the blacksmith's. Maggie and the girls dropped their bags and sat on the edge of a water trough to wait for him.

A deeper exhaustion took over them now they had come to a stop. Beth started to cry and Clare stared at the ground with her head lowered onto her knees.

'It'll be alright,' said Maggie to them.

'I don't feel well,' moaned Beth.

'We're here, won't be long now.'

'What if he don't get a job?' Clare asked sullenly.

'He will,' said her mother, 'We've not come all this way for nothing.'

'And where will we stay?'

'One of them huts I suppose.'

'I don't want us to be living wi a load of other men.'

'We'll see what happens.'

'I'm hungry,' Beth added.

'I know pet. We'll be getting you someat to eat soon.'

'When?'

'Not long now.'

Meanwhile Ethan was at the back of a queue of five other men. He could not imagine failing now, could not think what the consequences would be if he was not given a job. After walking so many miles, forcing his family to keep going, it would mean the worst failure possible. He felt dizzy with lack of food and his throat was sore. The men waiting in front of him were all in their work clothes. Another came out of the office, a short, thin worker who looked away as he passed by. Now Ethan felt nervous. His anxiety was a sudden pressure, a tightness in the stomach. Two men from the front of the queue were called into the office as he searched his pockets for tobacco that he had finished days ago. He had to distract his thoughts. If he carried on like this he would make a fool of himself. He glanced back at Maggie and the girls waiting by the water trough, the noise and stench of the site being blown around by the wind. He had seen the advertisement in a Nottingham shop window but it meant nothing now. Maybe they needed no more men. Maybe the journey had been a waste of time. Nobody in the queue was speaking. There was a tension between them. One was smoking his pipe, its odour breathed in by a grateful Ethan as he looked up at the brick factory's tall chimneys, their smoke being blown away down the valley.

Eventually he found himself in a small, cramped office. Deciding to take off his cap he stood waiting for the two men behind a desk that almost filled one half of the office to say something.

'You've come for work?' Joe Saunders the foreman asked.

Andrew Murray sat beside him and stared up at Ethan's filthy face. This man seemed all in, his features thinned down to the bone, weakly holding his cap with mud smeared hands. He gave the appearance of someone who had been working the cutting for days on end.

'I've come for work, yes,' Ethan managed, although to speak was painful.

'Where are you from?' Andrew wanted to know.

'I wrote a letter. I wrote a letter and posted it,' Ethan told them, feeling he had to somehow assert himself, to let the other two know they were dealing with somebody who had been educated.

'A letter?'

'Inquiring about the work I saw advertised.'

'And when was this?'

'Few weeks ago.'

'Posted where?' Andrew asked, wondering about what sort of navvy would send such a letter.

'From Nottingham, and I've brought the family, my wife and two daughters.'

The other two said nothing to this.

Eventually Joe said, 'We've had no letters from……what's your name?'

'Ethan Granger.'

'Well Granger we've received no letter.'

'I posted it.'

'That may be but we didn't get it.'

'I see,' Ethan responded emptily.

The residue of energy flowed out of him. He could hardly stand. He hated this situation. He felt embarrassed and angry at having somehow to sell himself now thinking he had been stupid to mention the letter.

'Tell us where you've worked,' Joe Saunders suggested.

'All over the shop.'

'Railways?'

'Mostly.'

'Are you a Trade Unionist?'

He glanced at Joe Saunders.

'No I'm not.'

'Glad to hear it. We want no nonsense here Granger.'

'So you're looking for work?' Andrew asked again.

'I am.'

'And you keep healthy enough?'

'I do.'

'Why I'm asking is because you looked washed out. You look more like you need a few days in bed never mind working for twelve hours a day.'

'I'm alright,' Ethan said back, mustering up the last shreds of his pride.

'So why did you bring your family with you? Bit risky that don't you think?'

'They've always been where I work. That's just how we do.'

'And where else have you worked?'

Ethan went through a list from the docks of Southampton to a recent Manchester branch line.

Nothing else was said until Andrew turned to Joe Saunders who nodded.

'Right Ethan Granger, you can start tomorrow. It's hard work but well paid so we expect full effort, alright?'

'I.....I was just wondering.'

'Wondering what?'

Ethan decided to take the plunge hoping that it would not jeopardise the job they had just given him. He had to try or it meant the family going hungry for even longer. He hated to have to ask. It left him even more vulnerable, more embarrassed.

'About a sub, I'm a bit short at the moment.'

'Bloody hell Granger!' exclaimed Joe Saunders, 'You've a bloody cheek.'

'I just.....'

'The answer is no,' Andrew Murray interrupted.

'I don't want much, just enough to tide us over until I get my first pay.'

'You'd better go now or we'll be changing our mind. What the hell do you think this place is, a bloody charity? We've over a thousand men working here and what if they all asked that question, a sub indeed.'

'Forget it then,' Ethan said angrily.

'And no need blowing so hot.'

'I said forget I ever asked.'

'Right,' Saunders said strongly, 'You'd better be off. But before you go, here's a key for hut twenty two,' he added after rummaging about in a desk drawer, 'There are four other men already in the hut so you'll just have to mek room for each other.'

Miserably Ethan took the key and turned to leave.

Outside Maggie and the girls stood up expectantly when he approached.

'And?' Maggie asked.'

'It's done,' he answered, 'but the buggers wouldn't give me a sub, not a bloody thing.'

'Well at least you've got work.'

'Ay, but nothing to feed my kids with,' he said miserably.

'You've no need to tek it out on me,' said Maggie at his critical tone of voice.

'I'm not teking it out on anybody. I'm just saying.'

'Does that mean we're staying?' asked Clare.

'Can we eat now?'

Maggie frowned at Beth's innocent question and answered, 'In a bit, just be patient.'

Ethan held up the key.

'I've got this, for hut twenty two they said. It's up near the top of the site.'

'Is that for us?' Clare wanted to know.

'Not just us.'

'What does that mean?'

'Maggie intervened, 'It means we have to share.'

'With who?'

'Not so many damned questions,' Ethan told her.

'I just want to know.'

'Well you'll know soon enough.'

'Where are we going now?' Beth asked as she held onto her mother's coat.

The interior of the hut when they finally found it was a filthy mess. The place had clothes strewn over chairs and the floor. A sheet had been pegged up to dry above the stove. The walls were bare wood and the stink from all the clothes and bedding was as bad as the stench outside. The table was covered in unwashed plates and bits of food. On the stove sat a pan of burnt potatoes.

'Good God,' muttered Maggie.

She had seen worse, a lot worse, but was so tired now that the hut seemed impossible.

'It stinks,' said Clare.

Maggie opened the door to the room on the left. In it were beds with filthy sheets on them and full piss pots beside as well as more clothes strewn about the place. The other bedroom was just as bad. Back in the middle room the girls stood there, their faces drawn down in disappointment and exhaustion.

'It's horrible,' Beth managed to say.

'Not as bad as some,' said her mother who refused to be depressed by this new situation.

Ethan stood making no comment. It was too much. They just shifted from one struggle to the next and still there was his anger and frustration at what life had thrown at them.

The family had dumped their bags which contained everything they had in the middle of the filthy kitchen floor. Suddenly Ethan stepped towards the door.

'Where are you going?'

'Just out,' he answered Maggie's question.

'Out where?'

But he was gone without another word.

'Where's our Dad gone?' Clare asked, her features so miserable and disappointed.

'Mum I'm tired,' Beth complained.

Her concern for the two girls forced Maggie to do something, telling them to strip the beds while in the first bedroom she started collecting all the damp clothes strewn around before returning to the kitchen where she cleaned the table and dumped all the wasted food into a bowl. Outside she discovered a water barrel full to the brim with rainwater than ran down from the guttering. She had to stand on the two wooden blocks to be able to reach into it with a bucket she had found. This she placed on the stove and then started on getting a fire lit from the coal and wood stacked at the side of the hut. She was surprised at how much was at hand. Gradually her mood began to brighten. Even the girls seemed more encouraged after the middle room floor had been swept and washed. They lifted all their things into the bedroom they had cleared, Clare having the job of taking the piss pots outside and emptying them onto the rough moorland behind their hut refusing to use the nearby privy. Maggie knew taking over one of the bedrooms might create problems with the men who already lived here but she had made the decision knowing that Beth and Clare needed to lie down somewhere. They lay on bare mattresses, each on their own bed. Maggie laid her own coat over Beth and an old dress and shawl over Clare telling them to try and rest.

In the kitchen she stood with her hands on her hips and looked around trying to imagine sharing this space with four other men. It was going to be tight but it had to be managed. She felt her strength returning, the determination to make things as best she could, still wondering how to get rid of the mixture of smells, rotten food, cigarettes and pipe smoke, the stink of piss coming from both bedrooms, damp clothes and the stench of four sweaty bodies.

CHAPTER FIVE.

Ethan stopped the first man he met.

'I was just wondering whether you could help us.'

'What is it?' asked the stranger, a small, squat man with his flat cap pulled down over his quick darting eyes. His hands and face were covered in mud and his shirt collar ringed black with dried sweat.

'I was wondering if…..if there was any way of making some quick money here.'

'I'm Arnold Wainwright.'

'Pleased to meet you,' said Ethan, 'I'm just new here. Ethan Granger.'

The men shook hands before Arnold pulled off his cap, took out a filthy rag from his trouser pocket and wiped his forehead.

'I'm sorry lad I've not got a penny to me name till payday.'

'No, I never meant that. I don't want to borrow money, more earn it.'

'So you've just been teken on.'

'I have.'

'Just yourself like?'

'My wife and two daughters have come as well.'

'I see,' said Arnold, his grizzled face squeezed in as he thought about the problem then finally added, 'Depends how quick you want it.'

'Today, now, this evening .'

Ethan waited for an answer. The noise of the work was decreasing as a gang of men appeared coming down from the embankment being built at this end of the viaduct and others trudging out of the brick factory.

'That'll be them finished,' Arnold remarked, 'Except them on the bridge. They'll keep going a while longer.'

They both watched the hundreds of men pouring into the uneven streets of Batty Green along the boardwalks that shifted under the weight of so many tired bodies.

'You'll have to come wi us,' said Arnold, 'I have an idea, just an idea mind yer, but it might work if you're that keen.'

'Where are we going?'

'To see a man who arranges things around here.'

Ethan felt he had no choice so started after Wainwright as they walked along the unsteady wooden boards by the side of the muddy road amidst all the returning workers. Some were already washing themselves down; others were seated on their front steps smoking while some had still further to trudge. Children were rushing all over the place as a few pigs snorted their way through the mud where the street was supposed to be. Women could be seen through open front doors busy in their kitchens where the smell of cooking added to the general stench of the place.

This was by far the biggest group of workers Ethan had seen. He had worked on many sites but nothing on this scale. It intimidated him. Already he was lost amongst so many workers. Following this stranger feeling so hungry and exhausted he wanted to just lie down where he was. But he had to try. He would do anything to get his children food by the end of the day knowing it would not be long before darkness set in. The sky was already turning grey with purple clouds to the West. Smoke poured from all the hut chimneys while more men were making straight to one of the many drinking places.

'Where we going?' Ethan wearily asked.

'Just here,' said Wainwright as he stopped at one of the end huts and was about to knock on the door when a navvy appeared, his shirt front unbuttoned and a cigarette in his mouth.

'What the fuck do you want?' he asked of Arnold.

'This is Ethan Granger.'

'And I'm Sam Oxton, so what?'

'So Granger is interested in tonight's entertainment.'

'Oh is he?' sighed Oxton as he flicked his cigarette away and smacked the back of a young boy's head rushing past into the hut.

Nothing was said for a few moments, all the time Oxton staring at Ethan trying to weigh him up.

'Don't look nowt but a scrag to me.'

'He's genuine though. Just been signed on and wants some ready cash and I thought you….'

'I've told you gobshite not to do such a thing. It'll be the death of yer.'

'He's only joking,' Arnold explained to Ethan who was feeling more uncomfortable.

Finally Oxton told him to strip to the waist.

'Bugger off,' said Ethan back at him.

'Suit yersell.'

'I will.'

'Come on,' interrupted Arnold, his filthy face screwed up with worry, 'Do as he says or you'll get nowt, nowt at all.'

'Sam! Sam!' came a woman's voice from inside the hut .

Silently Ethan stood there pulling off his coat, jacket, waistcoat, neck scarf and shirt, the cold air cutting across his skin.

'Fucking hell,' said Oxton who had started to roll another cigarette, 'Bring us a mug o ale!' he added as he turned to the open door.

He stuck the unlit cigarette into his mouth, stepped down and slapped Ethan across the face. Arnold had just the time to grab hold of him before Ethan had a go back, his arms taught, his neck muscles stretched as furiously he stared at his attacker.

'Oh I see, bit of a temper on him,' said Oxton as he walked around the two of them.

'Easy, easy,' Arnold was saying and then added, 'He'll have a go, at least that. Five bob for the man and the same for me.'

'Fuck off.'

'Five bob.'

'And nowt.'

'Suit yersell.'

'I always fucking do so fuck off.'

Ethan put his clothes back on, the slap having given him sudden strength. Anger could do that to him.

They were about to turn away when Oxton suddenly changed his mind.

'Half past seven or thereabouts. Half a crown for him and the same for thee.'

'No,' muttered Arnold and then thought more about it, 'Alright you bugger, five and a half for me.'

'He'd better be there.'

'He will be.'

'Right, so now fuck off while I get mesell some grub. Half past seven mind,' Oxton reminded them before he lit his cigarette and turned back into the hut.

A few minutes later Arnold was introducing him to the men who shared his hut. The idea was to get some food in him so he joined the rest of them filling themselves with burnt sausages, hard boiled potatoes and a few soggy carrots. He had been told by Wainwright about the weekly fights that Sam Oxton organised, bare fisted fights on which a lot of money was placed.

'You'll need some energy like so get as much down you as you can.'

But Ethan was so hungry he could not face the piled up plate in front of him. The five other men were greedily eating great mouthfuls, the food washed down with mugs of beer followed by intermittent farts and belches adding to the stink of their filthy kitchen.

'You can do it,' Arnold was saying in encouragement when later they walked between the row of huts with lamplight shining out of their small front windows. The mud was smelling and the air cold. They followed a growing number of men past the last huts out onto the open moorland to where the earth dipped forming a natural amphitheatre lit by a circle of lamps placed every few feet on the ground. This illuminated area was already ringed by a crowd who were shouting out different odds while money was being passed around.

'You'll be on first seeing as you're the novice.'

Ethan stood at the edge of the crowd and felt the cold rush of nerves. He was so frightened his body was numb and the sides of his head as cold as ice, hard ice clamped to his brain. He had no idea what he was doing. It was madness but he needed the money. It was the worst thing he could imagine, bare fist fighting with another man, especially the state he was in. There was no energy, no strength. He was scared and hated being watched by so many people, the crowd building all the time until he noticed Sam Oxton appear into the illuminated ring, an area of short grass where the noise from the men was even louder.

'No,' Ethan finally said.

Arnold stood beside him pulled a doubtful expression before he said, 'It's not no lad, not now.'

'I'm sick.'

'You'll be more sick after this but I'm not having Sam Oxton on me case, not a bloody chance, so come on, follow me.'

'I can't.'

'You can.'

'I'm sorry.'

'Bugger sorry. Come on, you're on.'

Finally Ethan could argue no more and started behind Arnold as he pushed through the crowd down to the front where he told Ethan to strip to the waist and get himself prepared for fighting.

If there was anything he hated it was to see grown men knocking lumps out of each other. It turned him cold whenever he saw such a fight. It was animal. It was barbaric, the worst state of all, violent, lost to it, wanting to destroy another human being and here he was agreeing to do exactly that. His body was shaking with the cold of the night as a half moon appeared from behind the clouds.

He looked across the area, the lamplight sending quivering shadows across it, at another man stripped to the waist, his opponent who looked twice as big and many times stronger, his white skin glowing in the strange light.

'Fucking hell.'

'Ay that's him, Tommy the Taff. I knew fucking Sam Oxton would try this.'

'What do you mean?'

'Nothing lad, you just get your hands in front of your face, your arms covering you ribs and whenever you get a chance try and jab him in the mush.'

Ethan tried to take deep breaths of the cold air as his name was announced and that of the Welshman who had ginger hair and a full moustache and was already bouncing about ready for action.

It lasted less than two minutes. To begin with Ethan managed to avoid any kind of contact. The crowd started cursing his tactics but he had no idea what else to do. The Taff just followed him around the ring, once kicking over one of the lamps in an attempt to swing at the retreating Ethan. He was ready to vomit, his breaths coming fast and shallow. His arms felt so tired as he tried to hold up his hands in some sort of pathetic defence. The fear was worse. He did not want to be hurt. He did not want to go down in front of all these men. He did not believe in any God so there was nobody to pray to except to himself wishing hard that he would survive this.

It was when Ethan stumbled that Taff stepped quickly forward and landed a punch straight into his face. The force of it created a momentary black out as Ethan's legs wobbled only for him to be punched again, hard knuckles slamming against his fragile skin and bone. Taff stood back to see what damage he had done and Ethan felt the rush of blood out of his nose and mouth. He was drowning in it. Slowly his legs gave way and he crumpled onto the cold grass, his head bouncing off the ground. There was a muffled roar from somewhere blown against him like a strong wind of sound, unconscious sound. He felt half of his face swelling while he laid there seeing the Welshman standing with his arm raised spinning around to the shouts of the crowd.

'Come on lad, up yer get.'

The voice was from a far distance, across miles of pain and a face that was thumping a pulse of agony. He could not move. He did not want to move. He wanted to stay where he was, to lie on the soft grass and dream all of this violent nonsense away. It was not him. He was in the hut with his family. He was the man, the one they depended on.

'Come on Granger, for fuck's sake,' Arnold was saying as he tried to get his hands under Ethan's armpits.

'Get the weak sod out of the area!' people were shouting.

'Get the bugger shifted,' Sam Oxton told Arnold as he walked over and threw a bucket of water over the two of them.

Ethan spat out a mixture of water and blood. He felt himself being lifted to a strange standing position. His legs were not working, his head spinning and faces shifted around him, their voices coming from far away.

'Here, tek yer money, not that neither of yer deserve it,' Oxton added as he flung the coins onto the grass.

Eventually Arnold managed to drag him away from the crowd and sat him down on a tuft of dead heather.

'Christ, you were bloody hopeless man, absolute rubbish. I'm surprised Sam Oxton kept his side of the deal. Here, this is what you did it for, meking a right fool of yersell. I can't see that anybody put money on yer so there'd be nobody losing that much. Here tek it for God's sake'

Arnold pushed the half-crown into Ethan's hand.

'And now what the hell are we going to do wi yer? Your Missus is going to go crackers when she sees yer like this wi your gob swollen, one of yer eyes closed and a bloody great bruise on your cheek. Surprised Taff didn't break some bones the way he smacked yer one. It was the worst ever. If I'd have known yer were going to put up such a poor show I would never have suggested it, not a bloody chance. You're either mad or really fucking sad Ethan Granger. Which it is I have no idea except both, ay both.'

There was no response to this fragmented speech. Ethan had his head down between his knees. There was nothing in his guts to vomit only a mess of phlegm and blood dribbling out of his mouth leaving a silver, maroon trail over the heather stalks. Pain was thumping through his head. He was a thing, numbed off from his surroundings, not hearing most of what Wainwright was saying. On the fringe of his shadowed consciousness he could hear the crowd shouting on the next fight somewhere down below the earth, down in a rocky darkness where men tried to kill each other for two half crowns.

'I'm done,' he finally muttered.

'You can say that again, but yer can't stay here all night so you'll have to get shifting. I'm knackered mesell as it is. Come on Granger, let's get yer moving. Stand up and lean on me. Come on man.

CHAPTER SIX

Maggie stood looking down at her two girls fast asleep. They were done in, pale and worn out. Both were still wearing their boots that were too small and had split at the front. They had been out on the road for nearly four weeks. Often she had thought they would not make it, but now they were at last here there was nothing but a feeling of exhaustion and uncertainty.

They needed a bath badly. Their clothes were splattered in dried mud and stains. Slowly she settled down on the edge of Beth's bed. The child's once round features had thinned down so much her cheek bones stuck out .But at least they were here wherever here was. The next hurdle for her would be the four men who already lived in this hut. She had no idea what kind of reception they might give her. For the moment she was too tired to bother. Her eyes closed as she slumped down beside her youngest one, the warmth of sheer exhaustion flowing through her. It was over. They had walked so far but now it was done and Ethan had got a job and all she wanted to do was quickly fall into a deep sleep.

It was the front door banging open that woke her. At first she thought it must be Ethan as she dragged herself up. The two girls were still fast asleep.

'Now then, we were told by one of the foremen we had company.'

In the kitchen were two men, caps in hand, wearing filthy clothes and boots. The older one who had spoken was stout with no beard or moustache just long grey hair. The taller one beside him stooped slightly. He was rough shaven and his mouth was set in an awkward position, slanted to the side with spit gathering in one corner. When he smiled he showed his brown front teeth, kneading the cap in his hands as he kept nodding at Maggie and smiling again.

'I'm Bill Asquith and this here is Jonty,' said the older man.

'Pleased to meet you,' replied Maggie.

'And you are?'

Maggie flushed as she gave her name and the rest of her family.

'Two girls, eh?'

'The eldest is near eleven and the wee one just five.'

'And we're to share so I'm told.'

'I hope....hope that's alright.'

Bill Asquith looked at her inquiringly and then smiled, his large face the colour of old straw with the weathering it had taken.

'Alright?' he repeated, 'What does to say Jonty lad, is it alright?'

The one called Jonty with his long neck and small head made a strange sound and then mumbled, 'Is it....is it alright Bill? Is it alright?'

'Don't see why not. We've shared before but not wi two lasses as well. That'll be different. And My hell, look at the place. You had no need to.....'

'I just gave the place a bit of a tidy. We've moved into this bedroom,' Maggie motioned to the door behind which the two girls were sleeping, 'and shifted the stuff from there into the other one.'

'That's how it used to be, us four dirty sods shacked up together in the one room. Next should be Fraser here soon but as for Jock, Jock Tarrant, well he's a world to hisell is Jock. We might see him tonight and there again we might not.'

Bill sat heavily down while Jonty remained standing.

'Come far have yer Missus?'

'Nottingham, and call me Maggie if yer will.'

'Nottingham's far enough.'

'So where's yer man then, a railway worker I suppose like the rest of us? Me and Jonty here work in the brick factory and that suits us grand, nice and steady work and out of the rain and cold. There's a lot fancy having our jobs but they ain't getting em, no chance. Are they Jonty?'

'Hungry Bill.'

'Wait yer hurry.'

'Hungry Bill,' Jonty repeated in his high squeaky voice.

'So have you and your girls eaten yet missus, Maggie?'

'No, not yet.'

'Well we've got plenty of grub if you'd like to have it with us.'

'Don't mind, that is if I can waken the girls. They're dead to the world.'

'Don't blame em. Now let's see,' sighed Bill as he got up again and went over to a roughly built cupboard nailed to the wall by the side of the stove.

Maggie had already come across the sausages, potatoes, two cabbages, some string beans, two loaves of bread and a jar of jam in the cupboard, more food than she had seen in weeks. She had cut the girls thick slices of bread and jam before they had gone to lie down.

'I don't mind doing the cooking,' Maggie thought she should offer.

Bill smiled, yawned and smiled again, 'Well if you don't mind we certainly don't. We usually tek it in turns. Not that anybody is any good at it. In fact we're rubbish. I think we'd better cook the lot if now we have eight mouths to feed, that is if Jock puts in an appearance.'

He brought out all the food, helped by Jonty and set it on the table.

'Will that be enough do yer think?'

Maggie thought it would be. The tone of Bill's voice gave her the sense he was the one who had taken authority in the hut. He sounded confident and comfortable with himself and was obviously looking after Jonty who Maggie already considered as being more like a child. She worried a little about how the girls might take to him but was more eager to start on the cooking, the sight of so much food churning up her empty stomach.

Fraser Henderson was the next to arrive. He worked on the tramway, was tall and very thin with wispy brown hair, a light moustache and incredibly long fingers. He had a southern accent and spoke softly and carefully. Maggie was introduced to him just before she started serving out the evening meal.

'Sit theesell down Fraser. Tonight we have a proper cook, one who knows what she's doing,' said Bill as he winked at Maggie.

'Pleased to hear it,' responded Fraser, 'I'll just go and get a wash down.'

'Never thee mind that for tonight. Have thee dinner before it gets cold.'

'I hope it's alright,' Maggie put in hesitantly as Fraser sat down with the other two at the long table,' Hope yer like it.'

'Smells grand,' said Bill.

'Yes indeed,' added Fraser as he glanced at Maggie with his very light blue eyes.

Maggie went in to check the girls who were still fast asleep.

Around the table the chat quickly got onto work and what had been happening that day. The lodgers had the usual moans and grumbles. Maggie thought of herself at being quick at estimating new acquaintances. The Grangers had lived in so many different places it was important for her to get an impression of people as speedily as possible, but Fraser Henderson had her baffled and unsure. There was something about him that immediately unsettled her. He did not talk like a navvy and he had such strangely refined features. Even the way he ate his food was much slower than the other two, especially Jonty who held his fork as if it were a shovel and was forcing in food as fast as he could, some of which mixed in with his spit kept dribbling down his chin.

They asked her no more questions. Establishing who she was and where her family had come from was enough information for them. They smelt of sweat, mud and brick dust, their faces and hands were filthy. Bill got up and went out with a jug to fill it from the water barrel by the side of the hut.

'That's one thing about Batty Green, the rain tastes good,' he joked as he poured some of the water into their jug of beer.

Maggie noticed how the swept and washed floor was again covered in muck off their boots. Jonty kept watching her as he started on another plateful. Again she expressed her worry about where Ethan could have got to.

'He'll be in the pub,' Bill suggested as he pushed his empty plate away, 'that's where he'll go like a lot o the men.

'Not my Ethan.'

'Well that'd be a first, don't tell us he's signed the pledge.'

'No, nothing like that,' she answered warily, 'He just doesn't often drink, that's all.'

'That's what they all say when they first get here, but it don't last long once they start to realise what a miserable place this is. We're miles away from anywhere up here. You'll know that already.'

'I don't think so, not Ethan.'

'Well you should know thee husband better than me,' Bill continued in his broad Lancashire accent.

It was then that the front door was kicked open and in staggered Arnold Wainwright holding up Ethan still with blood pouring down his face.

'For hell's sake!' exclaimed Bill as Jonty jumped up and started shaking with excitement.

'Ethan!' Maggie shouted, 'Oh God what's happened?'

'He'll be alright Missus,' put in Arnold who had managed to get him to a chair.

'Doesn't look like,' Fraser Henderson commented. He was the only one to remain at the table and continued eating as the others fussed around the bloodied Ethan.

Hurriedly Maggie washed his face to reveal an eye swollen shut and a huge bruise forming on the left side of his face as the blood kept pouring from his nose.

'What a mess.'

'What's he been doing Arnold or maybe I should be asking what has thee been doing?' asked Bill.

'It's just.....he just needed some money like. That's what he told me.'

'So what Arnold?'

'So the only way we could figure on getting some ready cash tonight was....'

'Don't say you had him fighting.'

'He agreed to it. I didn't push him or owt.'

'Fighting?' repeated Maggie.

'Ay,' said Bill as he got hold of Jonty's arm to try and calm him down, 'Every week there's bare fisted bouts up on the moor. The management turns a blind eye to the proceedings so long as nobody gets badly hurt.'

'And what would you call this?' she said angrily,' Ethan say something, speak to me.'

Painfully he lifted his head and looked at her with his one good eye, 'It's alright,' he managed.

'No it isn't. It isn't alright at all.'

'If I were you Arnold Wainwright I'd bugger off,' started Bill,' you've done enough damage for one night. And how much did you get out of the proceedings? I bet it was that damned Sam Oxton you dealt with. That man thinks he bloody well runs this place, well he don't and the next time you see him you can tell him that, tell him Bill Asquith said that and if he's got a problem with it he can come here and see me about it, do you hear?'

'Ay right Bill,' muttered Arnold, 'I hear.'

'Right, so bugger off.'

'I didn't mean no harm, I didn't.'

'Go! Get out!'

Sheepishly Arnold turned and left the kitchen.

'Worst person your husband could have come across. Arnold Wainwright will do anything to anybody for a few bob,' Bill commented.

Finally Maggie managed to staunch the flow of blood out of Ethan's nose before she and Bill helped him into the bedroom where he collapsed on the bed, turned his head and fell asleep.

'What were you thinking of?' she asked his sleeping figure later that night as she lay beside him, 'What a mess. What a start. And there was no need for it. There was more food than I could manage, lots of it. So you had no need to do anything, but that's always you, jumping at the first chance, never thinking, just going for it like a child who is scared if they don't it might disappear. I hope you're listening Ethan Granger. I hope you are.'

His breaths were long and slow. His head was towards her and there was blood dried over the mattress around his chin.

'God knows,' she continued in a whispered voice so as not to wake the girls, 'You're such a fool Ethan Granger. Nothing's ever right for you. You're always wanting more and wanting it straightaway, bare fist fighting. I've never heard the like. You who wouldn't say boo to a goose. You must have been scared silly. I just can't imagine it. I can't.'

She stroked the side of his face that was not bruised. With her other hand she touched her lower belly where the pain was always there. It constantly reminded her of how having Beth had destroyed so much internally. Even if they had the money to pay the doctors it would still never be mended. It was too late and now there would be no more children.

She thought momentarily about the four lodgers squeezed into the other bedroom. She had no idea if sharing the hut would work in the long term. In the past there had been places where they shared the same room with other families. She just hoped that coming to Ribblehead things might have been different. She wanted things to change as though they were starting over, beginning a new stage in their lives and not the usual trudge, the usual poverty. She was sick of it and knew how desperate it made Ethan feel. He had never been able to accept their lot. At least she got on with it whereas he despised himself for being who he was, living the life he had been forced to live. He could read, write, do his sums. He was clever enough but had never had the opportunity to show it and time was running out. They were already past the halfway stage of their lives. Whatever happened she hoped it could be different for the girls. Beth was more like her father, sharp and thoughtful. Clare on the other hand was the slower one of the two, was the girl who liked to be doing things, helping her mother with the house work and sewing in the evenings.

Gradually her thoughts began to merge into the deepening darkness of sleep. She curled up as close as she could to Ethan and closed her eyes.

It could have been a minute or hours later when she was startled awake by the sound of the front door crashing open. Immediately she checked on the still unconscious Ethan and then got up quickly to see if the girls were awake. Beth had opened her eyes before Maggie told her quietly to get back to sleep. She stood waiting, her breaths coming fast when she heard a chair falling over.

The only light in the kitchen came from the two small front windows. A figure stopped abruptly over the other side of the table as Maggie came into the room.

As the man straightened himself he said, 'Who the hell are you?'

Maggie made no reply.

'Fucking hell, it's an angel. It's an angel to look over old Jock. Fucking hell, an angel,' he repeated as he knocked over another chair coming towards her saying, 'Come on me angel, let me feel your wings. Come to Jockie now.'

The stench of drink came with every word as he tripped forwards and pinned her against the wall. Still she did not want to call out and waken the girls. By now he had his hands up her nightdress trying to force her legs open.

'Come on my angel, come on,' the man grunted as Maggie saw the figure of Bill in his nightshirt crossing the room.

In one move he pulled off the drunkard, spun him round and fisted him straight in the face jerking the man's head back before he crashed to the floor,

'Christ almighty,' Bill muttered as Clare appeared at the bedroom door.

'Mum, what's that.......what's going on?'

'You go back to bed pet. It's nothing. You go on now. I'll be there in a minute,' she said in a flustered voice, fumbling with her nightdress, her arms shaking.

Clare hurriedly turned away.

'Bloody Jock Tarrant. He's going to be the death of me one of these days so he is,' said Bill, 'Are you alright Missus?'

'No, not really,' answered Maggie shivering, 'No I'm not alright.'

'I was just hoping you might meet this sod sober instead of the usual. He's just a pig when he's had a drink inside him, an absolute disgusting pig. We should have thrown him out by now.'

Maggie took a deep breath, sorted her nightgown and watched as Bill dragged the unconscious Jock Tarrant into the other bedroom.

'You tell me,' Bill said when he returned.

'I don't understand,' she said, her voice almost a sob.

'Owt wrong and you tell me, understand?'

'Why you?'

'Why do yer think? I'm the only one here who can control that silly bugger.'

'I don't know,' said Maggie weakly, her head beginning to ache.

'Of course thee does. It'll work out right. It will. I can promise yer that.'

'I don't see how.'

'You will. You'll see,' he said, gently touching her arm.

Without another word Maggie returned to the bedroom. She wished more than ever that Ethan had never seen that advert for work at Ribblehead in a Nottingham shop window.

'What was all that racket?' Clare asked in a troubled voice.

'It was nowt, just that other lodger falling over a chair.'

'It sounded more than that Mam.'

'You just get back to sleep. Nowt's wrong. Go on, it's alright.'

She waited until Clare had settled back to sleep before returning to her bed.

Already regrets were dominating over everything else. Again she checked the girls, stood there at the foot of Clare's bed in the darkness, listening to her quick breaths. This was all for them. They had walked all those miles for them. Nothing else mattered to her. Now she was fearful they had made not just the wrong decision but one they could not change.

CHAPTER SEVEN

'We could go for a walk if you so wish, you mentioned Jane that you wanted to see the works up at Ribblehead, well I have discovered just the spot to view it all.'

Jane was always glad of an opportunity to be out of the house. She knew that James felt the same but for different reasons.

'Yes I'd like that,' she agreed.

'Well I suggest we go now while the sun is out.'

From the parlour she went off to fetch her bonnet, gloves and coat and to change her shoes into her outdoor boots.

Outside it was a sharp autumn day with a pale sun shining over the dale.

They walked down the lane, through the small hamlet of Chapel le Dale, past St Leonard's church and the vicarage. They crossed the stone bridge, its walls covered in thick moss. Flowing below was the beck that started below the Ribblehead works and ran down past the hamlet to flow a few miles on through Ingleton into the open, flatter countryside beyond. They crossed over the turnpike road that continued on to Hawes and Dent.

James helped his cousin through a narrow gap in the wall onto the first hillside. Above was a limestone escarpment with a pale grey colour that dominated the higher edges of the dale. No trees grew in this area only a few stunted hawthorn bushes remarkably pushing out of cracks in the stones that at some point in the distant past had been ripped away from the scree and had rolled down to the lower slopes.

Jane loved to be out, striding across this wild, barren land. Her spirits were uplifted. Here she felt free and more herself, more alive. Everything felt possible as though life was just beginning. The only problem was James and his dislike of her walking over the hills by herself. She refused to be imprisoned this way, refused to be so overprotected. There had already been several heated arguments between them.

'What do you see?' he asked her when they finally stopped for a rest.

She glanced at him. He had that superior look on his face that she disliked.

'I see what you see,' she answered.

'I don't think you do.'

'Why not?'

'Go on, tell me what you see.'

'This isn't another of your tests James, is it? I hate it when you do this.'

'Jane, I'm just.....'

'Oh alright,' she sighed, 'if you insist.'

But she found it hard to focus on any one aspect of the huge vista in front of them. Over the opposite side of the dale were the slopes of Whernside rising to over two thousand feet. The clear autumn sky gave everything definition. Below were the works at Ribblehead, the smoke from the brick works, steam from the cranes and engines using the tramway up to where she could see the gash they had made quarrying a dry stream bed. The first high arches of the viaduct were covered in wooden scaffolding. The many whitewashed huts of Batty Green were on the far side of the works and other settlements that had been built further up onto the moor. Along the Ingleton road she could see many carts being pulled towards Ribblehead while others were returning empty in the opposite direction. She knew this traffic continued all day and into the night. On a still, quiet evening she could hear the wheels of the carts from her bedroom window. On the lower slopes beneath them were a shepherd and his dog rounding up a flock of dirty, miserable looking sheep. The noise from the works dominated any natural sounds, such an isolated place overtaken by machines and human activity. It once must have been such a peaceful place. She felt fascinated and yet repulsed by so much industry here in this once empty valley. It was alien, artificial, all these people in their makeshift villages cluttering the countryside with their machinery and racket, but still she did not want to share this with her cousin so instead commented,

'I think Whernside looks higher than usual,' she answered evasively.

He was leaning on his walking stick as he turned to her, 'Is that all you see?'

'What do you want me to see James?'

He frowned and shook his head, 'Only what is there for you.'

'Well I've told you.'

'What a strange young lady you are,' he said condescendingly.

'You only say that because I obviously don't see what you see. So tell me James what.......?'

'Yes,' he interrupted, 'Yes, you're right. What I see is a terrible blight on the landscape, a hideous man made mess in what once must have been such a peaceful place. I can't help but regret what is happening here.'

'But surely the only reason you are living here is because of all this.'

'Yes, but that still doesn't make it right.'

She paused, enjoying the weak warmth from the sun's rays.

Finally his presence compelled her to continue as she said, 'You do God's work.'

His face was set in a serious expression. Sometimes she wished he could smile or even laugh.

'Up there, so many souls to be saved,' she added.

'People Jane who are struggling to find the right way.'

'I know.'

'Well don't make it sound so utilitarian because it isn't and I wouldn't wish it to be.'

Nothing was simple to him or light hearted. It was all so drearily significant. She knew the work he did was more important than anything else. He was dedicated and made sure everyone knew it. He could sound so sanctimonious as if his views had to be always accepted. The only occasions when he seemed more relaxed was on the rare evenings when he would accompany her singing on the piano or when he would play some of his favourite pieces of Mozart and Haydn as well as the works from his Methodist hymnal. Then he seemed happily lost in the music. Everything else was forgotten except concentrating on the next notes. These evenings for her were the most entertaining. It was the same when she accompanied him on some of his missionary work, more to get out of the house than anything else, an opportunity to meet other people. In the summer he had become interested in the garden, planting a variety of flowers and deciduous bushes. If he had any time to himself he would often be out there tending to the new plants that bordered the lawn. The rest of her hours with him were always a strain remembering to be appropriately serious. God was everywhere, something she had to ensure she did not ignore or forget.

'And it's progress,' she continued defiantly, 'in fact I find it exciting.'

His look was one of disappointment as he said, 'Sadly I can't agree with you.'

Nothing was said for a while. Even though she was standing close to him she felt such little connection between the two of them. Loneliness dominated her mood and the presence of James did nothing to change that. She had lost her mother and father to diphtheria and now here she was with a cousin she did not understand in a place that could be beautiful but which he managed to make so disappointing. There was so much space around her. Often she had no idea what she was doing here in Chapel le Dale. Even though she met people when helping James with his missionary work she had no real friends except the elderly Austwicks, no society to stimulate her intellectual needs. Her isolation frightened her. Somehow she had to change her outlook or become even more unhappy. She was unfulfilled and increasingly agitated and James did not help. His intensity and strange moods undermined her confidence with him. Yes he had been generous in offering her a home and yet had gone no further. He had done little else to make her feel comfortable and welcomed. She had hoped to be introduced to the local society of Ingleton and Settle but that had not happened. James was always far too busy with his mission work. Now she wondered if it had been sheer family pressure that had made him accept her in the first place. But whatever the reason she was here with no friends of her own age and no immediate prospects.

Dully she finally said, 'It at least gives people work James, and that's important, surely?''

He ignored the question and asked whether they should continue their walk.

The sun was beginning to dip behind a layer of clouds in the direction of the distant Lancashire coast as they followed a sheep track that cut diagonally across the rough hillside, returning to the house by way of a path by the valley's fast flowing stream.

That evening James went off to his meeting at the works leaving Jane trying to read in the parlour, wrapped in a blanket to give her some warmth in front of the empty fire. The house felt cold and empty. Tonight she was restless, even bored. She could find no interest in her book. Her thoughts were not on what she was trying to read but on yet another estimation of herself. She was sure she was pretty enough, intelligent enough. She had been given a rounded education and enjoyed discussing the usual topics. But here in the dale it was all wasted. There was nobody to appreciate her character and her talents. She could play the piano. She could sing quite acceptably and loved dancing whenever she got the chance. The more she thought about it the longer the list became and in consequence the more frustrating. What was the point to it all? Her parents had ensured she would be an attractive proposition except for the most important thing of all. She had no money. In fact she was almost penniless. All the family savings, which had not been great, had gone on her mother and father's funerals as well as paying off certain debts that had accrued. Her future was blighted. Unless someone found her attractions worth more than any pecuniary value she would be lost, abandoned. Then all that was possible was to find some job as a governess somewhere, an idea which she dreaded. Now the nightmare was the thought that she might be stuck in this house for years and even worse the terror that James might expect her to become his wife and follow him in his missionary work. The problem was not only James but the idea of having to marry any man. So far there had been not one who she had found attractive. She was being constantly urged by feelings that were warm but vague to respond to her body's needs but not with her cousin or it seemed any other man.

At night as she lay there in bed trying to get to sleep, her body started stirring a heat that spread from its centre down her legs and over her breasts. She knew such feelings were wrong but could not stop them, struggling not to succumb to such deepening needs. They frightened her. Only once had she gone so far as to produce such a warm rush of response. She had forced herself to stop, sensing that another world was there on the tip of her finger, a place where the fire was born.

She had too much time to consider such things, too much time to think about herself. Living here in this cold, dark house provoked her imagination to wander in any direction it chose. She was too often within herself, too often allowing herself a terrible freedom, a challenge to everything she had been taught to believe. It was not just her faith in God that was being questioned; it was faith in humanity, in her sense of identity. The idea of trying with James to discuss any of this was even laughable. She knew exactly how he would respond.

She rose, trailing the blanket behind her as she stepped into the narrow corridor outside the parlour door. Here there was darkness and the sounds of the wind and of Lizzie still at work in the kitchen.

The maid did not hear her descend the three stone steps into the kitchen. Lizzie was in her blouse and work skirt busily scrubbing the porridge pan. Jane was immediately fascinated by the girl's movements, the way her skirt shifted slightly from side to side as she worked her right arm back and forth. Her long brown hair had been taken out of its bun and was swaying in the same way under the light from the kitchen's oil lamp. Lizzie was just sixteen and had the perfect shape of a girl budding into fullness. She appeared so broad and strong, so natural and at ease with herself. She was singing away as she took up another sauce pan as though she had not a care in the world.

She sensed someone behind her.

'Why Miss Jane, you gave me a fright!' she exclaimed as she turned round, 'I hope I haven't been disturbing your reading?'

Jane noticed the swelling of her breasts and the smoothness of her complexion, the dark brown of her eyes, all this in a momentary fascination before she answered, 'No, not all.'

She knew she was blushing as she said these words.

Lizzie put down her pan asking, 'And what can I do for you Miss Jane?'

In an instant, without any planning, Jane knew what she wanted and said, 'I....I thought we could have a cup of tea together.'

'Tea with me?' Lizzie exclaimed and then laughed.

Her cheeks were perfectly moulded and her lips full and red. Jane could not stop looking at her. It was as if she had never really looked at her before, never noticed how attractive she was.

'Yes,' she continued, trying to control her voice, 'Yes here in the kitchen. I would like that.'

'Well if you say so Miss Jane.'

'I do.'

'Right you are,' Lizzie responded happily, 'I'll put kettle on.'

Jane sat at the scrubbed table while Lizzie busied herself making the tea.

'I could help,' she offered.

'No Miss Jane, you sit yersell there.'

There was a pause before, 'Do you like working here Lizzie?'

The girl stopped and turned, a worried expression on her reddened face.

'I......I haven't done anything wrong have I? Me Mam would murder me if I lost this job. I.....'

'No, not at all,' Jane had to interrupt.

'Are you sure?'

'Of course.'

'And Master James thinks I'm doing alright?'

'Yes of course he does.'

'Cos you'd tell us.....you would tell us if he weren't happy wi me?'

'Lizzie, you haven't done anything wrong. It's just that we've never had a chat, not a proper one and I just thought it would be nice to get to know each other a little more.'

'So Master James ain't been complaining?'

'No he hasn't.'

'Well that's alright then,' said Lizzie, obviously relieved.

When the tea was made they sat across the table from each other and Jane asked again whether Lizzie liked working in the house.

The maid looked uneasy, awkwardly shuffling in her seat before she said, 'Work is work Miss wherever it is.'

Jane, disappointed with this inquired, 'Had you another post before this one?'

'Just bits and pieces, couldn't get owt steady, helped me Mam with the weaving but there were never really enough work for the two of us so I suppose I was lucky that Master James took us on.'

Jane smiled and sipped her tea.

Lizzie frowned and seemed uncertain what to say next, glancing around the dismally lit kitchen, 'And you Miss Jane, where did you live before you came here, if you don't mind me asking?'

'I thought you knew.'

'Wouldn't be asking if I did. Master James has never said anything and you don't get much gossip around here seeing as the place is empty o folk. It's only when I get me Sunday off and goes home that I hear some o what's been happening.'

'Your mother and father help on a farm, is that right?'

They do. One o me brothers is still here while the other is away at sea and me sister Katie works as a chamber maid in some big house near Leeds so that just leaves Tommy, me and me Mam and me Dad who sheperds Mr Anderson's sheep up on the Topside estate.'

Jane tried to avoid those deep brown eyes as she said, 'Well I come from Sheffield.'

'And where would that be?'

'In Yorkshire like here but a lot further south.'

'Never been out o the dale mesell.'

'I'm sure you will.'

'Who knows? Me Mam I don't think has travelled more than ten mile from our house. Mind you everything is south of here Miss if you understand me. But I'd like to tek a look at what's going on up at Ribblehead, might get mesell up there sometime just to see. I still reckon it's daft spending all that money and time building a railway line north when there's nowt up there.'

'I see you have your opinions Lizzie.'

'Just what I think Miss.'

Jane was intrigued. Lizzie was only sixteen and yet already sounded well versed in Yorkshire sarcasm.

'So you think the work up at Ribblehead is a waste of money?'

'Don't know much about it.'

'I'm surprised you've never been up there?'

'It's just a big mess I hear.'

After another pause it no longer felt so awkward between them. The kitchen was mostly in shadow with its white washed walls, its blue slabbed floor and the pots and pans stacked up on broad shelves.

Jane was aware of just the two of them in the house. It was always better when James was not here. She shuddered to think what his reaction would be to her and Lizzie taking tea together. For once she was not bothered what he might think. This is what she wanted to do. She had no idea that Lizzie had so much to say for herself and expressed it quite confidently.

Without thought she reached across the table and turned over Lizzie's hand.

'Your hands are still so smooth,' she said lightly.

Lizzie looked at her coyly and smiled, 'Well that won't last long, will it?'

'That would be a shame.'

'Has to happen Miss, I'm only a servant lass.'

'I suppose so.'

'Can't be helped.'

'No.'

'Just how it is, a house maid finishes up wi rough hands just like any other working woman.'

There was a dryness in Jane's throat as she let go of Lizzie's hand, sat back and took up her tea.

'Not that I meant owt in saying that,' Lizzie put in quickly.

'I lost both my parents. They contracted diphtheria and there was nothing the doctors could do,' Jane continued, ignoring the maid's remark.

'That's terrible.'

'It was last winter.'

'How awful for yer Miss Jane.'

'Yes, yes it was and still is.......It took me a long time to fully realise what had happened. I was angry and awfully sad at the same time. It was hard. Death is so personal, so brutal, especially when it is so sudden. It took such a short time, such a very short time. Something was taken away forever, something in me. I loved my parents. They did everything they could to make me happy. I think I've been a little frightened ever since. I prayed and prayed for their souls in heaven. I went to church so often, several times a week and yet none of it did any good.' She looked up at Lizzie's concerned features, 'Now I'm here and sometimes I forget how I got here or why I am here.'

Lizzie, looking sad and bothered, made no reply to this. She poured out more tea and asked Jane if she wanted anything to eat there being some cold ham left over from earlier.

Jane shook her head, 'No Lizzie, thank you but I'm not hungry.'

'Got to keep yer strength up Miss.'

'I suppose so.

'And this place called Shef......Shef.....'

'Sheffield.'

'Yes this place Sheffield, what's it like? I bet it's nowt like up here.'

'Certainly different.'

'I reckoned so.'

'Here it is.....is a lot quieter, a lot emptier, such a contrast to a busy city.'

'This dale, Chapel le Dale, me Dad says is the emptiest of the lot. There's a few farms and nowt else, well there was nowt till this railway building started. They say there's a proper town been built up at Ribblehead wi shops and pubs and the like.'

'They call the main settlement up there Batty Green.'

Lizzie laughed, 'What a daft name to call anything.'

Momentarily they looked at each other, both smiling, one absorbing the other. This was far the best Jane had felt since coming to the house. Here in these moments she felt more real, more warm and relaxed. In such a desolate place was the surprise of Lizzie's beauty, her rounded features, soft unblemished skin, her full body and her long brown hair, strands of which kept falling across her face before she flicked it back into place.

'I should be going. Master James will be back soon.'

'There's still some tea left in the pot,' Lizzie tried.

Jane shook her head and took a deep breath that was almost a sigh.

'This....this has been nice,' she continued in a soft, easy voice.

'Ay, it has.'

'We should have tea together more often.'

'That's....that's up to you Miss Jane. Folk might think it funny, strange like, a maid having tea with the lady of the house.'

'I hope you don't think that.'

'No, but yer know what I mean.'

'And I hope Lizzie you don't find it strange.'

'No I don't, I don't Miss.'

'I'm glad to hear it.'

'But what about Master James?'

'I see no reason why he should know, do you? Let's keep it a secret between ourselves.'

'It's up to you Miss Jane. If that's what you want I'll say nowt about it, nowt at all.'

'Good,' said Jane, liking the idea of something shared between them that nobody else knew about.

At that she thought it was a good point to stop, leaving the kitchen then thinking how much her evening had improved, humming a tune to herself as she went along the hallway, happily taking up her book in the front room before trying to concentrate.

CHAPTER EIGHT

'Cracking goal you scored Mr Tranton.'

'I rather thought so myself Harry.'

'Wish you could be playing wi the lads regular.'

'So do I, but I'm afraid the Lord's business doesn't allow football as often as I would like.'

They were walking with other players off the boggy patch of ground situated the other side of the viaduct, all them covered in mud, James with his top shirt unbuttoned and hair plastered over his sweaty face.

'Well we're playing that Settle lot in two weeks so see if God'll give yer time off.'

James laughed, 'I'll have a word and see what he says.'

'We'll all pray for the reet answer,' another of the players put in, his jacket slung over his shoulder.

James enjoyed the usual banter and the way he was readily accepted.

'So where did thee learn to play, you being a missionary like?' another asked as they trudged along the boards beside one of the settlement's muddy streets.

'Well Fred, I just picked it up as I went along, played a bit at school but nothing serious.'

'It'll be serious alreet against that Settle mob. They reckon they're hard but they don't know what's coming to em.'

'That's right Harry,' James laughed, 'Confidence, that's what you need plenty of.'

'And a bit o skill wi the old one two thrown in to fool em.'

'That as well of course.'

'So you tell yer Lord and master what's needed for the boys up here.'

'I will Fred, I promise,' he said as the group started going its separate ways.

Later that evening he was in a predictably difficult meeting with Richard Stockton, the game of football far from his mind other than having to apologise for the state of his trousers and boots.

'You just don't seem to realise I have a lot more on my mind,' Richard was saying, 'than just....'

'A missionary hall,' James interrupted.

'I'm trying to build a railway up here if you hadn't noticed. I'm sorry Mr Tranton, your priorities are not mine. Of course they aren't. They can't be. So long as your involvement with the men is not interrupting their working day, well at least we agree on that much. Alright their spiritual life is important but they have to earn their wages first. Surely you understand that? You've been here long enough. The trouble is the amount of other societies, committees and others who want to be here at Ribblehead. They are all I'm sure working for a just cause but sometimes it becomes a hindrance. I'm afraid I haven't got the time to deal with all their demands.'

'And that includes me?'

'Unfortunately yes, I have to be seen to be fair to all sides.'

'So you are saying no to a hall?'

'No I'm not. I'm just saying it is not a priority.'

'It is to me.'

'And I respect that, but remember who has to pay for it and the fact the hall will be for the whole community and not one just for the Methodists. It will have to be costed and passed by the board of directors.'

'If you say so,' James stated in a critical tone.

Richard was trying to keep his patience but was finding it increasingly difficult. James Tranton was a perfect example of what he had to deal with. His approach was too sanctimonious as well as downright belligerent. He was so single minded that any alternative was not just beyond his understanding but beyond his consciousness.

They had been in Richard's office for the last twenty minutes, time that he could not afford to waste. He was sure that the likes of a James Tranton thought that all non-believers should to be damned. It was ridiculous what they imagined to be their rights over others and Richard was becoming tired of it. He was losing his temper because this missionary would not accept his answer.

'So you think it is suitable to have my people out on the moor when the winter sets in which up here will be in the next few weeks?'

'I'm not saying that.'

'It can't be postponed any longer.'

'I will write to the company and see what they have to say.'

'I thought you would have done that already, and I know the last thing you want is to have your men sick with illness caught standing listening to me in the freezing cold or the pouring rain.'

Richard looked directly at James' serious expression. As always the missionary was dressed in black from head to foot even though some of it was splattered with dried mud. Initially their relationship had been quite cordial, but over the last months he had come to represent all the other Christians who were desperate to bring more into their fold. They saw the railway workers as agents of the devil with all their drinking, womanising and fighting as though they were the last great challenge, just as great as any savages from Africa. They had to be brought back to the faith for their eternal good. Richard had no idea where these preachers got their endless optimism from. Ribblehead was to become the new Jerusalem. This was the last great battle ground in the industrial north. Over fifteen hundred people had to be saved and James Tranton was one of those who believed he could do it.

Richard suddenly thought he would change his approach.

'If it was up to me I would have no objection to one of the huts being turned into a small missionary hall. I know it wouldn't be big enough but at least it's a start. We already have our library and reading room. Next I want to see a school set up here and I don't see why a community hall could not be added to the list. It would mean the erection of more huts but more are going to have to be built anyhow with more workers being employed.'

James sat stiffly in his seat. He listened but his features showed no reaction. His face was still set in an unchanging seriousness much to Richard's dismay. It seemed nothing could alter this man's response until he unexpectedly said, 'Well I'm glad you agree Mr Stockton, very glad. I'm sure if you advised the company they would be willing to accept your recommendation, and I thoroughly endorse the idea of a school at Ribblehead. It seems your vision is wider than I thought, thank you.'

The condescension was in his voice but Richard for once did not mind it. At least his change of approach might bring the conversation to a close.

'So I promise there will be a decision within the next few weeks,' he added.

James stood up, shook hands with the engineer saying, 'I thank you for your time. These minutes have been more fruitful than I anticipated. I'm afraid I came here with little hope. Now I believe it is going to happen.'

'We'll just have to wait and see,' Richard said easily as he showed him to the door, 'Watch your step,' he added,' and just remember, it's still up to the company to make this happen.'

The unexpected visit had left him unusually thoughtful. He watched Tranton disappear into the cold darkness, illuminated for a few yards by the light shining through some of the windows and a half moon settled over Ingleborough in a cloudless sky. Richard took up his pipe and chewed on the stem thoughtfully. He was in no rush to leave the 'Engineers Hotel'. Andrew Murray would be in their shared hut for the evening and the idea of more talk about work was not appealing.

He was jealous of those with religious beliefs in one way and one way only, their faith in a life beyond death. He knew when his own terror of dying had started. He had only been three or four when he had entered the local graveyard. He and his friends had been playing hide and seek and he had been hiding behind one of the gravestones in the cemetery where a group of men were crowded around a large family burial site. Inquisitively he had pushed his way through to see one of the men holding a skull and other human bones exposed by their recent digging. He was roughly pushed away and told this was no place for a youngster like him. Unfortunately death at such an early age had taken on a definite vision. He had seen what it physically meant and he would never forget it. Death had haunted his life ever since, through his adolescent years, his time at university and on into his professional career. His Christian faith had been lost with nothing to help against the absolute terror of the fact of his own death. It was his one great fear, the one he had struggled all his life to control, refusing to allow it to undermine his professional confidence and the faith he had in himself. And so there had always been a resentment of all those wanting to spread the word of God and James Tranton was one of them, an example of a confidence and arrogance that he despised.

James on the other hand was going along one of the wooden walkways above the thick mud of Batty Green feeling surprisingly reassured by Stockton's response to the idea of a hall. He had achieved an agreement of sorts that now would be up to the board of directors. His breath clouded in the freezing air, his way illuminated by the moon and the lamplight of the huts. Children's' voices could still be heard out at play and the call of a cockerel obviously confused by what time of day it was. More lamps were being lit at the foot of the tramway as the mechanics worked on two small steam engines that pulled the trucks up to the quarry, their light glinting off metal and shadowing the shapes of the men and the noise of their hammers sounding through the cold stillness. He thought Richard Stockton was a hypocrite of sorts, someone who was too ready to pass on responsibility. He was too limited to understand the real importance of his mission. His responses always sounded hollow and slightly irritated. When it came to the religious needs of his workers he was not as interested as he should be. Once he had thought a friendship might have been formed between them. They were of the same age and a similar background and yet such an idea was finally abandoned when James began to realise that their concerns and personalities were completely different. Richard Stockton was a practical man. There was nothing of the spirit about him. His conversation was always blunt and to the point. Their meetings were always factual and rushed, a dull question and answer process.

As he approached hut twenty two he hoped this first meeting might be a positive one. There had been too many failures recently, too many blank faces and opposition to him. He was there to help people to discover the wonders of the Lord. They should be grateful for what he was doing. Whoever they were and wherever they had come from it was his duty to attempt to show them the light of the true Christ.

He passed a medley of noise coming from the different huts, a worker singing, a loud argument was going on in another, a child screaming in the next. People nodded to him or looked sheepishly away as they passed by. Batty Green was a stew of humanity, a mixture of sin and belligerence and stubbornness. It was his challenge and he had to force back any doubts.

It was Bill who opened the door.

'Why it's Mr Tranton,' he said loudly, 'the man with the beautiful tenor voice. I heard thee at the concert in Horton last month and thee sounded grand. Took Jonty for a treat and he right enjoyed hisell.'

'Thanks for that Mr Asquith, I wonder if I could just pop in for a minute,' asked James tentatively, 'I hear the Granger family has moved in with you and I would like to introduce myself if that's alright.'

'Come in, come in.'

The kitchen was hot and damp with washing hanging on a rope system that went diagonally across the crowded room. Maggie standing in front of the sink was drying her hands on her pinny. Fraser

Henderson was sat with the two girls at the table doing a jigsaw, Jonty sat across from them fascinated, watching their every move and trying his best to help. Ethan had as usual gone to bed.

'Mrs Granger,' James started as he held out his hand, 'Pleased to meet you. I'm James Tranton and I run a mission here on behalf of the Methodist church and I always try to meet any newcomers to the settlements.'

'Right, pleased to meet you I'm sure,' said Maggie, a little flustered, as she briefly took his hand that felt cold and bony.

'And these are?' asked James as he turned to the girls.

'This is Clare and our Beth.'

'And I see Mr Henderson is keeping them well entertained.'

'I am Mr Tranton.'

'We all do,' put in Bill as Jonty grabbed a piece of jigsaw and thrust it under Clare's nose, 'The girls have brought a bit o life to the place. We wouldn't swap them for anything, would we Jonty?'

He clapped his hands as Clare found the right space for the piece he had given her, his eyes wide and bright with pleasure.

'If anyone's the saint around here it's our Jonty,' Bill continued, as usual dominating proceedings.

Maggie had already accepted it. There was no point in doing otherwise. Bill Asquith was used to having things his own way and she was not going to challenge that, especially not after he had saved her from the drunken attention of Jock Tarrant. Already she felt Bill was someone she could rely on, a friend even.

'So Mrs Granger, how have you settled in?'

James had taken off his hat that he turned in his hands and smiled his thin lip smile.

'My husband's early to bed tonight.'

'I see,' said James, 'Not unwell I hope?'

'No, just tired.'

'Can't keep up with the pace,' Bill joked, standing there in front of the stove, his stout waist sticking over his leather belt, his feet apart and his pipe stuck between his teeth.

'Oh listen to him!' Fraser exclaimed in his higher pitched voice, 'you're not having to dig all day.'

'Neither are you.'

'I'm not saying I am. I know my job is easier than some. I'd be the first to admit it.'

'Well thee talk for theesell. Me and Jonty are one minute melting near the kiln and the next we're freezing to death loading bricks. You try it sometime.'

'I'm sure all your work is difficult,' James put in, feeling himself becoming suddenly uncertain. It was Bill Asquith who he found difficult. James knew of his reputation of being a violent man. He was brusque and his body seemed to dominate the room, something that James found challenging. It was not that he was intimidated by the man. It was merely his presence made him uncomfortable. He sensed a struggle going on, had felt it the moment Asquith had opened the door. His only experience of him had been when James had tried to talk to Jonty alone about coming to one of his meetings. When Bill Asquith found out he had been furious, telling James that he had not to pick on the weak and needy, that Jonty was his responsibility and no one else's.

'Say hello to Mr Tranton girls,' Maggie told them.

Clare at least gave a nod in response but Beth just glanced up at him and then back to the jigsaw.

James thought of a way of impressing them and their mother before he said, 'There seems to be a real possibility that Batty Green will soon be having its own school. What do you think about that Clare and Beth?'

'Is that right?' Maggie asked keenly.

'I don't want to go to school,' muttered Clare miserably.

'It would be a great opportunity,' James added.

'And what would that do for the wee uns?' asked Bill, 'Nowt but fill their heads wi nonsense. How would that help em to grow up as workers cos that's all they'll become like the rest of us?'

'I am sure Mr Asquith you wouldn't deride the chance of these two fine girls becoming pupils at our own school?' said James strongly looking at the mother of the girls for support.

'I think it's a grand idea,' put in Fraser, 'Nothing wrong with a bit of education, helping them read and write and stuff.'

He was in his collarless shirt and waistcoat like the other two with a dirty red scarf tied round his neck. He kept smiling at the girls, his eyes shifting from one to the other as they gradually began to put the pieces together. On the lid of the box was a perfect countryside cottage and garden with its thatched roof and colourful flowers.

'We've nearly done it Mam,' Clare announced excitedly.

'Very good,' James said believing that congratulations sometimes were better than any chastisement.

'They're clever uns,' Bill added as he lit his pipe, warming his backside from the heat of the stove that was making some of the washing steam.

'Would you like a cup of tea Mr Tranton?'

'No thank you Mam. I have a lot more visits to make this evening. I was just wondering whether you and your husband would consider attending one of our meetings. They are held twice a week and soon I hope will be in our own mission hall. I just......'

'We're Church of England,' Maggie interrupted.

James' face stiffened slightly, 'Oh I see.'

'Like me Mam and Dad before us.'

'Yes, of course.'

'We're glad the railway company see fit to hire carts and horses to tek them who want to go down to the service at St Leonards on a Sunday morning. We've been twice already and the reverend Smith does a fine sermon.'

'I'm sure he does.'

'So that's us.'

'So long as you follow the faith Mrs Granger, that's more important than anything.'

'I'd never thought I'd hear that from a Methodist.'

'And why not?' James turned to Bill.

'Thought they had to be all yours or they were lost, ain't that it?'

'No it isn't, although yes we would prefer it if they followed the word of our founder John Wesley.'

'There you are then.'

'But better a believer than not.'

'So yer says.'

'I do, one body in Christ. We're all his followers.'

'Well me and Jonty are doing fine wiout Mr Wesley as well.'

'Surprised you've ever heard of him' said Fraser sarcastically.

'Oh you've no idea what I know.'

'You're right there and I don't think I want to.''

'Right,' James interrupted, 'I must be going, but it's been good to meet you and your children Mrs Granger. Tell your husband I have been visiting and that.....'

The door swung open and Jock Tarrant appeared. His eyes were flushed with the drink, standing there unsteadily on his feet as his face contorted in disgust. Immediately Bill crossed the room, grabbed him by the arm, sat him at the table, went over to the stove and returned with a plate heaped up with food, 'Here, get that down yer and don't say a word, not one word do you hear Tarrant?'

The Scotsman looked at him angrily but made no response.

'Thank you and goodbye,' James repeated as he went through the still open door.

In the bedroom Ethan had been listening to the whole thing. The walls were thin and the men's' voices, especially Bill's were loud and too clear to get any sleep. He was tired more from the mental state he was in than exhaustion from work. The job was as bad as any he had taken on except there were more men working around him and the weather was awful and would only get worse.

He laid there, his arms and legs aching and his mind in a miserable confusion. He had never been right since arriving at Ribblehead. It had not been the fight with the Welshman but more the sense of starting the whole miserable process over again. He was sick of it, sick to the teeth with it. Work was just a ridiculous flog and he hated it. This was not for him. Navvying had never been for him. It was not enough. He was worth more than shovelling shit every day, but with every new start the chances of getting something different, some other kind of work faded away.

He turned over in the darkened room still smelling of stale piss. There had been comments made on the first days at work about his swollen and battered face but gradually they had stopped once his eye opened and the bruising had started to fade. Now he was accepted as just part of the gang that was working on the cutting towards the mouth of the Blea Moor tunnel where preliminary work had just started. The worst of it was sharing the hut. To begin with he did not think it would be such a bad idea but the reality was far worse than he had imagined. Bill Asquith had to be in charge. It often felt as though Asquith and Fraser Henderson were in competition to who had most influence over the girls and of course the other child Jonty. Henderson had more time and energy to play with the children than he ever did, their own father. Jonty was so innocent that in many ways he seemed younger than Clare and Beth. Initially the only one the girls had been wary of was him, but gradually they had begun to realise that he was harmless, a child like them, that he was just somebody who was more in his own world than anybody elses. Now the girls could laugh at him and with him. He enjoyed making strange noises with his tilted mouth and doing his impersonation of a spider crawling across the floor, long legs and arms everywhere as Jonty went backwards on all fours. Bill ensured that nobody bothered him. They worked together. Wherever Jonty was Bill was always right behind him.

Ethan listened to them talking. He turned onto his side then onto his back, his restlessness growing. It was this feeling of becoming increasingly irrelevant to his family, of being on the side lines of their experience that was fuelling his anger. In the past he had been the centre of their lives. He had made all the important decisions. They had followed his idea of coming to Ribblehead. It was he who had earned the money to keep the family going, but now all that was changing. Within a fortnight the four lodgers had agreed with Bill's suggestion that they each pay Maggie ten shillings a week for her to do the cooking, their washing and to keep the hut as tidy as possible.

Maggie was now earning. This had never happened before and he did not like this sudden change of roles, no longer being the sole breadwinner. Ethan was even sure she was managing to save some at the end of each week. He was worried that neither his wife nor his children would relate to him as they once had done. His position was being undermined. After all these years and within a few weeks everything was changing. He had to do something that showed his family that he was still at the centre of their lives, but he had no idea what to do. He could no longer let everything slide away from him and let these other men take over, not Bill Asquith, not Fraser Henderson. A month ago they were complete strangers and now they were part of a family in which he no longer felt included. There they were in the next room sharing their evening together as they always did. He knew slinking off to bed was not the way to affect things but at the end of each working day he was too exhausted to try anything else. The moment he walked through the door he felt defeated. Even the tone in which Maggie spoke to him had changed, now less uncertain in the way she spoke to him and it was the same with the girls.

'They should be in bed!' he shouted as he suddenly appeared at the kitchen door in his work shirt that came down to his knees showing the rest of his white, scarred legs.

'Ethan?' Maggie said back as she looked across the cluttered room at him.

'I said the girls should be in bed now!' he shouted even louder.

This unexpected noise upset Jonty so much he jumped up from the table knocking one of its legs so the jigsaw pieces scattered everywhere, most of them onto the floor.

'What's up Ethan?'

This was from Bill.

'You just keep out of this Asquith.'

'I'm only asking.'

'This is none of your concern,' said Ethan strongly.

'We were just finishing the jigsaw,' explained Fraser Henderson as he stared at Ethan disparagingly, 'No harm in that is there?'

Ethan waited a few seconds and then shouted angrily, 'Clare! Beth! You heard me! Now move!'

'There's no need for this,' Maggie tried.

'Get to bed! Bed!'

'It's not that late Ethan.'

'Hurry up,' he ordered the girls as they rushed past him, both with tears in their eyes at this unexpected outburst.

He slammed the bedroom door after them and stood there waiting until first Clare and then Beth had taken off their clothes, pulled on their nighties and quickly got into bed. He did not say another word as he too climbed under the blankets, his head on fire and his stomach churning over.

Then suddenly he shouted even louder, 'Bloody hell!'

'Dad,' whimpered Clare.

'Get to sleep!'

'I…….'

'You heard me. Not another word. Not another. I've bloody heard enough tonight. I've heard enough.'

Later Maggie lay stiffly beside him. She knew he was not asleep but she refused to say anything. She had apologised to the others but had not been able to think up a sufficient excuse for her husband's behaviour. All she could say was that he was tired. It had sounded feeble and that had made her even more bitter. She was sick of his sudden moods, his anger, his stupid reasons. He was an ordinary labourer just like every other man at Ribblehead and yet he had to show her he still had a brain, trying to prove to her that he was cleverer than the rest, just because he had gone to school when he was younger. According to Ethan there had even been talk of him going to university. But the money had run out, his father had been made redundant and he had had to find a job quickly or his younger brothers and sisters would have ended up in the poor house. That was his story. To begin with she had believed it. But later she had become unsure. Now there was no way of discovering the truth. According to Ethan it had been a change of circumstance that had ruined his chance of a proper career that had forced him to start working on the railways.

'I'm sorry,' he muttered with his back to her.

'No you're not. You say you are but it's happening too often. Tonight you upset everyone, especially the girls.'

'I said I was sorry.'

'Shouting at the girls like that in front of everybody,' she said in a harsh whisper.

'I wasn't shouting.'

'Yes you were. You can't hear yourself sometimes, mouthing off like a madman.'

'According to you.'

'Oh suit yourself,' she said sarcastically.

'I didn't mean to upset them.'

'For God's sake, what the hell did you expect? They're children, just children. They were having a nice time with Fraser and Jonty and you had to go and spoil it all, and why? Why did you do that? That's what I'd like to know.'

'Christ,' Ethan muttered as he rolled over to face her.

Her dark hair curled around her wide open eyes. She would not be beaten by him, not accept his feeble excuses.

'We're here now and we have to mek the best of it.'

'Nobody's saying different.'

'Yes you are. You Ethan Granger are saying different. You look as miserable as sin most of the time. We've only been here just over five weeks and we have to get on with it.'

'Oh I know it suits you alright.'

'And what's that supposed to mean?' she asked as she tried to move a few inches away from him.

'Doesn't matter.'

'So why say it?'

'I've apologised. What else am I supposed to do?'

'You say sorry to the girls first thing tomorrow morning, that's what you do.'

'I'm their father.'

'You apologise to them, and keep your voice down.'

'Like hell as like.'

'Well then, what's the point? It's just not me who needs an apology.'

'I suppose you want me going round each one of them as well, Jonty, Asquith and Henderson. I suppose you'd like me to do that.'

'I'm not listening.'

'Wouldn't you?'

Maggie made no response. She turned away, sick of his words, always words.

James Tranton meanwhile was on his horse Bess clomping along the Ingleton road that was sheened in moonlight. He had been visiting an old lady who was dying from old age and exhaustion. She lived in an isolated cottage a mile out of the village of Hawes, Elsie Brambles, a seventy two year old widow who lived by herself. Luckily her nearest neighbour who had a farm on the same hillside had popped in to see how she was getting on. The farmer had gone down to the ironmongers in Hawes where messages were usually left for James. That afternoon he heard about Elsie and decided to visit her before making his way home. He had not known his visit would last so long.

Elsie had been in bed, a shelf built into the wall of the one room cottage that had an earth floor and an open fire, one tilted table and two straight backed chairs.

'I....I can't mek thee a cup of owt,' she had said in her rasping voice, 'I can't cos I'm badly Mr Tranton, but I'm right glad you've come. I hoped you would, hoped you would come cos I think Elsie is on her way out. I think that and I reckon I'm not wrong. I'm not wrong Mr Tranton, but I pray to me Lord. I do.'

'That's all you can do Elsie,' he had replied, holding her dry, bony hand as she looked at him with watery eyes, 'You are in the arms of Christ, always. You are with him Elsie.'

'Will he tek me?'

'He will if you believe in the power of the Lord.'

'I'm not fussed, not frightened like.'

'There is no need for fear.'

'Cos I'm deeing. I'm tired and I'm deeing and I can't get warm, but I'm right glad you came and it being so late and all.'

'I heard from Mr Timmins the ironmonger.'

'All me children are dead before me. The eldest were only thirteen. Thomas went eight years ago now. I've not really been right since then, not really. I've kind of given up on it all I suppose cos I'm washed out wi just having to get up every day. Just want to rest like, rest away me time.'

'You will be in the arms of the Lord Elsie and he will hold you there.'

Her hand gripped his harder and she momentarily tried to sit up but sank back onto her stone bed, tears dribbling down off her hairy chin.

'Do you want me to pray for you Elsie?'

'Ay,' she nodded, 'I'd like that.'

James knelt on the cold, earthen floor, clasped his hands together, closed his eyes and had prayed for the journey of this old woman's soul, prayed for her salvation, for her coming into the bosom of Christ where all would be at peace, prayed in thanks that the worry and struggle were nearly over for her and that soon she would be absorbed into the warmth of the rays of eternity.

Before going he piled more pieces of peat onto Elsie's smouldering fire, made sure the bedding was up to her chin to keep her warm. Lastly he blew out the stub of candle that was on the floor beside her bed then gently touched her cold cheek and left her there knowing that someone would be coming in first thing the next morning to check on how she was.

Now as he thought on it Bess slowly took him down the valley. His horse was of wide girth, strong legs and a powerful looking head. Bess was always reliable, no stumbles or frights, no moods or awkwardness. He had bought her from a farmer near Horton and used her every day. James could let his mind wander and pay no real attention to the road. Bess would get him home.

In the small stable he wiped her down, gave her a bag of feed and locked her up for the night. Carefully he opened the front door and stepped into the hallway vaguely lit by the strong light of the moon outside. He took off his coat and hat and hung them on a hook behind the door. As he climbed the narrow stairs he stepped as lightly as he could. He was too tired to bother about anything to eat or drink. On the short landing he stopped momentarily outside Jane's bedroom and then went on to the foot of the stairs that went up to the attic where Lizzie had her tiny room under the eaves. He stayed there, his back straight, his hands clasped in front of him as he looked up the shadowed stairway. For several minutes he stayed in that position, his breaths coming slow and steady before he ascended three of the steps to the attic, turned and came back down again. He did this again, up the three steep, wooden steps, stopping, turning, and again waiting on the landing, his shadowed face tight in concentration before going up again. Eventually on descending the three steps he turned and went into his own bedroom preparing again to pray for his own salvation, a concentrated effort that could last for hours. He would remain kneeling in front of his window with the curtains open so the strength of the light outside shone across the room, his eyes shut so tight his brow was creased in a frown, his white hands held up before his face and clasped so tightly they were shaking. He was lost to his praying, to his supplications. Dawn was breaking before he was done, crawling over to his bed to get under the blankets and curl up into the growing warmth, into the place of sleep where his torment was silenced for a time.

CHAPTER NINE

The gang of over a hundred men were working on the cutting close to the entrance to Blea Moor tunnel. The rain fell incessantly out of a low grey sky as the men dug into the sodden blue clay. When it was like this there was the likelihood of the high sides of the cutting giving way as the clay changed into a sodden mess of unstable mud. You could dig into it and it would just pour off your shovel blade like watery glue.

Ethan's back, arms, legs and head were aching. He had pulled off his top coat that had become heavy in the rain and was now in his jacket, the water dripping off the peak of his cap. It was just another daily slog, another mindless, painful dig into the sponge like earth. He had his head down, trying to lose himself in the action of his work, the bending into the downward movement of the shovel, the tightness across his shoulders as he lifted up the heavy sludge, the tension in his arms and back as he swung and turned the shovel as it reached the edge of the barrow. Over and over again the action was repeated, trying constantly to will himself into this mindless action, to force himself to become the human automaton, just a process without thought, without feeling except for the drain on his body's strength. He had to stop himself always resenting what he was doing. He knew that to stop work would destroy him and his family. There were no choices. He was here. He had a job and he had to do it, to push every muscle to obey his will. His consciousness had been absorbed into the body's repetitive action. To survive he had to let go of his thoughts as he shovelled up another load, his clothes sodden with sweat and cold rain that dribbled down his face and hands. He was surrounded by others doing exactly the same thing but was not aware of them. He was cut off in a dark, physical world where there was nothing but effort and strain and growing exhaustion. The more the day went on the faster he worked. He realised that tiredness could weaken his resolve to keep going. He had to batter the mind into submission by forcing himself to work harder, no pauses, no rests, no break for a quick fag, only to go and on until the hooter went and another day was finished and he had won a victory against himself.

With the barrow full he wheeled it over to the start of the steep side of the cutting, attached a rope to the barrow and then with a call for the man at the top he started pushing as the other pulled on the rope. He slipped and slid, his feet dragging backwards against the slope of mud and rock, his arms outstretched as he pushed as hard as he could, shouting at the top man to pull harder. At one point the barrow nearly tippled over sideways, Ethan putting all his effort into keeping it upright. It was a good forty feet to the top of the cutting and yet it felt like miles of anguish and force, his heart pumping, his breath coming fast as his head was lowered so far down that his face was almost skimming the slope of blue sludge beneath him. So many times he had done this journey on this day and the effort it took made him sick and weak as finally the barrow came onto the top edge of the cutting and the other man released the rope and took it off to tip its contents away from the side. These few seconds were the only breather Ethan had, gasping lungs full of the cold air, waiting for the other to return. Nothing was said between them. The day was too long for that. Quickly Ethan holding onto the handles of the barrow slid down to the bottom of the cutting to start filling it again. The rest of his gang were doing the same like small pieces of activity in this huge daily jigsaw. They were in a deep hole surrounded by a dark blueness, the banks of sodden earth, the dull, blue, grey sky above and the sounds of the shovels and picks cutting into the earth against which they were struggling. One of the small engines went past along the tramway to the entrance of the tunnel its metal wagons full of bricks from the factory, its steam blowing heat against Ethan's legs and back as it went by. By this time in the late afternoon no one was speaking. All of them were just trying to get to six o clock when the hooter would go and another day would be finished. By this time of the year the work finished in darkness, only the oil lamps scattered about giving any light on what they were doing. But they did not need illumination. The men were working by instinct by now, fill the barrow, push and pull it up to the crescent of the cutting, get it emptied and back down to start all over again and again and again, a mindless flog draining them of their last energies.

Ethan refused to falter. His inner clock told him what time it was. The sun had gone down hours before. Along the tramway in the distance could be seen the lights from the viaduct shadowing the huge constructions of scaffolding and the steam cranes on the top lifting gear and stone. In the other direction came the muffled sounds of more explosions deep in the tunnel. This was his day to day world, the place where all his sweat and force were buried with the rest of the slag. Here was his gang cutting through a hillside, cheaper than tunnelling, but almost as difficult. The engineers and foremen were walking about the site constantly watching out for any sudden shift of mud that would start a huge slide of earth down the bank. Already this early winter there had been major mud slides in Ethan's section, slowing down the whole process as well as undermining any confidence the men might have had in the geologists and engineers who were supposed to avoid such things happening. Often the chief engineer himself Mr Stockton had been seen prowling around the area, his face a mask of seriousness and worry. He would stop to talk to some of the men as he passed in his ankle length mackintosh and wide brimmed hat. The men respected him for that. Instead of the usual silent looks from the bosses Stockton was at ease with his workers and seemed to understand what they were going through as though he had been in the same situation himself. There was no arrogance with him, not like with his second in command Murray who went about the works as though he was one of the company directors and had no time to look at never mind speak to any of the workforce. The men despised this attitude more than anything, which was why the mood at Ribblehead could often turn ugly with talk of strikes or downing tools for a day. There was a new belligerence in the work force nowadays. They were beginning now to realise the power they had. If they were unhappy they would certainly make it known whereas once of a day they would have kept their mouths shut and just got on with it scared of losing their jobs. Not that Ethan thought in such a way. He was not a radical. His pessimism meant he had no time for the ideas of huge changes, of revolution and the coming of a fairer and better world. To his mind nothing would ever drastically change. The British establishment was more solid than any other in the world. It absorbed challenges. It craftily compromised when necessary to maintain the status quo. It was not that Ethan was not interested or that he had not given it much thought. Like a lot of other things he had considered the different roles in society, accepting that his was the second lowest on the many rungs of the ladder of ambition. Beneath his position were those in the poor house, in prison, the vagrants and beggars. His whole purpose in life had become to ensure that he and his family never went there.

So often in bed at night when he was so tired he could not sleep he would try and understand how he had ever reached such a state. It had been the Reverend Barker, James Barker, the vicar of the Nottinghamshire parish where Ethan had been born. It was all his fault. He was the one responsible for passing on this disease of thought and consciousness, of giving the idea that so much was possible if you had a reasonable education. He had started taking a small group of local boys two evenings a week teaching them their alphabet. Ethan had been one of those boys and Reverend Barker had quickly seen his potential.

The next year he had started attending the junior school walking the three miles to Renton the nearest town and then when he reached the age of ten onto the big school which meant an even longer journey from his village.

'There's nothing wrong with ambition Ethan, but without a good schooling it is worthless to even consider it,' the Reverend Barker had once said to him, 'That's not to say you should not strive to become as much of yourself as possible, to fulfil all that you are capable of. You have been given this chance and you should take it.'

And he had been determined to ensure that the way forward would be not following in his father's footsteps and ending up down the pit. Even though he knew that was what his father had hoped. It had been his mother who had encouraged him to think differently, to believe that he was capable of a great deal more. There was even talk of university, something that the vicar was looking into.

The whole dream had crashed in pieces when his father had been taken ill and had died within a few weeks. Now he was the only one old enough in the family to earn a living. His mother tried her best taking in washing and sewing but it was not enough. One Friday in April Ethan had been a school pupil and by Monday he was working down the pit. It was the worst experience of his life. He felt as though he had been betrayed by circumstances, by life itself that had given with one hand and then had ripped it all away with the other. For months he had hated everything, especially his work down the pit, shovelling coal ten hours a day at the age of thirteen. The thought of endless years working in the sweating darkness had brought him low. His mother, brothers and sisters depended on the wage he brought in every week but necessity only bred contempt in him. His mind was being stifled. There was no time or energy for his books. For a few weeks he had tried to manage some hours a week reading but finally found it impossible, having to change himself into something that could function in the world of working men. Nobody was interested in anything other than earning money, drinking, gambling and finding a wife. That was all the miners talked about. From a man of the wider world Ethan had to shrink himself into this new miserable shape or he knew he would not be able to survive. But he hated being underground, hated the threat of the deep shafts and the way they made such strange, implausible sounds, creaks and clatters, wood groaning, rock falling, water dripping through the inevitable cracks. He wanted to be out in the fresh air, in space and sky and breath in a sense of freedom.

He was fifteen when he told his mother one night after work that he had heard about jobs building a new railway branch line near Manchester and that he was going to try for one. It would mean living away from home but the wages were good and he would send money home every week. To begin with his mother was distraught at such an idea. Night after night she argued and pleaded with him. Even his brothers and sisters had tried to persuade him not to go. But he could no longer work down the pit. It made him physically sick. He had to try something different.

The rain was getting heavier as finally the hooter went and the day's work was over at Ribblehead. Men trooped along the tramway before turning off, some to the other settlements, Surbiton, Jericho, Tunnel Huts and Sepastapol. The majority continued towards the embankment and the viaduct and then followed the diagonal track that took them down into Batty Green. Cigarettes and pipes were lit, a few conversations started, the men trudging along with their shovels balanced on their shoulders and some holding their lamps in the other hand to light their way. Some of the men owned their shovels, the others like Ethan went down to the shed where they were kept as well as the lamps. There was a crowd waiting to hand them over.

Suddenly the man next to Ethan as he turned away from the sheds said, 'Fuck this and fuck that as well.'

He tried to ignore these words but a face was pushed up close against his. He smelt the whisky before he realised it was Jock Tarrant.

'Fucking shit weather, eh?'

The broad Glaswegian accent and the stink of booze came off him and a smile was just discernible between the Scotsman's bushy moustache and thick beard.

They joined the rest of those going towards the pale whitewashed huts near the edge of the moor.

It was not just that Tarrant made Ethan uncomfortable, he was scared of him, scared of the constant threat he produced.

'So's?'

'Ay, filthy day.'

'Yer reckon.'

'I do.'

'Fucking right.'

This was the first time the Scot had picked him out to talk with. The man was intimidating. He gave the impression of being always ready for violence, his tone belligerent, miserable, angry. His words were forced out like small fists swinging at the listener. Usually all Ethan saw of him was in the early mornings before they went to work. Otherwise he was always in bed by the time the Scot had made his drunken way back to their hut. Sometimes he never appeared at all, lying somewhere unconscious in one of the settlement's many drinking dens.

Ethan wanted nothing to do with him but knew that made no difference. If Jock Tarrant wished to have a chat then that was what would happen.

'What about that big lump Asquith, what? He dotes on youse two bairns, him and long necked Henderson. Fucking hell. Mind youse Asquith had already got wee bairn Jonty in tow. Not all there, not the full anything. Should be in Bedlum so he should wi all the other fucking nutters. Now that's not me saying I dunnie like Jonty boy cos I does. What he needs is to get away from his fether Asquith. That bastard should leave him be, don't yer reckon?'

'I like Jonty too,' Ethan muttered back, feeling already stupid and inadequate.

'Ay,' Jock muttered and then smiled again, asking, 'What about us two going for a quick pint of the old frothy stuff? Don't look so worried Ethan Granger,' Jock was now laughing, 'I ain't going to force thee, Donnie worry yersell.'

Other men were shouting the odds as they turned off into their huts while the rest shifted along the walkways, the rain lashing into their faces and across the faint light coming from the hut windows.

Ethan knew he had to refuse but could not find the right words. He was nervous and confused by this unexpected bout of friendliness. He could tell the Scot was enjoying himself.

'No thanks,' he finally managed as a woman went by with two goats roped together followed by a group of boys who were rolling their metal hoops along the boards.

'What?'

'Don't fancy it.'

Jock stopped and turned, 'Well hell,' he muttered, 'Thought youse could manage a wee drink. Coming to think of it what the fuck can youse manage except getting to bed before yer own bairns?'

'Just leave it Jock,' Ethan said as calmly as he could, standing back to let another group of men past.

The Scotsman spat at Ethan's feet and without another word walked off in the direction of the Railway Inn.

Now Ethan felt even more intimidated, watching the Scot's squat, muscular figure disappear round the end of a row of huts. He was a worker and should be able to act like one but instead there was this feeling of always backing down, of letting the other dominate.

He walked past hut twenty one and continued to where the open moorland began, a huge swathe of rising ground that went right over to Dentdale.

His clothes were sodden through and he began to shiver as he turned to look over the full view of Ribblehead at night time, at the lights of all the huts and the vague outline of the scaffolding on the viaduct as well as more lamplight coming from one of the sheds where the tramway engines were housed. The heavy rain muffled all sounds. Ethan was desperate. The meeting with Tarrant had unsettled him. His nerves were screwed tight and his head was still pounding as he suddenly felt unsteady, his feet twisting in the heather. He forced himself to stay erect, trying to calm down with deep breaths. He could see himself standing there, that part of him that did the looking and the criticising, the persecuting, the part that created such dreadful dreams and daily frustrations, the part that never stopped questioning. His mind was his enemy and yet it was still him, still Ethan Granger, this one human being trying to blank out all sense of his identity and constantly failing.

He loved Clare and Beth more than anything in the world and yet sometimes found it hard to relate to them in the way he wanted. He was a married man who was trapped by his sense of duty. As a husband and a father he believed the pledge he had made to keep his family safe was unbreakable, something he would stick to whatever happened. He had a wife he loved who since the birth of their last child was unable to give him all he needed. Physically he was locked into frustration and a growing, more demanding desire, another piece of who he was that he did not want to recognise or accept. At the time there had been no other thought than to marry Maggie. She had been the daughter of the owners of a public house he used with a lot of the other men as it was situated close to where they had been working on a Manchester line. Some of the labourers had women who moved from one man to another. That was not for him. If he was to be with Maggie then it had to be a total commitment. With women he was always anxious, always lacking in confidence so when he had eventually managed to find one who was attracted to him and he to her then they had to be married. Only since the birth of Beth had he begun to regret such a decision, their vows made in a church which to Maggie meant they could never be broken. To her they were given in sight of the Lord. They still had feelings for each other. There were still remnants of the passion they had once experienced, but for him so much had changed. He could no longer physically love his wife and the more he struggled on to earn enough money to keep the family going the more he felt a stranger to himself.

Finally he came back into the settlement that smelt of cold mud, food being cooked, the stench of all the animals and the odour of sewerage coming from the sheds littered across the hillside. He would take off his boots before entering the hut, something they all had to do now that Maggie was responsible for keeping the place clean. He would hang up his sodden clothes with the rest and then sit down to eat his dinner before as usual going to bed early. Maggie would give him her worried look. Fraser Henderson would be entertaining Clare and Beth. Bill would be sat smoking his pipe while Jonty would be watching what the children were doing. This was the nightly routine. Only rarely was Jock Tarrant present. He was not part of this larger family that Ethan had begun to resent. He had not the energy or purpose to do anything about it. He just hoped that the day's work had tired him enough to give him a good night's sleep without the persecutory dreams he had been having recently.

'Oh there you are,' said Maggie as he entered the hut in his stocking feet, carrying his boots, coat and jacket that was dripping rain water onto the floor.

'Yes I'm here,' he answered emptily as the rest of them glanced up at him and then back to what they were doing.

CHAPTER TEN

The mud reflected a strange rainbow light. They had been told to keep up towards the moor side. The day was so cold any pools of water were frozen over, the ice creased and cracked. The more they were reminded to keep away from the valley bottom the more they were fascinated by it. The story of a woman was told who had been sucked down into Batty Floss never to be seen again.

'She's still down there,' Clare informed her sister, 'They say she's waiting for her fella.'

Beth pulled the scarf down covering her mouth and was about to ask a question but changed her mind.

Her sister was disappointed and so added, 'She were married to him.'

'Everybody's married,' said Beth confidently.

Clare laughed at her.

They had sticks and were swishing at the frozen grass as they ascended the moor side above the settlement.

Beth was anxious for something to happen. Her sister was trying to think of the right words for what she wanted to say next.

'Do you believe it?' she finally managed.

The sky was a ringing blue above them with crystal clear views right down the dale, all white under the new frost. From where they were walking they could see the last row of huts with washing hanging stiffly out on this the first fine day for over a week. Each hut had a pile of coal at the side. Some had pens for their chickens, geese, goats or rabbits. At the rear of their huts a few had a lean to under which they stored peat some of the local farmers sold round the settlements.

'I'm fed up,' muttered Beth.

'Fed up you?'

Beth was walking half a yard behind her sister, both in oversized coats bought cheaply from the Saturday market and badly worn clogs.

Clare's pale features, thin hands and narrow nose were emphasised in the low sunlight. She was never sure about herself. She knew Beth was different. She was nearly six years older so had to be in charge and at the same time had to show that she was responsible and caring. Both their heads had been washed, brushed and combed over and over again by their mother to try and rid their hair of all the filth and nits.

'I'll do yer plaits Beth. I won't pull too hard.'

'If yer like.'

'Here sit on this here stone.'

'It'll be too cold on me bum.'

'Alright then, I'll stand on it and don't you move.'

'Mam says me hair is clean as anything.'

'And mine.'

'Why.....why do we have hair?' Beth asked, her mind puzzling again.

'To keep our heads warm stupid.'

'So why haven't we got hair all over?'

'Cos we don't want to look like monkeys.'

'How do you know what monkeys look like?'

'That book, remember, that Fraser showed us.'

'He's nice is Fraser.'

'He's alright.'

'And Jonty, I like Jonty.'

'I like him when he laughs. He's funny.'

Below them all the smoke rose straight from the many chimneys and thicker clouds billowed out of the brick factory. Everywhere there were men working like clots of bluebottles. The metal trucks were being noisily pulled up the tramway to the quarry and the new one being built up to the tunnel. They could see women down at the Gayle Beck before it turned sharply down its narrow valley towards Selside and Horton and there was a line of carts coming along the Ingleton road. Added to this the confusion of the noise of cranes and steam engines mixed in with the sound of the men's shovels and picks.

'You're pulling too hard Clare!'

'Oh tosh! Stand still.'

'Are yer done yet?'

'Nearly.'

'Good.'

'I thought you liked me fixing yer hair. Yer lucky I can be bothered.'

'I'll do yours if you like,' Beth suggested.

'No thanks.'

'Why not?'

'Just.'

'Just what?'

'Stop asking so many questions.'

'Well how can I learn if I don't ask questions? That's what Bill told us, told us that to know things you have to ask questions.'

'There,' said Clare finally.

Beth patted the back of her head and added, 'You've made two plaits.'

'For a change.'

They looked down at the mob of boys who had suddenly appeared striding up the bank of moorland towards them.

'Crackers Clare Granger!' one called as they approached.

'Stinkers!' came another.

'Your arse is where thine head should be!'

'Show us yer crack! Go on show us.'

'Fuck off,' said Clare strongly as she grabbed Beth's hand and started trudging quickly over the frozen grass and down the hillside followed by more calls of derision.

'Mucky devils,' muttered Clare as they reached the track that led past the brick works and engine sheds.

'Where youse two going?' a worker from the brick factory wanted to know as he came out of the long building wiping his hands with a rag.

'Nowt to do wi you.'

'Yer cheeky bugger.'

'Cheeky you.'

'Whose your father?'

'He's a prince.'

'Never.'

'He is.'

'I never said he wasn't,' the man laughed as they strode away.

'Where we going?' Beth asked miserably.

'There's me Mam talking to that woman next door.'

They both looked up the slope where they could just make out Maggie talking to Shirley Stanton.

'So you're getting on alright in this place, settled down have yer?' Shirley was asking.

'I reckon so.'

'I don't know how thee manages wi a husband, two girls and four.....four lodgers.'

Shirley was short and stout with a large bosom and head topped off by a huge mop of ginger hair.

'Ay it's a fuss.'

'I should think it is, a lot of work fer yer.'

'Needs must and I'm not complaining wi the way they've wanted it.'

'And how's that?'

Maggie did not mind her neighbour's nosiness. It was how it was in the settlements, everybody wanting to know everyone else's business and making it up if information was lacking.

'They pay for me to do their cooking and washing.'

Shirley looked more than interested, her freckled face thoughtful and her eyes filled with curiosity.

'It's alright. It's owt fer nowt as they say.'

Maggie already had the reputation of thinking herself a little above the rest, a woman who had high standards and expectations and with a husband who seemed to do exactly what she wanted, quiet, steady, not a drinker, at home every night. It was Shirley who supplied this gossip if anyone was interested. She was fascinated as well as jealous and yet still had a liking for Maggie. Shirley enjoyed their chats which usually took place when they were hanging or taking down the washing. Maggie always had at least three times more clothes to do than she did. Shirley was desperate to know how much Maggie was paid by her lodgers. She knew what the going rate was and guessed that Maggie was probably paid more. Gossip in the settlements could be vicious especially round the women who ran the drinking dens, the ones who moved from one man to the next or those who sold themselves for a few shilling a go. Gossip became rumour that became downright lies, a web of insult and suspicion that wrapped around all of them. There were fights enough, women biting, scratching, tugging at hair, spitting and kicking as neighbours egged them on to more violence. The worst ones were well known and there were always new women appearing looking for which men would have them. Batty Green was big enough for a lot to be happening and small enough for everyone to hear about it, just the right balance for all the gossip mongers.

'I've only got Tom Bryson, our lodger, our kids and Arthur of course.'

'It was one o my lodgers that asked me, well Bill did.'

'Oh him, thinks he rules the roost that one does.'

'I suppose Bill does like his own way, but I find him right helpful at times.'

'He's just a big mouth and too old for any fit work. That's why they've shifted him off into the factory. How you put up wi that Jonty lad as well. He's not the full shilling if you don't mind me saying so.'

'Jonty's alright. He's meek and mild, wouldn't hurt a fly and Bill's always there fer him."

'I don't know,' Shirley persisted, her arms crossed under her ample bosom as the washing began to flap around them in the bright winter sunlight.

To begin with Maggie had wanted to keep as much to herself without being rude, but that had changed when she realised that whatever she said all of it would be distorted. Truth did not seem to matter. Opinion was everything. She knew if she told Shirley anything it would be round the settlements in minutes. She knew that soon the novelty of the Grangers' arrival would wear off and others would become the focus of her neighbour's attention.

'So how's your Ethan getting on?'

This question was more sensitive than most. Maggie was wary of saying too much and yet knew the inquiry had to be answered one way or another or Shirley would presume something was seriously wrong.

'I suppose he's a bit like your Arthur, just gets on wi it. Nothing else he can do.'

'No, you're right there. At least it's better paid here than most.'

'No wonder, asking folk to come and live and work in a place like this.'

'The wilds of Yorkshire!' Shirley laughed.

'It's certainly wild enough. This must be the first fine day we've had in I don't know how long.'

'So we have to mek the most of it while we can cos it'll be getting dark before we know it. I hate these long nights, always have.'

'At least we have the market tomorrow.'

'I should hope so. Need someat for a bit of a change.'

They went on to talk about the cost of bread and groceries brought up every day from the Bannister and Dicksen shop in Settle, part of the regular convoy of carts that came to supply the settlements, that and the rest bringing everything the building of the new railway needed. Most of it came from Ingleton that was on a branch line off the main London – Carlisle route. There was constant traffic from the small town, even late on in the dark evenings. It never stopped. It could not stop. There was also the blacksmith's, the cobbler, the temporary stalls set up through the week and the others on a Saturday that sold everything, clothes, leather goods, candles, fruit, meat, eggs, one selling meat pies, another a mixture of hot drinks and boiled sweets. The stalls were on either side of the road from the brick factory to the stone bridge over the Beck, each lit by a row of oil lamps when it got dark. Crowds would come from the other settlements, some travelling in the empty trucks brought down the tramway. Batty Green on a winter's Saturday night was busy, noisy, smelly, with the general reek of alcohol pervading the place as men tramped from one drinking den to the next, looking for a game of three card brag, a fight or one of the new loose women who had arrived that week. It went on until the early hours of a Sunday morning and was one of the reasons James Tranton complained about the lack of men folk at the first of his Sunday's meetings.

Maggie and Shirley were just discussing the arrival last Saturday of the fortune teller Nancy Mangini and her gypsy caravan when a boy called Billy Derkins came running along the boards.

'You missus Granger?' he asked breathlessly as he came to a stop.

'I am, said Maggie, 'what of it?'

'One of your girls she…….'

'What about her?'

'Stuck in the Moss missus. They're trying to get her out right now. I……'

Maggie threw down her basket of fresh washing, lifted up her apron and skirt and started running followed quickly by Shirley and the boy.

A crowd had gathered around the wide pool of black mud by the time they arrived. Maggie pushed her way through and saw to her horror Beth up to her chest in it with the surface ice broken in large fragments around her.

'Mam!' came from Clare who was there by the edge, 'I'm sorry Mam,' she started when she grabbed hold of her mother, 'She just…..just wouldn't tek a telling, wanted to walk across…..'

'It doesn't matter,' her mother interrupted strongly,' doesn't matter.'

'God help us,' said Shirley as she came and stood beside them and more people arrived to see what was going on, a silent crowd watching the young girl who was gradually sinking into the mud. The silence was one of a tragedy being close and all of them recognising the horror of the situation.

'I should have stopped her, should have stopped her,' Clare was muttering, 'It's my fault. Mine.'

'Beth!' Maggie tried, 'I'm here love.'

'Mam,' Beth said breathlessly back.

'It'll be alright. It will.'

'Mam I'm scared.'

'You'll be alright. They'll get you out. Just don't move whatever you do. Stay still, as still as you can.'

'I'm……..I'm trying,' Beth replied pitifully, her round face streaked with muddy tears and her mouth puckered up as she stared over at her mother and Clare standing there rigid with fright.

'Let them through! Let them through!' someone was shouting.

The crowd parted to let men with planks of wood come to the frozen edge of the Moss.

One of them shouted to lay them down and extend them over the surface of the mud before he ordered them to stand on the ends of the planks to keep them steady. With everything taken off but his shirt and trousers and with a rope tied around his waist he got down on his knees and started carefully going along the two planks that bent alarmingly with his weight. Everyone held their breath, intent on this man and the girl's terrified expression as she watched him crawl towards her. More men stood on the end of the planks to keep them from shifting although already the parts over the Moss were beginning to bend even more as the man got closer.

He was Tom Myres, a stonemason working on the viaduct.

'What's yer name lass?' he asked quietly.

Beth seemed not to hear as she slipped further down, the black mud now up to her shoulders.

'Yer name lass?'

'I'm…….I'm cold,' she finally managed in a shaky voice.

'Course you are.'

'It's cold.'

'Yes, I know, I know lass.'

Even Maggie could not speak. She knew they were reaching the critical moments. She felt Clare gripping her arm even tighter while Shirley could be heard panting rapidly beside them.

'Beth,' the mother finally managed, 'Her name's Beth,' she shouted to the man.

'Beth, right. I want…..want……No….no…….tek it easy, easy,' he added quickly as again the girl sunk down even further, 'Just keep as still as you can. Alright Beth? We'll have you out in a jiffy. You just do what I say.'

'Mam!' she called out.

'Just listen Beth, listen to the man.'

By now the Moss was completely surrounded by the crowd. Their faces were intent and focused. Even the children were silent, the peoples' breath rising into the frozen air as the sun dipped behind the viaduct's high scaffolding sending confused shafts of light into the squinting eyes of those on the far side of the mud pool.

'Now,' the man said gently as he shifted further along the planks that had now dipped beneath the mud and held out his right arm, 'I just want you Beth to just reach out…..just……'

'I can't!'

'You'll be alright Beth,' Maggie repeated, 'Just listen to the man. You have to do what he says and then you'll.....you'll be alright. You'll be alright Beth if you just do what the man says.'

'I'm scared Mam.'

'I know love. I know you are, but it'll soon be over. It'll be alright. It will. I promise you and Clare's here as well. Your sister's here.'

'I'm.......I'm......' Beth started as her shoulders suddenly slipped under the blackness. Some in the crowd gasped and others started muttering fresh advice which only seemed to confuse the girl.

'Steady Tom,' someone said.

Beth's face was so white, so terrified, her eyes full of fresh tears.

'I'll manage. I'll get yer Beth.'

'Please mister,' she said back.

'You're going to be alright.'

'Please.'

'You're doing grand Beth. You're doing grand.'

'No,' she moaned.

'You're alright Beth,' her mother said strongly.

'Beth, Beth,' her sister pleaded.

The crowd had seen enough dramas, tragedies and wasted lives. Danger was part of what they did and even if it was accepted it could still shock them as it did now. The Grangers were newcomers so not that well known but this was a young lass and she was slowly being murdered by the dreaded bog. They were men, women and children dressed in their drab winter clothes, the men filthy as always standing there concerned, held to these moments where death interminably shifted up towards the girl's terrified face. Around them the work on the line continued. The Moss was this silent centre of all the afternoon's business and noise.

Suddenly the sun disappeared behind the first clouds of the day. As the scene immediately darkened several things happened at once. Clare could manage no more and pulled away from her mother to lose herself in the crowd as she pushed her way out and away from it all. At the same time Richard Stockton and Andrew Murray strode to the edge of the Moss across from where Maggie was standing, and finally Ethan appeared, pushing his way through to his wife who gave him the briefest of looks before turning back to her Beth.

'I just heard,' he muttered, 'Oh my God, how the hell did she get there?'

Maggie made no reply.

More grey clouds came over the top of Whernside and descended towards the dale. An evening wind started and a deepening cold settled over the people watching. The broken ice over the mud turned into thin plates of steel as Tom Myres sank lower waiting for Beth to make a move.

'Bloody hell. No....no.....'Ethan was saying, 'What.....what was she.......?'

His voice trailed off. The only sound was of waggons coming down off the Hawes to Ingleton road, rattling over the bridge and following the track that skirted the Moss, some of the drivers stopping and standing up on their seats to get a better view of what was happening.

By now there was a large crowd who were constantly being joined by others. Time had almost stopped. Everything was becoming slower and slower as Myres waited and the blackness covered Beth's chin. And then at last she tried, suddenly jerking her head as she pulled out her right arm from the mud and reached over to the offered hand. But the movement had been so rapid that in a moment her head went under and the whole of her disappeared. There were different cries from the crowd. Ethan instinctively grabbed hold of his wife's arm as their daughter went under.

Myres lunged forward almost falling himself off the dangerously bending planks. Beth's sodden, melting face came up, her mouth opening to gasp for air before she slipped from his grasp and went under again only for Myres to make another lunge down for her, this time grabbing her plaits and pulling on them as the girl's head and shoulders emerged, Beth screaming and gasping as he dragged his arms under her shoulders, their shared weight bending the planks until at one point it seemed they were both going to slip away.

Myres was covered and sodden. Beth was half conscious as he tried to work backwards. The people watching made hardly a sound. Still it was not finished as with a familiar cracking sound one of the planks started to split. In a sudden rush and careful effort the stonemason twisted round with the girl behind him and as the plank split he already had his first foot on the frozen bank, dragging Beth up onto the icy grass. He laid her out. Mr Shawcross the company doctor had been called for. Ethan had his coat and jacket off and wrapped it round her as everyone started talking with relief. When it was certain the girl was safe Richard Stockton and Andrew Murray without a word made their way through the crush and left the scene. Maggie was on her knees stroking Beth's frozen face. Tom Myres was also down on the frozen ground trying to get his breath back as several men came up to congratulate him. He was sodden through, covered in the bog, mud dribbling off him like unwanted scales as he gasped in more of the freezing air.

It was over. Death had shifted away back into the depths of the Moss. The crowd started to disperse, a few staying behind to watch as Doctor Shawcross arrived and started tending to Beth who had now opened her eyes staring up pleadingly into those of her mother's.

'It's alright love. It's alright. You're safe now,' she said earnestly, still wiping the mud off her daughter's cheeks and chin.

'I'm......I'm sorry Mam. I'm....'

'No,' Maggie interrupted, 'You shhh now, quiet, let the doctor have a look at you and then we'll get you home and warmed up.'

The last rays of the sun merged into the horizon's greyness. The dale prepared for another cold night and more lamps were lit up on the viaduct and along the way of the line to where the rest of the men were still working.

CHAPTER ELEVEN

The Railway Inn, the only stone building in the area, was packed. Bill Arnold the landlord and his wife were serving up jugs of beer from the barrels behind the bar. In one corner a worker was playing an accordion as another joined in with his fiddle while the men worked their pipes filling the low ceilinged room with thick, floating smoke twisting into different shapes above their heads. Candles had been lit in the small window recesses and a coal fire roared below its stone mantelpiece sending shadows to dance with the pipe smoke.

Ethan entered and was immediately hit by the noise and fug of beer and tobacco smells. This was the first time he had set foot in one of Batty Green's many drinking establishments. For him there was too much of a social obligation once you entered a pub. On this night he felt shy and awkward with so many eyes glancing his way as he squeezed through the throng to ask the landlord if he could tell him whether Tom Myres was in tonight.

'Over there in the corner brewing up the next revolution,' the landlord had to shout above the din.

Ethan turned and glimpsed through the moving bodies of the crowded pub a group of men seated in the far corner of the noisy, choking room.

For a time he did not move, being pushed from side to side by more drinkers coming in. He was anxious, unsure as to how he was to manage this situation. Maggie had insisted that he found Tom Myres to thank him for saving Beth. Ethan was already feeling jealous and inadequate in relation to this stranger, the day's hero. In his mind it should have been himself who had rescued their Beth. He was utterly grateful and yet envious of this stonemason. Suddenly being self critical he forced his way to where Myres was seated.

Men were shouting and swearing at each other as he made his way through the throng. Beer was tipped and splashed about as the smoke stung his eyes.

Ethan held out his hand and Myres stood up at this unexpected interruption.

'I want to thank ye for what ye did,' Ethan managed, his throat dry with a deepening nervousness.

The stonemason with his thick brown moustache and short cut hair looked at him inquiringly.

'I'm the girl's father.'

'Oh, right you are. Now I understand. Saw you come in, never seen you in the Railway before.'

'No, I don't.....I don't.....'

'Anyroads, set theesell down.'

'I want to buy you a drink.'

Myres was aware of this man's uncertain tone. He found it amusing and interesting. There was decidedly something different about him.

'I could introduce you to all this lot,' he motioned to those seated in a semi-circle of straight backed chairs, 'but there's so many you'll have forgotten em in half a minute so I won't bother. So you are?'

'Ethan Granger.'

Myres said back, 'Well Ethan Granger I'll have a jug if you're offering.'

In his youth Ethan had often frequented the local pubs, one outside Manchester being where he had met Maggie, but since then, to ensure he kept the family away from starvation he had stopped drinking. It was a few years since he had last been in a place like the Railway Inn and it made him uncomfortable. It was loud, stank and was too noisy with the sounds of the accordion and fiddle that began to grate on his nerves. There were so many men here that he did not recognise, all of them still in their filthy work clothes.

One of those in the corner managed to find an extra seat for him after he had made his way back through the crowd with a jug in each hand.

'Good un Ethan,' said Myres before he gulped down a mouthful of the warm beer.

'I have to thank you.'

'You already have.'

'For what you did for our Beth.'

'So long as the lass is alright.'

'Doctor Shawcross said she'd be fine after a good night's sleep in a warm bed.'

'Best thing for her, help her to forget.'

'I was there, I saw what yer did.'

'Right.'

'Just heard up at the north cutting and ran down. I saw what you did. You were brave helping like that.'

'Anyone would have done the same,' said Tom.

'We're allays telling our two to keep away from the Moss, not that they listened. Beth was wi her elder sister our Clare. She should have known better. Now she's more upset than anyone.'

Ethan was aware that he was talking too fast. He took a sip of his beer that tasted sour and glanced around at the others who were also listening.

‘Yer lass was brave mind,’ Tom put in, his moustache covered with the froth from the beer.

‘I suppose so, her just having had her sixth birthday.’

‘She nair panicked.’

‘No, she didn’t, not like us, me and the missus.’

‘Couldn’t be calm in a situation like that, not when it’s yer own lass.’

‘We weren’t.’

There was a pause. Suddenly there seemed nothing else to say. The rest of the men started talking between themselves as Tom drank his beer.

‘You saved her life,’ Ethan finally added, knowing he was beginning to repeat himself.

‘My good deed for the day you might call it.’

‘Yes,’ he answered uncertainly, feeling the strain of being there.

The musicians stopped playing. The landlord was yelling at someone in the crowd as a jug was suddenly thrown and the men started looking around for the culprit.

‘Stupid bastard!’ another shouted.

‘Fucking shit!’ came another.

‘So Ethan, where do you hail from?’ Tom asked, ignoring the row that was brewing.

‘Nottingham.’

‘Do you know we’ve got the lot here? If yer listen carefully enough you can hear every dialect there is, Cornish, Welsh, Irish, Glaswegian, Geordie, Yorkshire and everywhere else they might have come from. It’s allays the same on a big job and they say this might be the last big one. There’ll be nowt much else after this for the lads. We’ll all have to be looking abroad. That’s where the work’ll be.’

‘I suppose so,’ said Ethan emptily.

Tom looked at him with an intrigued expression asking, ‘So you heard they were paying good wages at Ribblehead? They think they’re good wages although that’s debatable like everything else they tell us. Good for who? That’s the question.’

Ethan took hold of his jug not sure how to respond.

‘Sorry lad,’ Tom laughed, ‘after a few jugs I tend to go off on a rant.’

‘No, that’s fine wi me.’

‘We think we’re lucky having work but it’s as always the company who get the true benefit. So don’t think kindly on em cos they don’t deserve it.’

‘I don’t.’

'Glad to hear it Ethan Granger.'

There was a pause. Tom was trying his best not to pressurise Ethan. The cigarette and pipe smoke swirled towards the door every time somebody entered the place. There was a sudden uproar then as a woman appeared on the bar top.

'Christ, here we go,' muttered Tom.

'What she doing?' Ethan asked.

'If you ain't seen Mary Little dancing you're either in for a treat or you're going to be bloody disgusted. Mary is one of the cheaper ladies of Batty Green but has a heart of gold as they say but she lies rotten about her age, at least the other side of forty but pretends she's no more than twenty. The woman loves to mek an exhibition of hersell. You watch and you'll know what I mean.'

The accordion and fiddle started up again, their music getting faster and faster as the men pushed towards the bar and began shouting their encouragement, their eyes glistening in the fug of smoke, their mouths wet with drink as they stared at Mary up on the bar top spinning round and round, hands high in the air, her large breasts bouncing beneath a tight blouse and her skirt billowing out with the speed of her movements.

The men started to clap and shout out obscenities, their expression becoming serious with expectancy. Ethan felt their drink filled attention, a focus that disturbed him, hating to see a woman offering herself like this, her face red and sweating, her boots hammering on the top of the bar. This kind of entertainment was not for him and yet at the same time he found himself being roused by it. This Mary was so blatant with her flirting and laughing as her skirt swirled above her knees and a button burst off her blouse encouraging her audience to even more noise.

'Don't worry!' Tom tried to shout in Ethan's ear, 'There's only one nightly performance thank God. After this Mary'll have a queue of customers to get on with. She bloody loves the attention. Tries to tell everybody she used to dance in London variety shows, down the docks more like working up the dockers.'

Ethan was confused. The idea of any woman showing herself off like this bothered him. Her body was on show and she was enjoying it. She was enticing all the men who were open mouthed, drunkenly absorbed in her pathetic, crude performance. Mary began screaming through her thickly painted lips, then stopped, turned, stood with her legs parted before she lifted up her skirt to show her bare buttocks. The men roared and so she turned again showing all of it as she laughed back at her audience and finally dropped her skirt and fell off the bar top into the waiting crowd's arms.

'Thank Christ, that's over,' Tom Myres sighed.

'I'll have to be going,' Ethan told him.

'Nay lad, you've only just got here. Stay a while. Tell us where yer working.'

But Ethan wanted no more of this place and its loud congestion. His eyes shifted from side to side as he started to stand up, embarrassed with feeling himself hardening at what he had seen.

Tom grabbed his arm, 'I asked thee a question.'

Ethan looked down at him with a sudden defiant expression.

'Does it matter?' he asked irritably, pulling away his arm.

'Nothing matters if you think on it that way, not a damned thing.'

'You know what I mean.'

'It was just a bloody simple question.'

Ethan forced himself to sit back down. The rest of the men were watching him critically, their faces tense with sudden resentment.

'Let the man bugger off if he wants to,' one of them suggested.

'Mary's done for him!' another laughed.

'He's off for a quickie wi her.'

'I'm alright,' Ethan replied too loudly.

'Nobody said thee weren't.'

He turned to Myres and told him where he was working before taking another mouthful of beer, wiping the froth from his top lip with the back of his hand.

Tom pulled a doubtful expression, stroking down his heavy moustache thoughtfully.

'We're here to talk politics,' another of the men mentioned, 'that's what we do here, not like these other silly buggers who just come here to get pissed of a night.'

Ethan felt out of place, a stranger, somebody unwanted and yet now he refused to be pushed away. He would stay and show them that he could manage anything they wanted to talk about. If he left the pub right now he would be critical, disappointed and angry at himself so his decision was to avoid any more embarrassment. There had been enough already on this day.

'It's not just talk either,' said Tom, 'it's preparing for action. No good bloody just mouthing off. Someat has to happen, has to be done or nowt'll change.'

'So we don't blame thee if thee wants to go,' the worker sat on the other side of him said loudly.

'I don't mind,' he answered him, trying to sound calm.

'Don't mind what?'

'Anything you want to talk about.'

'Talk about?'

'Yes.'

'Right then.'

'So what do you reckon Ethan to the work up here?' Tom pointedly asked him.

'The work?'

'Ay, here at Ribblehead. How long have thee been here now?'

'Over two months.'

'Enough time to have an opinion, time enough to learn what's going on.'

'I don't see how I........'

Keep yer head down and say nowt, is that it?'

'No, not at all.'

'Well then?'

Ethan was becoming increasingly frustrated with being questioned like this, but he would not back down.

'At the moment I'm doing what I came here to do.'

'Which is what?'

'Work.'

'You don't say,' another of the men in the corner commented.

'That's what I came here for, work and better wages.'

'Well good for you.'

'Have we finished?' he boldly asked, a defiance in his voice.

'Thee's no need to tek it like that,' said Myres.

'I'm not taking anything. I've just said what I came here to say and now I'm leaving, simple as that.'

Nobody made a response while they watched him get out of his seat and push his way through the crowd to the door. Tom Myres sat there smiling to himself.

'Funny bloody accent,' one of his group added.

'Funny all round,' agreed Tom before he asked who was getting the next jugs of beer.

Outside Ethan took a large mouthful of winter air, the noise from the Railway Inn behind him. He hated to come away like that, somehow defeated and made to look and sound like a fool. He wanted to sound stronger, more definite and committed instead of being left sounding weak and unsure again.

On entering the hut Fraser was seated at the table, smoking his pipe and reading the Craven Herald, the local paper of the Dales.

'Evening,' Ethan muttered as he started taking off his coat.

'Cold one.'

'Ay it is.'

'Maggie is in the bedroom checking on the girls.'

The silence between them was based on uncertainty. After over two months they were still strangers.

'Terrible do,' Fraser finally added, 'Poor Beth and Clare in a right state.'

'It was, bloody awful. I got there just as a mason called Tom Myres pulled her out.'

'Oh I've heard all about Tom Myres.'

'In what way?' asked Ethan, immediately interested.

He had meant to go straight into the bedroom but wanted to hear what Fraser had to say. He sat down opposite him noticing the other's finger nails. They were the only ones he had seen that were clean and neatly cut. He presumed it was because of his job checking the tramway lines. He was not always covered in the filth of blue clay like the rest of the men. All he did everyday was walk the lines ensuring there was no shift in the rails or the ground underneath.

'Tom Myres stirs people up, he began, 'He might call himself a stonemason but he's here more to stir up trouble than anything else. He's a political animal who has a reputation of causing trouble. He calls himself a socialist or communist or some nonsense like that. To me he just likes the sound of his own voice. I'm not saying he ain't clever enough cos he is and he can get the men all hot and bothered with some of his speeches.'

'So why don't the company just get rid of him?'

Fraser's thin lips broke into a smile, 'Well yes you would think that, but Myres has got them caught cos he knows if they sack him then there really would be trouble.'

'You mean the men would back him?'

'Enough would I reckon. He's supposed to be the masons' representative or so he calls himself. The story is that they took a vote on it and he was chosen by a sizeable majority. More fool them, that's what I say. They're just digging a bigger hole for themselves cos eventually the company won't have it. There'll be a show down and guess who will win like they always do?'

When it seemed there was nothing more to add he awkwardly got up as he asked him where the others were.

'All of em out somewhere.'

'Right,' said Ethan, 'I'd better go and see how the girls are.'

'Let's hope they have a settled night.'

'Ay, let's hope so.'

In the bedroom Maggie had lit a candle and was seated on Beth's bed stroking her forehead. Both the girls seemed to be asleep.

'How is she?' he asked in a whisper.

'Asleep thank God.'

He came over and touched Beth's cheek saying, 'Well at least she's not burning up. What about Clare?'

'Cried hersell to sleep. Nothing I said made any difference. As far as she's concerned it's all her fault and she hates herself for it and is scared Beth will never speak to her again.'

'So we leave her, is that what we do?'

'I think so seeing as she's got hersell into a right state.'

'What a bloody mess.'

'At least our Beth's here. She could have died this afternoon, she could have. Luckily that Tom Myres knew what to do. Did you get to thank him?'

'I did.'

'Where did you find him?'

'In the Railway, supping with his mates.'

'And you thanked him properly?'

'Yes, I told you.' He said in irritation.

'Keep your voice down.'

He leant forward to kiss the sleeping Beth on the cheek and went over to do the same with Clare before he started getting undressed.

When Maggie finally joined him he was on his back still wide awake. Her body felt so warm beside his. He was thinking about Mary Little's dancing, showing her buttocks and the clump of black hair between her legs.

After a few minutes he said, 'I should have been there quicker.'

'You couldn't help it.'

'I know but it should have.......should have been me there instead of......'

'Don't be silly. Who cares who it was so long as our Beth was saved?'

'I suppose so.'

'It's true we have this Tom Myres to thank but you've done that. There's nothing more,' Maggie said quietly.

Later when she was asleep Ethan lay there with his eyes open in the darkness wondering if a man like Tom Myres ever had trouble going to sleep. Every night he was reminded how much he had failed himself, his dreams full of dread and a haunting. His own mind was persecuting him and tonight there was the added image of Tom Myres being watched admiringly by the crowd as he dragged Beth out of the Moss.

He was aware of Maggie breathing slowly beside him. Her body was still strong and firm but all she could offer him were her kisses, her warmth, nothing more and there never would be anything more. The birth of Beth had resulted in too many complications. It was something they never spoke about because there was no point. Their lives together had this problem and nothing could be done. The doctor had told her that becoming pregnant again would be too dangerous and however difficult it might be this was something Ethan had to accept.

'I should have been a teacher or an office worker, anything but what I'm doing,' he often told himself, the usual self recriminations.

The room was cold and dark. He heard Bill and Jonty return and then much later Jock Tarrant causing a row when he went into their bedroom and disturbed the others with his loud voice and stumbling about trying to get to his bed. It was another night with the usual routine leading to another day that would be just the same and on and on, all of them digging themselves to an early grave.

CHAPTER TWELVE

Jonty lived in a world of patterns. Bill and a fellow worker Sam Pritchard had found him on the Dent road around the same time the previous year. They had been bringing back a cart of peat from a local farm when out of the late afternoon's winter mist they had seen this figure walking along in the middle of the road. He had been bare footed wearing only a shirt and a torn pair of trousers. When they stopped and lifted him up onto the cart he was almost frozen to death, muttering away to himself as they took him back to Batty Green. Since then he had remained a mystery. Nobody including Jonty himself had any idea where he had come from and what he had been doing in such a state last winter on the road to Dent. Bill had pushed hard to get the company to give him a job guaranteeing that he would take complete responsibility for Jonty's welfare and his attendance at work. The two of them had been at the brick factory and staying in hut twenty two ever since that strange afternoon when this poor, half-witted young man had been discovered wandering about in the cold mist on the moors. Bill reckoned that if they had found him a half an hour later he would have been frozen to death.

But patterns surrounded Jonty. He could see them everywhere, in the frost on the windows, in the huge construction of the viaduct's scaffolding, in the way the bricks came out of the oven, shapes, jigsaw pieces, lines and blocks, squares and triangles. His eyes translated the physical world around him into his mind's perception. It was almost mathematical, but it was never expressed. Jonty had numerous images but few words. To speak was hard. It hurt his head and it hurt his throat. He had no past to remember; neither did the future exist for him. He was a child in a man's tall, gangling body with a tongue too big for his mouth and spit that constantly dribbled. His attempt at a moustache were a few scraggy strands above his top lip but his thick hair on top was parted down the middle and Bill ensured he was always well washed after work.

Jonty laughed a lot. He loved watching the girls playing games and doing the puzzles that Fraser brought them. In the morning he would be beside Bill on their way to work with his tongue stuck out catching the falling snowflakes that tickled as they melted. Nothing was boring. Nothing was without emotion. He was often scared and was unsure of any stranger which included nearly the whole work force at Batty Green. His whole existence depended on Bill; he was his father, mother, brother and everybody else that Jonty might need. To begin with there had been a struggle with the rest of the men in the factory. They had started to ridicule him but Bill would not have it. They had wanted to laugh at him but the first retaliation from Bill had stopped all their jokes. Now they left him alone, even respected the hard shift he put in every day. Jonty was dependable, strong, never tiring and eventually that was enough.

'I'm here,' he announced one Sunday morning, standing there in the kitchen with his best suit on and a face red and shiny.

This was now the weekly routine. Maggie would be up first followed by Jonty who would help her prepare the Sunday breakfast, the biggest of the week.

His collar was loose and his tie over knotted. He had tried to clean his boots with little effect but Maggie as always was pleased to see him. She enjoyed these Sunday morning moments together. She would tell him everything that needed to be done and he would follow every instruction as best he could.

Jonty felt calmer with Maggie than anybody else except Bill. He could feel how easy and relaxed she was with him.

'Ready,' he told her.

'Morning Jonty.'

'Morning Missus.'

'You look smart today.'

'Best suit.'

'I can tell. You look grand.'

'Sunday.'

'It is, all day Jonty.'

'Sunday best, going to church, me and Bill going to church.'

Such a long sentence he found tiring. Words would rush forward and then often disappear before he had time to catch them.

'So what's first Jonty?'

His eyes opened wide. He frowned and pursed out his thick lips.

Maggie waited. She was patient with him. He was the child trying to learn.

'Plates!' he exclaimed triumphantly.

'Not so loud, you'll wake em all.'

'Plates Missus.'

'Good.'

He went over to the shelves beside the stove, grabbing all the plates he could.

'How many?'

'Many?'

'How many do we need?'

Again he was lost before he tried, 'Seventy.'

Maggie laughed, 'We ain't got that many.'

He ignored her and began laying out as many plates as he was carrying.

After that he followed her around the kitchen doing all she asked until the table was ready and the bacon, sausage, black pudding and eggs were in the huge cast iron frying pan. Jonty stood beside her taking big sniffs, a huge smile on his face.

'Nice smell.'

'I hope so Jonty.'

'Hungry.'

'They'll all be. This'll get em up, you watch.'

The next to arrive were the girls, rubbing their faces, pushing hair out of their eyes, yawning, stretching in their long nighties, muttering good mornings.

'You need to get yersells washed and dressed before anything else.'

'It's too cold outside,' moaned Clare.

Since the near tragedy at the Moss the two girls had become increasingly dependent on their mother. They went out a lot less than they used to, preferring to hang about in the kitchen, looking at picture books or trying a new jigsaw. Clare especially had become a lot quieter, more uncertain whereas strangely Beth seemed less changed. She was growing up fast. Maggie knew she would be the cleverer of the two. Already she showed how quick she was, how ready with words. And the two of them enjoyed playing their games with Jonty when he was around. He joined in everything, running around the kitchen sometimes or joining Fraser and the girls on one of their walks so long as Bill was with him.

Beth and Clare returned to their bedroom to have a wash.

Bill appeared next, he too in his Sunday best with shiny grey hair brushed straight back.

'Is he behaving hisell?' he asked of Jonty.

'He's been right helpful this morning,' said Maggie, 'damned sight better than any of you lot.'

'Point teken Missus.'

'Well sit yersell down and Jonty can serve it up.'

'Smells good,' Fraser commented as he came into the kitchen.

The Grangers with Bill and Jonty would be taking one of the carriages supplied by the company to make the journey down to the church at Chapel le Dale.

'Bloody cold last night,' said Bill.

'And what about our drunken Scotsman,' added Fraser in his soft, disingenuous voice, 'what time was he clattering about? Surely it's time we did something about that man. He's just a nuisance, an absolute nuisance.'

'So what do thee suggest?'

Fraser looked sheepishly at Bill as Jonty came over with the frying pan and started to ladle out the breakfast food.

'Not so close, you'll be burning me next lad.'

Jonty scooped up a runny egg and smiled happily as he slipped it onto Fraser's plate.

'Where's yer father?' asked Maggie as the two girls came back in, they too in their best dresses and shiny boots.

'You look bonny girls,' said Bill.

Beth nodded while Clare looked away across the room to her mother.

Finally they were all squeezed round the table when Ethan emerged.

'Oh at last,' said his wife.

He gave no response, rubbing his face, pushing back his hair, looking distracted and still half asleep.

'I'll fry you up some more bacon. There's no eggs left so you'll just have to do without.'

Bill took up the job of cutting chunky slices of bread.

'Rough night?' he asked Ethan.

'Ay, with that bloody Scotsman barging about at God knows what time, making enough racket to wake the dead.'

'I was just saying,' added Fraser, 'We'll have to do someat about that man.'

'So thee can do it,' Bill said to him.

Fraser reddened and took a mouthful of bread, 'I'm just saying.'

'Ay, easy to say, not to do.'

'I don't mind,' Ethan muttered before he yawned, roughed up Claire's hair and then sat back with his hands on his knees waiting for Maggie to cook his breakfast.

When Bill was thoughtful his breathing slowed and his large features became still with concentration. He was twice as wide as the others with his collar cutting into his thick neck. His grey hair was yellowed at the sides and his eyes were a pale brown. It was only the deep lines down either side of his nose that gave away his age. For a navvy he was an old man and he knew it. If Jock Tarrant was to be thrown out then it would be up to him to either agree or not.

'I've already warned him,' he said then.

'Well he hasn't listened.'

Bill was already becoming irritated with Fraser's attitude.

'Well he will next time. Sit down Maggie,' he added.

'Just coming.'

'You do a right good spread.'

'Glad you think so,' she replied warmly.

'I tell yer, the difference since you took over the cooking. We used to eat like pigs but not anymore and it's all down to you.'

Maggie smiled and said, 'It's nice to be appreciated, thank you Bill.'

'Good break.......breakfast,' commented Jonty before he shovelled in another mouthful, fat running down the sides of his mouth.

'Won't be seeing him this morning,' Ethan said of Jock Tarrant.

Maggie came back with his breakfast plate. She and the girls would have theirs after the men had finished.

'Us being good Christian folk Sunday should be special,' she told them all.

Now that she was running the place and doing the cooking, washing, cleaning, it gave her more significance. The others had to listen to her. The last thing her lodgers wanted was for Maggie to change her mind and let them get on with everything themselves. Her work was well worth the money and they knew it. Now they had more time to themselves. At the end of each working day their effort stopped at six o clock. Maggie had seen to that. Even Bill was wary about any disagreement with her.

'You have to get yersell in yer suit,' she told her husband when the meal was finished and Jonty was scraping up the last bit off his plate with another huge chunk of bread, 'And you two can get yer hair brushed and yer coats on. We're going to be late if we're not careful.'

'Come on Jonty lad, that means us as well,' said Bill, 'have thee had a wash?'

Jonty looked up at him with his large watery eyes and answered, 'Had wash Bill, see,' he said lifting up his chin so Bill could get a good look for any tide marks.

'I believe yer lad.'

'Had wash Bill.'

'So you say.'

The door opened and Jock Tarrant unexpectedly appeared. The room was quiet as they watched him come over to the table and sit down. He too was dressed as though ready for a Sunday service although nobody had heard him moving about in the bedroom.

'Don't say you're going to church.'

Jock looked at Bill, his face unusually serious.

'And what if I was?'

His voice was deep and guttural. It was only when he was drunk that it became strangely lighter as his accent got thicker.

Jonty felt bothered. He could sense the changes in the atmosphere and it frightened him. He looked at Bill for reassurance but the older man was concentrating on Jock. As far as Jonty was concerned the Scotsman had broken the atmosphere into pieces. They were fractured all over the place, jagged lines between each person and nobody could cross them.

'You'll have to mek yer own breakfast,' Maggie told Jock who looked up at her and smiled.

'Right you are Missus, no problem.'

'There's stuff in the cupboard. Tell yer father to hurry up or we're going to be late for the coach,' she told the girls who went off into the bedroom, returning almost immediately with Ethan in tow.

'Come on then,' sighed Bill, 'Get yer coat on,' he told Jonty who was glad to be moving, wanting to be out of the hut quickly before the shapes broke into even more fragments.

When they had all gone Fraser started nodding as Jock moved over to the stove.

'You're a right one, do you know that?'

Jock turned and smiled again, 'And I know what your game is Henderson so don't start.'

'And what would that be?'

'You seem to forget that we go back a long way.'

'Unfortunately, yes we do.'

'So don't start the usual rubbish. One word from me and you'll be humming down that fucking road wi yer arse burning.'

'I don't think so,' Fraser said in an exaggeratedly calm voice.

Jock forgot about breakfast, rolled himself a cigarette and came and sat down at the table, his eyes glistening with the previous night's drink. His dark beard and moustache had even been combed this morning and his skin smelt of soap.

'I like it here,' he said expansively, 'I like having the Missus running around after us.'

'It was you only a few weeks ago remember who was totally against the idea and now look at you all happy and contented cos someone washes your stinking pants.'

'Been smelling em have ye?'

'How pathetic,' Fraser muttered, 'and don't you start threatening me.'

'My my,' sighed Jock, 'getting very sensitive in your old age.'

'Just tell me what you want.'

'Don't want anything.'

'So leave it then

'There's not a chance in hell o that.'

For a time they sat there staring at each other, the Scotsman's eyes gradually narrowing.

'Let's just say,' he continued in a consciously easy tone, 'we've both got stories to tell and you're as much a bastard as I am.'

'Same old stuff, same old words. Your brain is stewed in all that alcohol and I'm not sure whether it's working anymore.''

Jock got up, 'Well I've had a wash and now I'm going to have a wee bit of breakfast. Mind you if you're still here when I've finished eating I might spew the lot all over you.'

'Don't worry,' Fraser responded, stretching his tall frame as he stood up and went into the bedroom, putting on his coat as he reappeared in the kitchen, carefully adjusting his new peaked cap, pulling it further down to shade his pale eyes, 'I'm going for a bit of fresh air. You should think about doing the same thing some time, might do you good.'

'Fucking tosser! Jock exclaimed as Fraser shut the front door behind him.

CHAPTER THIRTEEN

As the four carriages bounced along the rough Ingleton road the snow began to fall out of a flat grey sky. The benches down either side of each carriage were covered in thick material held up by metal hoops. Every Sunday morning they made their way down to St Leonard's church at the bottom of the wide dale, a journey of over an hour.

Maggie was sitting between Beth and Clare with Ethan opposite. Ten other passengers were squeezed together including Bill and Jonty who was sat at the end of the bench sticking his hand out trying to catch the snow on his palm as fast flakes flurried in the cold air. The horses bent their heads against the worsening storm, plodding over the hard, rutted ground.

Maggie was tightly holding the gloved hand of each of her girls. Ever since the incident at the Moss she had felt closer to them, more kisses, strokes and cuddling to reassure them. She knew how much they were still bothered, especially Clare who still blamed herself.

Maggie enjoyed these Sunday trips. It was the closest the Grangers came to being a normal family. Like the Sunday breakfasts this was another ritual that she had asked for knowing how unconcerned Ethan was about religion. He came only for her sake. He had no real beliefs. For Maggie life's meaning depended so much on the existence of God and Christ. Even though both her parents had never attended any church she as a child had gone to worship with her friend every Sunday morning and had joined its Sunday school where she had learnt to read. Christianity for her produced the deepest sense of meaning, the deepest faith.

As she sat there being bounced about in the carriage she thought about the weeks since they had arrived at Ribblehead in such a miserable, exhausted state. Things had changed so quickly. So much was better now, especially she and Ethan earning enough money to be able to save a little at the end of each week, something she had never been able to do before. The girls seemed happy and there was even talk of a school being established at Batty Green. They were dressed in better clothes than usual, were better fed and had Fraser and Bill competing for their attention, both always buying things for them. Her daughters were healthy at the moment and that was more important than anything. Her worst fear was of anyone becoming ill. She had seen too many families shattered by illness. It only took one injury to Ethan while at work and their lives would be ruined. Constantly she was aware of such threats. Every night she prayed that Beth, Clare and her husband would remain free of all illness. It was just as crucial that she too remained strong and healthy. Her family and her faith were all that mattered.

She glanced at Ethan and the worries began all over again. Like the weather in these dales his moods came and went in an ever changing state of feelings. One day he was quiet and miserable, going to bed early and on another he could be chatting away, taking the girls out for a walk or helping with the shopping on a Saturday evening. Since coming to Ribblehead nothing about him was predictable.

Beside her Beth was wondering about a surprise Fraser had mentioned the day before. She was excited and impatient. Fraser had already given and made them so many things, picture books, jigsaws, wooden bricks, a cart with wheels, dolls, clothes, and Bill too, he had been just as generous. Her and her sister had never had so much. To begin with it had been strange to her to have grown men wanting to play with them, to enjoy their company and to give them things. But now they both had got used to it, so much so they had even begun to expect something from every Saturday market. They would be disappointed if nothing appeared.

Here Beth was rocking from side to side, holding her mother's arm feeling cosy and warm beside her. She looked over at Jonty with his hands stuck out the back of the cart. They were now used to his strange ways. She had once thought all grownups except her Mum and Dad were really stupid. Now Beth was not so sure, she no longer thought that even about Jonty. At least some of them could be kind and funny and interested. It was all strange and different. In her few years she had never shared things with so many people before. Her Mum seemed to enjoy it but not her Dad. He was either working or in bed. Except on Sundays like today they hardly ever saw him. Sometimes he could be funny and interested and at others not bothered. Now like Clare she was unsure of him. He made them uncomfortable and yet they did not know what to say to him. He was their father and they loved him but that somehow did not mean enough anymore.

The drivers stopped to light their lamps as the snow storm increased. Nothing could be seen except the white flurries flying across the road. The horses were unsettled, shifting about as they waited to get started again. All the passengers were covered as the snow blew under the canopy. The drivers congregated together to discuss whether they should turn back, their dark shapes huddled together.

With the decision to continue they climbed back up onto their seats and encouraged the uncertain horses moving again. Clare was not aware of what was happening. She was thinking about Bill. There was a lot she did not like about this old man, this one with the loud Lancashire voice telling everyone, especially Jonty, what to do. She thought he was a bit of a bully who liked having his own way and yet he was always bringing her and Beth things to play with. She did not trust him like she did Fraser. He was softer, kinder and was funny with the way he mimicked them sometimes. No, Bill was not like that. He was stern and scared her a little. He hardly ever went out except to work. He was in the hut with Jonty nearly every evening and all day Sundays except coming with them to the service. She really wished he lived somewhere else, but not Jonty. She felt sorry for him and was happy to have him watching their games. Even though he was always slavering and had such a strange way of saying things Jonty was still alright. Clare wondered why her father just let Bill be in charge all the time. She had heard rumours about Bill's fighting and hurting people if they ever crossed him. They said that even the bosses were scared of him and that he did as he liked in the factory because nobody dare tell him different. She could not understand how he could be so caring and careful with Jonty and yet not with anybody else except her Mum. Bill and her seemed to get on together in a way that was different. They were always chatting together, Bill often asking her how she was and thanking her for all the cooking and cleaning she did. She had even got him to agree to taking his work boots off before he entered the kitchen just like everyone else, even the horrible Jock Tarrant. No Clare would be quite happy to see Bill and Jock live somewhere else and leave Jonty with them. Anyway he was too old to be working, far too old and she hated the grey hairs on his chest when he sat at the dinner table with his shirt half unbuttoned showing a whole tangle of them. His hair was turning yellow and his hands were filthy black no matter how often he washed them.

The custom among the navvies was to have silly nicknames. They were never used in the hut but Clare knew they were outside. Every labourer had these other names. She had yet to find out what they called her Dad. Maybe he had not been long enough at Batty Green to have one. She had found out from some of the other children what their lodgers were nicknamed and all of them were weird and funny. Fraser was called Long Pole Henderson because of his height, Jock Tarrant was Highland Tadge, Bill Asquith was Plum Faced Jack because his face went beetroot red when he was taking the bricks out of the factory oven and finally there was Jonty who was known as Dent Boy, although nobody ever called him that if Bill was around.

Her thoughts were stopped by a sudden fresh flurry of snow blowing straight into her face. Jonty had seen it coming. He was at the back of the cart watching outside as so many flashing lines and grey white shapes flew across the roadway. It was a dance of numbers, a wild dance of so many snowflakes, up and down and around and back like a shiver of dull light jerking back and forwards and he could see it all in detail, his brain registering every fresh movement. It was so exciting that he found it hard to sit still. Back where the drivers had stopped to light the lamps he had jumped down and had started running about in it all to become a part of these dancing lines and shapes, these wonderful quick figures that flurried sound into his ears. Spirals suddenly shifted sideways, somersaults and jagged lines broke into a million new pieces. This was his music and he loved its accelerated sounds as the storm blasted across the thick whiteness merging into more whiteness while it all shifted round and came back at him.

'Sit theesell still,' Bill was telling him now he was back on the cart.

He was so happy. There was music and dance and beautiful cross lines and changing patterns of light flashing where the snow travelled.

'We'll bloody never get there at this rate,' Bill muttered beside him but Jonty was not interested. There was more going on outside in the wild early night. Morning had become night. Everything was shifting backwards and he was thrilled at such differences. His mind was within this furious white world as it moaned and shrilled across all the unseen distances he imagined.

He was not bothered as the ice snow stung into his eyes and blew over everyone in the cart, but Bill was. He was troubled in his mind and his face was stinging from the driving ice pellets. He tried to hide the fact of how tired he was, how his limbs ached now constantly, hating this sense of getting old, too old. But he was resolved to keep working as long as he could. He was the man the others sought for advice, the one who had made Jonty untouchable.

He was thinking about Fraser Henderson. He did not like the man. Jock Tarrant he could deal with anytime. He understood the Scotsman and his needs, his moods. He was just a drunk who often lost his temper. Not like Henderson. He was a mystery to him, smartly dressed with his soft accent. Bill could not believe the cheek of the man, telling him that it was up to him to do something about Jock Tarrant. He would take no orders or advice from Fraser Henderson who was always pushing his way in with the girls as though they were his responsibility. What Bill wanted was to work out a plan to have Henderson removed from their hut. Every day increased his irritation and resentment. He was growing tired of it. There was too much that was unknown about Henderson. He told everybody he was born in Norwich and that he had been a merchant seaman for some time which Bill thought was unlikely, Fraser coming across as far too delicate to survive at sea. How he got the job checking the tram lines nobody could understand. His days were a lot easier than anybody else's. There was something about the man that was too secretive. He never talked much about himself and yet he loved to gossip about everyone else. Bill could not understand how Maggie and the girls thought so much about him except for the fact he was constantly giving them things.

Ethan was looking across at the girls and Maggie all wrapped up in their Sunday best, bonnets and long coats, gloves and scarves, their shapes huddled so close they were merging into each other, peppered with the snow. At that moment he felt so proud of them. They were his family and he loved them. He had always loved them. They were the reason he was here in Ribblehead digging blue clay shit every day. He had never seen his wife so busily contented and the girls, so happy and involved in everything that was going on. Life had to be about family. It was the nucleus of all meaning, to give, always to give to them. If he had a religion then that was it, faith in the family, in his wife and his two girls.

And yet increasingly there was this feeling of separation, of being apart from the others. It seemed that as their lives improved his had grown worse. The space was widening between them and he could do nothing about it. There they were looking so together and he was not part of such closeness. He could no longer share with Maggie his needs and frustrations, not only the physical ones but his mental anguish as well, his ambition to become someone different. Now he was even jealous of the way his wife was so bonded with Beth and Clare. They were happy together and obviously enjoying themselves. And he resented the way Fraser Henderson and Bill Asquith seemed to act so naturally with them. They were taking over his role as the father and he was too lost and uncertain to do anything about it.

Suddenly Jonty could see a widening blue shape amidst the greyness. He laughed as the snow ceased falling and the storm passed on up the dale. It was over and he had lost all the dancing lines of light that were happily replaced by clumps of white and blue shifting over the exposed sides of the valley.

'Stopped,' he announced.

The rest of the passengers came out of their hibernation, shaking off the snow, straightening their coats, bonnets and caps. They were emerging from the dream of winter into this sudden cessation. Now they could see the horse and driver clearly and the other carts following on behind. They turned off the snow levelled road, down and over the stone bridge that led into the hamlet of Chapel le Dale.

The vicar was there to greet them at the church door, telling them all how glad he was that they had managed to arrive after such a terrible storm. All their snow filled minds were cleared as they found their pews and knelt to pray.

The tiny church was surprisingly full, those from the settlements taking the benches at the back behind the locals. As the service got under way Beth was imagining the silver lined clouds of heaven while Clare thought that Jesus must have looked like the reverend Smith. Jonty knew that God had to be someone like Bill seated beside him, his protector, his father, friend and the one who would never leave him. He could never tell him this. He had not the words but that is what he felt, the one certainty in his life.

As the congregation stood to sing the first hymn Bill was still ruminating on Fraser Henderson and how un-Christian like it was to hate the man so much and to want to do violence to him. Ethan was silent. Maggie beside him had a high, pleasant voice but he was not interested in musical poems to the Lord. They meant nothing. He looked at the lamps hanging from the cross beam above the altar, feeling the cold that had seeped into the stone flags of the aisle. He was pretending to believe. He was there because he thought that was what his wife wanted, to set an example for the girls. Now he was wondering how long he could keep up this pretence, this blatant hypocrisy on his part. In this small church there was only emptiness and nothing could change that.

CHAPTER FOURTEEN

Richard heard the man fall. He was at the foot of pier three with Joe Saunders, one of the foremen overseeing the stonemasons when they heard the crack of splintering wood followed by the man's scream and the sounds of his body smashing through four levels of scaffolding followed by a hollow thudding noise as his back was broken across a pile of freshly quarried stone.

With Saunders he rushed over to where the man had fallen, Richard shouting for someone to go and fetch doctor Shawcross. Men were scrambling quickly down the ladders while others looked over from the top of the unfinished piers. Everything was suddenly quiet except for the release of steam from the lifting gear pulling up a crate of facing stones.

'It's Archie Bates!' the foreman shouted.

There were shouts of shock and anger as the masons gathered around. The body was bent in a distorted position across the pile of stone. His backbone had been snapped so badly his body formed a triangle of flesh over the top stones. One of his shin bones had pierced through the skin and was sticking out below the knee. The left side of the stonemason's head had been crushed on impact, the eyeball hanging down the cheek on a thin thread of muscle.

'Fucking hell,' one of the men around the pile of stone muttered while his mate stood beside him started vomiting.

'Shit,' another swore as the group rapidly increased.

Richard felt sick and apprehensive. This was the third fatality this winter and each one he felt was his personal responsibility.

'Bloody hell Mr Stockton!' another mason began shouting as he came right up to the chief engineer, his fists quivering in frustration, 'Another one, another poor bastard smashed to bits cos of fucking weak wood. We've told yer over and over again but yer won't listen!'

'Buying it fucking cheap!' another added strongly.

'Easy lads,' Saunders tried.

'Let's find out exactly what happened first,' Richard said realising how weak it sounded, a feeble excuse to gain some time and to quieten the men.

'The plank split and Archie went down. That's what happened.'

'And he won't be the last one.'

'What yer going to do about it Mr Stockton?'

'You go and tell his missus and three kids that buying on the cheap killed her husband and their father.'

'There will be a thorough inquiry of course.'

'And what the fuck will that do?'

Richard noticed Tom Myres standing over the other side of the group. Myres was looking straight at him with a blank expression as if waiting until the men settled down a little.

Eventually he came over to confront Richard who could already predict how this was going to go. He had little fight in him. Another death undermined his confidence in the project. Nothing to him was worth a human life and yet terrible accidents were occurring in the new tunnel as well as on the viaduct. There had been too many. Of course railway construction had its dangers but so many incidents were unacceptable.

'You're always telling us Mr Stockton that the safety of the men is more important than anything,' Myres started in a steady voice that contrasted with the fury of the others around him.

'It is more important than anything, of course it is.'

'So why do we still have tragedies like this one?'

'I can't answer that at the moment. That's why we have to have an inquiry. There could be other reasons for what happened, you know that yourself.'

'Fucking hell!' someone exclaimed.

'I can't,' Richard repeated, 'We need to have all the facts first.'

'Weak planks.'

'We don't know that for certain.'

'So if we don't know that what do we know?'

'That we should wait until we have a proper investigation. But I want to repeat yet again that we do not buy wood on the cheap. That is not the company's policy and never has been.'

'Ay right!' came another loud comment.

'Fucking stories!'

'That's a fact,' Richard retorted as he sensed the mood of violence increasing.

He waited then to see what Myres' next tactic would be.

Momentarily they all looked again at Archie Bates' broken body. There were greasy strands of hair over the half of his face that was still recognisable, his filthy teeth showing as blood trickled from an unseen source down across the pale limestone blocks.

Shawcross arrived and the silence continued as the men watched him clamber up the mound of stone to where the distorted body was lying. They waited. More workers were arriving from different parts of the site.

'You don't need me to tell you what happened here,' the doctor said as he came back down and stood in front of Richard who by now had taken off his hat, holding it in front of him with both hands as he listened to Shawcross's brief report.

The air was so cold the breath of the men steamed around them rising and disappearing into the clear blue sky.

'I'll arrange for him to be taken to the mortuary,' the doctor said gravely.

It sounded appropriate and yet all the men knew the mortuary was only a shed built next to the two huts that were used as a makeshift hospital for the settlements.

'I should leave it for now Mr Stockton,' his foreman advised almost in a whisper, 'We can't do owt at the moment.'

'Yes,' he answered wearily, 'Yes I suppose so.'

'Arguing the toss here won't do any good.'

'We buy the best wood. The inquiry will show that.'

'The buggers know that.'

'So this should not be happening, not at all.'

'So?' Myres started, 'What's to be done Mr Stockton?'

'Nothing right now I'm afraid, but this accident will be thoroughly investigated. You have my word on that.'

'Well the men aren't going back up there unless you can give em certain assurances.'

'Assurances?'

'You heard Mr Stockton.'

'I think we'd better discuss this in my office.'

'Why not right here in front of us?' one of the masons wanted to know.

'Ay here!' a few others shouted.

Myres turned to them saying, 'No, leave it lads. If that's what Mr Stockton wants and you agree to me representing your wishes then he's right. I've gathered that there'll be no more work on the viaduct until this is sorted. Is that right?'

They all shouted back their agreement.

'Right then, get out of this bloody cold and we'll have a meeting later on this afternoon in the reading room so long as there's someat to tell yer. That depends on Mr Stockton here. Like I've told him lads, if we don't get certain assurances then we're not going back.'

Again they muttered their approval before breaking up into smaller groups and trudging off towards the settlements, their voices still full of anger and mistrust.

The few that were left were trying carefully to bring down the body of Archie, four of them attempting to lift him off the blood covered stone. At the foot of the mound they laid him on a canvas sheet. It took six of them to carry this towards the hospital with doctor Shawcross and the foreman following on. The first scream split the mournful silence, an extended shriek that wavered and then grew in power as a woman's shock and pain was transformed into this animal climax.

Richard and Tom Myres listened. All the workers and those in the settlements listened, this terrible sound of anguish drifting across the open dale, all of Ribblehead sharing in this awful, piercing scream that sounded as though it would never end.

'God help her,' Tom muttered, 'God bloody help her and her young uns.'

Richard could say nothing in return. He felt sick and emptied out. In his mind were those other sounds of the plank splitting and the body of Archie Bates crashing through levels of more timber to thud heavily down onto the pile of cut stone.

They were in Richard's office when Andrew Murray arrived.

'I've just heard!' he exclaimed breathlessly. When he saw Myres he forced himself to slow down.

'Yes,' said Richard, 'another accident, another tragedy.'

Andrew turned stiffly to Myres, 'I hope you're not thinking of using this as an excuse.'

Tom's careful expression did not change, 'Excuse for what Mr Murray?'

'You know.'

'I'm afraid I don't.'

'Yes you do, anything to undermine Mr Stockton's position.'

At that Tom laughed, 'Oh dear. I'm afraid if we're after anyone it's certainly not Mr Stockton.'

'You know what I mean.'

'Well yes it is a tragedy for Archie Bates and his young uns, glad you agree.'

And stop trying to be so damned clever.'

'Your condolences will be much appreciated.'

'I'm telling you Myres,' Andrew said strongly, his face flushing in anger.

'No you're not Mr Murray. You don't tell me anything.'

Richard stood there knowing that Andrew's confrontational approach was the worst possible. He wanted to intervene but felt so deflated and momentarily useless that he could only leave the other two to stoke up their argument, and yet realised he had to do something or Andrew might take a swing at the man.

'I think Mr Murray that will be enough,' he eventually interrupted, ' Mr Myres understands the doubts you have about this situation and how much you are upset about this accident happening to one of our hardest working men. I think you should just leave us two to sort this out if we can.'

'No,' Myres intervened, 'It's me who needs to go and talk to the men. I'll be back when they have come to a decision.'

'Decision about what?' Richard asked.

'We'll have to wait and see. All I know is that the men will have teken this bad, very bad,' he added before leaving the hut.

'That man is an absolute scoundrel!' Murray exclaimed.

'For God's sake Andrew, calm down. Abusing the like of Tom Myres will only make matters worse.'

'He'll bully them into some nonsense.'

'No he won't. The death of this Archie Bates means he has no need to stir them up. They're stirred up enough already and in some ways I can't blame them.'

Andrew looked shocked, 'What?'

'A man died.'

'I know that. I know how dangerous this work is.'

'Another accident, another death.'

'That can't be blamed on the company as Myres will try to do.'

'That's his job, to represent the men'

'Job!' Andrew exclaimed, 'He doesn't know what work is that man. All he seems to do is wander around the site trying to stir up trouble.'

'Please, just sit down and calm yourself. I'll boil up some water on the stove for a mug of tea with a drop of whisky in it.'

Andrew slumped down in his seat, 'The last thing we need is another setback. This winter has been bad enough as it is. We're weeks behind Richard.'

Richard wished he would stop stating the obvious. Sometimes the way he spoke seemed to imply that he was totally ignorant of what was happening on his own site. The man was too emotional, too ready to go to battle with the labourers who he saw as only causing trouble and dispute. But this was not the time for the two of them to start bickering with each other. There was going to be trouble enough without Andrew getting everyone even more agitated.

'Thank you,' he said miserably when Richard set a mug in front of him and then went back to poke at the coal in the stove to try and generate some more heat.

'So what do you think will happen now?'

'The masons will make their demands. I just hope this doesn't spread to the rest of the work force. Of course work on the viaduct will come to a grinding halt, but the last thing this project needs at this meeting tonight is work on the tunnel coming to a halt as well. We can't expect men to work one hundred feet up in a snow blizzard but of course work in the tunnel is different. There is no excuse there to stop work because of the weather. If the rest of the work can continue then we can hold out against the stonemasons until they start to see reason.'

'So you're sure they are going to.....'

'I'm not sure what they're going to do. I just know if Myres has got anything to do with it he will have them on strike unless we accept whatever terms he comes up with. There'll be issues about the men's safety and I can understand that Andrew.'

'How the hell do we prove to them that we only purchase the best timber?'

'I think whatever we say or show them they still wouldn't believe it. If Archie Bates did fall because of a weakness in a plank then that will be the second death because of such a problem. All we can do is double up on every level of planks, get them strapped together.'

'But that will mean....'

'Yes Andrew, increased expenditure.'

'But Myres will want more.'

'That's the nature of the beast. He sees an opportunity to do more damage to the company and he would be a fool to miss it. He is not a fool so we can certainly expect him to talk the men into demanding more.'

'Pay rates?'

'Probably.'

'And they are already the best paid men in the country.'

'To Myres and his like that means nothing. It's not about money, it's about power and who has it. This is an industrial battle that is growing and growing in every business, mines, shipyards, mills, everywhere. If I was a labourer nowadays I would be doing exactly the same thing.'

'You can't mean that Richard. Sometimes you sound more extreme than a liberal. Which are you?'

'I'm neither, but I think if you were over the other side of the fence and were an ordinary navvy you might see things differently.

'Well I'm not so I don't.'

'You make that very clear.'

'Any sympathy only leads to confusion and there's enough of that already in this day and age.'

'It's called change Andrew.'

'It's called uncertainty and that's not good for anybody. It means having to take more risks.'

'It's the company directors who put in the money.'

'Yes, the ones who have to gamble with their own funds and if they didn't nothing would get built.'

'A socialist thinks differently.'

'Well damn the socialists is what I say.'

'We will just have to wait and see. That's all we can do,' Richard finally added as he started filling his pipe.

'Surely we should be preparing some sort of response. We should let them have the rest of the day off and then get them back to work tomorrow.'

'Yes Andrew. I wished it could be that easy but I don't think it will. We'll just have to wait for the outcome of the meeting this evening and then see what happens and I'll go round later to see Archie Bates' wife and family. That's the least I can do.'

CHAPTER FIFTEEN

It was dark outside when Richard looked up from his account sheets at the sudden rap on the door.

'Come in!' he called and then waited for Tom Myres and two other masons to enter his office, Joseph Mordun a thin, short man and George Smith who had a full black beard and moustache.

Richard noticed that they kept their caps on as they stood there waiting for him to begin.

A few seconds went by while he refused to be the one to start. The three men smelt of the cold and the usual odours of stone dust and tobacco. George Smith was staring at him while Mordun's eyes wandered around the room. Only Tom Myres seemed at ease with the situation.

'There'll be no row,' he finally began.

'Glad to hear it,' said Richard as he set down his pipe.

'We just want what's right,' Joseph Mordun added in his broad Cornish accent.

'Of course.'

'Nowt else,' came from George Smith before he wiped his mouth with the back of his hand.

But it was Myres that Richard concentrated on. He did not like the way his face was expressionless, a blank stare.

Again he waited but nothing else was said.

'Sit down gentlemen,' he tried.

'No, we'll stand,' Myres told him.

'Suit yourselves.'

'It's not right!' Mordun suddenly exclaimed, 'Not right at all!'

'If you're referring to the terrible accident earlier this afternoon I agree with you.'

'Archie Bates has left a wife and three children,' Smith reminded him.

'And we'll do everything we can for his family.'

'And what about us?'

'That depends on how your meeting went.'

'Oh it went alright Mr Stockton, don't thee worry about that.'

'Pleased to hear it.'

'You won't be,' Myres finally put in.

'And why's that?' Richard retorted, trying to control himself, trying to find sufficient energy to deal with these men.

'Cos we've had enough,' Mordun answered, his eyes widening as he spoke.

'I thought it was you who was supposed to be representing the men here,' he said to Myres who smiled at this comment as he took out his pouch of tobacco and started rolling himself a cigarette.

Then he took out a sheet of paper from his inside jacket pocket and dropped it onto the table.

'And what's that?' asked Richard even though he knew already.

'I'd read it.'

He unfolded the paper which he quickly scanned before tossing it back onto the table.

'Well?' Myres inquired.

The other two started to become restless, scraping their mud clogged boots across the floor.

'This has nothing to do with me I'm afraid,' Richard said then.

'That's rubbish!'

'Nothing at all, you seem to forget I'm only the engineer here.'

'And the company spokesman.'

'But not in this capacity.'

'Capacity,' Myres muttered.

'You're to tell us what yer think Mr Stockton,' Joseph Mordun told him.

'No Joseph I'm not.'

'Well what then?'

'I'll pass this on to the company headquarters.'

'That'll mean a delay,' Tom Myres started, 'It's simple enough, we're not working until we hear what the company has to say so if you can't give us your response then it'll just mean days wi no work being done.'

'I thought that's what you wanted,' Richard said.

Myres looked at him showing no reaction, 'It's what the men want, not me.'

'Oh yes, of course, I forgot, you're just their spokesperson.'

'So you've nothing to say?'

'Only that I should think the company will look favourably on some of the safety issues but not when it comes to an increase in weekly wages. I would think that will get short shrift.'

'Short bloody shrift,' George Smith muttered, 'It's bloody danger money as I see it.'

'Not good enough Mr Stockton, not at all,' added Joseph Mordun whose beard muffled his words.

'So we're to go back and tell the men you've no comment to make?'

'Exactly, I'll get your demands sent first thing tomorrow.'

'And how long will all that take?'

'I've no idea gentlemen, but I can assure you there will be no delay on my part.'

'Christ almighty!' Tom Myres suddenly exclaimed, slamming his fist down on the table but then straightening himself, 'This is no bloody good!'

'Waste o time,' the two others added.

'I'm afraid that's all I can do, so if you're to advise your men that there'll be no work until the company reply then that's your decision.'

Mordun and Smith suddenly barged out of the office slamming the door behind them.

'What the hell are you playing at?' Myres asked then.

'Being realistic, these demands can't be considered before the inquiry.'

'Fuck that.'

'There's no need for swearing.'

'You know you've no bloody choice but to accept these terms so why the hell don't you just say so and have done with it and then we can all get back to work?'

'Because I know and you know Tom Myres that things don't work like that, so you can swear all you like but it won't make any difference.'

'Archie Bates is dead! Split in two!'

Richard tried to ease his breathing. He refused to be provoked by this man and yet he was tired of the endless conflict.

'What do you want me to say?' he asked then.

'Show some fucking concern.'

'I think you'd better leave.'

'Yes, just leave it all as it is.'

'I'll let you know the moment the company directors respond.'

'This'll not work Stockton, not a bloody chance.'

'We will have to see. Now if you don't mind I've got my own work to be getting on with and we have an inquiry to proceed with.'

Myres said no more. He waited for a few moments, flicked his cigarette onto the floor, stubbed it out with his boot and then left the office, closing the door loudly behind him.

Richard went over to the stove and stood with his back to it trying to get warm, his mind exhausted with so many thoughts and reactions. Everything was pressing against him like a force squeezing his brain until he felt sick with it.

The memories of Archie Bates falling off the scaffolding would not cease, the scream as he fell and the sound of his back breaking as it hit the pile of stones. However many deaths he had seen he had never got used to them. Archie Bates there up on the top level of scaffolding and then that terrible sound of splintering wood.

Taking a long breath he tried to settle himself. There were shelves on three walls of the hut full of files inside cardboard folders that were tied by ribbon just as you would see in a lawyer's office. They contained all the plans, drawings, reports, hundreds of them for this one stretch of line.

He went over and took down some of the files, placing them on the table and began studying them, his pipe between his teeth as he let the rest of the day drift away, feeling at last the warmth from the stove heat his weary limbs.

There was another knock on the door. He took out the watch from his waistcoat pocket and wondered who it could be so late. Just now he wanted to be left alone but the knock was repeated. It was irritating and unwelcome. He wanted to let his mind rest. He wanted no more problems but when he opened the door there was James Tranton and he knew immediately more was to follow.

'I'm sorry for calling in so late at night Mr Stockton but I've just been visiting the family of Archie Bates, the man who tragically died this afternoon.

'Come in,' Richard said abruptly, 'Yes, I was there when Archie Bates had his accident.'

'It's a terrible thing.'

'We will be looking into what could have happened.'

'Oh some of Mrs Bates friends have their theories already.'

'I bet they have. It's only to be expected.'

Richard watched him take off his long black coat, scarf and hat which he laid carefully on the back of a chair.

'We used to call each other by our Christian names, why did that change do you think?'

This was obviously not a question James had expected. He flushed slightly as he glanced at Richard, his eyes narrowing slightly.

'I.....I'm not sure, why do you think?'

'Our first few meetings used to be a lot more cordial than they are now.'

'Oh I'm sure things between us have not changed that much.'

'That's how I remember them James,' he said, emphasising his name.

'Well I'm not sure I agree with you.'

'Maybe it's when you started to hear the rumours about my objections to so many religious groups coming to Ribblehead.'

'We are here all working for the Lord, for the sake of these people. I am sad that you think that is an unnecessary interference.'

Richard was tired of the usual way their meetings went. He was bored by the usual banter. Tonight he was in an altogether different mood.

'You're just lucky James to believe what you do, very lucky. I wished I had such good fortune but I don't.'

'And yet you were the son of a well- known cleric I believe.'

'That made no difference, none at all.'

'Things can change Richard,' the missionary said tentatively.

'I'm afraid not,' Richard responded as he played with the stem of his pipe, 'Please sit down James.'

In the silence then between them Richard could smell the night's cold coming from the missionary's clothes. The lamps were flickering from a draft and the stove was beginning to cool. He was suddenly aware of the two of them sat there in these moments of time, on this winter's night with the settlement outside becoming quieter with most of the folk in bed.

'I'm going up there to see the Bates' family,' Richard continued.

'I'm sure they will appreciate that.'

'Let's hope so.'

'Such a sudden tragedy can affect people in different ways.'

'And Archie Bates' wife?'

'She has a strong faith, strong enough I think to get her through this.'

'With your help?'

'If I can offer any more assistance then I certainly will.'

'I'm sure she'll find that reassuring.'

'Do you Richard?'

He looked across at James, 'No, frankly I don't.'

'A pity.'

'It's nothing to do with you.'

'Only what I believe?'

'Something like that.'

'And yet it is a process that might help Mary Bates to avoid constant anguish.'

'You make it sound almost scientific.'

'No, no, it's certainly not that. No reasoning can understand the workings of the Lord.'

Richard made no response to this. He disliked the man's certainty, the way he had of fitting everything into place.

James clasped and unclasped his hands. His pale features were gaunt and intense, his black hair such a contrast to his white skin.

'I do pray for you Richard.'

'What?'

'I pray for you as I do everyone I know.'

'You must spend a lot of time praying as you seem to know most of the people in the settlements.'

'I only specify certain individuals and the rest are part of a general prayer.'

'So I'm one of the chosen?' Richard asked in a sarcastic tone.

'One of the fortunate ones I would say.'

'Don't you think that sounds a little arrogant?'

'It's not meant to.'

'Do you really think you have such power?'

'I have no power whatsoever, only God has it.'

'And yet you express it as his substitute.'

'I am the medium for the Lord's blessing. Yes, I believe that.'

'Well you've no need to pray for me. I'm sure there are a lot more deserving of your precious words than me.'

'Such humility Richard.'

'Not at all, just common sense. What's the point bothering about someone who is way beyond the pale without feeling you have to somehow save them.'

'You don't choose who is there to help.'

'Anyway, enough of this.....' Richard said.

'Nonsense?'

'Yes' you're wasting your time.'

'I don't think so.'

'Just leave it James.'

'May the Lord bless you and keep you,' he suddenly started, clenching his hands together, his moist eyes closed, 'May all sin be forgiven, may.....'

'I said no!' Richard exclaimed, slamming his hand on the table.

'Righteousness will be given to those who strive, to those......'

'No damn you James Tranton! Stop your nonsense before I have to.....'

'You would threaten me?' the missionary asked as his eyes suddenly opened and his face looked shocked, 'You would threaten me?'

Richard got up and returned his files onto the shelf, waited before turning and as he did so he attempted another smile.

'Why did you really come here tonight?' he asked, sitting back down.

James looked sullen and uncomfortable. He released his hands and set them flat on the table top. His long black hair reflected light from the single lamp hanging above them. From outside came the sounds of shouting and swearing, a sudden flurry of noise that stopped just as quickly.

'I am hoping to raise some money for the Bates family,' he finally said in a strangely subdued voice.

'That will be organised by the company in due course.'

'Has the family been told?'

'No, not yet.'

'It will be good news.'

'I hope so.'

Again they were silent. Richard was becoming tired, tired of having to respond.

'Anything else?'

'I'm afraid so.'

'I thought there might be.'

James glanced at him warily, unsure of this sudden shift from the spiritual to the practical.

'I heard that plans were going ahead for a school at Batty Green, something I welcome, but I just wondered if you had any news of the missionary hall we discussed.'

'Which is the more important James, a new missionary hall or a new school?'

'Has there to be such a choice?'

'Perhaps yes.'

'Both are important, of course they are.'

'And that's not an answer either. This job is about making difficult choices James. It is called financial reality, a stiff and unbending master.'

'The word of the Lord is more important than the word of man.'

'Is it now? I'd have been surprised if you had said anything different. And no I have no news from the company headquarters. I'm sure they will let us know when there is a decision.'

Richard rose again as if ending the night's meeting.

But James was not finished.

'There is something else?'

'I'm sorry to be taking up so much of your time and I know it is late so.....'

'So what is it?'

'I have spoken before about child labour. You made a commitment to me that here at Ribblehead it would end.'

'And it has.'

'I'm afraid is hasn't.'

'Says who?'

'I have seen it with my own eyes, boys under the age of ten breaking bricks and girls who take food to their fathers and find themselves pushing barrows up the slope, children in rags working in weather like today's. Shame on you and your company at.....'

'Shame is it?' Richard said loudly.

'It is. You promised Richard.'

'And I'll damn well keep that promise. If I hear of anymore of such practices then those involved will be walking down that Ingleton road before they know what day it is. I said I agreed with you then and I agree with you now. Let me tell you that in no uncertain terms. And now I have had enough of your complaints. However well meant they are it always saddens me that you and your like have never anything positive to say, nothing at all. We are trying to build a railway line here. I keep having to remind you of that. I just wish.....wish that you James and all the other religious groups could at least assist a little with such a project or if not that then stop their constant criticising, complaining, interrupting.'

As he was speaking James stood up and started putting on his coat and scarf.

'I am sad you think like that Richard,' he said when the chief engineer was finished, 'The men working here need spiritual assistance as much as anything else. I am here and I am not going away. Now I understand why we stopped using each other's Christian names. There is no trust between us and without that then any working relationship is difficult if not impossible. I have a job to do as well as you. I just hope in time that you can begin to understand how significant our work is here in the settlements. I can see this discussion is over and I thank you for your time, goodnight,' he ended abruptly.

Richard went over to open the door for him and said, 'Things will change. They always do but not perhaps in the way you hope for.'

'I only want change for the right reasons,' James answered.

Richard watched him descend the hut's wooden steps, steam coming out of the horse's nostrils as it shifted nervously at the approach of its rider. James put on his wide brimmed hat, easily mounted the horse and with a quick clicking noise had the horse turned and heading towards the track leading over the bridge onto the toll road.

Back in the hut Richard put on his coat, scarf and hat, turned down the lamps, closed the door behind him and set off towards Bates' home, walking quickly with long strides in an attempt to calm himself before seeing Bates' wife and children.

CHAPTER SIXTEEN

Mud was frozen between the uneven rows of the whitewashed huts. Shafts of light shone faintly from each window, the air frozen sharp. Desultory snowflakes drifted out of the winter darkness. Lamps were hanging across the front of the shops and stalls crowded with folk this December Saturday evening. They had come from all the other settlements, some making their way down in the empty tramway trucks as well as the local farmers coming over in their horse and carts.

Jonty strode along between the huts his head full of all these Saturday patterns of sound and smell, of lights and pale faces, the mixture that meant excitement. A man pushed a wheelbarrow past loaded with coal while another had a moving sack of noisy hens slung over his shoulder. Jonty looked up for stars but there were none. Tonight was different. Bill had agreed he could go to the market with Ethan. This had never happened before. It made him scared and happy at the same time. He was so used to Bill being beside him that having Ethan there instead made him worried Bill was no longer his friend.

'It's alright Jonty, Bill just thinks it would be a good idea if tonight you went to the market wi me and I was glad to do it. It's nothing bad. Bill'll be there when we get back. But we have to get yer boots resoled or your feet'll be sticking out of em and we don't want yer going to work in your Sunday best boots now do we?'

This was a lot of words from Ethan. Jonty thought he had understood but it still did not take away his anxiety. Now he felt that it was not a good idea. He did not like things to change. Him and Bill were always together and now he was not there and it made him feel lonely.

'Don't know,' he had to say as they saw flames from a fire in between two of the huts. Bits of furniture were being thrown into the flames that danced in Jonty's eyes, curved and shifted colours like moving fingers playing with the darkness.

'Thee'll be fine,' encouraged Ethan.

Around Jonty were the smells of burning wood, the cold mud beneath his thin worn boots and wafts of dirt from the privies. It smelt as though he could push his hands into such a thick mixture, fingers in the flames, hands moving through the stench of a Batty Green's Saturday night. His eyes reflected all he saw as he strode out beside his new friend.

'Boots,' he announced.

'Yes, going to the cobblers.'

'Boots.'

'Get em fixed Jonty lad.'

'Fixed.'

'So thee don't lose the soles of thee feet.'

'Hungry now.'

'Christ lad, thee has just had thee dinner. Where the hell does it all go?' Ethan asked.

As they approached the market Jonty could see many faces, yellow masks in the light from all the lamps. Shadows cut across the path that led towards the throng of people, loud and jostling, swearing and laughing. Their noise was music. The people were not talking, they were singing, sometimes loud and angry and at other times soft and funny followed by sudden small silences like stream water coming down the hillside. Even though he was hungry he was full of Maggie's food. His arms and legs ached as they always did after work and his mind was anxiously alert being with Ethan. He wondered what Bill was doing. He thought about turning around and going to check that he was still there in the hut.

'Eh, where are yer going?' Ethan had to ask as Jonty suddenly turned back.

'See Bill.'

'I thought we were going to get yer boots fixed.'

'Have to see Bill.'

'It's alright Jonty, Bill'll still be there when we get back, I promise you.'

Jonty stopped and was confused, his stomach ringing nervous bells and his head becoming warmer under his well pulled down cap.

Ethan waited knowing that to force too much would make things worse.

'Are we going or what?' he asked then.

Jonty shrugged his shoulders but did not move. Three children sped past him. A bell started ringing and laughter could be heard coming out of the darkness.

He started trudging again beside Ethan. There were so many people pushing and shoving. Faces twisted at funny angles. Long skirts trailed over the frozen mud. A young boy passing grinned at him.

The shop smelt of cows and was coloured grey and brown. Ethan started talking to a man in a long, thick apron with spectacles on the end of his nose. Their voices were easy to begin with but then they started to push against each other in a way that made Jonty confused.

The shop door was open and the noise outside was like a lot of birds squawking at each other. Shadows were birds with black wings.

'This is his only work pair.'

'Same as most around here,' Brock the cobbler said.

'Not really, some have two pair.'

'Lucky them then.'

Jonty waited smelling the deep odour of leather, of cows, of farms.

'Tek off thee boots Jonty lad.'

'Thy feet are a right colour,' said the cobbler as he inspected Jonty's ankles.

He stared back with his huge moist eyes.

Brock took up the boots telling the men to return in half an hour.

'We're beholden to you,' said Ethan as he took Jonty's arm.

'Half an hour mind, I'll be closed after that.'

Back out in the noisy night the two of them walked slowly past the line of stalls. Jonty laughed when Ethan bought him a sweet sugar stick to suck and one each for the girls. He gasped at the thick red cordial scooped out of a huge pot basin at another stall. It was warm and tickly going down his throat. There were so many colours and faces and voices stretching around his head like a merry go round with its own harsh music.

He now had his socks in his hand but did not mind, the tingly sensation of the churned up frosted earth beneath his bare feet.

'Put em in yer jacket pocket,' Ethan advised.

Jonty was looking at all the things on sale.

'Your socks.'

'Feet alright.'

'I know, put yer socks in yer pocket to keep em dry.'

'Cold a bit.'

'Jonty.'

Ethan waited and then gave up.

'New boots!'

'New soles, bottom of the boots, that's what they're called Jonty.'

Jonty glanced at him with a deep furrow crossing his brow underneath his dirty cap.

'Doesn't matter lad,' Ethan repeated.

They moved away from the market to where it was quieter, walking along the dark rutted roads between the dingy, whitewashed huts until on their way back to the cobblers they came across a screaming match between a group of women. The screeches immediately scared Jonty. His terror increased as out of the group staggered two women grabbing at each other's hair. Ethan took hold of Jonty's arm as he let out a strange wail of fear, his fists going up to his mouth as the two women egged on by the rest were tugging and pushing, shouting abuse, pulling each other onto the filthy ground.

'No! Want to go! Want to go!' Jonty was wailing as Ethan pulled him away, 'Not good, not good.'

'Come on lad, thee'll be right.'

'Don't like it!' he started shouting, 'Don't like it!'

'I don't blame you,' Ethan sympathised.

'Don't like it.'

A group of youths were flinging stones across the beck at each other. Further along this side of the stream the stallholders tethered their horses, the breath of the animals rising into the dark air, their heads bunched together as they patiently waited.

Jonty was quiet at the cobblers and on their way back to the hut. Inside it smelt of pipe smoke, fried meat and the washing hung everywhere across the room.

'So how did thee get on Jonty lad?' Bill was the first to ask.

'Jonty has new soles to his boots,' announced Ethan.

'Show us lad.'

There was no response, Jonty looking moodily at the floor.

'Thee's quiet. What's bitten thee tongue?'

'He saw a load of women fighting.'

'Christ,' Bill muttered, 'Bit early in the day for that ain't it?'

Fraser was down on his knees playing with the new bricks he had made for the girls. He stretched up, looked at the two arrivals and then went back to the game.

Maggie was standing by the stove with her hands on her hips watching and listening.

Ethan looked towards his wife, 'He says he's still hungry.'

'Well he can stay that way. There's nowt till breakfast tomorrow.'

'Did yer hear that Jonty? No more grub tonight lad.'

Jonty tilted his head to consider such a proposition before without another word he went off into his bedroom.

'He don't like fighting,' Bill said.

'Women fighting,' muttered Maggie, 'It's disgusting how they carry on.'

'Happens all the time. It's either about fellas or money or whose brat said what to who.'

'They ought to be ashamed of themselves.'

'Don't worry, they'll all be at the mission tomorrow. Tranton'll mek sure o that Maggie.'

'Ay, fat lot o good that does them.'

'No!' Clare shouted as Beth pushed down a tower of bricks.

'We'll start again,' said Fraser.

'She's allays doing that. She's so stupid.'

'Come on Clare, you start this time.'

'You alright?' Ethan was asking as he sat at the table across from Bill, still looking at his wife.

Maggie dropped her hands, wiped the sweat from her forehead using her piny and answered, 'About time the girls were in bed,' but her tone was easy as she said it.

'No Mam!' Clare immediately exclaimed.

'We're playing,' argued Beth, 'wi Fraser.'

'Now don't you two be getting me into trouble,' he told them.

'Five more minutes then.'

'Oh Mam!'

'You heard me Clare,' Maggie added knowing how her elder daughter enjoyed the games.

She went back to settle the fire in the stove down for the night. The heat in the room on this freezing winter night was overwhelming. It had to be to dry all the clothes and be hot enough for breakfast the next morning. In her mind were quick thoughts about the next day. She knew this being a Saturday the men would stay up later than usual followed by a long lie in on the Sunday. She always worried about the girls getting to sleep on such noisy nights. She felt a little easier when their father took them the next day after church on their walk out onto the hills. One Sunday Fraser appeared with two ferrets. The girls had been thrilled to bits, that night helping him erect a temporary cage by the side of the hut and then off with him rabbiting for an addition to their Sunday dinner.

'Bed,' Maggie reminded them.

'You'd better do as your mother says,' Fraser advised, smiling as he watched them trudge off to their room.

'Say goodnight,' they were reminded.

The two of them turned together to bid them all goodnight, their faces still disappointingly set as Maggie followed on behind.

It seemed Fraser was about to go to bed himself when Bill stopped him, 'And how do thee get on wi that Tom Bryant who's started working wi thee?'

Fraser's face stiffened slightly, 'Has a lot to say for himself, reckons he knows everything about everything.'

'He allays was a loud mouth that one.'

'But he doesn't bother me. I just get on with it.'

'That's the way.'

'And who's Tom Bryant?' Ethan asked unconcernedly.

'Used to be a foreman on the Trugton bridge but got hissell into bother and was sacked. I was surprised when he turned up here and then the buggers give him a tramway job.'

'What was he sacked for?' Fraser wanted to know.

Bill looked at the tall figure standing there but made no response for a few seconds.

'Probably boozing,' Ethan suggested.

'No,' Bill finally said, 'I heard the little sod was caught thieving, wouldn't put anything past that Tom Bryden. You just watch yersell lad or he'll have thee in trouble as well.'

'I try and have as little to do with him as possible.'

'Well I'd keep it that way.'

'Right,' said Fraser in his soft, uncertain voice, 'I'll go and see how Jonty is.'

'Oh I'd leave him. Anyroads he'll be well asleep by now.'

The other two watched him shut the door and then Bill said, 'Can't work out that rum bugger. Someat about him I can't put my finger on. I hear he likes the cards. Bit of a gambler. Doesn't like losing. He's a rum sort. What's says thee Ethan?'

'He seems alright to me. I know the girls like him. He's allays bringing em stuff, but they like thee just as much,' Ethan added easily.

'Oh I don't know about that.'

'You're just as generous, meks me feel like I've no need to bother wi two other fellas looking after em.'

'They're grand lasses, grand,' Bill enthused as he started packing his pipe with more tobacco, 'Thee's lucky to have such grand lasses.'

'Have thee never had any theesell?'

Bill seemed ready for this, stating easily, 'None that I know about. If there was I'm sure I would a heard by now,' he laughed.

'They've had a hard time have our girls.'

'Just the way o things wi being a navvy like.'

'But here seems better for em anyway.'

'I bet thee never thought thee'd be ending up in a place called Batty Green. Batty it damn well is but it'll do me for the time being.'

'Ay, you're right, can't see owt better.'

'There's never owt better, not for the likes of us. So long as thee keep well away from that Tom Myres and his lot, them who think they can change the world when they can't do nowt about it, not a bloody thing. Gets me going folk like that, thinking they have all the answers when they have no idea. You allays get em on any site. They're like rats scurrying about inside men's' heads, trying to get em to believe that they can manage anything they want, change anything, mek em all the money there is. Give it to the workers and fuck the rest.'

'He saved our Beth remember.'

Bill stopped at that before saying, 'Ay, he did that alright, and for that we're all beholden to him, but as for the rest Tom Myres is just another fool whose clever wi words, a clever dick whose mouth is bigger than his arse.'

Ethan looked up at some of the wet washing that had dripped onto his head. Bill had his pipe glowing as from outside came the shouts of men returning early from the pubs.

Later Ethan entered the freezing bedroom. It was such as contrast to the other room. It felt as though the night outside had managed to push its way through gaps in the walls to enclose everything in its coldness.

Maggie moved away as he climbed between the covers.

'You're frozen,' she muttered.

'Can't help it.'

'It's late,' she added.

'Been talking wi Bill.'

'And what's Bill got to say for hisell?'

'Just going on about Fraser.'

'He doesn't like him, does he?'

'You can say that again alright.'

'Nor Jock. Bill can't stand either of em.'

'I reckon they feel the same way about him.'

'Well not me,' added Maggie, 'Bill's alright. Me and him get on grand.'

'So I've noticed.'

She stiffened slightly at this, 'And what's that supposed to mean?'

'I'm just saying.'

'No you're not Ethan Granger. I know you and yer comments.'

'Give us a cuddle,' he said warmly.

'And I can't keep up wi yer at the moment, one minute as miserable a sin and in bed before the girls and the next sounding as if you hadn't a care in the world, teking Jonty to the cobblers even.'

'He needed new soles fer his boots.'

'Yer know what I mean.'

Nothing was said then. They could hear Clare's light snoring and the sounds of a low wind outside. Maggie shifted closer to him so he could put his arms around her.

'Bill likes being boss, that's his trouble.'

'That's what he's used to I suppose,' Maggie answered.

'Wi Jonty, yes, but that's what gets up Jock's and Fraser's noses. They can't stand him being the big man.'

'Oh Bill can sort them two.'

'I'm not so sure.'

'Anyroads he doesn't boss me.'

'That's cos him and you get on alright or so yer say.'

'He's a saint to look after Jonty like he does.'

'I agree wi that.'

My goodness Ethan Granger, steady yersell or you'll be saying I'm right about everything else as well unless yer careful.'

'That'll be the day,' he laughed before kissing her.

'I'm glad Bill and Jonty are wi us. Can yer imagine just having Jock Tarrant and Fraser Henderson in the hut? It'd be awful. I don't think I could stand it.'

'If they paid enough yer would.'

'It's not all about money,' she said sharply.

'Isn't it?'

'Anyway, we should be grateful they're willing to pay what they do.'

'That's cos they know they've got a bargain. Christ you never stop from morning to night.'

'Glad you've noticed.'

'Course I have.'

'It means fer once we can save a bit. Imagine us having someat to put by.'

'You just mek sure it's safe. There's enough thieving goes on around here.'

'I've done what some of the other women have done and kept it in the company office. They give us a book to tell us how much we have and it's signed every time we hand money over.'

'And you reckon that's safe enough?'

'Better than keeping it in a tin under the bed.'

'I suppose so.'

'It's someat I never thought would happen.'

'Well let's hope it keeps that way.'

'Oh don't worry, I never tek it fer granted, not wi the luck we have.'

'Are we lucky now do yer think?' he asked as he held her to him.

'We're a damned sight better off than we have been, but don't talk about luck wi what happened to our Beth.'

'But yer glad we kem here?'

'Are you?'

'It'll do fer now.'

'And that's all?'

'It's still shovelling shit every day.'

'I know Ethan.'

'And you working yer guts out.'

'The girls seem happy enough, that's what matters to me.'

'No wonder wi having two fellas fighting fer their attention. Bill and Fraser act like kids themselves sometimes.'

'I'm not sure about our Clare and Beth going off wi Fraser so often.'

'He teks em rabbiting and gives em a shot on the carts, what's so wrong wi that?'

'So you don't think there's owt wrong wi it?'

'If I did do yer think I'd let em go? Would I hell as like.'

'He just…….just…..'

'Just what?'

'Seems a bit shifty to me.'

'That's cos he sounds posher than most and doesn't get hisell so mucky. Fraser's just a bit different but I don't think there's more to it than that.'

'Well, she sighed, 'I hope yer right.'

'Of course I am.'

'You can be wrong you know.'

'Me, never!' he exclaimed.

'Sshhhh or you'll wek the girls.'

'It's not possible to wek them two. They sleep so heavy it's a miracle they don't sink through their beds and finish up on the floor.'

'We should be getting to sleep as well.'

'If you say so Missus, but give us another kiss first.'

Maggie put her lips to his and felt happier at that moment than she had in a long time. For once they were together and there was no edge between them. Their decision to come to Ribblehead had been the best thing they had ever done. All she could do now was to pray their luck continued and hope that God was listening.

CHAPTER SEVENTEEN

Later that night there was a loud crash followed by a shout that woke everyone in the hut.

Ethan was the first into the middle room holding a candle, its light revealing Jock Tarrant on his knees holding onto the front door handle for support, blood running out of his nose and from a deep cut down the side of his head.

Straightaway Ethan returned to the bedroom ordering Maggie and the girls to stay where they were. When he returned Bill was standing there with a candle in hand.

'Just look at the sod,' he said while going over to Jock who was muttering to himself, more blood dribbling out of his mouth, 'Get up!' he told him, kicking the Scotsman in the side.

'Let's get him into a chair.'

When Fraser Henderson came into the room they were pulling him up.

At the sight of him Jock suddenly broke away from his holders, took a couple of unsteady steps before throwing a punch in Fraser's direction.

The tall man jerked back so quickly he fell over a chair onto the floor. Jock lunged at him again shouting, 'You fucker! I'm going to fucking do you!'

At that Bill grabbed him by the shoulders, spun him round and slowly tilted his head back before head butting the Scotsman full on between the eyes. There was the dull crunch of his nose being broken before he slumped unconscious onto the floor half lying under the table.

'There was no need for that! What the hell are yer doing?' Ethan shouted.

By now Fraser was back on his feet and staring at Bill.

'Needed quietening down,' the older one commented before he spat in Jock's direction.

'You've laid him out cold.'

'So what? The stupid bastard is a disgrace.'

'Christ,' Ethan muttered, 'is he alive?'

'And what the fuck are you looking at?' Bill asked turning to Fraser.

'You,' he said boldly back.

'Bill, Bill,' moaned Jonty as he also came into the room.

'You get yersell back to bed lad. It's all done here.'

'What.....what?' Jonty tried.

'I told thee, get theesen to bed.'

Shivering Jonty slowly closed the bedroom door behind him.

'You might as well piss off as well,' Bill said to Fraser.

'Well done,' he said back in his strangely soft voice.

'Fuck off I said! You're as bad as bloody Tarrant!'

Fraser smiled and then added, 'You saved us all Bill. You saved us all.'

As he went into the bedroom there was a rap on the front door that was now hanging off its hinges.

'So the bugger is here. Last place I expected.'

They turned to Constable Archie Broad. He was one of three policemen based at Batty Green. Whenever more constables were required, especially on Saturday nights, they would come up from Ingleton police station several miles away.

He walked over to the supine figure of Jock before finding a basin, went back out to fill it with rain water from the barrel outside. He threw the water over the Scotsman's head rousing him enough to open his eyes and slowly sit up.

'That's right Tarrant, return to the land of the living. Nasty cuts we've got there. Been fighting have we?'

'Fuck off!' Jock gasped as he tried to stand.

'Just happened has it?'

The Scotsman grabbed hold of the table top and pulled himself to his feet. His face was a swollen mess, his nose already twice the size as normal and was turning blue.

'He came in a while ago,' Ethan tried.

'Come on Ethan Granger, don't you start wi yer bloody nonsense,' Broad told him.

'It's them Weegie bastards,' Jock managed to say between the bubbles of blood forming between his lips.'

'He fell on the front door step,' Bill added in a sarcastic voice.

Broad gave him a derisory look and then turned back to the Scotsman, 'Seems our lads from Bonnie Scotland are not seeing eye to eye at the moment. Our Jock here has been dishing it out good and proper. This is the second time this week the Scots have started knocking shit out of each other. Come on Tarrant, tell us what's been going on or I'll have you cuffed and in the cart before you know it.'

By now Broad had his face a few inches away from the Scotsman's.

Jock belched and spluttered blood.

'You shit!' exclaimed the constable as he jerked back.

'He's too drunk for God's sake to know what he's doing,' said Bill strongly this time, 'Why don't you leave him alone and if you want to ask him some questions come back tomorrow morning when he might have sobered up?'

'As if you'd know Bill Asquith. You just get on wi looking after that mad fucker who trails around after ye. Funty or Cunty or whatever it is you call him.'

Bill grabbed the policeman by the collar and almost lifted him off the ground, Bill's face turning red with anger as he held him tight, 'I think, I really think you should fuck off now or I'll fucking twist yer head off, snap it clean, clean I will so fuck off. You might think yer bloody Lord almighty around here but yer fucking nothing. There's plenty o dark nights when someone might shove a knife through yer fucking ribs.'

He pushed him away.

'Animals,' Broad muttered as he tried to straighten his collar, 'and don't you start threatening me Asquith.'

'Of course we are. Navvies are animals, that's right and we look after our own,' Bill said strongly, his chest heaving with fast breaths as he waited to see what the constable was going to do.

Again Jonty appeared at the bedroom door, his teeth chattering as he moaned, 'Want it to stop Bill. Want it to stop.'

'It's just Jock and yer know Constable Broad. It's alright Jonty lad. Get theesen back to bed before thee freezes to death.'

'To stop,' Jonty repeated.

'It's going to be fine,' Ethan put in, shivering there in his long johns.

'No,' Jonty answered.

'Constable Broad is just going so youse get yersell back in bed. You hear me? Go on, and there's no point pulling one of yer faces like that. Go on.'

Finally Jonty did as he was told.

'Christ almighty,' Broad muttered, 'what a bloody zoo this is.'

Bill came close up to him, 'I think thee should be going now.'

'And what if I say I still have business here.'

'Then I'd say to come back tomorrow morning when things might be a bit clearer like.'

'Don't you threaten me Bill Asquith, I've already told yer.'

'I'm just telling yer that I think yer should go.'

The constable stepped back, his expression uncertain as he glanced at the other two.

'Go on, bugger off, 'Bill repeated, 'and don't even think about coming back tonight wi yer fucking buddies. Do yer hear me?'

'This all has to be reported,' Broad said, 'You know that.'

'Well report it then.'

'Don't worry, I bloody well will.'

When he had gone and Bill turned back into the room Ethan was already bathing Jock's smashed face. The Scotsman moaned at every touch.

There was a strained silence for a minute or so before Ethan said, 'What a mess. You've broken his nose.'

'No,' answered Bill, 'that was a bastard from Glasgow or didn't you hear what that shit of a constable had to say? Fucking Broad needs bringing down a peg or two, walks around the place like he fucking owned it. Put a uniform on a man and he becomes a twat, a proper twat.'

'He'll be back Bill.'

'Not tonight he better hadn't. He'll be too ashamed o hisell to bother us again. He's like that, a yellow shite when it comes down to it. No, Constable Broad will be trying somewhere else to prove how important he is.'

'He'll just get more constables from Ingleton.'

'They can come as many as they like, meks no difference Ethan lad. This is Batty Green and there's too many of us. If they want a riot then all they have to do is start and we'll fucking finish it.'

Eventually Jock tried to speak, 'You miserable bastard Asquith. You know toss all.'

'Says you Jock.'

'Ay, says I and I'll say it as many times as you like. You butted me you shit.'

'Never.'

'Fucking butted me.'

'So what?'

'You'll.........you'll see.'

'Easy,' Ethan tried to intervene,' Stop talking. You're just making this worse.'

'Worse is it?'

'Couldn't be better could it Jock?' asked Bill before lighting his pipe.

He was there in his grey long johns and bare feet, his breaths slowing now as he took a drag of smoke and released it in a cloud across the room now freezing cold with the front door smashed wide open.

'And your Maggie and girls have to listen to this.'

Ethan glanced at Bill as he rinsed out the blooded piece of cloth.

'And it's not the first time.'

'So throw him out,' said Ethan, 'you seem to be good at doing that so go on throw him out. If he's such a problem get rid of him. There's plenty of other places he could find a bed.'

'I'm not so sure about that, but no I don't want the wee Scottie going anywhere for the time being. It suits my purpose to have him here.'

'And what purpose would that be?'

'You'll have to wait and see lad except I can say it's keeping a rat to catch another or maybe a ferret might do.'

'Christ,' Ethan muttered, 'I've no idea what the hell you're going on about.'

'And that's how I want it to stay Ethan Granger. Don't just get too smart yersell, that's all. Yer two girls are special like. I'd do anything for them two.'

'I never said you wouldn't.'

'You're fucking hurting me,' Jock interrupted.

'Just clean the fucker up and mek sure he shuts up cos I'm going to bed and I don't want any more carry on.'

Ethan watched Bill tap out his pipe on the stove top and then return to his bedroom.

'He fucking butted me,' Jock had to repeat.

'But saved you from being teken by the constable.'

'I can manage fucking PC arsehole Broad mesell, don't need no help from the likes of a shite like Bill Asquith.'

'Just take it easy. Your face is in some state. If yer nose gets any bigger it'll be closing yer eyes.'

Carefully he wiped the blood from the wound down the side of his head as Jock took each painful breath. His beard and moustache had turned ginger with dried blood and his lips were badly swollen. He had his head back to try and ease the throbbing from his broken nose.

'Why are you doing this?' he asked with difficulty, his voice sounding deeper and more guttural.

'Don't ask such a stupid question.'

'You don't know me. I live here but you don't know me.'

Ethan ignored this remark and went outside for more fresh water.

'It's allays the same,' Jock continued when he had returned.

'What is?'

'This....this carry on.'

Maggie appeared at her bedroom door asking, 'Is he alright?'

Ethan looked up at her with no expression, 'Got a broken nose and a few cuts but he'll manage.'

'The girls are really upset wi all the racket.'

'I don't blame em.'

'Especially our Beth.'

'Just tell em it's over with now and you go back to bed. We're nearly finished.'

Ethan's candle flickered light around the freezing room, its shadows shifting across Maggie's pale, worried features.

'It's the black dog,' Jock said after she had gone, 'It's that.'

'The black dog?'

'I'm frae Fife.'

'I know that much.'

'Me father was a miner and his father before him. That's how I started.'

'Same as me then.'

'You as well?'

'First years, yes.'

'It was alright.'

'So what about this.........?'

'It was when I was a wee un. This bastard black mongrel, huge bloody thing kem chasing me one day. Up on me back and trying to chew through me fucking neck and me screaming so the whole village could hear. One of the men hammered in the skull of the fucking dog there and then. But me, I was terrified and I showed it. I did the one thing you didn't do, not that, not to show as a wee lad how you're shitting yer pants wi fear. The whole village was there and me crying me bloody eyes out, hysterical like, me.'

'Careful Jock, keep yer head straight or the blood'll start again.'

'I lost it cos o that black fucking dog. But then it got worse. I used to dream about it all the time and then I started seeing it down the mine. I'd been shoving one o the trucks one day and I'd hear something, look up and see the black dog coming out of the darkness fast, coming fast at me and I couldn't stand it. Day after day this was happening, to me. I was fourteen and I couldn't stop seeing the fucking thing. I was spooked right and proper. I couldn't carry on. I med up some silly story for me Dad trying to tell him why. It was a load o rubbish and I left the mine. I couldn't stay down there any longer, not with that fucking black beast tearing around down there, tearing around in me head.'

Suddenly his voice quietened so Ethan could hardly hear him, 'I still see it. It's not the dog. I know that now. It just means old death is still chasing me. Out of the darkness it comes like a fast fucking shadow and it's after me and I can do nothing but try to drown the bastard in liquor, anything that'll shut me mind up and give me some peace. It's the only way. Now I have to get drunk enough so I go unconscious, out of it fair and square. I'm so scared of the fucking darkness I finish up in it anyway. Death to fucking death. But what's the use? That black dog'll get us in the end. I can never run fast enough. Jock is slowing down and that bastard is speeding up.'

He straightened himself and looked straight at Ethan, 'You know fuck all about me.'

'It doesn't matter.'

'Oh ay, it matters.'

'Just getting you patched up.'

There was a wheezing sound from his chest. His face was a swollen mound of blue and red flesh. His nose seemed to have spread so far that the rest of his features were a hidden contortion.

'You have to watch that bastard Bill Asquith,' he muttered, 'He'll fucking top anyone who crosses him.'

'He's not after you or so he says.'

'He's a lying bugger. He's an evil bastard so he is. I've come across the likes of a Bill Asquith before. The bastard is getting old and he hates to admit it. He'll do anything to prove he isn't. He'll still try and crush any poor sod who tries to challenge him. You....you have to watch him. Don't.....don't let him destroy yer family. He'll do it if he can.'

Ethan went to the door and threw away the dirty water.

'Can't do any more for you Jock.'

The Scotsman pulled himself wearily out of the chair.

'Means nothing what you've done, so long as you know that. I'm beholden to no one.'

'Never said you were. Why don't you try and get some sleep?'

Just then the candle spluttered out leaving them in darkness.

'Ay,' the Scotsman sighed before Ethan listened to his shuffling feet cross the room.

CHAPTER EIGHTEEN

The snow whipped into James' eyes. Muffed up in his thick coat and scarf he was sweating and shivering from the cold at the same time, his gloved hands gripping the reins while Bess plodded on through the thickening storm. This was not a sign of an oncoming illness but the consequences of his inner turmoil. He had always assumed that such challenges were part of being human. Life, society, history were based on obsession, ambition, desire, fear, depression. Each one of us is smitten with some mental disease or other. He was no different. Only God could save anyone from their passions, their insecurities, physical needs, fantasies, all of them the devil's work spreading such anguish and despair. The battle was in the self. Without the will to overcome and the support of religion life was doomed to be dominated by emotions. You were but a consequence of feelings. His struggle was to transcend his own weaknesses and become thereby purer and closer to God. Often he knew he was failing and yet he refused to take the easy way out. He could not take such a path because he knew his pride would regret it ever after. No, he would persist. Even though it meant reaching the edge of despair he would persist and either succeed or be torn to pieces in the attempt.

Dismounting Bess he led her quickly into the stables out of the snow storm that was whipping round the side of the house. There he took off the saddle and gave the horse a good rub down before filling half a bucket of feed and pouring fresh water into her trough. All was in shadow with the sound of the wind whining through the gaps in the slated roof as Bess nuzzled into her food. He patted her neck feeling the tightness of her huge muscles. The horse was the one reliable thing in his life. Not once had she been ill or injured since he had bought her. Bess the farmer had named her and so she remained, her flanks soaking wet from the melting snow. James loved the smell of the stable. It created a sense of security and warmth. Always at the end of each trip he recognised Bess as his friend, a creature of the Lord.

Lizzie and Jane heard him return that evening.

Jane was about to leave the kitchen when she heard her cousin going up the stairs to his room.

'I wonder if he wants some tea,' she said.

'He'll come down if he does,' Lizzie answered.

From the hallway they both stood listening to his low urgent voice in prayer coming from his bedroom.

'Wonder if it does him any good.'

'Lizzie, you shouldn't say such a thing.'

'Just thinking out aloud. You're allays telling me I should express mesell and then you're not happy when I do.'

'But not thoughts like that.'

'It just seems to me a waste of a lot of words and he does it all the time, praying.'

'He's a missionary and he's had another long day.'

'So why don't he come and have his tea like anybody else would do on a night such as this?'

'He.....he has a lot of things on his mind,' Jane said fully aware of what James was suffering.

'Come and finish yer soup,' Lizzie suggested.

Jane frowned and then sighed, 'So long as he......'

'He'll be up there for hours.'

'I suppose so, but don't start Lizzie worrying about him.'

Jane shivered with the cold of the hallway before they went down the stone steps back into the kitchen.

Even from here they could still hear him.

'Not being truthful is the biggest waste,' Jane added as she sat at the rough kitchen table, 'And James wastes nothing. That's what he says and I......I believe him.'

'Ay, truth can harm as much as mend me Mum allays says.'

Jane took a mouthful of the soup and then put her spoon down.

'Are you honest with me Lizzie?'

'Course I'm not.'

'Why?'

'Cos I don't like anyone knowing my business.'

'But I'm not talking about that. I don't know what your business means.'

'What's in here,' Lizzie said while touching her forehead then her chest.

'Thoughts and feelings?' Jane asked, 'Is that what you mean?'

'Feelings and thoughts, feelings allays come first. I reckon they do wi everybody.'

'And you keep them from me.'

'I reckon they're nobody's business but mine.'

The lamp hanging from the central beam flickered in the many drafts rushing slices of cold air through the room. Shadows moved across both their faces. Even though it might not be understood nor even recognised there was an intensity between them now. Everything said was of significance, every look and facial expression.

'So I am no different?' Jane said in a miserable voice.

'I never said that.'

'Lizzie you did.'

'You're........you're just looking for the contrary.'

'I want to know what you really feel, what's wrong with that?'

'You're greedy Miss Jane.'

Jane's features stiffened as she pushed away the bowl of soup and carefully wiped her mouth on a napkin. Lizzie had gone too far.

She decided to change the subject and said, 'Sometimes I hear you singing in here.'

'Got to do someat,' responded Lizzie sounding relieved, 'I just mek up the words as I go on.'

'You compose your own songs.'

'I wish I could sing like Master James, good enough to put hissell on the concert stage. I wish I could. A load of nonsense me singing and making up words, must be cos two minutes later I can't remember what I've been singing about.'

'Well next time I must come with pen and paper and write them down.'

'Never! I'd be too embarrassed so I would. I couldn't sing in front of you.'

'I don't see why not.'

' Anyroads you've got a lovely voice too. I've heard yer when Master James is playing the piano.'

'Oh that's just hymns.'

'You've a better voice than I have.'

'I don't think so.'

'Well I do. I just wish the master would play his piano more often. He hardly goes near the thing nowadays.'

'We're friends aren't we Lizzie?'

'I hope so.'

'Then you shouldn't be bothered about singing in front of me. In fact you should want to, especially when I am keen to hear you. Come on Lizzie, promise me you will. I would not be critical, of course I wouldn't. If you won't let me share in your feelings and thoughts then surely you can let me listen to your singing.'

The next morning was clear and blue as James set off yet again up to Ribblehead. The dale and hills were covered in gleaming white sparkling in the pale winter sun. Bess lifted her hooves to break through the surface crust that had hardened with the overnight frost.

Jane had waited for her cousin to leave impatient to set her plan in motion. It was something she had been considering for several weeks and now seemed the ideal opportunity. She stood at the door with her shawl wrapped around her shoulders and waved as James rode away. Quickly she went back into the house on into the kitchen to speak to Lizzie.

'Me, in the parlour?' the young maid asked.

'Yes, yes,' Jane answered, 'the two of us taking tea in the parlour and I want you to light the fire.'

'And what will master James say?'

'He need never know.'

'Miss Jane, you having secrets from him, whatever next.'

'I hope there will be a next Lizzie. I don't see why not so long as you don't say anything. I can trust you not to, can't I?'

Lizzie looked doubtful before she said, 'He wouldn't like it, would he? Master James wouldn't think it was right, me having tea with the mistress.'

Jane was disappointed, her eager features stiffening, 'Well I don't see what's wrong with it. I don't see what's wrong with me having tea with who I please instead of always having to take it by myself when James is not here and as you know he is away a lot. It seems so silly you in the kitchen and me in the parlour. Anyway it's been decided and you have no say in the matter,' she added playfully, trying to raise her spirits.

'And a fire?'

'Yes, absolutely, a large, blazing fire.'

Lizzie stood there, her breathing slow and her expression still doubtful, her hair tied back with a pale ribbon and her cheeks still flushed from scrubbing the kitchen floor. Now she was unsure what her mistress was suggesting. She knew it meant more than just sharing tea in the front parlour but Jane was so insistent that Lizzie did not have the mind to refuse her.

'Alright?' asked Jane.

'I suppose so.'

'That doesn't sound very enthusiastic.'

Lizzie blushed and wiped away strands of hair off her face, 'It.....it just teks some getting used to, that's all.'

'I'll help with the tea things if you light the fire and then everything will be nice and cosy. I think it will be splendid just you and me. I've been thinking of this for weeks. I so like being with you Lizzie. You know that, don't you?'

Again the young maid blushed and looked away.

'I tell you what Lizzie,' Jane continued excitedly, 'I want you to do something first before we have tea. I know you're not employed as a lady's maid but I would like you to brush out my hair once you have the fire lit.'

Lizzie could not refuse. The mistress sounded so enthusiastic. She agreed and followed Jane upstairs to her bedroom. Jane seated herself in front of her mirror after showing Lizzie her selection of brushes.

'Now I want you to unclip it and let it loose and then brush it out.'

Lizzie had never seen so many brushes, some with ivory handles. Carefully she started unclipping Jane's hair, 'You're sure you don't mind? I can do your hair after you've finished with mine if you like.'

'No I'm alright,' she answered abruptly, 'I'll just do yours.'

Jane's hair once loosened fell down to below her shoulders, a mass of shiny brown hair that flickered in the winter light coming through the bedroom window.

Repeatedly Lizzie brushed the hair from her temple down between her shoulder blades. Jane seemed to be lost to it, her body motionless, her eyes watching the maid's rhythmic action in the mirror. Her breathing became heavier and the silence deepened between them, only the sound of the brush smoothing through the hair could be heard.

'That feels so nice,' Jane finally sighed.

'A hundred times you're supposed to do it.'

'Oh I want more than that, a lot more. That's my trouble Lizzie, I always want as much as possible of what I like. I'm greedy like you said. I know I shouldn't be and that James would think it very sinful but I can't help myself. Have you ever felt like that?'

'No.'

'Oh I'm sure you have.'

'My whole family are greedy if you put it like that but not in the way you mean,' Lizzie said, smiling to herself.

So the brushing went on until Lizzie too began to enjoy it, the repetitive and soothing motion, the look on Jane's face in the mirror of pure satisfaction, her body swaying slightly to the action.

Eventually Jane expressed her satisfaction at how her hair looked before she added, 'I'm going to change my dress before you pin my hair back up and I want you Lizzie to choose which one I should wear for our special tea.'

She went over to the tall wardrobe and took out three dresses.

'These are them, which do you think?'

'They're lovely,' Lizzie said admiringly as she ran her hand over the delicate material.

'So, which should I wear?'

She picked up a light blue coloured dress and then laid it back on the bed before taking up a dark green one, holding it up in front of her and turning from side to side before picking up the last one which was a light crimson colour.

'What do you think Lizzie? It's your choice.'

'I like all three.'

'But you have to pick one of them.'

Lizzie frowned and crossed her arms over her chest trying to make up her mind.

'Come on Lizzie,' said Jane happily.

'The green one then.'

'Are you sure?'

'No.'

'Oh you're hopeless. I'll wear the green one then and get out of this fussy old thing I'm wearing. I only wear it because I know James thinks it appropriate. Can you help me with the buttons at the back?'

She turned to let Lizzie start unbuttoning her dress. She was aware of her standing so close, aware of the fresh odour of soap and the warmth coming from her skin.

Jane stepped out of the dress and went over to the set of drawers to light a candle saying, 'That's better. Now we can see what we're doing.'

Lizzie could feel the expectancy, the strange pressure that seemed to be growing between them. Here was her mistress standing in her under slip showing her bare shoulders that glinted in the light from the candle. Lizzie could only look and Jane seemed in no hurry to put on the dark green dress.

'Do you think you'd make a good lady's maid Lizzie?'

'Don't know nowt about it.'

'It means carrying out my personal wishes. I wonder if you'd like to do that for me?'

'Might do.'

Jane smiled as she held the dress up in front of her.

'Never thought owt about such a thing,' Lizzie continued, 'Master James just told us about washing, cleaning and cooking.'

'Yes, that's right. It's just that once in a while I would love you to be my lady's maid and help me with dressing and fixing my hair, things like that.'

'When Master James is not here you mean?'

Jane looked uncertain, her eyes closing slightly as she answered, 'I.....I don't want you to think......well yes, I do mean that. So long as you agree. You have to agree Lizzie or all this talk about a lady's maid is just a nonsense on my part, just a silly day dream.'

She stepped into the shimmering green dress and turned for Lizzie to fasten the hooks at the back. The maid watched Jane's shoulders moving up and down with every breath. For a moment she wanted to touch the skin on the back of Jane's neck, such a long, smooth neck hidden beneath her shining hair.

For a few seconds neither of them moved when Lizzie had finished. Jane could feel the young maid's breath on her neck and its low fast sound.

'Now my hair,' she finally requested as she returned in front of the mirror.

When they were finished Lizzie followed Jane down the steep stairs. The kitchen with its stone slab floor was very cold as later they carried the tea things into the parlour where the fire was now blazing.

'Yes!' exclaimed Jane when she inspected the table, 'Now we're ready. Lizzie you sit here nearest the fire and I will pour the tea. Do you like it weak or strong?'

'Anything'll do.'

'No, no. Today you have a choice, your choice, you must tell me what you would like.'

'Well let it stew for a bit.'

'Have a biscuit Lizzie.'

Lizzie did as she was asked, the heat from the fire warming her face and arms.

The table and chairs of the parlour sat on a faded oriental rug. The marble mantelpiece held a small clock and two dog shaped bookends.

Momentarily the young women became self-conscious and aware of what they were doing. Suddenly the house felt very quiet and empty with hardly a sound intruding.

Jane smiled. Lizzie could feel her excitement, the new passion in her voice as she started describing other teas she remembered from her childhood.

Awkwardly Lizzie ate a biscuit.

'Now, what else can we talk about?' Jane asked smiling.

CHAPTER NINETEEN

'Other than the weather being a bloody nuisance how are things going?'

Richard thought for a few moments, 'Yes, this winter has been bad so far. The ground is either as hard as steel and then we have a thaw and it becomes just running mud. It makes working conditions really difficult.'

'But at least you've got that nonsense sorted with the stonemasons.'

Elijah Armsworth was one of the Midland Company directors who took the most interest in the construction of the Settle Carlisle railway line. With Joseph Forbes the main contractor for the Ribblehead section of the line they were seated in the plush lounge of the Golden Lion Hotel in Settle. They had the room to themselves and a well stacked fire creating an intimate atmosphere on this winter morning. It was only with a sudden rise in temperature and the melting of most of the snow that they had managed to have this meeting. Up to the day before the road from Ribblehead had been blocked by high drifts in several places.

Mr Armsworth a staunch member of the Leeds Temperance Society board was drinking coffee and fully expected the other two to do the same. He was a short, tubby man with enormous grey side whiskers that emphasised the fullness of his face. Seated beside him Joe Forbes a quiet, taciturn character had a constant belligerent expression on his features, of medium height with light, ginger hair and beard and as usual a pipe stuck in the corner of his mouth. He was regularly up at the works, something that Richard was beginning to find difficult, especially as he suspected Forbes of constant cost cutting on supplies as well as badgering him and the other engineers to speed up the work.

Richard had had many conversations with these two gentlemen over the last months, either for a regular report or when a major problem had occurred at the site such as the accidental death of

Archie Bates. He knew that Armsworth was genuinely interested in the project while Forbes was only really bothered about keeping everything within budget. As he was the main contractor this was a natural concern especially when costs had begun to spiral upwards over the last weeks.

'It was an unfortunate situation with the stonemasons,' he continued.

'Two shillings a day more,' Forbes complained, 'what the hell they think they're about is beyond me. It was damned silly, that's what it was. Somebody's always stirring that lot up. That's what this is about. They're the best paid workers in the country and still that's not good enough. They should know better.'

Forbes and Armsworth both had broad Leeds accents.

'And a whole list of new safety measures that'll all cost you know.'

'Which I endorsed,' Armsworth put in emphatically.

'They still cost. It's them damned socialists or whatever they call themselves. Ever since that bloody nonsense in Paris last year they've been all fired up.'

The pressure Richard felt when with these two gentlemen had lessened. Whatever Forbes thought about him personally he knew he was doing all he could to keep the work progressing.

'In bad weather the job is as hard as it gets. We can only do so much when it's blowing a gale or we have two feet of snow overnight.'

'It's not always like that,' said Forbes poking the pipe in Richard's general direction.

'A man died Mr Forbes.'

'I know that Richard and we've paid compensation I believe.'

'There had to be consequences Joe,' Armsworth put in.

'But ones that weren't so costly. That's all I'm saying. I just find it rich that these socialists finish up costing us more. How does that help their damned cause? That's what I'd like to know if cause is what it is.'

'Tom Myres?' asked Armsworth.

'I'm afraid so,' answered Richard.

'And whose he?' Forbes wanted to know.

'One of those who like to stir things up, an agitator.'

'And before you say anything Joe it's not as easy as you think to get rid of such a man.'

'And why not?'

'Because of the influence he has. It's as simple as that. He's the one person the men listen to more than any other at the moment so we have to tread carefully.'

Joe Forbes pulled a face of disgust and took a mouthful of his lukewarm coffee as a waiter appeared to ask them if they were thinking of having lunch.

'I don't see why not,' Mr Armsworth said cheerily, 'I'm hungry after the long journey here.'

The other two agreed.

'Right gentlemen,' the waiter nodded before leaving the lounge.

'Do a grand steak and kidney pie here with all the trimmings.'

'So I've heard.'

'Been here a long time has the Lion and it's always had a good reputation.'

'Better than some of the muck I've been having recently,' Forbes complained.

The paleness of his face was emphasised by his light ginger hair. He was a man in his middle years who rumour had it was being stretched financially and might go under.

The last thing this project needed was for the money to dry up so what Richard was about to say he knew would not go down well.

'So the next six months Richard,' Armsworth started, 'how do you see it?'

'Better than the last six months I hope,' Forbes interjected.

'Yes,' said Richard trying to sound as positive as possible.

There was an awkward silence until Armsworth continued with, 'You wrote to me about your concerns with what happened last summer and how we try and avoid it happening it again.'

'That's what I wanted to discuss.'

Richard waited for Forbes to say something but the contractor for once seemed to be waiting for him to continue.

'Even though it lasts little more than a couple of weeks we did not expect in the summer for so many of them men to go off and help local farmers with the haymaking. We knew it was some kind of navvy tradition if you like. It was just the numbers we did not predict.'

'Should have sacked the bloody lot!' Forbes exclaimed.

'I'm afraid that would have been nearly half of the workforce and that we could not afford.'

'So what do you suggest for this coming summer Richard?'

He smiled weakly at Armsworth, 'We thought another advertising campaign in the spring might be the answer. The work force as it is will not be enough in spite of the haymaking.'

'Damn almighty. Come on Richard Stockton. Every time you open your mouth it costs me. You know how tight things are. You've probably heard all the gossip about how I'm financially stretched I am and all that nonsense, but if you carry on like this then the rumours will be proved correct and I'll be on my financial arse.'

'Steady Joe, you're talking to our chief engineer, not the board of directors. This is nothing to do with Richard. He is on site so he's our first port of call when we're looking for information. You can't build a railway line without things having to be flexible. You know that as well as I do. Up there at Ribblehead is a bleak God forsaken place and it's not easy to keep the work force we have. However good the wages might be it's still an awful bloody place to be stuck there month after month working in every weather imaginable. You were up there before you put in your bid Joe so you knew what you were taking on. This is a challenge whichever way you look at it and we're all wanting it to succeed. It has to succeed. There's no going back now.'

'Which means I suppose,' said Forbes, 'that no matter what happens to me there'll be somebody willing to put the necessary money in. Will there or not?'

'I should hope so. The directors would take over the contract if necessary. They would have to.'

'Sounds like a threat to me.'

'Don't talk nonsense man. It's called being realistic. I thought that's what you were Joe Forbes.'

'Ay when it suits anybody can be realistic as you call it.'

'Well to go back to Richard's point the advertising campaign last year seemed to go well.'

'Especially in the Midlands and Wales,' Richard put in, feeling the strain deepening between the two of them.

He usually looked forward to these gatherings of the wise as Armsworth called them but on this occasion he felt drained and unable to be as sharp as he wanted to be.

'So just in case,' Joe Forbes persisted, 'some of the workers bugger off to help with the haymaking we have to employ more men.'

'Something like that, yes.'

'Well I've heard everything,' he muttered in exasperation.

'It also means we require more men whatever happens. The haymaking is just one factor in all this.'

The contractor lit his pipe and puffed away in irritation as though he wanted nothing more to do with the conversation.

Armsworth sighed exaggeratedly and poured himself another cup of coffee. From outside came the noise of horses and carts going along Settle's main street and the whistle of a shepherd to his dogs as he took his flock of sheep towards the market square.

Richard walked over to the window and stood watching them. The travellers' guides stated that Settle had a feel of a French town about it but to Richard it was as Yorkshire as any other place on the edge of the Dales with Castleberg rock stuck up behind the place's rooftops, a sheer cliff of limestone that dominated the town. The discussion had reached a natural break where the three of them needed time to absorb what had been said so he would stand there and watch the folk of Settle go about their business until the other two were ready to continue.

'The board has agreed to establish a school at Batty Green,' Armsworth started, 'and of course the company is going to pay for the building and for a teacher.'

'It's needed,' Richard said as he returned to his seat, 'and it'll be good for the company image.'

'Education is always needed, I agree with that.'

'So say some,' Forbes finally became involved again, 'But giving the workers the ability to read and write will only get them thinking too much. They're not paid to think. Give the young uns something to do, something they can work at that will help the railway line. Why not? I don't mean them dragging trucks along Blea Moor tunnel. I mean doing bits and pieces wherever it's needed.'

'I think Joe those days are behind us.' commented Mr Armsworth who looked a little disappointed with his contractor.

'But you know what I mean, a little knowledge can be a harmful thing.'

'And we have a teacher, helped interview her myself, a Miss Lucy Ormskill and very attractive too I might add. She comes from Burnley and has excellent references. I wanted to be part of the interview panel just to see what kind of teacher would answer our advertisement. Miss Ormskill came immediately across as experienced, sensible and dedicated to her job and sounded like somebody who would take no nonsense from her pupils. I was impressed by her and I'm certain she'll do well. So we have a teacher but no school room.'

'Last week's blizzards stopped everything coming through from Ingleton so our carpenters are just waiting for more wood to get started as long as the weather holds,' Richard added.

He was already wondering about this Miss Lucy Ormskill. Ribblehead would certainly be a challenge for any teacher with some of the roughest, wildest children there were who were just roaming around the settlements getting into trouble. He certainly did not envy anyone attempting to educate such a filthy mouthed bunch and yet initially it had been his idea to have a school. He wanted Batty Green to have everything a small town would have and that included a school. It already had a library and reading room, a temporary hall for evening entertainment and all the other clubs that had been established. It certainly had enough drinking dens and loose women in the settlements and their own police force. Some of the men had been trained as fire fighters. There was doctor Shawcross's surgery and the small hospital he had established. No, a school was the only thing missing and the sooner that situation changed the better.

'So Richard, when do you think Miss Ormskill will be in her schoolroom teaching the young ones?' asked Armsworth.

'We have arranged for her to lodge at the Johnstons farm. It's a bit of a trek down to Batty Green but it's the best we could do. I think we should be ready by the beginning of March.'

'Is she church or chapel?' Forbes suddenly inquired.

Armsworth gave him another critical look, 'She's Church of England.'

'I should hope so, there's enough of them Methodists already up there.'

At this point Richard thought he should mention James Tranton's missionary hall.

'Oh him!' the contractor exclaimed, 'I've come across missionary Tranton alright. You'd think to listen to him that he was the only damned person in the world to have discovered God. He has an arrogance about him that turns me hot. Why doesn't he and the rest of the Methodists, Quakers, Independents and the rest of them just clear off to some foreign country where the heathens have not yet found Jesus? Our workers don't damn well need any of it. Oh ay they drink and they fight when things get stirred up, so what, so what I ask? Wherever you have a load of navvies working together that's bound to happen. They don't need saving. They need to be left alone to get on with what they're being paid to do. Right at the start I told the company they should have built a proper church at Batty Green that had a proper vicar. Oh I know the folk use the church down at Chapel le Dale but that's miles away and who's going to bother with that journey there and back every Sunday? No, we should have built a proper church and not some converted hut and told all the rest of the do gooders to pack up and try somewhere else.'

'Anyway,' Richard said calmly, 'that will be happening when the weather improves.'

'To have the worshippers indoors in weather like we're having has to be better instead of the men and their families catching every illness there is going,' added Armsworth before he took out his watch from his waistcoat pocket to check on the time, 'Right gentlemen, lunch.'

The three of them stood up and on the way to the door Armsworth took Richard aside to tell him about a visit the directors were arranging for some of the good folk of Leeds who had bought shares in the company.

Such visits were just an added worry to Richard knowing that if anything happened it would be his responsibility. He wanted to be proud of what they were doing at Ribblehead. On the last visit of Armsworth's guests two ladies had wanted to be lowered down one of the air shafts to the work on the Blea Moor tunnel below. For him it had been like a slow nightmare waiting for the ladies to be brought back up safe and sound after such an adventure with Forbes there on one of his visits on the same day. Never did he want to go through that again.

'You hungry Joseph?' Armsworth asked loudly as they left on their way to the dining room.

CHAPTER TWENTY

Mrs Hislop's hut was generally known as The Drunken Swan. Tommy Hislop her husband ensured the rowdy did not get out of hand and kept a look out for the customs men who prowled around the settlements looking for the illegal sale of alcohol.

On this night The Swan was packed with men and women drinking mugs of beer and glasses of gin and whisky. There was as usual a lot of shouting and cursing. Any sign of a fight would have Tommy and his henchmen throwing out the culprits. The hut was thick with cigarette and pipe smoke and the stench of beer and spirits as women shifted from customer to customer looking for free drinks for the price of a cuddle.

'He's at it, the bastard,' muttered Jock Tarrant who with his swollen nose sat crouched in a corner next to the tall Fraser Henderson who was finding it hard to hear what the Scotsman was saying because of the racket.

'He'll try but he'll get nowhere,' Fraser had to shout back.

Jock took a quick drag of his cigarette and glanced at him suspiciously as he asked 'So you've said nowt?'

'Of course I haven't. Why the hell would I say anything to the likes of Asquith? The old sod hates my guts. He thinks I'm taking the girls off him.'

'Well you are, aren't you?'

'I'm not doing anything.'

'Oh ay Fraser, I know yer tricks.'

'Just wanting the girls to enjoy themselves.'

'Oh they'll enjoy theirselves alright.'

'That's not the point Jock. It's what Asquith can find out.'

'He needs fucking doing, that's what he needs. He's been after me since I got here. I upset his little kingdom so I do cos I don't listen to a bloody word he says and the old faggot can't fucking stand it. King Billy is the boy. I hear he always has been. That might be the case when you're in yer prime but the old sod is way past it.'

Fraser thought of saying if he was so past it how had Bill managed to break the Scotsman's nose but thought better of it and said instead, 'That's what he's scared of, just that.'

Jock took a mouthful of beer, wiping the froth from his moustache. A woman came over and leant between them asking if there was anything she could give them.

'Ay, you can toss off darling,' said Jock.

'Charming,' muttered the woman who pulled up the front of her blouse as a gesture of disapproval, 'And fuck you as well Jock Tarrant,' she added, laughing as she rejoined the rest of the chaos.

'Jonty's a way in.'

'And how's that?' asked Fraser as he sipped at his whisky.

'Asquith needs him, depends on him in his own way.'

'So?'

'So we tek him away from him.'

'There's no chance of that.'

'How no?'

'Because Bill watches Jonty like a hawk. He's his child, his follower. Nobody is.....'

'Nothing nasty like, friendly. Jonty likes friendly,' Jock interrupted.

'Can't see it,' said Fraser.

'That's because you don't understand how Asquith works. The bastard doesn't want to be seen as getting Jonty to do everything he wants. That's not how it is wi him anymore. He wants to pretend that he's trying to give the lad some kind of freedom whatever that fucking means so he can look like the big man trying to improve things for the half wit. Don't get us wrong, I'd rather have Jonty than most of the other buggers around here. At least he keeps stum and waits to be spoken to. He's my boy. Oh yes, me and Jonty are going to get on just grand.'

Fraser looked at him inquiringly, 'You're a scheming bugger Jock, so you are.'

'We have to stop that old bastard, have to get him gone out of here before he thinks he's found something about you or me, doesn't matter which.'

'Yes it does. You wouldn't be bothered if you thought he had nothing on you. Don't forget he's been around a long time and has worked plenty of sites wi people who'll have come across you sometime or other. It stands to reason you're known.'

'And you as well, remember.'

'That's possible I suppose.'

'So we have to stick together on this because if I think you're bending in the other direction I'll have you fucking blutered before you can say happy child again. Do you get me?'

'Oh come on Jock, for God's sake,' Fraser sighed, 'This is me you're talking to, not some bloody ninny out of the sticks. I know you and you know me and that means we're sticking together no matter what and in the end I don't care what happens to Bill Asquith so long as he keeps out of my business.'

'Right!' exclaimed Jock, 'On that we'll have another drink.'

'So lads, what'll it be? I'm on tab,' came a sudden loud voice.

They both looked up at Arnold Wainwright bending and swaying as he leant on Fraser's back to steady himself.

'Arnold!' exclaimed Jock.

'Me, ay, that's me, here I am.''

'It'll be a wee whisky for me and a mug of beer for my friend here and none of the watered piss.'

'Beer, one, whisky, one, one beer and……one whisky,' Arnold repeated.

'Correct smart man. Don't forget where we are and if you do ask old bag Hislop she'll give you directions,' Jock told him.

'Right you are,' stuttered Arnold as he attempted to turn round before disappearing into the throng.

'What are we bothering wi him for?' asked Fraser.

'Arnold knows a lot of people.'

'So? He's a fool.'

'Doesn't matter when he's one of the only ones who gets close enough to Jonty, not friendly, just close enough.'

'And Bill doesn't mind?'

'Bill like everybody else thinks Arnold is a harmless arse. Probably thinks he's on Jonty's level. Arnold's a messenger boy, always has been ever since he got here and that suits us fine.'

'You asked him here?'

'Did I hell. Just fortune is smiling Fraser lad. Up pops fucking Arnold Wainwright and things become a little clearer, well to me anyway. You just keep being an ignorant twat and everything'll work out if you leave it up to me and you will leave up to me won't you Fraser? You will cos you know that suits your interest as well as mine and you've always been good at hiding behind some other sod's back. Ain't that right friend?'

'Shut up for God's sake! You just like the sound of your own voice, that's all.'

'I want you to be nice to our Arnold boy.'

'I'll try,' Fraser muttered, his face yellow in the sickly light of the Swan's lamps.

Arnold Wainwright was known around the settlements as the fixer, the messenger, the go between, the one who took the bets to the bookies, who organised the card games and yet never played, who looked out for any new custom officers. Arnold spread gossip and was paid to take any news to Andrew Murray the engineer about Tom Myres and his followers. Nobody trusted him and yet he was given many tasks around the place. Murray had got him one of the top jobs on the site, maintaining a steam crane up on the viaduct. Arnold was always filthy and went around with his mouth full of pipe tobacco. He had a rough Leicester accent and was the same man who Bill had allowed to befriend Jonty and take him on a weekly visit to the reading rooms where they played dominoes or draughts.

'So Arnold lad, sit yourself down,' Jock told him when he unsteadily returned with their drinks.

'Stinks worse than ever in here!'

'That's cos nobody bothers to wash, same as you Arnold,' the Scotsman joked.

'Get on with it,' Fraser said impatiently.

'So...so what is it I can do for you?'

'That's right,' Jock agreed, 'someat you can do for us, well not do, more keep as it is for the time being.'

'You've lost me.'

'And me,' Fraser added drily before sipping at his drink.

'You and Jonty.'

'Ay, Jonty's me lad.'

'He likes you.'

'I hope so.'

'And Bill Asquith doesn't mind?'

'Was Bill's idea in the first place, that I should get friendly like wi him. No idea why, just happened.'

'That's because you're not a threat Arnold to his kingdom.'

Arnold belched, picked up an ashtray and emptied out his mouthful of tobacco, the brown juice squirting everywhere.

'For God's sake,' muttered Fraser in disgust.

'Me and Jonty go on a Tuesday night up to the reading rooms for a game of doms or draughts. Never miss. He's allays ready for me when I turn up. Have to get out o that hut quick cos the Missus has never teken to me ever since that fight with Ethan, and me doing them a bloody favour as well. Miserable woman so she is.'

The noise in the hut was increasing as the night drew on. There was a constant coming and going as the place disappeared in a fug of smoke and beer smells.

'Well you just keep Jonty nice and sweet, that's all Arnold, that's all we want.'

Arnold looked puzzled, his filthy forehead creasing in uncertainty, 'Nowt much then.'

'That suits us.'

'So why?'

'Nothing to do with you at the moment,' Fraser said strongly.

'We might just suggest someat to you one Tuesday night and if we do then we want to make sure you do as requested.'

Again Arnold took his time as he considered this vague suggestion.

'I won't have Jonty hurt.'

'No lad, nothing like that.'

'I won't,' Arnold repeated.

'We....we just want.....well, let's just say this has nothing to do with Jonty, not really.'

'You're after fucking up Bill Asquith.'

'Could be, what of it?'

'Oh I'm all for that!' Arnold exclaimed, 'That bastard could do wi a fucking scare.'

'That's me lad,' agreed Jock, 'And so not a word, not one word to anyone about this.'

'Or you'll be in trouble as well as Bill Asquith,' added Fraser.

'Do you understand us?'

'Just keep Jonty sweet, that's all you have to do.'

'That's it.'

'Right.'

'Right, so how about another mugful Arnold lad before you get thirsty?'

CHAPTER TWENTY ONE

Jonty liked the sounds of the animals, the sheep, pigs, hens, ducks, geese, a few cows. Were they singing he wondered? Or sometimes they sounded in pain. They and their smells were everywhere, especially in the sharp winter air that dark morning as he walked beside Bill on their way to work. As always he had asked Bill whether it was Tuesday today and when the answer was yes Jonty had become immediately excited. He asked the same question every morning. Tuesday meant Arnold coming for him that evening and that was a good feeling. It was his one time away from the factory or the hut. He was going to the library and the reading rooms. Arthur would be with him. They would sit at one of the tables and play games just between the two of them, although sometimes now Arnold suggested he played against some of the other men who were there. He did not mind so long as Arnold sat beside him.

'Slow down lad, thee's fast this morning,' said Bill as they joined some of the others on their way to work in the morning darkness.

Lamps were lit up on the viaduct and more light was coming from the work sheds. One of the shunting engines pulled its load up the tramway to the tunnel as on another line an engine with its trucks came down with stone from the quarry. Many of the huts' windows were lit as more shadowy figures moved towards the sheds where the tools were handed out.

Sleep was still fogging Jonty's mind. He never liked his dreams. He did not remember them but they always left him with a feeling of being scared. Still he felt warm beside Bill. With him he knew he was safe. His friend was all around him like a soft comfort. He had no memory of a father or mother nor any other relative. There was nothing of his past except for strange shapes that sometimes came into his head, houses, streets, fields, trees that were like ghosts. They were there and then not there. He had once tried to tell this to Bill but he had found it too difficult and had instead started to cry. Otherwise there were no thoughts about anything except for this tight feeling in his stomach now that he knew it was Tuesday and he would be meeting Arnold.

Arnold was funny. He was not like Bill. Arnold laughed a lot showing his brown teeth. His hands were always dirty as was his neck and ears which stuck out from the side of his head like those of a piglet he had once seen with the sun shining pink straight through the young pig's flappy ears.

'Cold,' he thought he had better say something to Bill who he knew did not like it when he did not try and speak.

'Thee has to tell us what you're feeling lad then I know if owt's bothering you.'

Often he forgot to try and then went at it too hard so that too many words stacked up. They got stuck in his throat like bits of chicken bone.

'It is Jonty, bloody cold, but not as bad as it has been.'

'Alright Bill, Jonty?' one of the other factory workers greeted them.

Jonty never remembered peoples' names. Bill had to remind him all the time who they were even those men he had been working with for months now.

'Look at their miserable faces. Look at their hair and beards and moustaches. Listen to their accents. We've got a right mixture here. Try to concentrate lad. You wouldn't like it if everyone was always forgetting your name, would you?'

It never sounded harsh. More than anything else Jonty wanted to please Bill. That was all that mattered to him.

'I'll bloody make sure that nothing bad ever happens to you lad. Let's just say it's my second job. I mek bricks and I keep thee out of trouble.'

'Jonty likes Bill, likes Bill a lot,' he would often say much to the older man's embarrassment.

'I know lad, but best keep that between you and me.'

'Is it....is it alright?'

'Ay it's alright so long as you don't go mouthing it off in front of everybody. The fellas will only take it wrong like. They won't understand. The poor buggers won't understand Jonty so it's best left between the two of us, just us, alright?'

'Bloody freezing,' another of the men complained as they approached the factory doors.

'It'll be hot enough when we get them kilns going,' another responded.

The factory was a long, low building where thousands of bricks were made every day, bricks to line the Blea Moor tunnel and the arches of the viaduct, its two high chimneys belching out smoke from the kilns that could be seen far down the dale.

For Jonty nothing about the work had to change. If it did Bill would tell him what was happening and try and explain why. It had not taken him long to get used to his routine and now he enjoyed everything about it. He loved his work. Every day he looked forward to being there. Recently the bricks had reminded him of those Fraser Henderson had made for the two girls. Jonty was proud that he could name everyone who lived in hut twenty two. Best of all was to sit and listen to Bill telling Clare and Beth a story before they went to bed. He would tell them such stories about things that had happened in places all over the world. Jonty absorbed every word. He sometimes could see the pictures Bill was describing and at the end of the story the girls would always have questions to ask. The story Jonty liked the most was the one Bill told several times about the sailor who is shipwrecked and lands on a small island in the middle of the ocean and how he manages to keep alive before he is finally rescued and brought back to England. The girls were always asking for that story and Jonty especially liked the part where the shipwrecked sailor made a shelter for himself and lived off fish and fruit.

Fraser bought the girls sweets on a Saturday and he got a bag as well. This Christmas with the help of Bill Jonty had made Clare and Beth a proper card and had signed it with his name or that is what Bill said he had done. To him it had just looked like a squiggly line that Bill had helped him draw by holding his hand and guiding the coloured pencil, a red pencil so the line had looked like fine thread on the yellow paper.

Jonty loved colours. The winter was the most disappointing time for him. There were so few colours. But there again even the summer months at Ribblehead could be almost as dull. There was gold in the hay fields and dull green on the few stunted hawthorn bushes or white when they were in blossom and the heather on the moors came out purple for a few weeks. They were the only differences. The strongest colour of all was there all year. It was the flames in the furnace, such a deep, deep crimson that Jonty loved to watch dancing and flickering as the heat from such colour made him feel as if it was going to melt him into liquid red.

His job was to load up the freshly baked bricks onto a flat handcart that he would push out to the tramway. There he would lift the bricks into the trucks to be pulled up to the tunnel. For the viaduct where less bricks were needed they were loaded into horse drawn carts. Jonty was friendly with all the horses even if he repeatedly forgot their names. One especially, dark brown with short thick legs, would nuzzle up against his chest. The horse would smell strong with its warm breath snorting through its nostrils.

When he tossed the bricks into the handcart he looked for the different patterns they made. Some were pleasing but mostly they were a mess. He liked the colour of the bricks that reminded him of summer suns and of a peat fire in the winter. If possible things had to be placed in a way that he felt satisfying. If no one was looking he would quickly rearrange the bricks into a more pleasing pattern.

Everything was shapes and lines and connections. The world for Jonty was made up of numerous diagrams that fitted with the puzzles in his brain. Constantly he was discovering new intricacies of shape and colour.

With people it was different. Usually they formed ugly constructions which could only threaten him. Their presence was messy and unpredictable. Only Bill saved him from the others. There were now no jokes about Jonty, no smart comments. Bill made sure of that. The men were friendlier to him than they had been at the start. He had seen Bill knock a man flat out on the factory floor. Another time he had watched him take on three of the workers so hard and fast that quickly their faces had turned red with blood. In the factory Bill ruled over the others. The threat of violence was his power over them.

Only once had a man called Red Jed raised his fists to him when for some reason Bill had not been there. So Jonty had done the same, raised his fists and had been ready to fight. He had been more curious than anything else about what it would feel like to be punched in the face. Red Jed had swung at him but had missed so he had tried a punch hitting his opponent so hard he had knocked him off his feet much to the amusement of the other men who had been shouting out odds as to who would win. After that he had never been challenged again, not that it would have bothered him because he had actually enjoyed smacking somebody in the face and would have done it quite willingly again.

'Have you drunk yer tea?' Bill asked him at the morning break.

They were seated on a bench near the open oven doors with some of the other men.

'I have done,' he answered, proud of being able to express himself so readily.

'And have yer eaten?'

'I have.'

'So now you'll be wanting out for a pee.'

'Might do.'

'Well don't forget.'

'Won't forget Bill.'

Shadows moved across the walls of the factory and the roaring sound of the ovens being fired up filled the air. Everywhere brick dust coated the hands and faces of the men.

He was warm and easy here listening to the men mouthing on about bets and weather and the coming football match between the settlements and some farm lads from nearby Horton. He did not understand all they were saying but that did not matter. His thirst had been quenched and his belly felt fuller. He felt excited but could not understand why.

'Whenever you're not sure, whenever you're not happy or confused about someat, then you tell me straightaway,' Bill was always telling him, 'And if some bugger says someat you don't understand then you ask me and I don't want you going off by yourself. That's why I don't mind thee and Arnold

Wainwright going to the doms of a Tuesday night. At least that's a start. I want thee to have more freedom like but not if it gets you upset or into bother. I'm here to look after you and whatever happens I'm damned well sure that's what I'm going to do. Are thee listening lad?'

Jonty always listened as carefully as he could to Bill. He knew it was important because he knew Bill loved and cared for him and would do anything necessary to keep him safe.

Spittle formed in Jonty's mouth as he stood up and stretched himself. His shoulders were rounded so he walked with a slight hunch. He was tall with long arms and had a head out of proportion to the rest of his gangling frame. If he ever got upset his eyes would moisten and his bottom lip quiver. He would lower his chin onto his chest trying to hide his feelings.

'I suppose so then,' Bill sighed as he stood up as well.

'Excited Bill.'

'About what?'

'Don't know.'

'Well neither do I.'

'Excited.'

'Lucky you.'

Jonty walked towards the factory doors, his mind a confused attempt to discover why he was feeling like this. Then he stopped as a cold wind whipped brick dust into his eyes and everything turned red.

PART TWO

CHAPTER TWENTY TWO

Richard was waiting for the new teacher. The benches and desks were in the new hut that was still smelling of fresh wood and paint. A blackboard was on the end wall in front of the teacher's raised desk. The school room would accommodate up to fifty pupils aged from five to ten. Looking around he knew this was not enough but at least it was a start.

Stupidly he had imagined a middle aged spinster would be Batty Green's teacher, stocky, hard and a little severe. Surely there could be no other sort of candidate to take on a post in such an isolated place as Ribblehead. So he went outside the schoolroom built at the top edge of the settlement and waited to see who would arrive from the Johnston farm high up on the other side of the valley.

He felt a strain of anticipation, an uncertainty that caused him to hold himself tightly erect, his wide brimmed hat in hand, one foot placed neatly in front of the other as though this was the appropriate pose to receive the new person. His thoughts on this new teacher were not exactly subtle but Ribblehead was not a place for subtleties. It was grim, barren, wild and relentless and he thought that anyone applying for such a post must either be very foolish or escaping from something. He was waiting and she would soon be coming and somewhere in between those two points was an unexpected nervousness. Even before meeting this woman he was concerned that he made an impression. The suggestion had been his to establish a school at Batty Green as a matter of principle and humanity. The young ones needed more than just roaming around the settlements all day getting into trouble.

Today the sky was a clear blue and the air was the warmest it had been since the previous autumn. More men had answered the company's national advertising campaign and the work was back on schedule. James Tranton had his meeting hall and Mr Armworth's guests had come and gone but unfortunately not without incident. It had occurred when they were being shown around doctor Shawcross's hospital. Next to the doctor's surgery was a store room where a few coffins were stored and some drunk had managed to get into the room and lay down in one of them for a sleep. The ladies were shocked to see a dead body in an open coffin but even more so when the corpse suddenly sat up, opened his eyes and had started swearing at them for disturbing his rest before lying down again and falling back into his stupor. The shock for the ladies had necessitated smelling salts to help revive them after they had rushed out of the hut in a state of some confusion.

Richard smiled at the memory of it. A navvy would lay his head anywhere when he was approaching drunken unconsciousness. One of the tramway trains sounded off its hooter as it reached the rise before the approach to the tunnel. Five huge pillars were complete at the viaduct and three more under construction. In the far distance he could see the procession of horse drawn carts coming up the Ingleton road with the daily provisions. Ingleton station was where the new teacher would have been met by Andrew the day before. He had some business there so had volunteered to take her up to the Johnstons' farm.

He saw an unfamiliar figure passing between the line of huts, smoke blowing from their chimneys and washing hung out on such a good drying day. This must be the teacher and yet could not be. Even from such a distance it was obvious that this lady was taller than he had expected, walked so erectly while carrying a large leather bag. As she got closer his first impression was enhanced by the sight of her long neck, blond curls fringing under her grey bonnet and the manner of her smile as she looked up at him. Her coat, scarf and bonnet were all a shade of grey and yet the whole impression seemed to be one of colour and brightness.

'Miss Ormskill?' he found himself saying, 'Let me help you with your bag.'

'That would be kind,' she laughed easily as she put down the bag and shook his offered hand.

'I'm Richard Stockton, the chief engineer and manager here. I wanted to make sure the school had all you required.'

'Oh I'm sure it will suit very well Mr Stockton. I'm Miss Ormskill but please call me Lucy.'

Momentarily he was lost for words. Her impression had made him temporarily speechless. He desperately wanted to start the conversation again and sound manlier, more mature.

'It was finished only two weeks ago.'

'So recently,' she responded, looking at the freshly whitewashed hut that had yellow flowered curtains at its small windows.

'And you had a good journey here?'

'Yes, I was met by Mr Murray at Ingleton station as arranged, thank you.'

'And what about your rooms at the Johnstons'?'

'They are more than I expected and already I have been introduced to Mrs Johnson's custard tarts.'

She laughed lightly as he tried to stop himself staring at her greeny blue eyes and perfect mouth. This was not supposed to be happening, not at all. He was immediately disturbed by this woman for being so attractive, disturbed at the way she totally disrupted his mood. She was so at ease with him, so natural and charming in ways that he found hard to respond to.

'Should we go in?' he asked as he picked up her bag.

She followed him into the large classroom with its desks and benches neatly in lines. There was even a map of the world pinned to the wall bright in the pink of the British Empire's colonies.

'How fresh it all smells, paint and wood and new pens and pencils on my desk,' Lucy exclaimed, 'how very thoughtful, a lovely welcome. I'm sure this will all be fine,' she added as she ran her hand along the top of the sloping desks. She walked to the back of the room and turned to him, 'And what do you remember of your first days at school Mr Stockton?'

The question threw him completely. 'School,' he muttered, 'I'm....I'm not sure if I can remember.'

'Oh everyone remembers their first day at school surely.'

'It was too long ago I'm afraid.'

'Nonsense. It is obvious that cannot be true.'

'I'm glad you think so,' he answered weakly.

She waited a little before returning to the front of the classroom where she unbuttoned her coat and laid it on the desk. She was wearing a plain dark blue dress but again its plainness could not hide the shape of her long limbs and full bosom as she took off her gloves and scarf and started emptying her bag.

'So is there anything I can do for you at the moment?' he asked, wanting his stay to last as long as possible.

'I don't think so Mr Stockton, thank you.'

'I'd....I'd like you to call me Richard, if that's alright,' he managed to add.

She looked at him for a moment, her eyes widening slightly as she said, 'Fine Richard, and please remember to call me Lucy.'

'Lucy.'

'For my sins.'

'Which I'm sure are very few.'

She smiled again. He offered his hand before turning to leave.

'Oh Richard,' Lucy said as he reached the door, 'Thank you for coming to meet me here this morning. You've even had the stove lit.'

'It's still cold up here, even in the spring sunshine.'

'Thank you anyway,' she repeated.

'My pleasure,' he answered.

When he had gone Lucy sat at her desk thinking she had no idea what she had done taking on this job in such a God forsaken place with chief engineers who seemed as stiff as a board and the children she had already seen as filthy as city urchins. She put her hands on the desk and tried to control herself. She had always been told by her father that one mistake inevitably leads to another and another until there is a huge equation of difficult consequences. Coming here to Ribblehead seemed already a perfect example. The rooms at the Johnstons farm were cold and stank of manure and animal feed. They had such low roofs she could hardly stand up straight and the kitchen was a mess of dogs, cats and hens roaming in and out and a young, gormless labourer who could not stop ogling her. The idea of having to spend months and months in such a place was disgusting and miserable.

She had come here in a panic. She had been scared and had acted without thinking. There had been nobody to guide her, nobody with whom she could discuss what she should do. As always she had been alone and desperate and had made decisions that had been blatantly wrong. This was always the risk for a woman by herself. Society was not there for women to be making decisions by themselves for themselves. Husbands were supposed to do that.

Her eyes moistened as she took out a handkerchief and looked at this simple room with its simple furniture. It was a classroom and a prison already full of the future echoes of rowdy, stupid children who struggled against everything she would try to do for them. It was unnatural for them to be educated. Her job was a mission and a battle of endurance. Back in Burnley she had failed to remember how a teacher had to act in society. She again had lost her way through dreams and desires that were inappropriate and corrupting. Having an affair with a married member of the board of governors had been stupid and threatening to everything she had strived for and now she was paying the price. This miserable place was the punishment that she deserved. She was guilty and was proud of it when her mood was defiant and she would stand up against the rest of the masculine world. But just now there was no such strength.

Automatically she emptied the rest of the bag, arranging her teaching materials over the desk top. Enrolment for Batty Green School would begin tomorrow and Andrew Murray had said he would help her. At least he was better looking than Richard Stockton but just like the manager he had appeared so solid and reasonable and all he had wanted to talk about on their journey from Ingleton was the building of the railway line. He had been too nervous to ask her any questions except about her trip to the Dales.

She dried her eyes and started pinning pictures and posters up on the wall. She believed that a learning environment should be as colourful and stimulating as possible so here she was in the middle of nowhere already beginning to pretend that civilisation was all around her. Batty Green looked like some shanty town from the far west of the United States of America, once the country of her young dreams.

Suddenly there was a clatter and three boys almost fell into the room in their shorts, bare feet and filthy faces.

'Shit!' one exclaimed.

'You the new teacher?' another asked.

They seemed no more than eight years old and were breathlessly confident and cheeky.

They came to a sudden stop in front of her desk, their large eyes emphasised by the dirt around them.

'We don't want no school,' the third said strongly.

As he spoke there was the sound of smashed glass and a stone rolling across the floor.

'Fucking hell!' one of the boys shouted.

A man rushed in asking Lucy whether she was alright as the three boys ran around his legs and out of the door as quickly as they could.

'I'm....I'm fine,' Lucy managed.

'They're little buggers,' the man said in his broad Yorkshire accent,' You're sure yer alright?'

He took off his cap and screwed it in his hands while waiting for her to respond.

Lucy made no comment. Already things were going too fast. She looked at him in his jacket, moleskin trousers tied up below the knees and filthy boots that had left dirt along his track from the door. There was a clear line between dirt and the white skin where his cap should be. He had a handsome face and bright, brown eyes, taller than the usual worker and seemed confidently set.

Finally she said, 'I hope the rest of the children are not as bad as those boys.'

'I'll tell the foreman about the window, and no they're not all as bad. Mind you most of them ain't that brilliant, not when it comes to their behaviour. They're bored most of the time. Nothing in the settlements for them to do except get into trouble, like most kids I suppose.'

'Unfortunately, yes.'

He paused although it was obvious that he had more to say.

'Well thank you Mr.....'

'Tom, I'm Tom Myres and you're Miss Lucy Ormskill from Burnley where you last had a teaching post, and yes we hear things fast around here. There are enough folk in the settlements for things to be happening but few enough for everyone to hear about them or make it up as they go on. Rumours Miss Ormskill are more important than money around here and I'm afraid you'll be a centre of attention, such a fine looking woman if I may say so also being the first teacher at Batty Green. You're just what the rumour mongers have been waiting for.'

'I hope not,' Lucy said lightly, already struck by this man's fluency and directness.

'It's a certainty, as certain as them lads'll have tanned hides if I get hold of em.'

'I'm afraid you're a cynic Mr Myres.'

'I'll be anything you like if you call me Tom.'

'Why should I be so informal?'

'To be friendly like and also the fact that I have no time for social conventions.'

'Am I to take that for a warning?'

'Go on, tell me you've known me for ages already.'

'Not when that would be untrue.'

'My, my, Miss Ormskill has a way with her, an unexpected way, trying to play word games I'm sure.'

'And what word game would that be?' she asked.

'Well the one of course when a lady is interested in a gentleman at first sight but pretends that is not the case by hiding behind clever words.'

'And you sound as though you are well experienced in such matters.'

'I should hope I am.'

'And I think you are too forward for your own good.'

'Agreed,' Tom answered happily smiling as he stood there enjoying himself.

'How generous for you to agree.'

'So it's agreed. Some evenings I will walk you back to the Johnstons farm where you're staying just in case you have any more trouble with the young riff raff of this community.'

'I'm sure I can manage myself.'

'Well at least you could thank me for my generous offer.'

'Was that what it was, generous? You flatter yourself Mr Myres.'

'I'll be trying again. It's in my nature not to give up too easily.'

'I'm afraid I'm not interested in what your nature is.'

'And that's the first thing you've said Miss Ormskill that is untrue!' he exclaimed in a mockingly shocked voice.

She looked at him critically and said somewhat abruptly, 'That's one thing I never do.'

'So I gather from that you are trying to be a religious person.'

'All I believe in is trying to give children the best chance they can have.'

'How laudable.'

'And you Mr Myres, what do you believe in?'

'The coming revolution of the working class,' he answered boldly, smiling at the same time.

At that she laughed, 'Oh dear, a socialist!'

'And proud of it.'

'Obviously.'

'And you, may I call you Lucy? Have we spent enough time together?'

'No, you may not.'

'Why not?'

'Because I don't know you.'

But she felt that was not true. She was already crossing boundaries, the one thing she promised herself she would not do. But this Tom Myres intrigued her with his good looks and his fast talk, his humour, his dark hair and eyes, his lean, strong body.

'We've been chatting away for what feels like hours already. By now we're almost old acquaintances, don't you think?'

'I'm surprised you're quite so open about your politics Mr Myres.'

'Perhaps I'll refuse to continue this conversation if you can't call me Tom. Nobody else need know. Whatever we say to each other will go no further than these four walls.'

He said this smiling, scratching his nose as he waited for her response.

Lucy felt his confidence was both flattering and unexpected. If this was the first navvy of Batty Green she had met it made her wonder about the rest.

'Do you work here at Ribblehead Mr Myres?' she finally asked as she tidied the books she had brought.

'Oh, now it's getting nasty.'

'I just thought at this time of day you would have your work to go to.'

'I'm a stonemason who has been to the tunnel to hear about certain problems up there.'

'Work problems or political problems?'

'Everything is political Miss Ormskill.'

'So you are in a union?'

'Not exactly.'

'Well,' she sighed,' what are you then?'

'An obliging man who is not allowed to escort you home of a night. You refuse to call me by my Christian name. Oh you're a hard bitten woman, one I might regret making all this effort to get to know.'

She rose from her chair, smoothed down the sides of her dress and stepped down off the dais and offered her hand, saying, 'Alright. I succumb to your wishes Tom because I have the sense that you are not someone who will easily give up on something once they have they set their mind on it.'

He took her hand and held it there for a few moments looking at her bright, green eyes, 'And all I'll have done is filthy your hand,' he joked when she finally stepped back, 'Lucy,' he added warmly.

'How sincere you can sound.'

'It's called unmasculine enthusiasm. I never try and hide my soft side Lucy. Every socialist has one. It's the reason he has such concern for his fellow human beings.'

'But soft can be vulnerable.'

'Not necessarily. To me it can be a kind of strength, one that a lot of men do not allow themselves. It gives me an advantage and they don't understand why.'

'But do you really think it would be a good idea you escorting me through Batty Green, and how would your work timetable fit in with the ending of my day?'

'Well I intend to make it work.'

'I don't want to be embarrassed Tom. I have not even started yet. You might not accept social conventions but most people do and I don't think the people who employed me would look favourably at me out walking with one of the workers. Surely you can see that?'

He frowned and nodded before putting on his cap, pulling the peak lower over his eyes, saying, 'I can Lucy. I want only what's best for you so we'll have to have a think about it. There might be one or two days when I can fiddle my time and get off early, make some excuse or other. The management tend to give me a wide berth here.'

'So you think yourself that important?'

'Of course!' he laughed.

Suddenly the classroom door was pushed open followed by a young one shouting, 'Tom Myres is kissing the teacher!'

'Dirty bugger!' another of them added loudly.

'Right, that's it!' Tom exclaimed, 'Wait till I get hold of them little sods and I'll get someone to fix your window. Bye Miss Ormskill!'

Lucy could do nothing but smile at this last remark. She went to the open doorway to watch him step quickly down the boggy slope with the boys running off in all directions. Her depression had been abated, her mood lifted in a most unexpected way. The boundary had been crossed and she did not care as she watched this Tom Myres disappear between the first rows of huts as the low sun glinted orange light across the valley.

CHAPTER TWENTY THREE

Ethan was going running, fell running as they called it in these parts. The challenge had come from the local farmers. Already there were the football matches, some boxing and strength competitions between the navvies and the locals, events where a lot of money was exchanged and a lot of drink consumed. As most of them took part on a Sunday this was frowned upon by the Temperance Society and all the other religious groups whose members were disgusted at such things being allowed by the Ribblehead management. Richard Stockton had had several visits from their representatives including James Tranton and expected another one once the fell race was announced for the first Sunday in April.

Arnold Wainwright had proposed the idea to Ethan on their way back from the cutting after work was finished for the day.

'Come on lad, you're as fit as any of the others and you have a good turn of speed, I've seen ye chasing your girls.'

Ethan looked doubtful, 'After you got me into that filthy fight how the hell do you expect me to listen Arnold to any of your cock and bull ideas?'

'Nay Ethan, this is a bit of fun like, not that those bloody farmers will be thinking that. Just cos we beat them at the football last Saturday they'll be wanting to prove a point so I say we should show these buggers and beat them at this too.'

'So why aren't you volunteering?'

'Christ lad, can thee see me trying to get up bloody Whernside. It'd kill me. It'd be murder so it would.'

'This is why they call you Badger you old bugger, never stop badgering honest folk, do you?'

'There'll be money on you.'

'Oh here we go, more of your devious schemes or in this case maybe not. Some bugger has put you up to this. There's someat going on Wainwright.'

'Not at all, just a few of the lads interested in the odds. Anyway there's practise this Saturday evening.'

'Practise!'

'Well if thee is going to do it might as well do it right. Need to get them old lungs cleared out of all that blue shit you've been breathing in for the last months. The lads who'll be running are going to tek a turn down to the Hill Inn and back.'

'And I won't be one of them.'

'Oh come on. What can thee lose? It'll be a bit of a laugh.'

'Ay, for the spectators watching our lot fall about in heaps. Whose stupid idea was this?'

'The famers' lads think they can beat the shit out of us and we have to mek sure they don't, so come on Ethan lad and buck up. You don't smoke. You hardly ever have a drink. You're in your prime, in your prime and you should show these so called mountain goats what thee can do.'

'Up Whernside and back?'

'No bother.'

'It's bloody madness, that's what it is.'

'So you'll do it?'

'I'll.....I'll think it oer.'

Arnold slapped him on the back as he had exclaimed, 'There you go! I knew thee would do it. I knew it.'

'I haven't said whether or no yet.'

'Saturday night. I'll be there to see how thee gets on.'

'That's big of you.'

'I should think it damn well is.'

Maggie was not at all impressed by the idea. As far as she was concerned anything from Arnold Wainwright had to be suspicious.

'I just can't understand how you could agree to anything that man suggests. You watch, there'll be someat in it for him. There allays is.'

'This is me doing it, not him, me. Can't do any harm.'

'Oh no, all it will tek is you injuring yerself and then what? You don't get sick pay. You don't ever get sick pay and where would that leave us?'

'I'll be careful.'

She had pulled a doubtful face.

'And where are the girls?'

'Playing next door.'

'How did they get on at school today?'

'Beth loves it and she loves her teacher, not sure about our Clare though. She don't seem that fussed. She's still as much a young un as her sister. Sometimes I think there's no difference between em. Our Clare just ain't growing up as quick as I reckon she should be, but she's still a grand lass and that's all that matters in the end.'

'So you'll be down on the road supporting us on Saturday night?' Ethan tried.

'Like hell as like.'

'And there was me hoping you'd bring the lassies as well to see their father.....'

'Meking a fool of himself.'

'Not at all Maggie, I'm fitter now than I've ever been.'

When the girls came in they rushed up to him, Clare shouting, 'You're going in fer that race!'

He lifted Beth up, spun her round and then carefully put her down again before tousling Clare's hair, 'And what if I am?'

'You running Dad.'

'That's me.'

'You'll win Dad!' Beth exclaimed.

'Well I don't know about that.'

'Course yer will.'

'You two should be coming running wi me then.'

'Can we?' Clare asked.

He looked at their two eager faces before saying, 'Not this time, but I'll tek thee, just us three. I'll have to do some serious training and you two can help.'

Maggie was relieved there was at last something that seemed to have lightened his mood. Even the girls getting a place at Batty Green's new school had not roused as much interest from him as she had hoped. This was one of the best things that had ever happened to her family, having her girls receive some kind of education in such a place as Ribblehead, the last thing she had expected when they had first arrived here.

So on Saturday evening she, Clare and Beth, Bill and Jonty with the rest of the crowd were up on the toll road to watch the athletes depart for their first training run. There were at least thirty of them even though the word was that most of them were only going as far as the Hill Inn and no further. A group of boys shouting and laughing followed on behind as the men started off into the twilight that had settled over the dale, the sound of their boots and clogs clattering away into the distance. Some managed no more than half a mile and turned back, others broke away in ones and twos, the group spread out along the rutted road as it started to rain.

'Fucking hell,' one of them muttered jogging beside Ethan.

'Give us a pint and a fag any day,' another added breathlessly.

The calls and shouts from the young boys running after them were silenced. They too saw no point in going any further as the rain began pouring down.

As expected at the Hill Inn most of the others turned into the pub while about ten who were left started back along the rutted road.

Now it was serious. It was plain those still running were focused and unwilling to stop. Some were making a race of it disappearing into the wet darkness. Ethan with a few others stayed together at a steadier pace. To begin with his chest had been on fire and his legs felt like heavy weights taking so much effort to lift up one after the other. Worse were his boots, too tight and hurting his feet at every step. It got so bad he thought of stopping at the Hill Inn like most of the others but instead had forced himself to continue. The last thing he wanted was to become one the crowd would joke about, one of those who had never managed and should never have bothered in the first place. Pride and a bloody mindedness took over.

His clothes were sodden, the water and sweat dribbling into his mouth. He realised that this run in comparison with the proper race up Whernside was easy, mainly on the flat with no obstacles, but at least it was giving him and the rest a sense of what running was all about, a steady rhythm of steps, arms and breathing, a mental concentration and a refusal to stop even if most of the brain was telling him to give it up and walk.

Because of the rain there was nobody waiting at the finish except for the few organisers and those who were looking to put serious money on its outcome. When he took off his boots in the hut Ethan's socks were sodden with blood.

'Oh my God look at them!' Maggie exclaimed as she went for a bowl of water.

'They're horrible,' Beth said as she and Clare gave his feet a close inspection.

'Well yer can wash em if thee like.'

'No we won't!' Clare exclaimed in disgust.

'But yer did it Dad. Yer ran it.'

Ethan nodded to Beth and said jokingly, 'I suppose I did, not that I think it's done me much good.'

'I know you'll win.'

'No lass, I don't think so.'

'I tell em all at school you're going to win.'

'Well you'd better tell em someat different.'

After the girls finally went to bed Maggie complained again about the state of his feet.

'Need some larger boots,' Ethan said, 'or I'm buggered.'

'New boots tek some wearing in.'

'Well I can't bloody run in these. I'll get some new uns from the market and then I'll have time.'

'You shouldn't be running at all. Look at the state of you.'

'Don't start woman,' he answered moodily.

'I'm not. I'm just saying.'

'There's three weeks to go yet so I reckon that'll give us chance at another couple o runs. The girls can come wi us part o way if they like.'

'Our Clare'll beat yer.'

'Ay she probably will,' Ethan agreed, enjoying Maggie's sudden interest.

On the Sunday of the actual race everything was different. Nobody had been prepared for the crowds or the fine weather. What had started as a bragging match between some of the workers and young farmers in a Horton pub had turned into the biggest event the settlements had seen. Even Mr Armsworth had agreed to start the race and brought a large number of guests with him.

People had come from miles around. Every coach, cart and gig had been hired for the day so by the time of the start there were hundreds of people on the route that ran across the valley before the steep undulating rise up to the top of Whernside and back, a climb of over two thousand feet.

What to wear had been the main topic of debate for the runners. Arthur thought Ethan should stay in his long johns and wear a knee length pair of shorts over the top.

'I'll look a right bloody fool in them,' Ethan had complained.'

'You just see what the young farmers'll be wearing. It'll be the same. Thee doesn't want to be overheating wi too many clothes on.'

He had decided to wear his old boots after all. Some of the runners had hammered in more studs for grip and one of them had decided to put on his wife's boots because they were made of finer leather and so were a lot lighter, something that caused a few sarcastic remarks.

Ethan with his family walked nervously towards the start. Maggie noticed Mr Stockton in the crowd with the new teacher Miss Ormskill. The rumour was that they had been seen on several Sundays in Mr Stockton's gig going about the district. Andrew Murray was organising the starting tape and gun that Mr Armwsorth would use to get the runners going. The din of hundreds of voices filled the air including those of all the farmers and their families who had come to see their sons in the race. Stalls had been set up selling hot food and mugs of beer or cordial. The school had made a bunting strung over the start. There across the valley and up the first slopes of Whernside could be seen a dark line of people ready to cheer the racers on. Uncertainty and expectancy were in the spring day atmosphere. Children were running around everywhere. Rows and rows of horses had been tethered up alongside the Beck next to the carts and carriages. The whole area had been quickly churned up into a huge bog, the ground sodden from the previous days' rain which would mean the descent of Whernside would be treacherous.

'Thee ready lad?' Arnold wanted to know as he stood beside Ethan trying to ignore Maggie and the children.

'Christ, why I ever listen to you Arnold Wainwright, Badger bloody Wainwright.'

'Now don't be like that. You're running for all of us now and we don't want to be beaten by a load of sheep shaggers. Remember, first you has to finish cos there's points for that and then it's up to what position you come in the race. That means you just keep going whatever happens. Even if you're last, it doesn't matter so long as thee finishes. Just be steady to start with and then see how it goes.'

'Listen to you!' Ethan exclaimed, 'Trying to sound like a bloody expert!'

'Well I wouldn't go as far as that.'

'Neither would I.'

'Right, come on, the runners are being called to the start. Don't look up to where thee are headed. Just keep thee head down watching for the next step. That's what you do.'

'Bloody hell Arnold, shut up for once.'

'I will when you've started. Right show today. Never seen so many folk, and Mr Armsworth here as well with all his hob nobs from Leeds. Seems there's all the police constables from every town around here. Must be expecting trouble if we don't win or if we do. It'll still be the same I reckon. The pubs'll be stacked tonight alright.'

Ethan got away from him at last to join the rest of the runners. Suddenly this was important. He did not want to make a fool of himself in front of all these people, hundreds of them, all in their Sunday best. There was the mixed smells from the food stalls, the mud, the privies and the new grass on the hills. He took in deep breaths trying to calm himself then shook hands with some of the other runners before Mr Armsworth called them to the line.

The gun went off and with it a huge cheer, a mixture of alternating sounds from the children, women, men and old folk, some who continued shouting their encouragement until the runners were crossing the valley.

As Arnold had predicted the young farmers looked lean, fit and were all in shorts and vests. There were ten in each team and by the time they had reached the first slopes of the valley side it was a group of young farmers who were in the lead.

Just before the gun Ethan had looked unsuccessfully for Maggie and the girls in the crowd. He wanted to prove to himself that he could at least once stand out from the rest of the men. Usually he hated such bravado, this need to compete, but on this occasion he had committed himself.

Tommy Watkins, one of James Tranton's congregation, was the youngest at eighteen in the navvy team. Most of the young famers seemed under twenty, all thin and muscular. Ethan was one of the oldest out of the twenty runners and it began to tell when they reached the first slopes of Whernside. This was no jog down to the Hill Inn and back. This was serious, no jokes, no stopping for a quick breath. Already four of the young farmers were well in the lead, bouncing up the slopes like young sheep. Ethan was near last, his chest burning, his head and worst of all his feet thumping out pain. Even though Maggie had bandaged them up as best she could he could before the race he could already feel they were bleeding again, the toes bruised against the front of the boots.

The slope steepened. He had to stop pretending to run and started to walk, head down, hands on knees, concentrating on the next step, lost in a delirium of exhaustion such as he had never known before. All his digging and shifting had not prepared him for this, especially the pressure on his legs that were aching with the effort of every movement. Ethan refused to give in. The others were still battling on and so would he. He was drenched in sweat, feeling he wanted to wretch, the sides of his head pulsing a new kind of pain like everything was being stretched until it would snap.

When they he was roughly halfway up the steep hillside he tried to check what was happening around him. Only a few spectators had made the effort to come this far, their desultory calls drifting away across the barren hillside. At least he was not last, but there again the leaders were a good distance in front. He remembered Arnold's words that finishing was more important than anything else. He had to keep going at his own pace and not break himself. There was a way of doing this, of balancing his need to keep going with what his body's strength could manage. With every step he was learning how to control his breathing, to mentally relax and believe that he would get to the end somehow or another.

Whernside was one of those hills where you thought you had reached the top only to have another rise in front of you, repeated over and over again until it began to sap the confidence of all but the most experienced runners. Now the first batch of young farmers passed him as they started on their way back down, bouncing and stepping quickly over the rough ground. It was obvious those four would be finished before anybody else. At one point Ethan passed Harry Fletcher, one of the drillers in the tunnel, who was obviously struggling. Ethan wanted to say some words of encouragement but could not as Harry was slowly left behind, his breath sounding like a dog's swimming with a stick in its mouth.

Up here there was more of a wind and some of the slope was covered in scree. He thought again of Maggie and the girls. To have them in mind was a huge encouragement. The last thing he wanted was to walk in hours after all the rest. His pride was still there, his anger at his own physical weakness. There were no thoughts about how he would feel the next day. All that mattered was pushing himself on and on until the uninspiring summit was reached and at last he could turn and start on the downward run. At the top were a few men to check that all the runners actually reached the top of the hill and that there was no cheating going on. Ethan passed five runners still struggling on their way up, four of them from his team. His mind was telling him that the navvies were going to be well beaten but that no longer mattered. All he wanted was to get down as quickly but as safely as he could, down to where he could see all the crowds, down to where at last it would be over and he could lie on the earth and gulp in fresh spring air and know he had survived. But it was not yet over. Suddenly he heard a scream and less than a minute later passed a small crowd huddled around the figure of young Tommy Watkins who was screaming and writhing on the ground, one of his legs twisted at a strange angle. For him it was over and for two other navvies he passed who were sat hunched up on the hillside, their heads down between their knees gasping for air. The whole thing was becoming a madness of endurance. Now he could hear the crowd. Now he had reached the lower slopes without incident, sliding and slipping his way down, his mouth as wide open as possible, his hands bleeding from his attempts to steady himself against the outcrops of limestone. His boots were shredded and he could no longer feel his feet. They were like so much else of his body, numbed off from sheer exhaustion.

'Come on! Come on! Keep going!, he could now hear from the line of people and it was as if all their cries were for him, all for him, all eyes watching him, Ethan Granger, one of the navvy team almost finished. He was the child happy to compete, the young one running free in an old body that ached and stretched and felt bruised all over.

He cross the finish line and crashed to the floor and everything went momentarily blank. He rolled over and spewed out everything in his stomach. Without thinking he sat up and started taking off his boots. By then Arnold was beside him.

'You bloody did it lad!' he was exclaiming, 'I bloody knew thee could do it. You finished. Yer did it.'

His words were lost in Ethan's sickening state of mind and body. Everything was reeling and spinning, his guts tight, his legs humming, his mouth so dry, sweat pouring down his face and blood dribbling from his fingers.

Arnold helped him with his boots and unwrapped the crimson soaked bandages. His feet were a mess. Huge blisters had burst on the back of his heels. There were deep cracks in between each toe and most of the nails were bruised and stained with blood. But at least they were in the air. Their thumping pain free of restriction as he lay back down to look at all the figures shifting around him until the faces of Clare and Beth appeared followed by Maggie.

He looked up and tried to smile.

'You didn't win,' Clare complained.

'I know lass, I'm sorry,' he gasped, bent forward, hands on knees with sweat dripping off his chin.

'I thought you'd win.'

'Arnold said you would,' Beth added.

'What a mess,' Maggie put in as she looked down at his feet.

'They'll mend.'

'What, by tomorrow they won't.'

'I'll manage.'

'And there's Tommy Watkins with a broken leg. That could have been you,' she said critically, shocked at the state he was in.

'Well it isn't.'

'He did good Missus,' Arnold tried to intervene.

'And what would you know?' Maggie said back strongly.

By the time Bill and Jonty had supported him back to the hut the unsurprising news was out that the young farmers' team had won the race easily. Four of the navvy team including the poor Tommy Watkins had not managed to finish. Most of the others had been well behind the winners.

'Well I hope you're proud of yersell,' Maggie said when they were both in bed that night.

Ethan was so tired he could not sleep, could only lay there taking an inventory of all the different pains he was experiencing. He felt as though his feet had swollen to three times their normal size and his hands were nipping from all the cuts. His legs were stiff and aching and even his back felt as though it had been on the rack. His head was still thumping and his throat felt as though it had been scraped by a dull knife.

'That could have been you with a broken leg and then what would we have done?' she continued.

'I did finish Maggie,' he managed to say.

'You finished! So what does that prove if anything at all? You should never have gone in it for such a thing in the first place, listening to that Arnold Wainwright.'

He waited miserably to see if she would continue which she did, 'You should have nothing to do with that man. All he does is get you into stupid situations, really stupid. And what does he get out of it? That's what I'd like to know because don't you worry he will do. The likes of his type always do.'

'He's.....he's a friend of Jonty's, remember.'

'And I don't know why Bill allows it.'

'Isn't it....it up to Jonty?' Ethan asked wearily, emptily.

'Of course it isn't. Jonty can't be expected to mek up his own mind. Anyway, that's got nothing to do with it. I don't want you involved wi such nonsense again. It's too dangerous. Of course it is. How often have we talked about trying to keep the family healthy at all costs? How often have we seen other families destroyed through illness and accidents? I won't have this family put under threat because of these stupid games men want to play. You have a job that depends on you keeping well, and now I'm taking in some money the same is for me. But there you go and risk the whole thing on some stupid race. There you......'

'For God's sake Maggie, leave it won't you? Leave it,' he said as he turned away.

'Easy for you to say.'

'Nothing's easy.'

'Well stop trying to mek it harder.'

Again he went through the race, remembering so many details of it. Now it all seemed slightly unbelievable. Whernside was so high and he had run up and down it. He would never be able to look at that side of the valley again without thinking about what he had done today. All the rest had been so pleased for him. Even Fraser had come up and congratulated him in the reticent way he had. Jonty had been excited by the whole thing and wanted to express what he felt over and over again. It was only the girls who had been disappointed he had not won and here was his wife so against the whole thing that what he had done felt in so many ways now meaningless. She had taken all the worth out of it, all the effort and strain and had left only a resentment. He could never do it right for her. She pulled apart every positive moment he created and he was tired of it, tired of always failing her.

CHAPTER TWENTY FOUR

'Miss teacher, Sam Johnston has peed hisell again!'

'I'm sure that's not true George.'

'It is Miss teacher. He stinks.'

Lucy stared at the boy causing this sudden outburst as the class started laughing and calling out. She was not sure whether to ignore this.

Weeks before enrolment day had been a long one with queues of mothers trying to prove the age of their children, some attempting to enrol ones too young, others too old, which had led to many arguments. She had been glad that Andrew Murray had been there to help with some of the angrier disputes. Because of such a demand they had managed to squeeze in another row of desks and benches which meant the class now had sixty two pupils. Initially the plan was to use some of the ten year olds as helpers but as Lucy quickly discovered they were not up to the task. One of these had been Clare Granger. By the next day it was obvious that Clare could not cope herself at school never mind trying to help some of the younger ones.

'Fuck off Smithens!' came a shout from the back of the room.

'Quiet!' Lucy demanded.

These children were even worse than those from the back streets of Burnley, even rougher and dirtier. To Lucy such children as these were not ready for schooling. It was impossible. Of course it was expecting too much of herself. She knew she needed more adult help so asked Andrew Murray to try and find a couple of teenage girls who could read and write who might assist her. Here she had been lucky. There had been three candidates and all were accepted and paid a small amount of money each week by the company. They were just what she had been looking for, sensible, hardworking, not taking any nonsense and more than anything else they enjoyed all their tasks which was a minor miracle. Shirley Tibbins, Angela Mould and Sarah Bickerstaff were on time every morning and stayed late to help her clear up the classroom. From near disaster these three girls had offered the possibility that the school might actually work.

'Now letters!' she said loudly over the din, 'Slates, chalk and eyes to the front and nobody out of their seats. My monitors are there to help so use them and no more calling out, no more! I won't have it!'

For a few minutes her words seemed to have some effect as she started writing out the alphabet on the blackboard sounding out each letter as she did so.

Lucy had always refused to use any kind of corporal punishment. The idea of inflicting physical pain on a child was abhorrent to her. She knew the class took advantage of this. Once it got around that the teacher was a softy then everything was possible. She loved her pupils and hated them at the same time. She would often wake up in the middle of the night after hideous dreams of their wild, outrageous behaviour, all of them working a conspiracy against her. It was the nature of the job.

Some saw the teacher as the enemy. Others fell in love with her, had crushes, thought she was wonderful. Beth Granger was one who adored her and looked forward to school more than anything. Beth was entranced by this tall, beautiful, clever lady who actually spoke to her and seemed to care for her. Beth would do anything for Miss Ormskill and hated it when some of the others started telling filthy jokes about her. She would block up her ears and run away.

One of the problems of Batty Green's new school was that it had no designated playground area. The class would disperse over the top moor, playing through the heather, along the gulleys of sodden peat, jumping pools of black bog water. Lucy's helpers would be out there trying to supervise them but at the end of each break most of the class would return caked in mud or would not return at all, some of them having run off back into the settlement. Everyday a few went missing, most of them turning up the next day. For those who regularly did not return she would try and talk to their uninterested parents. The rest would drag their children back up to the school intent that they should get some kind of education.

The classroom stank of wet earth and filthy bog water, many of the children with scrawny faces still black with yesterday's playtime mud. They had no idea how to converse with each other or their teacher. Their means of communication were either a string of swear words or hitting out whenever they felt it was necessary. It took weeks for Lucy to understand a word they were saying, broad accents from all over the country with guttural sounds that started at the back of their young throats and sounded like an anthem of ignorance.

'My God,' she often thought to herself, 'They sound so stupid, so limited. The girls are just as bad as the boys. Everything merges together into a claggy mess of deep Yorkshire or Lancashire accents and goodness knows what else mixed in with a lot of swearing.'

She was not shocked. She had been teaching too long for that, but still found it depressing. Everything about their young lives was miserably stunted and it seemed without any possibilities of change. They were all tiny navvies acting like their elders, ready to grow up into a world of work, poverty and drink and never to expect anything else. Education was supposed to give them a chance but here at Ribblehead Lucy was unsure as to what that chance might be.

'The Jesuits thought that having them up to the age of seven would ensure that their pupils would remain from then on as good Catholics,' she remembered telling Richard Stockton on one of their Sunday afternoon trips, 'and they were right. They start with me at the age of five and I feel it's already too late, far too late to make any kind of real difference.'

Richard thought about this, his forehead creased and his lips drawn tight before he had said, 'You do yourself an injustice Lucy. I'm sure you do. I'm certain that in the coming months you will see what effect you are having on them all, and I mean all. They will not escape your ability to change them, to civilise them. But we don't expect miracles.'

'Well I hope not!' she had laughed, 'I really do.'

She had seen nothing of Tom Myres since their first provocative meeting, but with Richard things were very different. He had suggested they take a trip out so he could show her the local area and this had become a regular fixture of her weekly routine.

On the first occasion he had picked her up in the cobbled yard of the Johnston farm with hens and geese scurrying all over the place and the stench from the barn where a few cows had been kept through the winter. The Johnstons had come to the door to wave them off. His rig was sleek, painted a shiny black and pulled by a strong horse. Lucy had been all muffed up in scarf and gloves to keep out the chill of the early spring day. Beside her Richard had been anxious to make the right impression.

Now as they set off down the steep track from the farm he was quietly pondering what he should say. Lucy was quite happy with such reticence as though just another's presence was sufficient on such a sparkling afternoon when the brown and dull green of the hills contrasted with the clearest of blue skies. This country was both alien and exhilarating. It lifted her spirits. The memory of Burnley and all its dark streets and belching chimneys were quickly lost to this other world where as they slowly rode away from the Dale and its settlements it became more remote and empty.

'Are you comfortable enough Lucy?'

'More than that,' she had answered, 'It's lovely. I never imagined it could be so empty of people.'

'So you like this sense of isolation?'

'For me, yes it is isolation. I'm only used to city living I'm afraid. I very rarely travelled out of Burnley except to go shopping in Manchester once in a while.'

'Sometimes space like this is necessary I think, puts a completely different perspective on things.'

'In what way?'

The question was not expected. Later he would come to learn that this was something Lucy often did, asking instead of just accepting. He wanted to impress her and felt he had to take care with his answer. Sounding too intellectual would not be right but on the other hand he did not want to sound trite either.

'It's so easy to get caught up in the rush of things you risk losing who you really are. Up here there is more time for individual thoughts. I worked in London for a few years and I know how easy it is to get carried along with the crowd and the bustle of the capital city.'

'What did you do in London?'

'Worked on the underground Metropolitan Railway, a devil of a job that took months longer than expected.'

'Our capital city,' Lucy said, 'Unfortunately I've never been. I'd love to visit it.'

'I'm sure you'd be impressed but even then it can still be a monster overwhelming everyone, forcing them into its busy life.'

'How very descriptive Richard. I don't think I like the sound of that,' she laughed and then was jerked sideways as the wheel of the rig hit a lump of rock on the road.

Instead of being pleased with his own response to her question Richard was now worrying about whether he was dressed in the right clothes for the occasion. Earning good money meant he had a choice and was unsure that what he was wearing was too formal for going out riding on his rig, too much his Sunday best for a trip around the Dales.

Eventually they approached the small village of Dent with its cobbled, winding main street, the Sun public house and Queens's hotel surrounded by small stone built houses.

'How quaint this is,' Lucy commented as they rattled over the cobbles along the almost deserted street.

'We'll ride around the place and then turn back if that is alright with you Lucy,' he said before adding, 'To think that Dent, this little place, was once a centre of strong opposition to the monarchy, that this tiny village had numerous radicals living here and in the local area.'

'And when was this?'

'In the reign of Henry VIII,' he answered as they returned through the rest of the village and out onto the main road. The sound of a hymn being sung came from the nearby church. 'It was at the time of the dissolution of the monasteries,' he continued, 'The folk round here were solidly against such policies and joined what became known later as 'The Pilgrimage of Grace', thousands of men from the villages of Yorkshire and elsewhere against the King's men to save the monasteries.'

'And they failed I assume?'

'Absolutely. Promises were made. The men returned to their homes and then Henry not only continued with the destruction of the monasteries he had their leaders executed as well. In fact he went back on every single promise he made.'

'The Pilgrimage of Grace,' Lucy had repeated,' what a lovely title for such a tragic event.'

'Yes, for once a rebellion when people wanted to hold onto the past.'

'Oh I'm sure the likes of a Tom Myres would not agree with any of that!' she laughed.

Richard stiffened, 'And what do you know about the likes of a Tom Myres?'

Lucy understood immediately the mistake she had made.

'Oh someone mentioned him as one of the socialists you have at Ribblehead,' she had quickly lied, 'They can't make your job any easier Richard.'

She felt him still wary as he said, 'No, they don't, but it's to be expected. As far as I can gather they're now in all major industries, just something we have to tolerate at the moment I'm afraid.'

'And is that what you do, tolerate them?' she asked, still criticising herself for mentioning Tom Myres in the first place.

'If it was up to Andrew Murray he'd have them all thrown off the site.'

'But you don't agree?'

'Not necessarily. I'm unfortunately one of those liberal minded people who respect other peoples' opinion even if it is contrary to what I believe.'

'How very broad minded Richard.'

'Oh I don't know about that, just being practical I think.'

'You are a man of compromise.'

'Oh yes, that, I hope that, certainly.'

'Fanny Jane is crying Miss!'

Lucy turned from the blackboard, her thoughts on Richard Stockton so suddenly and loudly interrupted.

One of her helpers Shirley Tibbins went over to the six year old who was by now bawling her head off.

This had set the class off again. They were becoming restless. Concentrating for more than a few minutes was beyond them. If it was getting out of hand she would suggest a song she had taught them in the first week. Sometimes this worked or she would have them put their hands on their heads or try to get them to listen to a story. Thankfully Richard had agreed to her suggestion of having a piano in the classroom as well as more large picture books. Constantly changing tactics seemed to work. The map of the world fascinated a lot of the boys who were keen to ask questions about it and the girls were desperate to learn more songs. At least sometimes there were possibilities beyond the grim, daily grind.

When at last the school day was over and everyone had left Lucy would sit at her desk trying to shift the painful drone of children out of her mind. Sometimes the residue would remain for the rest of the evening and night, the noise, the anxiety, the reprimands, the shifting atmospheres so unpredictable from one day to the next. The mood of the class was constantly changing and often there seemed no apparent reason for it. So she remained trying to breathe deeply, slowly and relax when all that happened was that she started to think about Tom Myres and wonder why he had not been round to see her as he had promised. She knew there was already a lot of gossip about her weekend trips with Richard but the fact was that he was in charge of the whole Ribblehead project and the rumour spreaders could criticise all they liked. She was safe. If he was not bothered with the gossip then she certainly was not. He gave her that kind of security and of course she enjoyed being pretty and attractive to him. She had always understood how to use her powers to challenge, aggravate, seduce and dominate certain men. It was something she used skilfully. The more Richard paid her attention the better. Even though he held little interest to her in any meaningful way at least she had something to do on a Sunday instead of moping around the Johnston farm. Also such a relationship would certainly enhance her reputation around the settlements, to be seen with the chief engineer and for him to show so publicly how interested he was in her. More importantly she hoped if any stories about her time at Burnley started to emerge her friendship with Richard Stockton might deflect them. Richard had made his interest in her so obvious right from the start it had made her realise quickly how useful he could be.

She got up and started walking around the classroom that smelt strongly of many unwashed bodies. The navvies here might be the best paid in the country but that did not mean their children were not tainted with the usual signs of poverty. Like so many others the folk of Ribblehead were struggling. It might not be quite as desperate as in some of the cities but it was bad enough. Suddenly she felt the children as a memory. Only half an hour before they had been filling the room with their noise and movement but now they were gone her concern for them was stronger. They were like the ghosts of the love she felt for them. It could be like this when they were not there. Then they produced all the feelings she used to have when she first began teaching, emotions about the sudden past, the time just gone, the class just departed, their noise and swearing fading away as they had set off towards the settlements. Only they could lift her depression and sense of loneliness and yet be the cause of it at the same time. Richard Stockton was merely an appendage. He was too formal, too eager to please, so steady and careful. Nearly all the men she had met were like him, practical, unemotional, slightly condescending. Their lives were made up of one step after another, planned, thought through with an ambition that had a conclusion. They knew what they wanted and thought they knew how to get it including the woman of their choice. In their world passion was dangerous, the spontaneous a threat and all because they did not trust life and they did not trust themselves. They would remain the children of their other side which would never be expressed because it was hidden so deeply. She craved for excitement, for a relationship that could not be so easily predicted. And yet she knew such feelings always led to disaster. It had to be checks and balances like someone's bank account, added up at the end of each day credit or debit.

She looked out of one of the classroom's tiny windows as another shower swept down the valley. The noise of the steam driven cranes on the viaduct and the rattle of the trucks being pulled along the tramways were the sounds smothered by distance and the rain. It was all so dreary and meaningless to her when she was in one of these reflective moods. She would walk down the rough track, through Batty Green, over the bridge, across the Hawes road and up the steep climb to the farm. Tea would be laid out in the kitchen with Mrs Johnston fussing about as her husband and farm hands sat there waiting. She would enter and they would all stop and stare before greeting her. Upstairs she would put down her school bag, take off her coat and bonnet, wash her face and hands in a earthenware bowl using water from a jug and then descend into the overheated kitchen and try for half an hour to hold some sort of conversation as the men gulped down their food. It was the same routine every day creating the same hopeless response in her. Not that she disliked the Johnstons. They were generous and friendly enough. It was just the topics of conversation never wandered from the farm or what was happening on other farms in the area. They seemed worried about asking Lucy any direct questions as though what she did at the school was none of their business. She had been employed by the company to do a job and that was all there was to it. She was their lodger and brought in extra money and for that they were grateful to her. There was nothing more and there was no reason why there should be.

CHAPTER TWENTY FIVE

After she had received an invitation to visit Chapel Le Dale Jane met Lucy Ormskill off the Ingleton coach. She was waiting beside the road as the coach came to a halt.

'Miss Ormskill, glad to meet you,' she said as she helped Lucy down from the carriage.

'Pleased to meet you too,' Lucy said in return, smiling as they shook hands.

'Jane.'

'Yes, Jane.'

'And I can call you Lucy?' she asked before they set off towards the house.

'Of course.'

'Good,' said Jane warml y.

They stopped for a few moments to watch the beck running fast under its moss covered bridge, listening to the wheels of the carriage clattering away into the distance.

'Now take off your coat and hat and Lizzie will hang them in the hallway,' Jane added as they entered the house.

Lizzie's face looked miserably stiff as she turned back to the kitchen to prepare tea.

'Goodness is that your maid?' Lucy started after they had seated themselves.

'What about her?'

'Well I would say brusque is the only way to describe her. Is she always like that?'

'Not usually.'

'She looks so cross.'

'I'll have a word, I've no idea why she's so out of sorts.'

'I don't mean her to get into any sort of trouble. I was just rather struck by her attitude.'

'I'm afraid she's still learning.'

'Not quickly enough I'm afraid. I sympathise completely with what servants have to do nowadays but there is no point if they cannot find anything positive from what they do. I suppose she's from the local area.'

'Yes.'

'Well she should think herself lucky to have employment. Anyway, don't let's talk about her. I wanted to say how grateful I am for your kind invitation. I'm just glad we can get to know each other, two single women in the wilds of Yorkshire.'

'But you at least have your pupils.'

'Batty Green's first and only teacher, not that my class creates any kind of civilised society, far from it I'm afraid.'

Jane frowned and asked, 'Is it so terribly hard?'

'To be honest Jane the first weeks were a nightmare. They were like little primitives.'

'How dreadful.'

'It's only recently I've begin to feel we are getting somewhere and that's only because I have the help of three older girls from the settlements. I don't know where I would be without them. Well, that's not true. I know exactly where I would be, on the next train from Settle.'

They both laughed and then stopped as Lizzie appeared with a full tray. They waited as she set the tea things out, her actions clumsy and loud.

'Careful Lizzie,' Jane told her.

Lizzie ignored the remark, plonked down the teapot and left the room.

'Goodness,' Jane added, reddening perceptively, 'I've no idea what's got into her.'

Lucy only nodded and waited for her hostess to pour the tea.

'I hear your cousin is one of the missionaries for the settlements.'

'James, yes he is ever so busy. He never stops and the bigger the population at Ribblehead grows the more demanding everything becomes. He intends to meet every new family or individual worker. Now the summer is approaching he is holding more and more outdoor meetings and always takes time to visit those who are sick or in need of what he calls spiritual sustenance.'

'I think we all could do with more of that,' Lucy joked.

'James would agree with you.'

'I've heard so much about him but so far we have not met.'

'Oh I'm sure you will.'

'I am told so many good things about him.'

'That's kind of you to say so. I'll mention it to him when he returns.'

'So it's only you, your cousin and your grumpy maid living here.'

'That's it.'

'And how do you like it, actually living in the wilds of the Yorkshire Dales?'

'I could ask you the same question.'

Lucy thought for a moment and then answered, 'I'm still not sure yet. It's such a contrast to my last post in Burnley. I must admit I never imagined it would be so....so......'

'Isolated.'

'Exactly, that's the only word to describe it and yet sometimes it has its own special beauty.'

'That it certainly has,' Jane agreed.

'And barren. No trees or flowers, hardly any wild life, just limestone, grass and moorland.'

'And sheep. You mustn't forget the sheep.'

Their laughter was shared and genuine. Lucy already beginning to feel easy and relaxed whereas Jane was under more pressure to ensure their meeting was a success. She knew that such opportunities would be rare and wanted to make the best of it, to establish a friendship with Lucy if that was possible. She had to impress but at the same time not make it too obvious.

'Unfortunately James is my only close relative. I lost my parents last year from diptheria and James was good enough to ask me to come and stay with him to give me a chance to consider my future.'

'And have you come to any decision?'

'Not really. In fact the choices seem so limited.'

'That is because they are limited for a woman.'

'I have no funds.'

'Is there no one else in the family who could help?'

'Oh no,' Jane said weakly, 'No one.'

They were silent then as if such an admission had created a sudden obstacle to their conversation, an awkwardness.

Lucy sipped at her tea. Jane attempted to nibble at a sandwich as the late spring sunlight shone through the parlour's two windows.

'You have your teaching,' she finally mentioned, shading her eyes from the piercing light, 'I envy you such a vocation.'

'You wouldn't think that if you saw the little foul mouthed scallywags I have to deal with every day.'

'Oh surely Lucy they can't be that bad.'

'You should visit us and then again maybe not. You might be shocked and think me a failure.'

'And how many pupils do you have?'

'Sixty two at the moment, although there are more parents desperate to enrol their children.'

'Goodness!' Jane exclaimed, 'That sounds a lot.'

'It is, believe you me.'

'But you have your helpers, the girls you mentioned.'

'And I now have my piano, my secret weapon. If all else fails, to get them singing along helps calm things down. They love the sound of their own voices. Mind you it took me weeks to understand a word they were saying. There is every accent in the country in my Batty Green classroom. I just wish they wouldn't all want to talk at once.'

'But you still.......still enjoy it if that's the right word?'

'No, not the right word,' Lucy answered humorously, 'It is a challenge. That's what I'd call it.'

'But I can tell you'll succeed. I'm sure you will.'

'I wished I could be as optimistic.'

'And are you Lucy?'

'Am I what?'

'An optimist.'

Lucy's eyes opened wider than usual as she pondered on the question.

Hesitatingly she began, 'No......no I don't think I am.'

'Oh,' said Jane in surprise.

There was another pause before Lucy continued, 'I don't know if there is anything more to add. I just think that life and society in general are difficult for most people and very difficult for some.'

'Cousin James would agree with you.'

'But not you Jane?'

'I think I'm too much of a coward to be so pessimistic. I...I have to believe that things can improve for each one of us.'

'But you don't sound so sure.'

'That's because at the moment I am in a situation that is precarious. I can't keep on depending on James for my sustenance. I know it can't be easy for him.'

'But that's not how a man of God would consider it, surely? Like you said, he is here to help people as much as is possible and that I would think includes his cousin.'

'I don't.....don't want to live off his charity.'

'But he will not see it like that, I'm sure.'

'I hope you're right.'

'Listen to me,' Lucy laughed, 'talking away and I've never met the man.'

'I'm afraid he'll be out until late today.'

'It being a weekend.'

'Yes.'

'No day of rest?'

'Not for James. For him there is no such thing.'

'I can tell you admire him.'

At that point there came a banging and clattering from the kitchen. Jane decided to try and ignore it, grateful that it had interrupted their conversation before she asked Lucy whether she was warm enough now that the parlour fire was unlit.

It was then Lucy decided to mention Richard Stockton.

'It was his idea to have a teacher at Batty Green in the first place. Since then he has been more than helpful. That's because he really wants the school to succeed. His views are very strong about education. I think he was becoming increasingly embarrassed by the fact of there being such a large population at Ribblehead and with it so many children who were being offered nothing at all.'

'He obviously believes in social progress. It sounds like it.'

'He believes in giving people chances, all classes of people.'

'That's what I could do with,' Jane sighed before wiping her mouth with her napkin.

'I suppose I just refused to accept my situation. That's what gave me the impetus to do something about it. I was very unhappy at home. My sister and I were always arguing, always blaming each other for everything that went wrong, so many petty arguments.

'Good heavens!' Jane exclaimed, 'I bet you're so clever Lucy.'

'Not at all. Next you'll be making me out to be an intellectual.'

'I thought that's what all teachers were supposed to be.'

At that Lucy laughed, 'Not at all!'

'How disappointing.'

'Now you're being disingenuous on purpose.'

'No, I mean it. I so used to look up to my teachers. I thought I could never be as clever and I think I was right.'

'Nonsense Jane. You underestimate yourself.'

'Do I?'

'Absolutely.'

'How do you know? How can you tell?'

'I just can. Let's put it down to female intuition.'

'If there is such a thing.'

'Of course there is.'

'Well if there is obviously some women have it more than others.'

Just then Lizzie came in, 'Carriage for Ribblehead'll be soon.'

'Oh Lizzie, that's an hour away yet,' said Jane, glancing at the clock on the mantelpiece.

'Just thought I should say, remind you both like.'

'Well alright, I won't let Miss Ormskill miss it.'

'I think she wants me out of the house as soon as possible,' Lucy remarked when the girl had gone.

'Let's not bother about her. I agree she's in a funny mood, but one that I hope is not affecting you too much.'

'Not at all.'

'Good, I'm glad to hear it.'

They chatted on for the next hour, Jane describing her friends the Austwicks and their house at Selside, Lucy talking about some of her time at Burnley before they again returned to the question of Jane's future. Lizzie brought in a fresh pot of tea and Jane played on the piano for a while after Lucy had taken some effort in persuading her.

Eventually it was time for her to leave and Jane escorted her back onto the Ingleton road.

'I've so enjoyed this afternoon,' said Lucy warmly as they stood there waiting for the coach.

Jane smiled at this, 'I know we can be friends.'

'Of course, it's the two of us against the rest.'

'We should try and make this a regular thing if that's alright with you?'

Lucy took Jane's hand saying, 'Yes, I would like that.'

After the coach had picked her up Jane stood beside the road watching it disappear along the valley. She felt anxious and pleased at the same time. So rarely had she felt that there were possibilities, that things could actually change. Lucy Ormskill was obviously someone who believed in her own self worth. Jane just hoped she would not be a disappointment to her.

When she got back Lizzie was in the parlour clearing up the tea things.

'Well, I think that went well Lizzie,' Jane said to her.

The young girl looked at her, a glint of fierce anger in her eyes as she picked up the tray, 'So you'll be kissing and things with her next then!'

Jane was so shocked that to begin with she made no response. It was only when Lizzie made for the door that she said, 'What an earth was that about? Lizzie, what are you saying?'

'Nowt.'

'Tell me Lizzie.'

'Doesn't matter.'

'Yes it does.'

'Nowt really matters.'

Lizzie stalked out of the room with Jane following her along the corridor into the kitchen saying, 'This is ridiculous.'

Lizzie plonked the tea tray on the table and turned, 'I see you didn't want me at tea. Oh no. Not this time.'

'Lucy would not have understood.'

'No she wouldn't. So it's alright sometimes but not others, not when you have visitors, not then.'

Jane hated when Lizzie's accent was so loud and broad. It sounded so primitive and ignorant. The girl's face was flushed and her hands clenched as she continued, 'Posh visitors. No I'll just stay in the bloody kitchen. I know me place.'

'I'm not listening to this anymore.'

'No, you go and slink off back to the parlour.'

At that Jane slapped her across the face only for Lizzie to slap her back. Momentarily they both stopped, shocked at what they had done, both breathing heavily. Jane touched her cheek as she said, 'You.....you don't speak to me like that.'

'Come on then,' Lizzie muttered.

'You don't.'

'Come on,' she repeated, going up to her and grabbing her by the back of the head to pull her into a hard, almost brutal kiss.

CHAPTER TWENTY SIX.

Maggie was hanging up the washing beside the hut, a warm breeze flurrying the clothes and sheets in the bright sunshine. With the girls at school for once she had time to herself. Ever since waking there had been a shift in her mood. She was more aware of herself, a rare experience these days. Usually she was too tired. Now she had a few minutes to consider things, a process that she felt was important but one that also worried her. The mind could play tricks when it was trying to think through something and Maggie was always prone to unnecessary fears and doubts, especially about the children. Now they were at school she knew that they would be more likely to catch any infection that was doing the rounds of the settlements. With so many children squeezed into the one room they were sure to pass on everything. Even though there was nothing she could do it did not stop her constantly worrying.

She finished pegging up the washing, now a daily task. With the mud everywhere around Batty Green keeping things clean was a regular battle. She wanted her hut as respectable as possible. It was important for her own sense of herself and the pride she had in her work. The worst was where the four lodgers slept. Having refused bunks their beds were pushed against each other and there was hardly any space for keeping their other clothes and belongings. Earning money meant she had to keep on top on things. She was not like some of the settlement women who let their huts become a cluttered mess. For Maggie she had to keep control of the place in which she and her family lived.

She decided to go for a walk, quickly putting on her coat and bonnet before setting off down towards where everything was noise and activity, all of it loud and confused in the fresh morning air that was tinged with coal smoke from the brick factory chimneys and from the engines pulling the trucks up the tramways. At the weekends Fraser would take the girls for a special ride in the trucks up and back down from the entrance to Blea Moor tunnel. It was such a treat for them, something that none of the other children were given. Even though she had her doubts the last thing she wanted was to undermine the pleasure Clare and Beth were experiencing. For once they were happy. For once they were being given attention by other adults and also attending school which Beth loved and Clare hated. The young one could never stop talking about the wonderful Miss Ormskill whereas Clare was desperate to think of any excuse she could not to have to go at all.

She passed some women on their way to the stalls and some going to the beck with their baskets of washing. By now she knew most of them and of their reputations. It was the usual mixture from those who attended church to the sluts who sold themselves to any man who had the money. There were even husbands she had heard about who would sit at the hut door and take the cash paid for their wives. Inwardly Maggie judged, it was in her nature, but outwardly she kept her opinions to herself knowing how gossip could easily lead to arguments and fighting. Every weekend there would be the screams and abuse of women tearing at each other goaded on by the crowd. She hated such behaviour. They were just animals who could reach such a disgusting level. Her God would take cognisance of it all when it came to the final reckoning. Life had to be lived with the sense that everything led to a judgement. Maggie believed in righteousness, in a proper conscience, without them then there was only depravity.

But today there were no such thoughts. On this bright spring morning she was happy and glad to be out of the hut. There was a smile on her face as she climbed up the steepening hillside to where she could see over the whole site. She stopped for a time, the sun's rays warming her face, the breeze blowing strands of loose hair across her forehead as she looked over Ribblehead with all its noise and business. These were the best of moments. She felt free and for once at ease. This time was hers and she relished it.

Later as she came along the path towards where the huts had been built closer together she felt tired. Her back and legs ached and her hands were throbbing with a pain that was beginning to affect all her finger joints. She stopped to chat to two of the women who were returning from the stalls about the price of meat that day, Maggie hoping to buy a leg of pork for the men's' dinner. Smoke from the settlement's chimneys was drifting down the valley as she left the women and reached the butcher's. She bought her meat and went to the bakery for three loaves of bread and then on to a new haberdashery stall where she purchased laces for the girls' boots. It was a new experience not to have to consider every penny as she shopped although the old habits were difficult to lose.

'Fine morning Mrs Granger,' Earnest Grimshaw one of the the blacksmiths smiled as he came out of his work shop for a breath of fresh air, his arms heavily tattooed.

'You look busy Earnest,' she replied.

'Always busy missus.'

'Well that's good.'

'It is, it is and I'm not complaining. This won't last forever Missus.'

He looked directly at her waiting for a response but Maggie just smiled and carried on in the direction of a line of wooden office buildings where the administration of the site was housed.

Everyone seemed to be out on this spring morning. There was Sally Langton and Alice Yates standing at the end of their row of huts, the two of them well known for selling beer and spirits and anything else that made them extra money. Maggie nodded to them and passed on, the two women watching her critically, their arms crossed over their working clothes and the breeze blowing their hair about their faces.

The place was alive with noise and smells, this town in the middle of nowhere erected so quickly once the decision to build the Settle Carlisle railway line had been made. To Maggie it was at last familiar, a place where she felt established. All that she wished for was a few more years of such prosperity, enough to set up a small shop somewhere down south, the one dream she had always retained, a secret that she had shared with no one, not even her husband.

She turned at the sudden shout from Bill who was rushing up the path towards her.

'Jonty! Have yer seen him?'

'No, why?' Maggie asked, immediately concerned.

'The silly bugger went off for a pee half an hour ago and nobody has seen him since.'

'He can't be far Bill.'

'Far enough,' said Bill, 'the little sod has done this before. Wait till I get hold of him. Just when we've a fresh stack of bricks ready he has to do this. I've told him over and bloody over.'

It was half way along the road to Dent that he finally found him. Jonty was sat in the ditch with only his trousers on and tears dribbling down his filthy cheeks.

'No! No!' he started screaming the moment Bill went into the ditch to help him out.

'Come on Jonty lad, for God's sake, you're alright, you're alright.'

Jonty was shivering and he had peed himself, a huge stain over the front of his trousers.

Bill tried to slow himself down, anger and desperation mixed together in a way that only Jonty could produce in him. He waited, giving time for him to calm down.

'And where's your shirt and boots you daft haporth?' he tried.

Jonty would not look at him, his arms and back shaking uncontrollably, his head down between his knees and his feet covered with the dark brown ditch water.

Finally Bill decided to fill and light his pipe, nodding to a carter as his wagon and two horses went slowly by considering whether to say something to this man he did not recognise before letting him rattle past.

'Come on Jonty lad. You can't stay here. We're supposed to be at work.'

Every time something like this happened Bill felt deeply responsible. When Jonty made off like this Bill knew he had failed him, making him both angry at himself and Jonty. He alone was supposed to be ensuring his safety. Never had he been so committed to anyone like this. He had never been married, never had any real relationship with any woman or had ever called a man a true friend. Bill did not believe in such friendships. In the end there was only yourself you could rely on. Nobody else was that interested. Why should they be?

'Are you coming?'

Jonty eventually stopped crying and looked up at him, 'Not coming Bill.'

'And why is that?'

'Fed up Bill.'

'We all get fed up. Doesn't mean we jack everything in every time it happens.'

'Fed up,' Jonty repeated.

'So I heard the first time.'

'You're.......you're angry,' Jonty said in a shaky voice, his cheeks covered in the tracks where his tears had dribbled down the russet stain from the factory's brick dust.

'No I'm not. I just want you out of the bloody ditch, that's all. Now come on,' Bill said strongly as he again climbed down into the ditch and managed to get his hands under Jonty's arms so he could lift him up, his pipe clenched between his teeth as he got him to his feet and dragged him up the bank onto the road.

'There, look at you. You're bloody soaking and you've wet yersell. What a sodding state Jonty. Not good, not good at all. What will Maggie say when she sees yer?'

'So where was he?' she asked as half an hour later the two of them approached, Jonty in his shirt and boots that Bill had found further along the Dent road. She was standing outside her hut with Shirley Stanton her next door neighbour.

'Up on the top road. God knows what the hell he thought he was doing.'

Jonty had his head lowered, listening.

'Well at least you found him. Jonty, what a daft thing to be doing,' Maggie said lightly, stepping towards him.

He made no reply, only started walking away.

'Right, we're back to work,' said Bill before he went to catch up with Jonty.

'What a lad,' Maggie commented, 'He teks some looking after. If it wasn't for Bill God knows where he would be.'

'Well he wouldn't be here at Batty Green, that's for certain,' replied Shirley.

Maggie nodded, 'No, he wouldn't. I just feel so sorry for him. We all do. The girls treat him like a brother. Usually he wouldn't say boo to a goose and then things like this get into him and nobody knows what to expect. He did the same thing a few weeks ago, found him in the stables.'

'He's just a big lad.'

'Nobody knows where he comes from, not a thing. Bill has tried his best to find out but has got nowhere.'

'Well how did he get here then?'

'Found him last winter wandering along the Dent road wi no boots on and wi nothing else, no belongings, just Jonty in his shirt and trousers and not a penny to his name.'

'And now he's wi you.'

'He is and I'm not begrudging him that, not at all. He can be right helpful when he knows what to do.'

'My Arthur says the rest of the men feel sorry for him.'

'Better than making jokes at his expense.'

'So will the girls be round later?' Shirley asked before turning to her one year old asleep in a washing basket beside her.

It was nearly four o clock when there was the usual screams and shouts which meant the children's' day at school was finished. There would be a mad rush in all directions, some having to hike up to the Tunnel settlements nearly a mile away.

'We're hungry Mum!' Clare was calling before she was even through the door.

Maggie turned from the stove where she was preparing the leg of pork, her face covered in sweat.

'Billy Fisher was chasing us!' Beth added as she rushed into the kitchen.

'And what were you doing?' her mother asked.

'Nowt. It was him Mam.'

'It always is Beth.'

'I'm starving hungry,' Clare repeated.

'I heard you the first time.'

'Can we go out?' shouted her sister.

'Not until you tell me how you got on at school today.'

Clare pulled a face as Beth answered, 'Miss Ormskill told us about butterflies.'

There was such a contrast between their responses. She knew by now that Clare would never take to schooling and wondered if it was a waste of time her being there. But Beth loved every minute of it and was already telling everybody she was going to be a teacher like Miss Ormskill when she grew up.

'And what about you Clare Granger, nowt to say for yourself?'

'I ate me piece in the morning and I've had nowt since.'

'Well that's your own silly fault. And before you two go anywhere I want you to tidy up yer things in the bedroom. If Fraser or Bill get you two owt else I don't know where it'll be put. There's your stuff piled everywhere.'

'Do we have to?' moaned Beth.

'Oh no, I just said it for someat to say. Yes you do!'

'Come on,' Clare muttered to her sister.

'And no just stuffing it under yer beds, do you hear?'

In the evening for once everyone including Jock was at home after work. The mixture of coal and peat for the stove meant the hut was so overheated the men were in their shirt sleeves. Clare sitting cross legged on the floor was watching Bill work on the farmhouse he was building for her and her sister, working on a thin piece of board divided up by wooden fences into fields.

Beth was seated on Jonty's knee looking at one of her picture books with him, 'Here's a castle.'

'Castle,' repeated Jonty.

'That's called a forest.'

'A forest.'

'And that's princess, a princess.'

'Pri……princess.'

'That's right. Now you tell me what this is?' Beth asked as she turned the page.

Ethan with Jock and Fraser at the table were playing a game of cards, a pastime of which Maggie did not approve. She was cutting meat off the bone of pork that would make sandwiches for the following day.

For once there was no washing hanging from the lines. The floorboards had been scrubbed that day and the night before Clare and Beth had stuck up new pictures from newspapers and magazines which added colour to the walls.

'What's Jonty been doing?' Clare asked Bill in a whisper.

'None of your business Miss nosey,' he replied.

'Go on, tell us.'

'No I won't. Now hand me over that glue brush and don't get it over yersell.'

Maggie watched them for a few moments.

'You're doing a right grand job there Bill.'

He looked up at her, smiled and nodded, 'It's coming on Maggie.'

'Teaching em to be farmers are yer?'

'Could do worse.'

'I suppose so. Mind you I wouldn't fancy farming in the Dales, not wi the weather they get up here.'

'Ay, yer might be right. It's someat I never reckoned mesell.'

'Oh I can just see you wi a dog rounding up yer sheep,' she laughed.

'He'd never mek it up the first hill,' Ethan put in.

'Oh listen to you,' Maggie countered, 'just cos you were daft enough to run up Whernside.'

'He weren't daft!' Clare exclaimed.

'You tell her girl,' her father said strongly, 'like a mountain goat I was.'

Maggie shook her head before returning to the stove glad that Ethan for once had not gone straight to bed after his tea and seemed to be absorbed in the cards. So long as money was not involved she did not mind that much. She knew that Fraser had a reputation for gambling and was one of the reasons he would work at weekends when the opportunity was offered so he could pay off some of his gambling debts. It was another reason why he caused disquiet in her. She wanted to accept him but found it impossible and the more she got to know him the more uncertain she was of him.

Clare was watching every move Bill made as he continued building the farm house. Beth conscientiously kept repeating to Jonty each word that described something from the picture book.

Momentarily everything in the room stopped as there came the sounds of a bagpipe being practised further down the settlement.

'Listen to that racket,' Bill had to say, 'Sounds like some old cow with gut ache.'

'That's the finest sound there is,' countered Jock, 'so don't you be saying anything bad about it. The lad is trying his best. It's Duncan McGregor and he's just got started wi the pipes so give him a chance.'

'Not if he carries on making that……'

'Music,' interrupted Jock.

'Oh ay,' Bill muttered in disgust.

CHAPTER TWENTY SEVEN.

'I know I'm a disappointment.'

Tom Myres was standing at the classroom door in his work clothes, a blue scarf tied round his neck, his cap tilted at an angle emphasising his dark brown moustache and hazel eyes.

Lucy looked up from her desk, 'If you don't expect anything then you can't be disappointed,' she responded stiffly.'

At that he laughed, took off his cap, brushed his hair back and said, 'I apologise.'

'You've done nothing wrong, have you?'

'I promised I would escort you to your lodgings.'

'That was far too long ago Mr Myres, I hardly remember.'

'I see we have returned to the formal.'

'That's what the passing of time does I'm afraid.'

Lucy turned to the two girls who were tidying up the classroom.

'You can go now Shirley and you as well Angela, thank you girls.'

They put the last of the slate boards away before taking up their coats hanging on the back of the main door.

'Good afternoon Miss Ormskill,' they said in unison before pushing past Tom Myres on their way out.

'You have em well trained I must say.'

'No I don't. They're just like that.'

'For you maybe Lucy.'

'I just know they're extremely helpful Mr Myres.'

'Aren't you going to ask me why I'm here?' he put in.

'Why should I?' she said strongly before pushing back her chair as she stood up.

'I would have thought it was obvious,' he quickly added.

'So I am supposed to puzzle it out?'

'Yes, if you like.'

'No thank you Mr Myres. Not today. I've had a busy, I would say stressful day and have no time for puzzles at the moment. I'm sure even you can understand that.'

Tom walked further into the room, standing with his feet apart and with half a smile on his face that was as dirty as his hands.

Lucy disliked the confidence of the man, disliked the assumption that she would be interested in such a display of masculine bravado. He obviously thought he was attractive, stood there displaying himself even though she could smell the mixture of sweat and rock dust off him. After all he was only a worker, a navvy who happened to be articulate and who seemed to enjoy this verbal repartee.

'I'm intruding am I?' he said then.

'You're doing nothing, absolutely nothing.'

'Surely more than that?'

'I don't think so Mr Myres.'

'How harsh you are Miss Ormskill.'

'I'm a teacher. Unfortunately it's necessary to be harsh sometimes.'

'But as you've just informed me your teaching day is over. You no longer have to fulfil that role. You can be yourself.'

'Can I? How very generous of you.'

'Oh come on, you know what I mean Lucy.'

'And why you Tom Myres? There are over a thousand men working here at Ribblehead. So why is it you standing here in my classroom and not somebody else?'

He nodded thoughtfully, mockingly rubbing his chin.

'Do you think my question implies that you are any different from the rest of the men?' Lucy quickly asked.

'I don't think I am. We are all basically the same, all of us, men or women.'

'And is this part of your socialist creed?'

'If you like, yes it is.'

'It still doesn't answer my question, why you?'

'I saw you first. It's a simple as that.'

'No. I don't think it is. I don't think someone else would have had the audacity to think that such an opportunity gave them any rights.'

'You had only just arrived.'

'Did I ask for your help or attention?'

'No.'

'Well then.'

'But I offered, didn't I?''

'An offer I did not accept if you remember.'

'That's not how I remember it.'

'Well I do. Now if you don't mind I still have things to do here.'

'I can wait,' he replied easily.

'Wait for what?'

'To escort you up to the Johnstons' farm.'

'No Mr Myres.'

'Why not?'

'I would like you to leave.'

'No you don't.'

'You are audacious!' Lucy exclaimed.

'Be honest Miss Ormskill.'

'Just go please.'

She waited. For a few moments he did not move and then smiling he put his cap back on before asking, 'Are all teachers as attractive as you? I'm only asking because I was never given any schooling so I wouldn't know.'

Lucy ignored his remark, sat down and opened her book.

Tom went and seated himself on the first row, his hands clasped together as they rested on the scarred wooden surface of the desk.

She tried to ignore him. The sounds of children shouting came from outside. Late afternoon sunlight shafted through the classroom's windows turning everything a deepening gold that glowed on Lucy's concentrated features.

The minutes passed, Lucy carefully turning the pages of her book. Tom never took his eyes off her. A loud noise of metal clanging against metal sounded from down the hillside, the constant drone of activity as the two of them waited to see who would move first, their persistence lasting nearly quarter of an hour.

Finally he got up and approached the desk.

'Here,' he said, 'I want you have this, stuff that's more important than anything else around here.'

He took a piece of limestone out of his jacket pocket and placed it on the desk and then without another word left the classroom.

Lucy momentarily did not move. Her nerves were tight and stretched still waiting for something to happen. Then she picked up the piece of limestone and smiled to herself. It was not even that unexpected. She already realised that unpredictability was part of Tom Myres' attraction. He would tease her but thoughtfully, carefully.

It was a few minutes later when Richard Stockton knocked on the door and came in.

'Richard! I never expected you,' she said quickly as he came towards her.

'Sorry, did I interrupt you?' he asked with a serious tone in his voice.

'What brings you to the schoolroom?'

'You do of course. I was on my way up to the tunnel and wondered if you'd be still here.'

'That's very kind of you.'

'Not at all.'

'I can even offer you some tea if you like.'

He smiled, 'No thank you Lucy, I'm fine.'

He turned and started walking around the room, 'It already feels like your room. Your presence is here Lucy. That's because you have worked so hard. I know you have. I do hear reports you know.'

'Who from?'

'The parents.'

'You ask them?'

'Sometimes.'

'Are you inspecting me Richard?'

'Not at all, it's just hoping that everything is as it should be for you and the children.'

She made no response. There was a strain in his voice that made her alert to his mood. Something was not quite right but she had not to wait long to discover what it was.

'I thought I saw Tom Myres leaving here,' he suddenly started.

'Tom Myres,' she repeated, 'yes, he was here?'

'For any particular reason?'

'Yes, he came to see how one of my pupils from Jericho settlement whose parents are both ill is getting on. The boy also lost his sister last year,' she lied, looking straight at him.

'And how is he getting on?'

'As well as can be expected I suppose,' she lied again, aware of how easily and quickly it came to her.

'He was supposed to be working.'

'Who was, the boy?' she asked not so innocently.

'Myres. I'm surprised he didn't hand you one of his political pamphlets. That man is a rule to himself and someone I would keep a distance from Lucy. I've known Myres from way back. People think of him as a socialist but he's more than that. Given the chance he'd be one of those revolutionaries who would kill for his cause.'

'But he still works for you Richard, why?'

'Unfortunately yes, but I don't think for much longer.'

'I don't really know the man.'

'And that's the way I suggest you keep it. I suggest you as the teacher should not be too sociable with any of the work force. I'm sure that would have been mentioned at your interview.'

'Is that one of your rules Richard?' she asked strongly.

His expression changed at the force of her tone, 'No Lucy, of course not. It is just a piece of advice.'

'From one who knows best.'

'I do know more about things around here than you. Surely you would accept that?'

'You'll find I'm not very good at just accepting other peoples' rules. That's not the way I am.'

'I see,' he responded carefully, nervously running fingers around the rim of his hat.

'I'm not sure if you do. I believe that everyone is entitled to their own opinions.'

'No Lucy,' he interrupted, 'that's got nothing to do with it.'

'I hope it hasn't. I was just going to say merely because I'm a woman I……'

'Surely you know me better than that by now?' he interrupted, looking directly at her.

'And I would have thought that by now you would understand Richard that I will listen to advice, to someone else's opinion but not necessarily agree with them. I am in a vulnerable position here at Ribblehead being a woman alone.'

'Of course Lucy, but I think you are taking this to too much of an extreme.'

'Am I Richard?'

'I only meant to say that things are more simple here than in a town or city.'

'And why should that be?'

'Because there are nearly fifteen hundred workers here and their families and only a handful of others.'

'You mean the middle class, people like you and me Richard.'

'I mean the professional class and there are so few of us we have to be careful how we act. If there are unspoken rules at Ribblehead then I suggest they are different from elsewhere. They have to be. This is a unique situation we are all in, you included.'

'You make it sound ominous, almost threatening.'

'That's because in some ways it can be.'

'And you are here to what, protect me?'

'Keep you safe, that beyond all else, safe and I hope as happy as possible.'

He came back to the front of the room and picked up the piece of limestone off the desk.

'Is this one of your geological specimens to show the children?'

'Something like that.'

'Well there's plenty more where that came from.'

'Indeed,' she replied coldly.

Richard helped her on with her coat. As she was fastening her bonnet he said, 'I could walk with you if you like.'

'What, and keep me safe? No I'll be fine Richard. You are on your way to the tunnel and I feel quite confident that I will be able to reach the Johnstons without mishap thank you.'

'Shall I see you on Sunday?'

'Of course, why ever not?''

'I'm already looking forward to it.'

'Yes,' she answered vaguely.

Outside the schoolroom he took her hand for a moment, asking, 'You don't mind this?'

'Mind what Richard?'

'Me holding your hand.'

'And why should I?'

'I just thought.....'

'It's just a gesture of human friendship, nothing wrong with that.'

'Is....is that all it means to you?'

'Of course Richard, why what else should it mean?'

'I.....I just......just hoped.....'

'Hoped what?'

'Oh nothing,' he said, leaving her hand in his for a few more moments before quickly releasing it and turning to start on his way up to the tunnel.

Lucy waited a few moments and then set off in the opposite direction thinking to herself how easily some men could be manipulated especially when one of them was desperate to believe every word she said and how easy it was to lie to him.

CHAPTER TWENTY EIGHT

Richard reached the start of the tunnel which eventually would run for nearly a mile, five hundred feet under the surface of Blea moor.

'A week at the most and we should be joining up to the first air shaft,' Charlie Saltcoats, the foremen, was telling him as they walked into the semi darkness.

The tunnel was lit by the bobbing lamps of the men and those attached to hooks hammered into the walls.

'That's quicker than when we last talked,' Richard said as water dribbled from the roof onto his hat and shoulders.

'We're shoring up the sides now and the factory has caught up wi the bricks we need so we're doing the top lining a lot quicker.'

'That's good work Charlie.'

He was careful to avoid stumbling over the tracks of the tramway. The sides of the tunnel glistened with moisture and the calls of the men and the rattling of the trucks was accentuated the further they went underground.

He needed the work to dominate his mind, to focus away from Lucy Ormskill. He had never felt like this before, never felt such desire and anxiety. No woman had ever had such an effect.

'So how far?' he asked the foreman.

With all the workings we're about a sixth of the way there, roughly speaking. The surveyors will be on the moor tomorrow and then we should have a clearer view of our progress, but so far there have been no major problems, although I shouldn't say that because as you know once you say that then someat bad'll happen.'

'Well we hope not.'

There was a sudden shout as everything stopped before the next blast from an explosive charge set off further along the tunnel, its echo bouncing along the walls into the unseen distance.

'Can rattle the old ears if you're too close.'

'Yes,' was all Richard could manage, coughing while smelling the burnt gunpowder wafting towards them.

The air was warmer here, the men stripped off to the waist, their bodies shining from the light of the constantly moving lamps. These were his men, the workers who would get the job done and he was proud of them. That is what he wanted to concentrate on and nothing else, but Lucy was there always shadowing him.

'It's certainly impressive. I was only here a few days ago and yet a lot of progress has been made since then, such good work Charlie.'

'I wish I could say the same about the cutting. We're still not through to solid rock so we desperately need more timber to shore up the north side before the lot collapses and we have to start again.'

'Yes, Mr Murray told me about it. They're having the same difficulties south of the viaduct. The geology is more complicated than we expected.'

'Why would that be?'

'Just how the land is I suppose, the rock is overlaid by all this clay.'

There was a pause before the foreman said 'Right, if there's no more questions I'll get on if you don't mind.'

'No, you go on Charlie. I'll be here for the next half hour or so. I want to look at the top edges of the embankment and see how they're holding up.'

'I can get one of the men to show you the new path up there.'

'No, it's alright. I'll manage myself thank you.'

He watched Charlie's lamp merge with the rest as he stepped aside to let one of the trucks past. It was being pushed by two men bent low with the effort. The truck was piled high with rubble from one of the latest blastings. Another truck behind was just as quickly approaching. Here in the semi darkness the work felt steady but intense. Being underground gave emphasis to every movement and noise. Water was dribbling constantly down from the roof forming long pools beside where the tunnel was being layered with bricks.

He inspected the rest of the tunnel without interrupting anyone although he knew his presence could still put the men a little on edge. At least by now he believed they were more relaxed with him. He wanted to be fair and appreciative when possible, an approach that he firmly believed got the best results.

Finally he drew near two of the carpenters who were setting up a new stretch of scaffolding for the brickies to work on the roof.

'Afternoon Mr Stockton,' one of them said in a broad Lancashire accent.

'How are things Simon?' he asked, priding himself in knowing many of the men's names.

'Well other than standing in a permanent shower of water it's alright. We're getting done now we've got the wood we needed.'

'So I see. You've been making good progress over the last few days.'

'It's a bit stop and start,' said the other carpenter, his filthy face flickered in the light of the lamps, 'What wi the blasting. There was a bad un yesterday.'

'Yes, I heard.'

'Young lad, Georgie Simpson, drilled onto an explosive cap that some silly bugger had left in.'

'I visited him at the hospital,' Richard told them.

'And how is he?'

'I'm afraid he's lost his right eye, but it could a been a lot worse.'

'Lucky to be alive then.'

'I should say so. It's something we tell the men all the time, but I know it's not always their fault.'

'Well I wouldn't do that job whatever you paid me,' said Simon strongly.

'Too much of a gamble,' his work mate agreed.

'Yes, of course, any way I'll let you get on,' Richard responded as he stepped away.

Out in the cutting he took deep lungfuls of the spring air. Inside the tunnel it was warm and fetid with the stink of sweat. Now he could look up at the sharp sided valley being dug out by the hundreds of men swarming all over the steep embankments. Trucks here full of rubble were pulled along the tramway by the small steam engine down to the viaduct site and then when empty were filled with bricks on their return journey. Men were on the top of the two sides pulling ropes attached to the wheelbarrows full of the blue clay that the workers at the bottom were digging out. Here was the noise of the trucks over the temporary lines as well as the clunk and grating noise of so many shovels digging into the earth. Here the men had their coats and jackets off, their shirts smeared in the clay that stuck to everything. By now it was predicted that the sides of the cutting would have reached solid stone but as yet it had still not been found which meant this constant battle against the hard mud that could melt in minutes when it started raining.

'Afternoon Mr Stockton!' several men called as he went past them.

He nodded and responded knowing that a few words from him could make at least a little difference to their mood.

'We're getting there,' another of the workers told him as he stopped to chat.

'So nothing to complain about James at the moment?'

The man grinned, his teeth whiter against the rest of his dirty face, 'Oh I wouldn't go as far as that, this clay's a right carry on so it is.'

From on top of the cutting came the cries and groans of those pulling up the full wheelbarrows. The start of the tunnel seemed much smaller from where he was standing as another truck appeared out of the dimness.

'Right, I'll leave you to it James,' he said then.

'If there is owt to tell thee I'll be the first to let thee know Mr Stockton,' the navvy called after him.

He passed Ethan and Jock who that afternoon were on the same gang of diggers and then climbed to the top edge of the cutting to make his way back down to the settlement.

Now he had the full view of the Ribblehead site below him. The smoke from all the huts had formed a thin grey cloud above the settlements. There was no wind today to blow it away up to the head of the dale as usually happened. The noise and bustle of the work gave him a sense of pride and certitude. He felt inspired and determined. Once that would have been his full response to the work, but instead there was now so much inner doubt. How could a woman destroy so much confidence so quickly? How could another human being undermine him like this? He loved Lucy Ormskill but had no idea what that really meant.

He walked past the first line of the huts of Belgravia and over the other side of the track those of Inkerman and Sebastopol and noticed that they needed a fresh coat of paint after the weathering they had taken over the winter. Women wrapped in shawls and children playing were out on the boards set over the mud. Washing was hanging limp from their lines. Some watched him as he walked past down to the offices and workshops. But today instead of going into meet the junior engineers he went on under the viaduct to the huddle of buildings at Salt Lake, another of the smaller settlements. It was a walk he took every few days. It was necessary to ensure he saw where all the work was being done but also where the men and their families were living. A line of carts was approaching and others returning to the station at Ingleton. Eventually when the new line reached the southern end of the viaduct everything would be brought up by train from Settle leaving many carters and suppliers out of business.

He had once thought about living above the Railway Inn but had decided to stay in the hut on wheels. The drawback was that Andrew Murray shared it with him, their beds across the room from each other with only the long work table separating them. To begin with they had enjoyed their evenings together, determined not to talk about work, playing chess, drinking port and smoking their pipes. Gradually the differences in their characters had begun to emerge and with it a growing awkwardness between them. Andrew was impatient. He was thorough in his work but aggressively so as he was with the men. He gave off a too obvious sense of superiority and would be furious at any mistakes or miscalculations others made. Richard had experienced Murray's anger too often with the other engineers and surveyors and he was even worse with the navvies. It was as though he felt there was a constant conspiracy to slow down the work.

Murray had been away for a few days visiting his family in Shropshire but was there when Richard climbed the steps and opened the door.

'Good timing Richard. There are spare chops if you want some. I have new potatoes on the boil and I've brought back a grand chunk of Shropshire cheese.'

He was at the stove in his stocking feet, his braces hanging loose over his trousers.

'Smells good,' Richard replied, taking off his jacket for once glad of the others presence, especially if it meant having his dinner cooked for him.

'Bill Arnold sent over a jug of beer as well so we're all set for this evening.'

'And how was Shropshire and the journey back?'

'Tedious,' said Andrew, 'The quicker this line is built the better. The journey took forever and the carriage from Ingleton was freezing.'

'And your mother and father, how are they keeping?'

'Mother complains of stiff joints all the time and father is certain he has gout. Other than that they were their usual cheery selves. Right, how many chops?'

He dished out the potatoes, set the jug of beer and mugs down as well as a loaf of bread and large chunk of cheese.

'So what have you been doing today?' Andrew asked.

'This afternoon I took a walk around the whole site. It reminds you of how big we've become, how many people actually live here now. All the settlements together make a sizeable population, such a huge responsibility for us all. I don't usually feel it like that but today I realized fully what we are dealing with here, not just a building project but ensuring that everything holds together.'

'We're big enough now to have a town council except if it was up to a free vote, God forbid, then Myres and his like would be quickly running the place.'

Richard thought to himself how it did not take long for Myres' name to come up.

'Yes, there's a new batch of leaflets circulating around the settlements at the moment.'

'The usual nonsense I suppose, more money less work.'

'An increasing number of the men take them seriously.'

'Those who can read.'

'And listen.'

'I suppose so,' Andrew said.

Later with the meal finished, the beer jug empty they were seated in the two more comfortable chairs preparing their pipes.

Casually Andrew asked, 'And how is the new teacher getting on at the school? I hear good reports.'

Richard took a moment responding before he said, 'Miss Ormskill seems to be doing well. We will not know how good until the school has its first inspection. Then we will have a better idea on how things are going.'

'She certainly makes Batty Green a more attractive proposition altogether.'

'How do you mean?'

'Oh come on Richard, even you must have noticed what an absolute beauty Lucy Ormskill is. If I was not spoken for I would certainly be interested.'

'Yes, she is rather good looking,' Richard said vaguely.

'Rather!' Andrew exclaimed, 'Listen to the man! Talk about understating the case.'

'Steady Andrew, you're getting quite carried away.'

'Yes, you're right. I have to remember my Janet, my dear Janet and the commitment we have made to each other, married next year.'

'And will she live with you up here?'

There was no response to this. Richard noticed a sudden taught expression on Andrew's face. For some reason it irritated him.

He poured them both a glass of port before they sat for a while smoking their pipes. Eventually Andrew said, 'It's been a mistake.'

Richard looked at his serious, doubtful expression and asked, 'What has?'

'This engagement to Janet, I went at it too quickly. I was worried if I didn't do something I might lose her and now I'm not sure if I want to marry her at all. In fact I don't think I do. What a bloody mess,' he muttered before taking another mouthful of port.

'Well don't do anything rash.'

'Do? Do what rashly? I haven't done anything.'

'But you're thinking about it.'

'And what if I am? Surely I'm allowed to rectify my own mistakes.'

'And make Janet suffer because of it.'

'Come on Richard. If I don't love the girl what would you suggest I do, still go through with the marriage? Surely that doesn't fit with the liberal opinions you hold, with all the liberal newspapers and books you read? You think I should still marry Janet even when I don't love her?'

'I don't see why not.'

Andrew stared at him for a few moments before saying, 'You don't mean that.'

'You've made a commitment, a serious one.'

'For God's sake, you don't know anything about the situation. You've only met Janet once.'

Momentarily they both looked at the stove that was gradually cooling down, tension there between them.

'You're right,' Richard finally said, 'you and Janet, that is your affair.'

'Yes it is,' Andrew answered strongly.

'Maybe it's working up here that makes everything too clear cut.'

'I was thinking about what you said a few weeks ago, that there are no big projects left in England and that your next job could be in the United States.'

'Yes, what about it?'

'Oh I don't know. It....it just sounded.....'

'Surely not for you Andrew?' Richard interrupted, appalled by the idea of Murray coming with him.

'No, you're probably right, jumping at another idea as usual.'

'You need to slow down, to think things through carefully.'

'Like you I suppose.'

'Not at all,' Richard responded.

'It's just who I am.'

'Well that can change, we can change ourselves surely.'

'If you believe it's possible.'

'I do. I believe anyone can fundamentally change if they put their mind to it, if they really want to.'

'And I don't know whether that's a good thing or not,' Andrew added.

'There has to be that possibility or the future is going to be just a repetition of the past.'

'Now you've lost me.'

'I'm only saying.'

'Yes, that I should slow down and behave myself.'

'Something like that,' Richard tried to say in a lighter tone, tapping out his pipe before standing up and adding, 'Well, I'm for bed, what about you?'

'Not just yet.'

'I've got an early start in the morning.'

'And I've still got another day's leave so try and keep it quiet when you get up.'

'Not easy in a place this size.'

'You sure you don't want another glass of port?'

'No thanks Andrew, I've had enough.'

Nothing else was said while he prepared for bed. Richard closed the stove door and extinguished the lamps before trying to settle down for the night.

Later he listened to Andrew's slow, heavy breathing coming from across the room. He was still critical of him and yet as he lay there his mind was full of more urgent thoughts about Lucy Ormskill. Even after their argument Andrew had gone straight to sleep when he knew he would be awake thinking over and over again about how he was going to manage Lucy, how he could interest her enough in ways that would not reveal how stupidly obsessed with her he was.
Several hours went by before he finally got to sleep with a new wind coming off the moors rattling the hut's window frames and the sound of some of the settlement dogs barking at each other.

CHAPTER TWENTY NINE

'The Lord is with you. You know that. You have faith and he will repay you for such faith and comfort you.'

James was holding the hand of the young Georgie Simpson who had lost an eye in the recent tunnel accident. With half his face bandaged Georgie was propped up in his bed in the makeshift hospital adapted from two of the huts. There were other men in their beds listening and watching.

'Georgie is doing very well,' said doctor Shawcross standing behind James.

'Of course he is. He's a strong young man doctor.'

'Just feel thirsty all the time like,' the young navvy confessed.

'Your parents are Methodists you told me,' James said.

'Ay, allays have been Mr Tranton. I'm right glad you came to visit,' the young man told him in a weak, dry voice.

'I wanted to see how you were and thought we could pray together. Your work mates have been asking of you.'

'Ay, some of em kem round earlier this evening.'

'The ward was crowded out,' said the doctor before he moved on to another of his patients.

The whitewashed room was lit by two lamps hanging from the ceiling. Most of the other men were dozing by now as the tall, blue suited Shawcross did his rounds.

'You have had a terrible accident but now you must concentrate on getting well. The Lord will give you strength. You have your other eye and we must thank God for that.'

'Yes Mr Tranton,' Georgie agreed, squeezing hard James' hand.

His face was sheened in sweat, the skin chalk white in contrast to his dark, close cropped hair.

'And....and me Mum and Dad have been told.'

'Doctor Shawcross has written to them. They'll be getting it soon.'

'They'll be sick wi worry, especially me Mum. She's never wanted me to leave home and neither me Mam or Dad can read nor write but they'll get someone to read out doctor's letter to em.'

'Yes, of course, but you must not worry about your parents. Doctor Shawcross will have explained everything.'

Georgie began to cry, his chest jerking up and down as he tried to speak through the sobbing, 'Bloody blind in one eye. Me! I know I.......I know I have to accept what's happened.'

'You must,' said James strongly.

'But.....but it's hard and half o me face feels three times the size it should and the pain keeps on and on until.....until I can hardly bear it Mr Tranton. I want you to pray for me. I want you to do that.'

'That's why I'm here, to pray with you, to share in all your troubles and anguish. He will take them away from you and make you feel whole again. His kindness and love has no boundaries. Circumstances, terrible circumstances can challenge our faith but we must be strong and not waver in our belief in the true Christ. He is with you, now and always. The Lord understands everything and shares in our grief and we have to feel him within us and know that he is our saviour, our strength, our everlasting benefactor. So we will pray and our prayers will be heard. Whatever happens we must never doubt the Lord's overwhelming goodness. He is with you Georgie.'

On his was back down the road to Chapel le Dale James thought of the young worker and the dreadful pain squeezed into his features. He had lost so much and yet had survived. He had been so unlucky and yet blessed with good fortune at the same time. The last time James had come across Georgie had been in a football match some weeks ago, both of them playing in attack for the Ribblehead team.

Bess clattered along the rough track. On the far horizon was a faint line of yellow light, the last of the sunset out to the west. The darkness of the hills on either side of the road was accentuated by the lighter sky above, a late spring evening that was merging into night.

James was tired. He had been visiting most of the day, going from hut to hut before finishing with Batty Green's makeshift hospital. He felt emptied out. It was in such a state that he was at his most vulnerable, where images and guilt filled his mind with such desperation. The congregation at Leeds had chosen him as the missionary for Ribblehead. He had been chosen and his mission had filled him with optimism, his first such responsibility and still only twenty seven. But now all of it was threatened, all his work jeopardised by his own miserable weakness. He lusted and such passion created dreadful ideas that he could not control. The devil was testing him. There he was on his usual journey back to the house and all on the surface was normal, Mr Tranton the Methodist missionary riding his horse passing the supply carts going in the other direction, their lamps swinging to the rough motion of the wheels bouncing over the rubble on the road. He would bid the carters good evening and they would respond and all would seem as it should be and yet within this normality were dreadful, aching doubts. The devil was in the terrible need that he was struggling to control. The devil had him in his grasp and he could not break free.

He rode along brooding on his miserable situation. Everything was now out to undermine him. Only the evening before he had passed the front window to see Lizzie sitting there with his cousin apparently having supper together. By the time he had opened the door and was in the hallway the maid was already there, red in the face, obviously flustered, holding a tea tray, telling him that his own supper was ready and that she was about to make a fresh pot now he had returned.

'I see now you're taking supper with the maid Jane,' he said the moment he stepped into the parlour, his face stiff and critical.

'Nonsense James, she only sat down for a minute. I told her to take a break from rushing in and out. I have no one to talk to all day so having a chat with Lizzie is something I enjoy. Surely you can understand that?'

'But I saw the two of you taking supper together, you with Lizzie,' he had persisted.

'And I say you have misunderstood what happened.'

'I saw you.'

'Oh stop it James and accept my explanation before you make this into something a lot more than it is. You're tired. You've been exhausted for weeks now. You're doing too much.'

He knew she was lying, his cousin lying to him, she who had been homeless, she who he had taken in. It disgusted him that she could be so deceitful. He would have to get rid of Lizzie. She had to go and yet still he wavered. He would have to dismiss her. There was no other option.

Just then Bess jerked to the right as she stood on a large rock that had fallen off the wall running by the side of the road. The walls were in a poor state of repair after the long winter with gaps appearing in places where they had collapsed altogether.

'Steady, steady,' he said to her softly.

A light drizzle began to fall as he pulled his coat collar up to his chin and his hat more firmly onto his head. He was hungry and yet felt sick at the idea of food. Pain throbbed in his fingers and his left leg was going numb. The rain made him squint to see the next few yards of road. It was coming straight up the Dale that became a tunnel for the increasing wind. He lowered his head in defiance as it began buffeting him backwards and forwards while Bess trudged stubbornly onwards. The wind whined through the gaps in the dry stone walls and further up the valley sides moaned and shifted across the open ground of grass and scree. The sounds were of this Northern night. He was used to them, once relishing their sounds and disturbance but now they were a deepening irritation as he tried desperately to clear his mind.

'James, you're soaking wet!' Jane exclaimed as she came out to meet him in the hallway carrying her blanket as he took off his sodden coat and hat, 'Come into the parlour and I'll get Lizzie to make a cup of hot broth for you.'

'No, no thank you. I think I'll go straight to bed,' he said wearily.

'But have you had anything to eat up at Ribblehead?'

'Yes I've eaten,' he lied.

As he started mounting the stairs Jane reminded him that she was going to meet the Austwicks the next day.

'They're picking me up at two in the afternoon tomorrow and I'll be staying at Selside for tea.'

'Yes, yes, alright,' he answered bluntly before continuing up the stairs.

Jane went back to the parlour and tried to carry on reading. Now there was no fire she had to sit wrapped in a blanket, the rain lashing against the windows. Even more she hated her cousin's miserliness. It was ridiculous to have to be wrapped in blankets with her thick woollen dress in an attempt to keep warm. She refused to go to bed so early. It was depressing to have to climb under the blankets such a short time after the sun had set. And yesterday James had almost discovered her and Lizzie taking supper together. They had stupidly forgotten the time and he had come home earlier than they had expected. She was tired of having to hide everything from him. It was supposed to be as much her house as his or so he had told her, but she knew the idea of Lizzie sharing meals with her would be totally unacceptable to her cousin. However much he went on about the Lord's love for all humanity he was very aware of his own social standing. The last thing he would allow was for his position to be jeopardised in any way, for rumours to circulate about strange goings on at his house. That would truly mortify him. He would never understand how lonely she could be by herself day after day. Lizzie was her only company except for the Austwicks and now Lucy Ormskill who she met once every two weeks or so. It was not enough. It could never be enough for someone like herself who thrived on being with people. Chapel le Dale had become a prison from which she found so few ways to escape. There were only the walks she took by herself over the hills of which James disapproved. The rest of her days were taking up with sewing or reading except now for time spent with Lizzie, the most precious time of all.

So the next day she was even more pleased than usual to climb up into the Austwicks' carriage.

'Up you come Miss Jane,' laughed George Austwick, 'You look right pretty today.'

George was short, rotund, red faced and had made enough money to retire to his favourite part of the country by selling the family's woollen mill. His wife Eleanor had been the daughter of a well known solicitor in Halifax and they had bought a long, low seventeenth century house in the hamlet of Selside only a few miles from Ribblehead on the main Horton to Settle road. It was a large, cluttered house and Jane loved it, such a contrast to where she lived. Every room was full of ornate furniture, mirrors, pictures, antiques, tapestries, Indian carpets and exotically designed wallpaper. There was so much warmth, colour and richness in the Austwick's house that when she was there she never wanted to leave it. Jane had met them at a fund raising night for war widows in the small nearby town of Dent. Although they were so much older they had quickly formed an easy friendship with Jane who they quickly realised lived a very isolated existence at Chapel le Dale. They were drawn to her sense of life and humour, the open way she had of talking about any subject and the obvious warm feelings she had for them. She was like the daughter they never had.

'The fire is lit in the dining room and Mrs Rathbone is making us a cup of tea,' Eleanor said as her husband and Jane entered the house.

'Just what I need,' Jane told her happily as she hugged Eleanor before they went into the lavishly decorated dining room.

'And your journey was alright Jane?'

'She never stopped talking,' interrupted her husband who was never afraid of saying what he thought, much to his wife's embarrassment at times.

'That's not true!' Jane exclaimed, 'I could hardly get a word in edge ways. Your husband wanted to tell me about the iniquities of quarrying in this area.'

'Oh that,' Eleanor sighed.

If her husband was a prosperous robin his wife was a half starved starling, so thin and stretched with sunken cheeks.

'I suppose I did go on a bit,' George admitted as he stood in front of the blazing fire.

'On this I agree with him,' his wife continued, 'it would be a travesty to see the hills of these beautiful Dales gouged apart.'

'Yes,' said Jane.'

'Bad enough what's going on at Ribblehead.'

'And it's happening so quickly.'

'Progress Jane waits for no man. Must get on, that's what this age is all about, getting on and who cares about the consequences,' said George strongly.

There was a pause in the conversation. Mrs Rathbone their housekeeper served the tea before they continued discussing a variety of topics from quarrying to the state of the local roads, how James' mission was going, the school at Batty Green, the recent outbreak of smallpox in some of the Lancashire mill towns until Jane with so much talking began to have a headache.

'You're looking pale Jane, are you feeling alright?' George eventually asked her after she had been quieter than usual for a few minutes.

She forced a smile and answered, 'I'm afraid I've got an awful headache coming on.'

'Can we get you anything for it?' Eleanor inquired.

'No, not if it develops like my headaches usually do. Then nothing seems to affect them, nothing at all. It's a pest. I'm sorry but I really don't feel well.'

'Not well enough to stay for something to eat?'

There was a pause before Jane said, 'I.....I'd rather go home and get to bed if you don't mind. I.....'

'No, of course not,' George interrupted, 'I'll go and get the gig ready.'

'I apologise for being such a nuisance.'

'Not at all, if you don't feel well you don't feel well, nothing worse than a blooming headache.'

Jane closed her eyes for a few moments to try and stop the dizziness and nausea she was experiencing.

'I'll get your bonnet and coat,' Eleanor said, getting up quickly.

On their way back she hardly spoke a word. Even George for once was quiet.

'Do you want me to take you right to the door?' he asked when they finally approached the turn off down into Chapel le Dale.

'No, I'll walk the rest of the way, but thank you for asking.'

'Not at all, don't want you fainting on me before you reach your house.'

'I'll manage, I promise,' Jane said after the carriage had come to a stop.

She waved as George set it off back up the road. At the bridge she stopped, leaning on the stone to look down at the stream water swirling around the rocks that were covered in thick, bright green moss. The pain down the sides of her head was being stretched ever further. She felt sick and unsteady. Pushing against the stone parapet she tried to gulp in deeper breaths of the afternoon air.

Finally she straightened herself and started walking slowly towards the house, each step ringing dully in her brain as she tried to concentrate.

In the hallway she relaxed a little, taking off her coat and bonnet and straightening the front of her dress. Then she did not move sure she could hear James' voice coming from upstairs. There was nothing unusual in this. When he was at home James spent a lot of time in his bedroom praying or preparing his next sermon. In the semi darkness she searched for the peg near the front door to hang up her coat. Her head was still painful as she went to the kitchen for a glass of water. The room was empty. She supposed Lizzie was cleaning the parlour or out the back taking in the washing. The water revived her a little. There was no one in the parlour when she looked. Again she waited in the hallway listening to James' incessant flow of words that seemed to fill the otherwise silent house. Only then did she have her first misgivings, a strange sense that something was not quite right. Images of the Austwicks' house flashed through her brain as though that was where she really belonged, in the warmth and colour of their beautifully furnished rooms. Slowly she started mounting the steep wooden stairs, holding onto the bannister, a shadow squeezed across her vision as though her eyes were only half open. Suddenly she felt cold and exhausted. As she reached the landing she steadied herself, trying to slow her breaths, remaining as quiet as possible

The door to James' room was ajar, light from the gap in the door forming a bright shaft of gold across the landing's threadbare carpet. Consciously she stepped across it, suddenly acutely aware of everything, the mood of the house, his voice, the pain down the sides of her head, the tightness in her chest as she approached his door. His voice was fast and urgent, his words rushing forward with such intensity. By now she was frightened, a cold fear in her as she gently pushed open the door a little more. The one thing James would not tolerate was to have his prayers disturbed.

She knew something was badly wrong. It was instinct accentuated by her heightened state of consciousness. Part of her wanted to go no further, wanted to turn and go into her bedroom but the fear in her was too strong. If she was ill then it was distorting everything so much that she hardly trusted her own sensations as she took another step.

'Oh Lord give this young woman strength. Oh Lord give her strength. Oh Lord give her strength,' James was repeating over and over again.

He was on his knees with his back to the door. Facing him Lizzie was in the same position, her hands gripped tightly between his and held high in supplication, their knees almost touching and their faces so close to each other. Lizzie had her eyes shut and her mouth set rigidly as James continued with his loud, vibrant prayer. It was too intense, too passionate. Jane had never heard him so forceful, his arms quivering, his neck stretched as he continued.

'Help this young woman to overcome all evil oh Lord, to banish all evil thoughts from her mind and live in your grace. She has sinned but seeks forgiveness. Give her strength oh Lord to find true redemption.'

Jane could not move, stood there frozen with shock. What she was witnessing was disgusting in its intensity, in the closeness of their bodies. The shock of it made her turn cold. Lizzie was so apparently involved and accepting with James clasping her hands tightly between his. But this was not true prayer. Even though she wanted to stop them she could not. She felt numb and too helpless to interrupt.

Lizzie suddenly opened her eyes, looking straight at her and a small smile formed on her lips in acknowledgement of her standing there. This was even more shocking, the sense that Lizzie was quite happily going along with this charade. The pretence somehow made the young woman seem more vulnerable, lost to James' need. And yet in Lizzie's look was an awareness, an acceptance. And then the expression in her eyes became more challenging. She was daring Jane to interrupt and stop what was happening, her mouth softening, her lips parting slightly as she continued to look over James head straight at her. Jane was lost in a confusion of desire and disgust. Her cousin was playing his own hypocritical game and she was in no position to do anything about it.

'Oh Lord give her strength. Oh Lord give her strength to overcome all evil. Oh Lord give her the strength to be pure and strong. Oh Lord give her strength to know thy salvation and never to wander from the way of purity and faith. Oh Lord give her strength,' James continued and all Jane could do was listen and look until she could stand no more, quickly turning away and going along the landing to her own bedroom where she sat on the edge of the bed, squeezed her hands tightly together as the tears started down her flushed cheeks.

CHAPTER THIRTY

Jane took to her bed for the next weeks hardly eating or drinking anything. At one point James was so worried he got Doctor Shawcross from the settlements to come and see her.

'It's influenza, bad dose of it,' Shawcross told James who was waiting on the landing outside Jane's bedroom, 'She's very weak and needs as much rest as possible as well as plenty of fluids and lots of light food, broth and such like and I must say it is very cold in this house Mr Tranton.'

Lizzie brought up everything the patient needed, moving daily from the kitchen to Jane's bedroom with jugs of water, lightly done toast, vegetable soup, a basin for washing her face and arms, broth and cups of tea and everything else that was supposed to be good for recovery. In the evenings whenever he could James would come and sit with her, reading from 'Pilgrims Progress' or a selection of John Wesley's sermons. In all this time Jane said not a word. Whenever Lizzie tried to talk to her she made no response just stared with sunken eyes across the room, her face drawn and pale with the illness.

Eventually after the doctor's last visit and some slow improvement Jane was helped downstairs to sit in the parlour for the afternoon. James allowed Lizzie to light a fire even though it was now early May. She wrapped a blanket around the patient's legs before bringing in a fresh pot of tea. Jane seemed moulded into the chair, her breathing slow and steady as her eyes followed Lizzie around the room. The faint tick of the small clock on the mantelpiece and the rattle of a cart going along the Ingleton road in the distance were the only sounds. A warm sun was shining through the windows. The house was settled into its early summer stillness. Finally after so many days of silence Jane finally said something.

'I....I can't believe you two were praying together like that,' she said slowly in a quiet, weak voice.

Lizzie turned from the window, 'Goodness Miss Jane, you've said something!'

'I can't understand.'

'What can't you understand?' Lizzie asked as she came and stood in front of her, wiping her hands on her apron.

Jane did not look up at her. Instead she wiped her tongue along her dry lips and sighed.

'You haven't spoken for ever so long. The doctor said you were on the mend. Mind you there were days when you were awfully weak and wouldn't eat a thing so now look at you, as thin as a sparrow so you are. We'll have to get you fattened up. Is there anything you want?'

Jane's eyes lowered but she made no reply.

'I'll pour yer tea.'

'Go away.'

Lizzie continued pouring out the tea.

'Go away,' Jane repeated in a low, dismal voice.

When she slowly put the tea pot down Lizzie asked, 'And why should I do that?'

'I don't......don't want you anywhere near me.'

Lizzie laughed, 'My, you never used to say that!'

Jane said nothing more until she gasped as Lizzie suddenly grabbed her under the chin jerking her head up saying strongly, 'So don't start now, do you hear? You don't change your tune like that. You don't Miss Jane.'

She let her go, poured herself some tea and went and sat in the opposite chair.

There was nothing said for a few minutes. Lizzie gulped down mouthfuls until the cup was empty and then belched before wiping her hand across her mouth.

'He asked me so I agreed and it wasn't the first time,' she started.

'He's done it before?' Jane forced herself to inquire.

'Lots of times.'

'Has he....has he.....?' she started muttering to herself.

'I reckon he just likes the idea of saving my soul.'

'You know it's more than that.'

'Well he ain't done owt if that's what yer mean, not really.'

'I love you,' Jane said quietly.

'So you say, doesn't stop your cousin saying his prayers, and oh he sounds so earnest so he does and repeats hisell over and over again. I have to listen to it for goodness knows how long. So if it's so wrong you'll have to talk to the master not me. I'm just the maid remember. I just do what I'm told. That's what me Mam said, just do what they ask and then you can't go wrong so it's not me going wrong, is it? It might be others in this house but it ain't me. I've only just come seventeen so I can't be blamed. No one would blame a lass as young as me.'

'It's.....it's wrong.'

'You're just jealous, jealous that I do what he says

'Stop, stop it Lizzie, please.'

'Don't see why I should. Cos you'd know what to do wi it wouldn't you? The master has no idea what it's for except to play the devil's tune.'

'Our.....our love........our love is not like that,' said Jane as she tried to push herself out of the chair, falling back with the effort.

'You're still poorly Miss Jane. You have to tek it easy like.'

'You must promise me that you......'

'No!' Lizzie exclaimed, 'I'm promising nothing! Not to you or anyone else!'

'You have to Lizzie.'

'I don't have to do anything.'

'We are....are different.'

'Oh you can say that again. I reckon the folk around here would agree wi you.'

'Please Lizzie.'

'There's no please. There is what there is, that's all, so stop going on. Rest, you're supposed to rest not get yersell all worked up like this. Drink yer tea and then in a few days you'll be able to get that Lucy Ormskill round and you can love her.'

'Stop it!'

'Yes you can.'

'Stop it Lizzie.'

'Because that's what you want and me master James as well cept he is trying to fight against it and using me as the devil's kind. I'm the devil's woman and he has to hate me first. But oh he knows what I can offer him. Just like thee does Miss Jane. You know better than anyone. You should feel proud of that, Lizzie's first. Yer might be surprised but you are and I'm being honest so I am, telling the truth, not that me Mam told us to do that. If lying gets you somewhere then lie yer head off is what she said to me, tell all the lies yer need.'

Lizzie finally stopped, her face red with anger.

Jane began slowly shaking her head but the young maid paid no attention.

After a few minutes when nothing else was said Lizzie took up her tea cup and crushed it in her hand, the pieces of china splattering over the floor.

'You have to want it bad enough,' she said bitterly.

'I love you,' Jane murmured with difficulty.

Lizzie went up to her, bent so she could kiss Jane hard on the mouth before asking, 'Isn't that what you want?'

She stepped back and went off into the kitchen for a brush and pan, 'Can't have a mess that master James might notice. Everything has to be neat and tidy for him so it has,' she continued as she brushed up the shards of china off the carpet, 'So he'll never know cos I don't think he has any idea how many china cups there are in the house or anything else for that matter cos he is a man of the Bible, a man of the Lord who is not interested in such nonsense as things in a house, isn't that so Jane? Isn't it right that he is such a studious man that this won't be of interest to him? Not like you. Everything's of interest to you isn't it Miss Jane?'

'I....I don't understand what you're.....'

'Oh I'm sure you do. Anyroads it don't matter if you don't. Does't want another kiss? Would that suit yer, or maybe a bit more? No, cos I don't think yer up to it.'

'You would never tell anyone.'

'Wouldn't I?'

'Lizzie, you couldn't.'

'I can do anything Miss Jane. You should know that by now. I kem here not knowing what I could do, not knowing anything really, but the two of you have taught me so much in such a short time. It's amazing how much I understand. So don't try and tell me what I can or can't do.'

Lizzie went back to the window humming to herself. Jane never took her eyes off her. From the garden came the sounds of a flock of sparrows feeding in the bushes that surrounded the small square lawn.

'Wi you poorly like,' she started again without turning, 'I've had plenty o time to think. Not that I like thinking cos I don't, not usually. But I was getting bored and I hate that more than owt. I hate having nowt to do and no one to talk to. It's not right for a lass my age to be stuck in a house wi the mistress ill and the master out all the time. Anyway, I got to thinking about things, lots of things, not that I could tell yer what thoughts I had cos I've forgotten most of em. They've just left me wi a feeling, a bad feeling and it meks me angry. I get upset you see and I don't like getting me sell all worked up. Me Mam always said I kem out of her already talking. I might not be able to read or write so good but I can talk for Adam. So cooped up here wi nobody to talk to is like a torture. Oh I've not said much before but that's cos I was learning. I was the maid and maids aren't supposed to open their gobs unless spoken to. Hell even I could understand that. The last thing people want is some young maid mouthing off at them. They'd lose their place straight away. And this is me first job and me Mam and Dad said I had to do it right, that I was getting a good chance and not to mess it up, and I haven't have I?' she asked as she turned round, 'have I?'

Jane's sat there expressionless.

'I asked yer a question.'

'No.....no you haven't,' she said miserably.

'There you are then.'

'I....I think I'll go back....back to bed now.'

'Oh right. Miss Jane wants to go back to bed.'

'I'm tired of all this.'

'Miss Jane is tired.'

Lizzie watched while Jane struggled out of the chair, 'I don't need your help. I can manage.'

'Of course you can. You're the mistress and the mistress always manages, ain't that right?'

'Just leave me alone.'

'Right you are Miss Jane.'

Lizzie waited as Jane struggled to cross the room, managed to open the parlour door and make her way out into the hall but when she came to the stairs she hesitated, one hand on the bannister with her head lowered and her breaths coming fast.

Lizzie was now standing at the parlour door, 'Up you go then.'

'I will.'

'Go on then.'

Jane managed the first two steps before she had to stop to catch her breath.

'Not easy is it when you feel so weak?' Lizzie added, 'But you're the mistress so you know what you're doing.'

It took Jane many minutes to force herself up to the landing and finally into her bedroom leaving Lizzie standing at the foot of the stairs still humming to herself.

In the following week James allowed his niece to have visitors. The Austwicks came on the Wednesday afternoon with gifts of flowers and sweets while Lucy came on the Saturday morning for a couple of hours and brought her a selection of books. The following Tuesday James had gone off to Settle to a Methodist meeting leaving Jane sitting out in the garden reading, a small parasol fixed on the back of her chair to shade her from the sun. It was one of those rare early summer days in the Dales that were warm enough to sit outside. Regularly she turned the pages, a Gothic novel that Lucy had brought for her. She was unsure what James would think of such a piece of literature so only read it when he was away. The afternoon sounds of human activity from the toll road made her feel strangely secure. Life was going on around her. So often here at Chapel le Dale there was only a widespread silence. Except for a few birds or the bleating of sheep even nature made little difference to the place's emptiness. It was the sounds of humanity that gave these hours their richness as she followed the book's words of mystery and romance listening to everything going around her at the same time.

Lizzie called from the house asking her to come in for a minute. Jane put down her book and anxiously crossed the lawn always unsure now as to Lizzie's moods. They made her apprehensive and uncertain.

'What is it?' she asked hesitantly.

'Come with me,' Lizzie said, taking her hand and leading her along the hallway and upstairs to Jane's bedroom.

Jane nervously let her take off her dress. Lizzie pulled back the blanket for her to get onto the bed. She then lay there anxiously watching every move Lizzie made as she took off her skirt and blouse, carefully and slowly as though it was a ceremony.

Finally they lay on their sides, their faces a few inches away from each other, the one looking at the other for a long time without a word being spoken.

The curtains were open allowing a strong light to fill the room. Both had their hair down, Lizzie's tumbling over her shoulders.

Eventually Lizzie started to trace the shape of Jane's cheek with her finger as she said, 'I was angry, very angry. I was boiling, raging and I didn't really understand why. Why Miss Jane? Why do we feel things? Why do feelings tek over?'

'I don't know,' Jane answered in a low, unsure voice.

'You're so beautiful.'

'As you are.'

'But too thin, too thin mistress Jane. You need to eat more.'

'Do I?'

'I say you do.'

'Well then I shall.'

'But you're still so lovely, your skin so smooth and soft and meking such lovely shapes, yer cheeks and then yer mouth,' she added as her finger traced along Jane's lips.

'This is our secret,' Jane tried, feeling a little more confident now.

'Yes,' Lizzie agreed.

'That nobody will ever know.'

'Yes.'

'The most precious secret and you're perfect Lizzie, absolutely perfect. Please don't change. You mustn't change.'

'Oh I don't know about that! I suppose I have to grow more and then who knows. I might finish up like me sister Betty and she's colossal, a big, girt thing.'

'No!' exclaimed Jane.

'Yer never know.'

'Kiss me.'

'Might do.'

'Kiss me Lizzie, please.'

After their kiss Jane said in a relieved voice, 'This is such a beautiful day. You make it feel like that.'

'Feelings do everything.'

'Yes.'

'We can't stop them.'

'No, we can't.'

'Nothing can stop them.'

'Nothing,' Jane repeated without hesitation.

CHAPTER THIRTY ONE

The rain had been falling constantly out of a lead grey sky for nearly two days as Jock and Fraser trudged up the muddy path beside the tramway line leading to the quarry workings. Whernside, Ingleborough and Penyghent were shrouded in low cloud. The settlements were a mess of running water, mud, the stench from leaking privies and coal smoke that filled the air. The two men said nothing as they followed the path in their long coats and caps pulled down over their faces to shelter from the incessant rain. Visibility here on the moor top was down to a few yards. It was past seven o clock in the evening. The shift had finished over an hour ago so there was no one else around as the two of them approached the stream that had recently been diverted. They went over the newly built stone bridge and left the tramway. Here Fraser started leading the way. His job being to check the tramway line meant he knew this area of the work site better than anyone.

He started up a short rise of new heather with Jock close behind and then climbed around a small hillock. Eventually he stopped. They stood together on the edge of one of the hundreds of swallow holes that littered the area, steep dips in the earth formed by water flowing off the hills and down underground cutting through the limestone. This one had a clutter of stones at its bottom. Fraser clambered down and started shifting some of them revealing a gap between the stone like a black wound in the earth formed by thousands of years of running water. Below where the two of them were standing was a chaos of underground tunnels and vertical shafts permeating this area of the Northern Pennines. Like a massive brain it had a labyrinth of arteries, huge chambers, narrow cuttings, hanging stalactites and stalagmites that rose up from the sodden, constantly dripping stone.

'Here, this looks alright.'

Jock scrambled down beside him, 'Ay, it'll do,' he said as he looked at the gap that was like a black wound cut through the limestone.

He watched while Fraser started replacing the rocks over the hole.

They stood together for a short time, neither of them speaking as the rain continued to pour over them before they climbed up onto the moorland to begin their way back down the mile and a half to Batty Green.

'You drink like a fucking vicar,' Jock said to Fraser after they had been in the Railway Inn for a time later on that night.

Fraser thought how little the Scotsman knew about the drinking habits of vicars but accepted it would be hopeless to try and keep up with his pace of drinking. So far he had downed two pints to Jock's six.

'The bastard knows,' Jock added then.

They were squeezed together in one of the corners of the overcrowded pub with the usual fug of beer smells, pipe smoke and the stench of men in their sodden working clothes.

'He's been talking to Freddie Shipton.'

'And that fucking sod from Derby, that Jason Donally who we worked wi two jobs ago.'

'So you think he knows?' Fraser asked.

'The bastard must by now.'

'So what's he waiting for?'

'No fucking idea, but Asquith is a scheming old sod so he'll be biding his time for some reason.'

'Maybe he hasn't got all what he thinks he needs.'

'Let's hope he hasn't,' Jock said.

'But it has to be soon.'

'Soon enough.'

'And you've talked to Arnold Wainwright?'

'He says he's got Jonty round his little finger and that Asquith don't mind. Took Jonty to watch a football game last Saturday and Asquith wasn't wi em.'

They drank down their pints and Fraser went off through the scramble to get two more. When he returned Jock gave him a critical look saying, 'It'll be the bosses and the constabulary he'll go and see just to mek sure he gets us either way. Asquith's been after us for fucking years and now he's almost past it he's making a last effort to get us nailed. That's how it'll be. He's getting on and he soddin hates the fact that we ain't and we're still here. Got to keep this going Fraser lad, don't want any softening up.'

'Not me,' Fraser answered, his features still calm and thoughtful, that was until Stan Woodson, one of the tallest and broadest workers at Ribblehead suddenly pushed his way out of the crowd with two of his mates.

'So where the fuck is it Henderson?' the huge navvy asked in his deep Welsh accent.

'Stan,' Fraser said back, 'How can I help you?'

'The money, where the fuck is it you little piece o shit. You said last Friday.'

Jock got to his feet before Fraser could stop him, 'Eh Woodson or whatever your name is,' he started, 'me and me mate are having a drink and don't like being interrupted so why don't you fuck off back to the Welsh bog you came from?'

'You must be fucking joking,' Woodson answered grinning with his two minders standing either side, the three of them being jostled by the throng behind.

'You either heard me or you didn't and if you didn't I'm not repeating meself so fuck off and leave us to our pints before....'

'Before what?'

'Before I fucking do for you,' Jock told him.

'Is this thick shit wi you?' Woodson asked Fraser.

Suddenly Jock leant over to the next table and grabbed a bottle of beer, smashed it on the table edge and rammed the broken neck up into Woodson's face, its glass just touching his skin below his eyes.

'You ain't got it yet you dumb fucker, have you?'

The big navvy remained stock still, his eyes bulging as the broken, jagged glass quivered slightly against his skin.

'So this gets pushed through yer fucking face if you don't just go away and leave us in peace, you got it?'

'If yer say so.'

'Right then, fuck off,' said Jock angrily as he pulled away the broken bottle.

For a few moments Woodson seemed unsure until he finally said, 'The money Henderson. You've got till tomorrow.'

Fraser waited before the three disappeared into the crowd.

'You've just made things a lot damned worse,' he said then.

Jock pulled a hard face and answered, 'I don't care what I've fucking done. That big bastard is not going to disturb my drink.'

'I owe him money.'

'That's your problem.'

'A lot of money.'

'So do what I do, just drink and nowt else then thee can't get into debt. Wi the drink the money's either there or it isn't. Can't see the likes of Bill Arnold subbing anyone. If he started that racket he'd have no paying customers left. They'd all been on tick.'

Fraser made no reply, just sat there thoughtfully turning his pint pot round on the table.

Across the room in the far corner of the pub Tom Myres was sat with his usual group which now often included Ethan. Ever since Myres had rescued Beth from the Moss Ethan had spent more time with him usually at these weekly meetings where the talk was either to do with the working conditions at Ribblehead or to do with wider issues that were facing the country.

'Two this week, one's lost an arm they reckon and the other had half his cheek blasted away.' Tom was saying.

'Wouldn't get me working in that bloody tunnel,' one of the others commented.

'Someat has to change,' said another.

'They're even talking about making the cemetery bigger down at Chapel le Dale. The Reverend Smith is running out of space so there's need for another graveyard next to the old one, has to be consecrated or whatever it's called, and now wi this rumour about smallpox in some of the mill towns well it won't be long before it'll be needed.'

The men looked thoughtful as they drank their beer and smoked their pipes. Ethan had gradually begun to enjoy their company, becoming increasingly interested in these discussions.

'Can't even give us a decent burial,' continued Tom, 'There'd be no bloody railway line without us workers. They depend on us to get it built. We have that responsibility. In a right society no man should earn more than another. What makes any job more important than another? That's what I'd like to know. But it's always been the same since the dawn of time, the head men and his followers, the kings and their serfs, the chiefs and the ones that do the fighting and do the work. Meks me wonder why the ordinary working man has put up with it, thousands of years and because of fear and violence those in charge have kept the rest under their control. They've been damned good at it, sometimes giving just enough to keep the masses quiet, especially in this country. They're bloody brilliant at sniffing out trouble and changing things just enough to calm people down. Look at the bloody Reform Act, only brought in because the establishment was scared of the rumours about riots and civil strife. They were scared and so thought they'd better appease some of the mob before things got out of hand.'

'Christ, you're on form tonight Tom,' said John Noble, another of the group.

Every time the door opened it brought in the smell of the rain still rattling against the pub's dingy windows.

'But there's talking and there's doing,' Melvin Stannard, an older man in his forties, said before puffing on his pipe.

'You're right there Melvin,' Tom agreed, 'But the pot's being stirred and the more accidents in the tunnel the more likely the lads'll start to listen.'

Bill Arnold the pub's landlord started shouting over the din that the dominoes match between the Batty Green boys and a combined team from the rest of the settlements was about to commence. He was standing on the bar ordering tables to be moved so that eventually the crowd managed to create enough space. Here it would be games of two against two that involved ten players from each team.

Most of Tom's group went off to watch.

'There they go, they love their doms,' he commented.

'Yes,' agreed Ethan who decided to stay where he was.

'I was going to ask you,' Tom said, 'how the hell you put up with the likes of Jock Tarrant and Fraser Henderson in your hut. I've just noticed em over there in the far corner. Living with them must be damned hard going.'

'Fraser's not so bad, but Jock, Christ he's hardly ever sober as far as I can tell and he's got a right mouth on him. My Missus can't stand him.'

'Don't blame her.'

'He's alright when he's not been drinking, but that doesn't often happen.'

'And what about Bill Asquith, and you have Jonty wi you as well?'

Ethan frowned. There was already the noise of doms being shuffled or slammed down as the crowd shouted their encouragement. He had to think about a description of Bill Asquith.

'He's getting on is Asquith, must be well into his fifties by now,' Tom put in.

'He's right good wi Jonty and the lad idolises him but I don't know about the rest. He can be a moody bugger can Bill, and he likes to get his own way, and there's someat been bothering him recently. That's what it seems like to me, someat he can't get off his mind. It could be Jonty. I just don't know.'

'There's talk that he's struggling to pull his weight in the brick factory.'

'I know he's knackered every night. Mind you we all are.'

'Starts to tell on a man, thirty odd years of navvying, grinds you down,' said Tom, 'I've seen too many men die the moment they stop working.'

Ethan took a mouthful of his sour beer and thought about what had been said.

'I'd trust Bill though to do what he promises. He's honest that way.'

'You've not said much about Henderson, what's he like?'

'Quiet most of the time. He's champion with the girls, buys and meks loads of things for em, can't fault him wi that, generous like is Fraser except me Missus doesn't think so. She's wary of him for reasons I don't understand.'

'Can't see why the hell he hangs around wi the likes of Jock Tarrant.'

'That's been only for the last weeks. No idea why, but at the moment they're close. Someat's brewing between em and it'll be to do wi Bill I reckon.'

'It'll be Jock planning some nonsense. They say he killed a man outside Manchester but was never charged. All I know about Fraser is that he likes a game o cards.'

'You seem to know a lot about the men,' Ethan added.

'I allays think I should. I should know whom I'm talking to instead of just seeing a load o strange faces in front of me. I want to know as much about the men here as I can. If that missionary James Tranton prides himself on knowing just about everyone's name in the settlements then I want to do the same. It's important or why should any man listen to me if I'm not even bothered enough to know who they are.'

'Suppose so,' agreed Ethan, the beer numbing his mind in ways he was still not familiar with.

They were silent for a time as the smoke and beer smells wafted around the densely packed pub and there were more shouts at the games of doms. From the solid crowd around the tables bets were being taken on each game and money changing hands so quickly it was hard to tell who was giving and who was receiving. It was the same with any competition between the settlements. The rivalry was intense, even moody and always there was gambling on the results. As usual Fraser Henderson was involved, stood jiggling a handful of coins while keenly watching one of the games.

Tom was rolling himself a cigarette as he looked inquiringly at Ethan knowing that he had to be careful even cautious with him.

'It's not easy,' he began, his voice low and serious,' being political. Some of em think all you have to do is wave a few flags around and that'll change the world. But I think you're interested or you wouldn't be here.'

'I am,' Ethan said tentatively.

'I could lend you a couple of books if you like seeing as you sound like an educated sort of fella. The more people like yourself in the group the better.'

'And what good would that do?'

Tom laughed, 'Well you read the books and you learn. That's the idea.'

'I used to read a lot, but that were years ago.'

'But you're interested in things changing?'

Ethan pushed his beer mug away, his face straining at the question, 'I.....I suppose so because if I'm not satisfied wi my own lot then I can understand how others feel.'

'Yes,' said Tom encouragingly. His dirt covered face still looked young and yet hard. He lounged back in his seat, one leg crossed over the other, his cap tilted on the back of his head. He wanted to appear relaxed and not to push Ethan away by his intensity. 'Not satisfied, eh?'

'No, not really.'

'You're a navvy Ethan. That's all there is to it and you're well paid up here and you have yer family wi you. What more can a man ask for?'

'A lot more,' he answered, knowing that Myres was pushing for a reaction.

'Such as?'

'Well, a proper education for a start off.'

'But you told me your girls have started the school here.'

'Until they're ten and then that's it. That's no damned good. It's not enough. It's the same as owt else. Everything's kept to the least it can be. We work lousy hours in lousy conditions, queue outside the office at the end o the week to be paid like a load of kids being given sweeties. There's no bloody pride in that, none at all.'

'And what else leaves a family man like you dissatisfied?'

'The fear me and the Missus have of getting ill, knowing that if I go down wi someat then we're buggered. Who brings in the money then?'

'A good question that nobody has yet answered because we know there isn't an answer.'

'And I suppose whatever happens my life will come to nowt. Like you said you work for thirty odd years and then you're done. Your life is over. For what? What will I have achieved except line someone else's pockets? It's that feeling of bloody hopelessness knowing that there are some people in this country who are well off, who can do what they like, achieve what they want and they don't care a shit about the likes of us. Why should they?'

'Well said Ethan, now you're talking.'

'That's why I'm interested.'

'And you're not an informer?'

Ethan's face stiffened in shock at this, 'What?'

'It's another thing I have to be prepared for.'

'I'm not a bloody informant!' he answered strongly,' and if you think I am then I'll just go.'

'No, no. Tek it easy. I'm only saying cos there's allays traitors in any political group who tell it all to the bosses and are paid for doing so. You have to know and trust who you're speaking with and even then they'll have you, even then you'll be surprised at whose betraying us for a few bob.'

'Well not me.'

'I never thought you were.'

'You shouldn't have mentioned it then,' Ethan complained, doubt still in his voice.

'Just someat you need to face. However committed someone sounds they might be just covering themselves while they learn as much about a group as they can. They're the real bastards.'

Ethan took up the beer mug and forced down another mouthful.

'And what about you, what got you started?'

'Oh that's easy,' answered Tom, 'I was eight years old or thereabouts and me Dad worked down in Earlby pit, one of the South Yorkshire mines outside Wakefield. There was a bad accident in the mine and I was told to go and tell Fletcher the mine owner. It's was maybe cos I was a fast runner they sent me. Anyway his house was two miles off and I remember I was in bare feet that were cut to shreds running up his driveway that was covered in loose gravel. His house was huge, a mansion. I managed to just reach the door bell and this fella came to the door and I asked him if he was Mr Fletcher. You should have seen his face. "No," says he, "I'm Jones the butler." Well I had no idea what the hell a butler was but I told this Jones the story. He left me on the doorstep and came back shortly to inform me that Mr Fletcher was having his breakfast and would be down at the mine in an hour or so. And that was it. Bit that got me was the size of his house. I never knew people lived like that and then there was Fletcher not even bothered enough to leave his breakfast. There were men stuck down the mine and he had to have his bloody eggs and bacon or whatever. It got me, really got me. I never forgot it. Later just to remember it made me angry and I suppose I've been angry ever since.'

'And you believe change is possible?'

'It's not about believing. This is not a religion. It's about reality and facts.'

'But you know what I mean.'

'Yes, radical change is possible, but not through getting the vote and all that. Nothing will be changed that way.'

'So how then?'

'Through a real revolution. It's the only way the establishment can be smashed. All this talk of democracy is another ploy on the bosses' part to keep the workers happy. It'll do nothing. If you can't imagine yersell killing for the cause then you're wasting your time. This is a serious business. We're not playing at it. I'm not playing at it you can be sure of that. Don't look so worried Ethan!' Tom exclaimed, slapping him on the leg, 'We've a long way to go yet. But don't ever think we'll be successful without having to do a lot of things you might not like. Those with the power will never give that power up without a bloody great struggle. Of course they won't. It's about who meks the decisions. It should be us and in the future it will be. So welcome to the struggle,' Tom laughed, 'Welcome to a life of anger and frustration cos that's what it's like.'

'So no real difference then to how things are at the moment,' Ethan responded.

'If that's what you think Ethan.'

'I do.'

'What about another pint if I can get through this mob?'

'No thanks. I've drunk more than I meant to already.'

'You're right. I've had enough as well. No point forcing it down,' Tom said as another game of doms ended with a lot of shouting and swearing from the crowd.

CHAPTER THIRTY TWO

That same evening Maggie had taken Clare and Beth to visit a family the Grangers had known from their days in Nottingham who stayed over at the Sebastopol settlement. It gave Bill the opportunity to try and have a serious talk with Jonty. He settled him down and then sat opposite, their knees almost touching, and started by saying, 'I want to talk to you Jonty lad and I want you to listen carefully, alright?'

'Listen to Bill,' Jonty muttered back, his large eyes bulging in worried anticipation.

'It's nothing to be bothered about.'

'No, no.'

'I just want you to listen carefully Jonty.'

'Haven't.....haven't done owt wrong.......haven't Bill.'

Bill took his hands in his, 'I know that lad.'

The saliva from Jonty's drooping mouth dribbled off his chin as he hunched even further forward as if to shield himself.

'Do you know how old I am?' Bill asked, 'Do you know?'

Jonty stared at him and then furiously shook his head.

'Fifty two, I'm fifty two. I'm getting old Jonty, too old.'

Jonty suddenly looked around the room. With all the rain lately Maggie had washing hanging everywhere and with the stove stoked up to help it to dry the room was hot and steamy. The windows were covered in condensation and both men were sweating. The pages cut out of magazines and newspapers that had been used to paper the walls were turning brown and curling at the edges.

'That means I'm at an age,' Bill continued, 'when men have to think about stopping work, stopping Jonty, stopping for good which means no more working at the brick factory. Do you understand that?'

Jonty's huge eyes moistened and he nervously began to rub himself between the legs which he often did when he became anxious.

'Do you understand?' Bill repeated.

He was finding this harder than expected. For weeks he had been putting it off, even fooling himself into thinking he could manage another year at the work. But in his heart he knew he was done. There was nothing left to give anymore. He was well and truly knackered and understood that he would never make it through another winter, not here in a place like Ribblehead.

'Two….fif…..fifty……' Jonty tried as his eyes roamed around the room filled with washing.

'Yes, too old, too old now for working. I have to stop. I have to stop.'

'No.'

'I have to.'

'No!' Jonty exclaimed, squeezing his hands together before rubbing himself again.

'Steady now. I just want you to try and understand that I can't carry on at the factory. I can't Jonty. Me old body is done for. It can't tek no more or it'll kill me. It'll kill me Jonty.'

Just then Jock and Fraser returned from the pub, barging into the room with Jock shouting, 'That lot are a load of shits!'

They stopped before Fraser asked, 'Where is everyone?'

'Gone visiting,' Bill answered as Jonty jumped up, pushing over his chair and rushed off into the bedroom.

'What's wrong wi him?' Jock asked.

Bill sat there deciding how much to say to these two.

Jock dragging off his sodden coat went over to inspect the contents of the pans on the stove. Fraser hung his coat on the nail at the back of the door and then seated himself at the table and took up the Craven Herald.

'I was telling Jonty I was thinking of packing up here,' Bill finally told them.

Jock gave Fraser a quick look.

'No wonder he was upset then.'

‘Ay, I suppose so,’ said Bill emptily.

‘And what’s brought this on?’ the Scotsman asked as he came to join them at the table.

‘I suppose it’s nowt to do wi you but seeing as you’re asking it’s just time, that’s all.’

‘You’d leave Ribblehead?’ Fraser asked as he set down the paper.

‘I’m going down south to stay wi me sister and I’m teking Jonty wi me. She lives outside Winchester wi her husband, a wheelwright, and they have a crippled daughter Elsie. She’s allays said that’s what I should do when I stopped working.’

‘Bill Asquith giving up work!’ Jock exclaimed, ‘I don’t fucking believe it. You’ll never stop.’

‘That’s the way it’s going to be.’

‘Never, not you Asquith.’

‘I’m trying to get Jonty to understand what I’m planning.’

‘He wouldn’t stand a chance without you,’ said Fraser.

‘Don’t I know that? It’s why I’m teking him wi me. Whatever happens I’m not leaving him here wi you buggers. Jonty is coming wi me even if I have to bloody well drag him the whole way to me sister’s. I’ve allays known that. I promised mesell long ago that I’d allays look after the lad and I will, I bloody well will.’

‘And what’s your sister going to think about that?’ Jock asked.

‘She’ll be fine wi it will our Betty and Jonty can allays get hisell some work down there.’

‘Not wiout you holding his hand he can’t.’

‘Anyroads,’ Bill sighed, ‘that’s what’s going to be happening. I just have to get me lad here to know what’s what. Not that it in the end it’ll mek any difference. He’s coming and that’s final.’

Fraser shook his head and glanced at Jock again who was staring at Bill with his beer moistened eyes. The Scotsman undid his scarf and hung it on the back of the chair, his moustache glistening with raindrops as he passed his tongue over his lips and then belched. His breath stank of beer and cigarette smoke, ‘You’re fucked wi that one old man just like you’re trying to fuck us and why is that? Why are you trying to fuck me and Fraser here? What’s it about Asquith? You do us and then bugger off. Is that the idea? But we know you see, we fucking know what you’ve been doing, asking around, digging about like a fucking mole, no, like a bastard shit stirrer cos that’s what you are.’

Bill half rose out of the chair in anger when Fraser held his shoulder, ‘Don’t listen to him Bill. You know Jock, a few beers and he mouths off a load of nonsense.’

‘I’m doing nothing.’

‘Oh of course you aren’t.’

‘Nothing, do you hear you fucking bent bastard?’ Bill shouted back.

'He hears you Bill, he hears. Don't you Jock? You hear what Bill's saying?'

'Jonty, get theesell to bed,' Bill ordered when he noticed Jonty sheepishly stood in the bedroom doorway.

Jonty was in his long johns, his bulging eyes shifting around the room.

'To bed lad,' Bill repeated.

'Bill....Bill alright?' Jonty asked in a stuttering voice.

'Ay lad I'm alright. You just get theesell to bed and we'll talk later on, alright Jonty?'

'Me go to bed?'

'That's it.'

The three of them watched as he turned back into the bedroom with his head lowered and his arms held stiffly by his side.

There was a tense silence for a few moments, the rain rattling against the hut's small windows. Jock kept staring at Bill while Fraser was beginning to look uncomfortable.

'You've been talking to Murdo Dorks,' Jock started in a quieter voice, 'You've been asking Sean Johnson a lot of questions. You've been bothering Simon Trotter and the list goes on. We know cos they've all come to tell us that old Bill Asquith has been trying to find out as much as he can about what we've done in the past. If you suspect someat why the fuck don't you just come out and say to our faces instead of scratting around for information or stories cos wi the likes of you it don't fucking matter which, does it?'

'Just what are you going on about?' Bill asked calmly.

'So all these men are talking rubbish, is that the idea?'

'I don't know what the hell they're saying and I don't care.'

'Trouble is we do, me and Fraser do care cos this is about us. You think you've got someat on us both and we'd like you to tell us what that is.'

Fraser lit a cigarette while Jock rubbed his dirty fingers together. There was the intermittent sound of water dripping off the washing that was gradually soaking the floor. Bill looked straight ahead, his breaths coming firm and steady. In his waistcoat with his shirt sleeves rolled up, his long grey hair was sheened by the light from the lamp hanging above the table.

'I couldn't care less about you two,' he finally said, now staring straight at Jock.

'I wish.....I wish that were true Asquith,' answered Jock in his broadest accent.

Fraser with his pale face and pale eyes slowly shook his head as he exhaled smoke in Bill's direction.

'You want us rolled over by the constabulary,' he told him.

'And why the hell would I want to do that?'

'That's what we want to find out. That's what this is all about. Come on Bill, you're acting fucking stupid when we know you aren't. You know exactly what's happening here and you also know that we won't give up until you tell us why you've been going around the settlements asking questions about me and Jock.'

'Or what? Or you'll do what?' Bill asked strongly.

'You know that as well,' Jock intervened.

'Piss water, that's all you two can manage so bugger off and leave me alone. I'm going to see how Jonty is,' he added as he stood up.

'No,' Jock told him.

'No what?'

'You stay here.'

'Here,' repeated Fraser.

'I'm going to……'

'Just sit down old man.'

'I damned well won't,' said Bill.

'So you can tell us what you've been doing or we can play the guessing game, so sit down or we'll fucking go in and see how Jonty is, but I don't think he'd like it.'

'You don't go bloody near him!' Bill exclaimed.

'Well sit down then so we won't have to disturb him. He's probably having another pull at hisell cos that's what the poor sod will be doing. Christ you can't get a night's sleep with the noise of that simpleton working away at it. Thought you would have taught the dirty bugger to control himself Asquith by now. Haven't you told him it's a sin?'

Bill sat back down, his face stiff with anger, his eyes opened wide as he rested his thick tattooed arms on the table and tried to steady himself.

Again there was nothing said for a time, each silence creating added pressure.

'There's just rumours, this place is full of em,' Bill finally mentioned.

'Rumours about what?' asked Jock.

'You.'

'What about me?'

'That you've killed a man, that you're a murderer.'

'I've killed a man?'

'Yes.'

'Says who?'

'It's.....it's just what some people are saying.'

'Just saying are they?'

'Yes they are.'

'And me?' Fraser put in.

Bill glanced at him uncertainly.

'Go on, what about me?'

'If I ever thought you'd.....'

'I'd what?'

'You'd ever touched either Clare or Beth I'd fucking stick your balls down your throat so help me God. I would do that if it was the last thing I ever did.'

'Steady old man,' Jock said, 'Steady.'

'So that's me is it?' asked Fraser, 'That's what I'm supposed to have done, is it?'

'That's the.....'

'Rumour?'

'Yes.'

'And you believe these stories?'

'Don't see why I shouldn't, and I'm not the only one.'

'Oh of course you aren't Bill. How could we fucking suggest such a thing, that it was just you stirring all this shit up by yourself?' asked Jock in an exaggeratedly sarcastic tone of voice.

'I don't start rumours,' Bill announced, 'I'm not one who goes mouthing off all over the place.'

'And yet you're running around wi your arse on fire trying to get as much out of every man who's ever worked wi us as you can.'

'The past is the past and it don't go away. I know that much.'

'And where's the evidence for all this damned nonsense?'

Bill glanced at Fraser, hating him more than ever and said, 'This ain't a court. This is what folk think.'

'You bastard,' Jock muttered just as Clare and Beth rushed breathlessly into the room followed by their mother.

'Uncle Bill!' Beth exclaimed, 'We've been eating toffee, proper toffee.'

'Oh you have, have you?' asked Bill, forcing himself to sound interested.

'It's stuck to me teeth,' complained Clare as she went for a mug of water.

'Is Jonty in bed?' Maggie asked.

'Ay, went a while ago.'

'And you two have been drinking. I can smell it from here,' she added as she looked challengingly at Fraser and then Jock.

'Just a few pints missus, nowt special.'

'Anyway, it's late and you madams should be in bed.'

The girls pulled faces.

'Come on. You've no need to bother wi a wash tonight,' Maggie said as she chivvied them into the bedroom.

'Just remember,' Jock said menacingly to Bill, 'Any fucking more of your nonsense and you'll be fucking nailed.'

'Bugger off,' Bill muttered before he got up, crossed the room taking deliberately slow steps into his bedroom.

CHAPTER THIRTY THREE

'Beth, Beth, slow down. Tell me what happened.'

'She heard........'

'No Clare,' said Lucy, 'Let her tell her own story.'

'But it was Sally Middleton.'

'No Clare,' she had to say more strongly.

School had just ended with a terrible fight outside. Beth's nose was dribbling blood and Clare had scratches down her left cheek. Their clothes were plastered in mud and one of Beth's boots had its sole flapping loose.

'Sarah Fanshaw started it, said our Clare was a prossie who slept wi our lodgers and then Sally Middleton called her more names so I hit her and she hit me back and then Sarah Fanshaw grabbed me hair and then our Clare saw us and kem over to pull em off and another of the girls started on her and they were all scratching and biting until you kem out Miss and they ran off!'

It was described all in one breath, her little chest heaving up and down. Lucy then tilted Beth's head back to try and staunch the flow of blood.

'They're all bitches so they are, all of em,'Clare muttered.

'That'll do Clare Granger.'

'They started it Miss.'

'So you've said.'

'Sally Middleton hates our Clare,' put in Beth still with her head held back, her voice sounding strangely nasal.

'And I.....I don't.....don't wi the lodgers. I don't Miss......'

'Right,' said Lucy, 'Let's look at you.'

She dabbed at her scratched face with a damp cloth before looking at Clare's left hand that was swollen and bruised.

'Called her a mucky slut Miss.'

'Yes, you've told me that already. You know I don't allow such language in or out of school.'

'No Miss.'

'It's disgusting talking like that.'

'Yes Miss.'

'I'm going to fucking do that Sarah Fanshaw and Sally Middleton,' Clare said later on their way down the mudded path to the huts.

'Me too,' agreed Beth whose nose had finally stopped bleeding even though it was splattered all over her pinafore dress.

Clare licked her lips and then tightened them, 'You stuck up for us.'

'Suppose I did.'

'You went fighting cos of me.'

'I've done that before,' Beth confirmed.

'I know, but not like this, not serious like this.'

'Any roads, I hope Miss Lucy gives em a right thrashing tomorrow.'

‘You know she won’t. She don’t believe in using the cane.’

‘Well she should. She should have Sarah Fanshaw and Sally Middleton wi their knickers down screaming wi pain in front of the whole class.’

They set off again looking warily about for groups of children who might be ready to ambush them, but there was nobody around except for a line of men on their way up to Blea Moor tunnel, their shovels and pick axes slung over their shoulders as they trudged up the slippery path.

‘Why do all the men have such stupid nick names?’ asked Beth as she watched the men go by, ‘What about me Dad? What do they call him?’

Clare shrugged her bony shoulders and then remembered, ‘Midland Eddie.’

‘Why’s that?’

‘Cos like us he’s from the Midlands, where we were born.’

‘So I’m a middle as well and you are.’

‘If you want to be.’

‘I don’t think I do.’

‘Better than bloody south or north.’

‘Suppose so.’

‘I don’t want to go home just yet,’ Beth announced as they came to the end of their line of huts, ‘We’re just going to be in trouble wi me Mam.’

‘Neither do I, we’ll go down to the beck.’

Beth looked at her sister so tall and thin with her black hair tied tight in a bunch. She was one of the tallest in the class. Beth thought she was the prettiest. She was proud of her sister’s looks and wished her own face was as lovely. Instead hers was a round pudding sort of shape with ears that stuck out too far and a nose that bent down at the end as though someone really had smashed it hard with their fists just like Sally Middleton had tried to do. She knew that Clare had been bothered by something for weeks now. She seemed always moody with her except for today when she had saved her from a worse beating. Often whatever she did now Clare would be angry with her. She wanted to ask her what was wrong but was not sure how to say the right words, but she knew something was niggling at her.

‘You alright?’ Clare asked her.

‘Me nose hurts.’

‘So does my bloody hand. I wished I’d have knocked that fucking Middleton into smithereens.’

They reached the Gill, the pool where the women did their washing. By this time in the afternoon the day’s clothes were finished and hung out on hundreds of lines around the settlements.

Beth crouched down and scooped up some of the water to wash her face.

'The sheep have shit and pissed in there.'

'Don't care.'

'You will if you get poorly.'

They watched two carts cross the bridge as a group of children appeared over the other side of the stream.

'Bugger off Grangers!' one of the boys shouted.

'No, leave em alone!' another responded.

'Clare Granger is a bully. She's a shit!'

'She beat em all today.'

'What, them babies?'

'Fight them your own age you smelly shit!'

They shouted more abuse for a time but when neither of the girls responded they carried on further along the stream bank where it flowed under the stone bridge and down the Dale.

'Why's it allay us?' moaned Beth as she threw a stone into the brown, peaty water.

'It ain't. Just feels like it today. Tomorrow they'll start on someone else. Today it's been our turn, that's all.'

Beth thought about this, pulling a face as she did so. Clare sometimes wanted to just hug her for a long time. Her sister was short and strong looking but she knew that Beth got upset easily. She was her responsibility. Beth's face was all pink now with the blood's deeper red dried under her nostrils and her brown hair cut short as her mother liked. The sole was still flapping off the front of her boot and her woollen stockings were wrinkled round her ankles.

'What about when me Mam hears about the fight?' Beth suddenly asked with tears welling up.

'She'll probably have heard already.'

'Oh no,' Beth muttered.

They turned from the stream and headed up onto the moors. From there they could see the line of men working on the far side of the viaduct and the steam cranes lifting huge pieces of stone up onto one of the high pillars. Children were running around the settlement, some with metal hoops, others with skipping ropes tied round their waists. On a flat bit of grass near the brick factory the daily football game was under way. They could hear the noise of the tramway trains, the distant shouts of the football players and the vague clunking of shovels where the cutting was being finished.

Down in a dip was a small stone hut that was half demolished, its short roof beams sticking from under the slates and the front wall broken down. It was a place to which the girls often came. It was their secret place that they imagined nobody else knew about. A strong, high sun was shining down as they clambered over the rubble into the broken down hut. Its floor was covered in sheep droppings and wool was straggling down off broken pieces of wood. Clare crouched down against the back wall while Beth sat herself on one of the fallen beams.

'Mind yer don't get splinters in yer arse,' her sister laughed.

Beth made no reply. She pushed her finger through a spider's web that was glistening in the sunlight and then started rocking her head from side to side. Clare suddenly looked serious and worried, her face pulled tight and even paler than usual.

'Fraser…….' she started.

'I like Fraser,' Beth said.

'I know you do.'

'He's good to us he is.'

'Yes.'

'And uncle Bill.'

'About Fraser,' Clare tried again.

Beth sensed a sudden serious mood, 'What about him?'

'Has…..has he ever……?'

'Ever what?'

'Asked yer……asked yer to do someat you didn't….didn't want to do?'

'What do you mean?'

'Has he touched yer….touched you….you know…..down there…….?'

Beth shook her head furiously, asking, 'What are you saying that for?'

'I'm just wondering, that's all.'

'About Fraser?'

'You haven't answered my question.'

Beth gave out a long sigh and squeezed her nose before picking out some of the dried blood.

'He……he might have done.'

'Beth!' Clare exclaimed, 'You tell me.'

'Don't want to.'

'Tell me Beth or I'll never speak to you again. I'm eleven and you're just six so tell me.'

'It weren't anything.'

'What wasn't?'

'I....I was just itchy......itchy....you know......down there and Fraser said he'd rub it for me, that's all.'

'And did he?'

'Just a bit.'

'A bit?'

'Not much. It wasn't owt really.'

'He touched you there?'

'Yes, but I didn't mind. I didn't Clare,' Beth almost pleaded.

'And what about asking you to.....'

'I don't want to hear any more!' she shouted, 'Just leave us alone!'

'Because he has with me.'

Beth looked straight at her, 'What has he done?'

'Touched me.'

'On your bibby?'

'Yes.'

'And you let him?'

'Yes?'

'Why?'

'Because I was.....was scared I suppose and didn't know what else to do.....I didn't want to say no to him cos he's been so kind to us.'

'I don't know,' Beth said miserably, anxiously.

'It was alright. He didn't hurt me or anything.'

'How....how can it have been alright?'

'I just mean he was.....was gentle like.'

'I want to go back now.'

'He's a man Beth. They.....they do things like that.'

'Well it's horrible.'

'I suppose so,' said Clare.

They were silent then. Beth had tears in her eyes as she picked up a shard of wood and threw it over the front wall. Clare did not move, staring down at the ground her breaths coming fast. Then she lifted her swollen fist and put it against her mouth as though to ease the pain. More calls came from down in the settlement as a flock of crows flickered across the shafts of the sun. The stone of the hut was warm and the place stank of the sheep droppings.

'Don't you ever tell anyone,' Clare finally said.

Beth made no response, just wiped her eyes.

'Did you hear me Beth? No one. This is between just us forever, forever and forever, understand? You understand what I'm saying?'

'Just leave me alone!' Beth exclaimed, 'I don't believe you!'

'Why should I mek up someat like that?'

'Don't know?'

'Well I'm not making anything up. I'm not lying and I know he'll want to do it again. He teks me them special journeys on the tramway and says you're too young cos he wants to be just wi me.'

'Shut up!'

'I'm not telling lies Beth.'

'He's kind to us, as kind as anyone.'

'Yes he is. He says it has to be our secret, says we have to tell no one.'

'I'm not listening anymore.'

'And if anything else happens you tell me. You must tell me, do you hear?'

'No I don't hear owt. I'm going.'

Beth started climbing over the pile of stones when Clare grabbed her by the arm and spun her round, 'You tell no one, no one,' she stated in a low, insistent voice, 'do you hear me?'

'Alright, alright,' Beth muttered.

'Promise.'

'I promise.'

'On our Mam's grave.'

'On our Mam's grave.'

'So help you God.'

'So help me God.'

And then Beth pulled away, clambered out of the hut and started running down the moor side.

CHAPTER THIRTY FOUR

It was the beginning of June and Richard had already had a busy week. Here he was in the lounge of the Golden Lion hotel with Mr Armsworth and Mr Friar two of the company's directors most interested in the railway line. On Monday he had attended a lecture in the missionary hall, on the Tuesday he had taken the train from Ingleton to Carlisle to see about extra supplies for the works. Seven of the directors had come to visit the Ribblehead site on the Wednesday and Armsworth and Friar had stayed over in Settle so they could discuss things further. So on this dull Thursday morning, drinking his coffee, Richard reflected on a successful visit.

Adam Friar was a short, stout, robust looking man with huge side whiskers and thin brown hair that was swept from one side of his large head to the other. It was rumoured his family had made its money out of sugar cane from the West Indies. He wore a thick golden watch chain across his highly decorated waistcoat and several gold rings on his stubby fingers.

'I'm afraid,' he was saying in his London accent, such a contrast to the broad northern tone of most of the other directors, 'that Josiah Forbes is going under. The man has bitten off more than he can chew and he's having to face facts.'

'Yes,' put in Armsworth, 'Josiah I'm afraid has got his sums wrong.'

'He's damned well struggling.'

'So what would it mean if he went under?' Richard asked, 'Josiah being the main contractor?'

The two directors looked unsure until Friar said, 'I should think the company would have to take over the contract, the position we are in this year, don't you think Elijah?'

Armsworth agreed, 'It might be complicated but I can't see any alternative at the moment.'

Richard felt a dull ache begin in his stomach. Even though he was not surprised this was the last piece of news he wanted. Without Forbes' ready financial support the whole project might be slowed down by months, even years.

'I wouldn't like to see cut backs, not now,' he remarked, his voice as steady as he could make it.

'Nay Richard, you've no need to be thinking in those terms, not at all,' said Armsworth.

'Of course not,' agreed Friar, 'Of course not. We want this new line opened on time and we know that depends on your section. The rest have not the same challenges and they'll be waiting for the Ribblehead work to be completed.'

'That's the pressure gentlemen.'

'Nobody on the board expects your section to go at the same pace, not with the viaduct and the tunnel, not at all Richard. You just do your job and keep things progressing as they have been recently and everything should work out. It's unfortunate that we might be losing our main contractor for the section but that doesn't mean great changes are afoot. They can't be. It's as simple as that. We're too far down the line if you don't mind the pun to stop now.'

Friar sipped at his coffee glancing at the other two over the rim of his cup. Armsworth looked at Richard and smiled before saying, 'You've got enough on your plate. You just leave the financial side of things to us and our accountants. If things go wrong we'll blame them.'

There was a pause. The lounge was busy, Settle being full of summer visitors as well as farmers in town for their weekly supplies. Many were crowded into the Golden Lion filling the place with loud voices and the bustle of maids and waiters serving. Dust floated in the sunlight coming through the lounge windows that looked out onto the main street. Here there was a steady flow of horses and carts and two shepherds with their dogs guiding a large flock of sheep along the road.

'So I hear there was another lecture up at Batty Green,' Adam Friar mentioned, 'It's becoming a right academic centre is the place. I'm all in favour.'

'Yes. That's another thing we discussed yesterday but I want to expand on a little this morning if you don't mind,' said Richard, glad of this opportunity.

'So what was the lecture about?'

'It was a Mr Framish talking about the history of lead mining in the Dales.'

'And was it interesting?'

'Well I thought it was. I'm not sure what the rest of them thought.'

'So what did you want to expand on?' Armsworth asked.

'Just that I think we need to create a larger hall, a meeting hall or whatever it would be called if it was bigger. Once or twice dances have been tried in the hall we have at the moment but it's just too small. Even on Monday the place was packed to overflowing. There's a real need for learning, for entertainment, good, appropriate entertainment and this necessitates a bigger hall.'

The directors paused in thought before Armsworth said, 'Don't see why not Richard as long as it's at a reasonable cost.'

'All it would take would be four huts put together without two of the supporting walls.'

'And that could be done?'

'According to our carpenter and Thwaite the builder they don't see why not.'

'So it's already been discussed?' asked Friar.

'I've talked to them, yes. I hope that's alright. I didn't mean to be presumptuous.'

'I suppose it's alright,' Armsworth responded.

'You think I should have discussed it with you first?'

'Anyway it doesn't matter who you've spoke to about it, you're mentioning it now. That's what matters and I think it's a good idea, a very good idea so long as it won't cost a fortune and it shouldn't. What do you think Adam?'

Friar smiled, his reddened face pushed out at the cheeks, 'You know me Elijah. I'm one of the more liberal directors shall we say. In fact Richard I think you've picked us two on purpose.'

'Not at all,' he answered smiling.

'Well we agree with the proposal and I don't see why it has to be taken any further even though I suppose it should be discussed with the rest of the board. I think the quicker you get started the better so long as we get an invitation to its opening event whenever that'll be.'

'Good, I'm pleased.'

'And that's what we want, our site manager pleased, isn't it Elijah?'

Armsworth agreed before catching the eye of one of the busy waitresses to ask for another pot of coffee.

It was the following Sunday when Richard told Lucy about his meeting with the two directors.

'They just agreed, just like that with no real discussion.'

'Well that's good Richard, well done.'

'I couldn't believe how amenable they were.'

'But you've always said that Mr Armsworth supports you.'

'Yes he does and now he seems to have got Friar on board as well. I don't think any of the other directors are that concerned with the welfare of the men. That's the trouble with this country. The majority of the people have been taken for granted and left behind. Britain cannot compete without an educated workforce. It's as simple as that but seems to have taken some people a long time to realise it.'

Lucy looked at him with a different expression, 'You sound....sound....'

'What?'

'Well, you sound very convinced and convincing Richard.'

'Do I?'

'Quite eloquent in fact.'

'Is that so unusual?'

'I don't mean it that way. You're being too sensitive.'

He stopped the rig up on the top moors near where the Dent road forked off from the main route from Ingleton. The June sky was without a cloud. For once there was not even a breeze. It was such a warm and still afternoon. Regularly they were passed by other carts and people from the settlements out for their Sunday walk. Except for haymaking the Dales were now at their busiest. Richard was hoping for a little more privacy but had to accept that it being such a fine day there would be nowhere in the area where there were not folk about. Inevitably they would be noticed and comments made.

'But what a boring lecture on lead mining it was on Monday. I was bored stiff,' Lucy laughed, 'and so was everybody else.'

'Well I wasn't,' said Richard, surprised by her tone.

'You must have been the only one who wasn't.'

'At least it gave us the opportunity to meet Andrew Murray's lady friend.'

'Elizabeth Sellars, yes, interesting,' Lucy remarked.

'Andrew has mentioned her a few times recently.'

'And who is she exactly?'

'The daughter of a big landowner Malham way. He met her at a young farmers' dance.'

'One of those mad affairs they hold in barns?'

'That's the idea.'

'Andrew Murray dancing in a barn.'

'Seems to have brought him a piece of luck.'

'And is it serious?'

'Don't ask me. I'm afraid Andrew and I are no longer as close as we used to be. He has or had a fiancée down in Shropshire, I know that much. I've no real idea why things have turned out the way they have. It seems to have happened over the last year or so. I suppose it's because we disagree on certain fundamentals. Andrew has no time for universal education. He thinks it's either a waste of time or even dangerous by raising the workers' expectations. Andrew imagines riots and revolution are waiting just below the surface. I think he is wrong, sadly wrong, but there are still a lot who think like him. He is what I would call an extreme Tory. I'm sure he must have read Carlyle at some point and has been heavily influenced by him.'

'What he would like is a return to the middle ages?'

'Something like that,' answered Richard, laughing.

'Carlyle is dreadful. How can anyone believe in his nonsense?'

'So he won't be taught in your classroom,' he joked.

'Never!' Lucy happily exclaimed, feeling this was by far the most relaxed and interesting conversation they had shared so far. No longer did it feel that Richard was trying to impress. He was saying what he actually felt. Their friendship had lasted for months now and gradually she was beginning to understand who this Richard Stockton was.

He started the rig towards Dent. Richard had booked them a dinner at the Sun Inn. Now the evenings were lighter there was less pressure to return to Ribblehead early.

'I wish, just wish for once it was all plain sailing, but I suppose that's impossible,' Richard said after a few moments' silence while they both had taken in the wide open, barren scenery around them where the brown, hazy moors stretched to the horizon in all directions.

'Why, what's wrong?' Lucy asked, curious that he was now willing to share his worries about work.

'Oh it's just some of the men are being stirred up about the accidents in the tunnel. They're unfortunate but they don't happen that often. It's just that in the last three weeks there have been several explosions and men being injured. Thankfully no one has been killed but the men are angry and some of their leaders are making things worse. I have to accept the situation and yet at the same time it makes my job so much more difficult. If I think the men should be given more responsibility, more involvement in their jobs then I have to accept that they might want to push things in a direction that certainly does not suit. And what's happening at the moment does not suit, not at all.'

'So what can you do?'

'I Just hope we don't have any more accidents in the tunnel and that the men see that getting angry and all stirred up, threatening to down tools and all that nonsense does not help the situation. It only makes it worse because if work comes to a halt in the tunnel everyone suffers. In the end we will have to try and catch up and inevitably corners will be cut and that means more accidents are likely. It's a trap and at the moment I can't see any way out.'

'Poor Richard,' she said vaguely.

'Poor everybody.'

'But the men are still working.'

'So far, but if Tom Myres has anything to do with it that won't be for long.'

'You really don't like him, do you?'

'He's a navvy, one of thousands. He's nobody in particular,' Richard said strongly.

'And yet you often mention him.'

'That's because he's always on the lookout for the first sign of dissatisfaction. He's a parasite living off the troubles of others, that's who Tom Myres is and yes I do resent him for it.'

Lucy knew not to prolong this line of conversation.

'What's that over there?' she asked then at a plume of smoke rising in the distance.

'It may be the farmers burning back the heather. They do it regularly to give new shoots a chance to grow, the ones the sheep like the best. The problem is that the farmers start the fire and then have all sorts of trouble putting it out. Last year we nearly had half of Whernside going up in smoke, so much of it you could not see the mountain at all.'

To Lucy the smoke looked like some ominous message being sent from one area of the Dales to another. She had read somewhere that this is what some of the native Americans did and yet found it hard to imagine a group of feathered savages seated on their war horses in the middle of the north Yorkshire moors.

She wanted their talking to stop for a while so she could just absorb the atmosphere. It was one of her favourite experiences, here up on the high moorland with only the call of a skylark overhead.

For these moments she wanted to forget herself and just breathe in the warm summer air and listen to the sound of the chattering bird that was following them high in the clear sky. She felt the tension ease away with each breath. Happiness existed only when you could forget everything and just be within each moment.

'Are you alright Lucy?' he asked.

She wanted to answer that she was not there, that her mind had left her body and was only aware of this tiny segment of time.

'Yes,' she had to answer, 'I'm fine. It's so lovely up here.'

'You must be hungry by now, we've been out for hours.'

'Have we? I hadn't noticed. It's such a beautiful day time doesn't seem to matter very much.'

'But my stomach does,' he joked.

In the Sun Inn the tiny dining room was full except for their table by the small front window. Richard ordered a bottle of claret. Lucy wanted only a piece of chicken lightly cooked with some bread and butter whereas Richard decided on the largest steak they had with potatoes and vegetables and a custard pie to finish with.

'That should do,' he said warmly after he had ordered.

'Do you know anyone here?' Lucy asked as she quickly looked around.

Richard glanced about and then answered that he did not.

'But this is where all those rebels came from for the Pilgrimage of Grace you told me about?'

'You remembered.'

'Don't sound so surprised.'

'No, it's just that I only mentioned it once and that was some time ago.'

'It surprised me that such a small place as Dent could produce so many rebels.'

'And its surrounding area. They came from all around here.'

'Yes,' she said while watching the waiter serve another couple.

As they started eating Lucy said, 'I had a visit on Tuesday from James Tranton.'

'And what did he want?'

'What a strange and intense man. It was quite extraordinary. For a start he came when the children were in the classroom and I had to tell him that his visit at the time was not suitable so he came back at the end of the day. He's persistent, I'll give him that. He wanted to know what parts of the Bible I taught. I told him about the government's guidelines but Mr Tranton had to argue. The man was incorrigible. He just would not give up, going on about how the children of his congregation were not being given a proper religious education.'

'Yes, he's like that, thinks the settlements should all be Methodist by now. I've had a few run ins myself. It's the arrogance of the man that gets me.'

'All I can say is that I'm glad I'm not one of his congregation.'

Richard laughed and then added, 'Well in a few weeks' time, after the school holiday I should think you'll have fewer pupils to teach anything.'

Lucy frowned, not understanding, 'Why should that be?'

'Well, a lot of the men will decide to leave the works and go and help with the haymaking on the farms around here. It happened last year. I could not believe it and then they all traipsed back and expected their jobs to be waiting for them and because there were so many who had gone off taking their wives and children with them to help with the work we had to just accept the situation.'

'So did they all get their jobs back?'

'According to them they had never given them up in the first place, just taken a summer holiday, unbelievable!' Richard exclaimed.

'And when does this happen?'

'August time usually.'

'When the children have just started school again.'

'Just like I say, be prepared for an empty classroom.'

After the meal Richard had a brandy with his coffee while Lucy preferred a pot of tea. She felt strangely sad that all this effort on both their parts would come to nothing in the end. It was easy and interesting but completely lacked the intensity she sought. Richard Stockton was not that kind of man and it was a pity, a deeply felt pity for the two of them that their relationship could never progress any further. She knew he loved her. He recently had made it so obvious and she had had enough experience of men to tell when they had reached the point where only one thing mattered and that was being his wife. He would never begin to understand that she wanted to be no one's wife. She wanted her own independence more than anything and yet would never say this to him until he forced her to do so, until he actually proposed.

Driving back in the rig the sun was still high above the horizon. The road was quieter now. The food and the drink seemed to have quietened Richard. She leant slightly against him as he chivvied the horse along. Now the evening had come she could smell the moors, the soil and the new heather. There was the chuckle of pheasants hidden away and the softest sound of a breeze wafting the air around them. Today was the Dales at their best. They could be barren and isolated but today they offered something completely different. For once they felt connected to the rest of the country and more on a human scale, more gentle. She was warm and tired and content so long as she just absorbed the atmosphere and thought about nothing else. Only the present existed. Only she existed. It was a pity that the man beside her was less than that.

They joined the Ingleton road and it was as they turned the next corner to start down the long slope to Batty Green and the other settlements that they could see the crowd of people on this side of the beck.

'What....what are they doing?' Lucy asked, roused from her thoughts.

Richard pursed his lips before saying, 'I have no idea.'

He slowed the rig as they approached the crowd gathered a short distance from the road. It consisted mostly of men with a few women and several children running around. Richard recognised most of them, his workers in their Sunday best clothes listening to Tom Myres standing on an outcrop of rock with a group of his companions close behind him.

'We wait. We always wait,' Myres was shouting to be heard by all of them, 'For Mr Stockton and the bosses to do someat about it. Yes Mr Stockton, this is about you!' he called over the heads of the crowd when he noticed the rig stopped on the road, 'You and them directors in Leeds who have no idea what's happening here. First we have men killed on the viaduct and now we're having one accident after another in Blea Moor tunnel, an arm lost here or an eye or scarred for life. And what's being done about it? What the hell are you doing Mr Stockton to ensure our men are not in constant danger? Come on! Come on up here and tell these people what you're going to do about it because they've had enough, enough! Do you hear Mr Stockton? So come and tell us. We're waiting. That's right, just bugger off!' Tom called as Richard hurriedly set the rig in motion, 'Just say nowt as usual, tek the coward's way out! Are you listening Mr Stockton? Are you? Well all I can say is you better had be. You better had be because these folk here have had enough!'

'Not so fast Richard!' Lucy exclaimed as he forced the horse to speed up.

Neither of them spoke until he stopped the rig at the foot of the track up to the Johnstons farm.

'I'll leave you here if you don't mind. I've a lot of work to do,' he said curtly.

'Richard, are you alright?' she asked, turning to him.

'Fine,' he answered in a false voice, anger in his face that she recognised straightaway.

'No you're not. I can tell. I thought you…….'

'Lucy, I have to get on, I'm sorry. I have a great deal of work that has to be done.'

At that he came over to her side of the rig to assist her down and then went to open the gate for her. Without another word she watched him drive off.

In his office he threw off his hat and jacket and was about to lift the table and toss it across the room when Andrew Murray and his new friend Elizabeth Sellars entered.

'Richard, didn't expect you to be here,' Murray said, a little flustered, 'I've just been showing Elizabeth around.'

'Hello Elizabeth and what do you think?' Richard forced himself to say, his voice straining with the effort.

'There's so much happening here, so much and I don't know how you sleep at night you two with so much on,' said Elizabeth happily.

She was tall and slender, her hair so fair it was almost white. She had a small mouth, a shapely body and was wearing a bright, pink summer dress. At any other time he would have found her attractive.

'Well he sleeps alright,' Richard said abstractedly.

Andrew laughed, 'And how would you know? You're always the first to go to sleep.'

'Never, not me.'

'And are these some of your plans?' asked Elizabeth as she scrutinised the diagrams on the table.

'Here,' Andrew said, 'this is the overall plan where our southern section starts and this is where it ends at Blea Moor.'

She leant closer and looked carefully, mesmerised by all the fine detail on the map.

Richard was trying to slow his breathing. He had to get out, his anger so strong he just had to get out of the hut.

'I'll leave you to it,' he said.

'Oh no, don't go because of me,' Elizabeth responded.'

'I have to go down to the carpenters and then on to the brick factory.'

'Surely people aren't working on a Sunday evening?'

'No, but unfortunately I am,' Richard said before he took her hand for a moment, nodded to Andrew and stepped out of the hut, his anger and resentment burning up inside him.

CHAPTER THIRTY FIVE

On the same evening Maggie was sitting outside their hut in the low summer sun mending one of Ethan's work shirts. Other women were also out chatting on their front steps with children running around them. From the direction of the shops and offices came the sound of fiddles and a drum. The shafts of the sun ran straight along the row of huts and Maggie was turned sideways to avoid its glare. Calls and shouts came from the children and mothers chiding them with dogs barking and sheep bleating in the distance. It was Sunday evening in Batty Green, the one day when the work stopped and all the noise from the viaduct, tunnel, cuttings and embankments was quietened. Instead there was music. Maggie smiled to herself at its fast, rhythmic sounds that reminded her of when she and Ethan were courting and went to the local dances in Nottingham. She could remember the fast, regular banging of clogs and boots on wooden floors. It was exhilarating, exciting and something that was at the centre of her memories. It seemed so long ago. Now she could not imagine herself or her husband ever dancing again. There had been a few dances recently at the mission hall but they had never gone.

She squinted at her sewing and considered again whether she needed glasses. Bill used them for reading. She had often wanted to ask him if she could try his out. Perhaps it was the angle of the sun that was making it hard for her to focus. There was little smoke coming from the chimneys of the huts now dinner was over and the stoves had been left to cool. There was always the stench of the privies and the smell of all the animals. It was like being on a big farm with hens, pigs, goats and sheep everywhere.

Maggie remembered happily when a few weeks ago Sally Middleton's mother came banging on their door after the fight between her Sally and Clare and Beth up at the school when Clare had come back with a scratched face and Beth a bleeding nose.

Annie Middleton had been as usual all red faced with her loud voice and big bosom there ready to continue the fight their daughters had begun.

'I've come to see what you're going to do about what happened this afternoon.'

'Why, what did happen?' Maggie had innocently asked making the woman even more furious.

'You know Maggie Granger what's been going on, your Clare picking on my Sally and leaving her wi hair tugged out and a tooth loose. I want you to give that girl of yours a good lathering.'

'I will if it's true what yer say,' Maggie said.

This had caught Annie Middleton by surprise.

'I want her punished.'

'And she will be.'

Again the woman did not know what to say next. Maggie had used this strategy before when parents came banging on the door looking for a row. She always agreed with whatever they said. They could not continue. Their attack immediately faltered leaving them uncertain as to what should follow. Usually they made a few more threats before leaving just as the Middleton woman had done.

'And I don't want no more, do you hear?'

'I do.'

'Right.'

'Yes.'

'I'm off.'

'Good day Mrs Middleton.'

Maggie had enjoyed their confrontation. That night she had bathed Clare's scratches and told her what had happened.

'You're not going to give me a lathering are you, when it weren't my fault?'

'Of course I'm not. You just mek sure next time you pull out more of that Sally Middleton's hair. She's as bad as her mother.'

Momentarily it warmed Maggie to remember, but then her mind shifted back to the usual worries. There was smallpox in the settlements. Like many diseases this one could kill so quickly. Five days ago she had heard of a child in Jericho who had contracted smallpox and ever since then she had been brooding on it, trying to decide whether to take Clare and Beth away from school and keep them with her at home like some families had already done.

She released a deep breath and set her sewing down on her lap. The Timson boy came hobbling along on his crutches and said hello as he went past. He had been born with his right leg deformed and could only walk with the help of crutches. A few minutes later he was followed by a group of girls in their Sunday dresses. They were laughing and giggling and trying to talk all at the same time, paying no attention to Maggie as they made their way down towards the music. Nancy Allbright three doors along waved before she went inside her newly whitewashed hut. Everything was fraught and fragile. The pressure of the work and the closeness of so many people living together gave Ribblehead all the problems of any other Northern town. The whole country was unsettled with a sense of change everywhere, a feeling of tension building and yet no one knew which way things would go. Ethan had explained to Maggie that the Reform Act had only unsettled people. The workers wanted to be heard and she was interested in such things. Ever since her husband had started talking more and more about politics lately Maggie had begun to think about what it all meant, about why so many people were angry and frustrated, but more than that it had made her wonder at Ethan's changes of mood.

She had never known him talk about somebody else so much, Tom this and Tom that. Myres had captured his attention and had given him a new lease of life. Now in the evenings instead of bed straight after dinner he would be off to meetings or reading one of the books Myres had given him.

Still sometimes there would be the sudden miserable moods where he hardly spoke but these happened less frequently. Something had captured his interest and once that happened everything with him was taken to an extreme as it always was. There were no half measures. Once Ethan was committed to something he would take it as far as he could.

'And where do women come into all this?' she had asked him one night when they were lying in bed, the only place where they could talk freely with each other.

'No difference,' he had answered, 'there should be no difference between women and men, none at all. We have to work to where the ordinary man and woman control their own lives and make the decisions that affect them. Like Tom says, you can't have liberty and equality together at the same time. It's impossible. Equality has to come first, always first. There is no freedom when one man has power over another.'

'Listen to you Ethan,' she had said.

'It's me Maggie. This is me. This is what I believe. It's not just words.'

'I know that. It's just all happened so quickly.'

'Not really. I've always felt mesell as a radical, it's just now I have the ideas, the words as well as the feelings.'

'Just tell me it won't mean trouble,' she had insisted.

'And how can I promise that when nobody knows what's going to happen?'

'I don't.....don't want things threatened, not what we have now, surely not now Ethan after all we've been through to reach a better life, especially for the girls. I've never seen them so happy, never. You wouldn't destroy what we have. Tell me.'

'You're more important than anything. That's what this is all about.'

'Not if these ideas of yours mean trouble.'

'If you want change then everything has to change.'

'Well I don't want it then,' she had said miserably.

'For God's sake Maggie, nothing is happening.'

'It will.'

'You don't know that and neither do I.'

'If that Tom Myres persuaded enough to go on strike what would you do?'

'What a stupid question.'

'What would you do?'

'Go on strike as well. What else could I do, just ignore what was going on, pretend it didn't exist?'

'And fight?'

'Yes, fight.'

At that she had turned away from him.

'It has to be like that,' he had said strongly, 'I have to believe what I'm saying, believe that I would do what was necessary otherwise there's no point.'

'You'd risk everything, even your own family after you've said many a time we were more important than anything else.'

'Why the hell have you got to always make everything so damned personal?'

'Because in the end that's all there is.'

'That's not true. What about everybody else? What about those in a damned sight worse state than us and there's a lot of em in this country.'

'And Clare and Beth?'

'They come first.'

'Not in your mind they don't.'

'It would be for them.'

'No it wouldn't. It would be for you Ethan.'

'Rubbish woman.'

'For you.'

'This isn't just........'

'You've no need to say anymore,' she had interrupted, 'I don't want to hear any more.'

It had been a miserable end to their talk. She had hardly slept that night imagining all the things that could happen if men like Tom Myres had their way.

Now she was sitting there in the bright sunlight feeling confused. Part of her was relieved at Ethan's new mood and yet at the same time felt it threatened all they had worked for. Ideas could destroy everything. She had never thought about anything so much as she had recently, thought about the consequences. And then she saw him come round the end of the row of huts with some of the other men. Their meeting must have finished and now they were all talking and arguing about it with raised voices, excited, involved voices.

'Where is everybody?' he asked when he approached.

'Clare's gone with Fraser to the music and Beth has gone for a walk with the Stantons.'

'I hear the music is just a ploy by the Independents.'

'Well that won't please our Clare.'

'Imagine her singing hymns or Fraser for that matter.'

'Might do em both good. So how was the meeting?' she thought she had better ask.

He laughed as he sat on the step beside her chair, 'It couldn't have been better cos Stockton came along with that Miss Ormskill from the school in his gig and he made the fatal mistake of stopping. Tom didn't half blast him. It was champion to hear him and there was Stockton as red faced and angry as could be before he was off as fast as he could go and that Miss Ormskill hanging on for dear life. It was one of them moments that just happen, pure chance, but it made the meeting. Stockton got the message alright. He couldn't avoid hearing it! Priceless Maggie! Absolutely priceless!'

'Look at yer, yer look like the cat that's found the cream.'

At that he was on his feet again pulling her off the chair and swinging her round in time to the distant fiddle music, swirling her round and round until she was dizzy and out of breath.

'Come on Mrs Granger!' he kept repeating, 'dance wi yer husband!'

'Give up yer daft happoth!'

A group of children further along the row were calling out and clapping.

'What an exhibition,' Maggie complained happily.

'Shocking,' agreed Ethan.

'Get yersell inside.'

'I will not. How thee doing Freddie?' he asked another worker walking past.

'Grand meeting,' he answered.

'That it was.'

Maggie smoothed down her Sunday dress, wiping her brow then before she said, 'Seems the meeting's gone down well wi em all.'

'The men are angry.'

She sat down with her sewing and he joined her and rolled himself a cigarette, its smoke drifting straight upwards. Now instead of the fiddle music and drum they could hear singing coming from down near the factory.

'Clare and Fraser must have stayed,' Maggie said, suddenly worried.

'Unless they've gone for a walk or someat. Fraser's allays showing her things to do wi nature. He's a right one for that.'

'He seems to know a lot, every flower and sorts of sheep. Don't know where he gets it all from.'

'Maybe meks it all up.'

'Ethan!' she retorted.

'Where's Jonty and the rest?'

'Oh Bill's gone off to see someone and Arnold Wainwright has teken Jonty to watch the football match.'

'Don't say Jonty's thinking o playing.'

'Not if Bill has owt to do wi it.'

'You're right there, can't see Bill letting that happen. So what the hell are they doing up there?'

'Bill said it would do Jonty good.'

'Bill, always Bill lately, and what's got into him? He's as miserable as sin. Never seen him so bad and every night he's out off somewhere or other dragging Jonty along wi him. Where does he go?'

'Don't ask me,' said Maggie.

It was good to sit with him like this. It rarely happened when there was just the two of them. It reminded her of the time before the girls were born. Then they had such a lot to say to each other and Ethan had introduced her to so much, some poetry and music and books that she had never heard of and they had gone to concerts and public lectures in Nottingham. It had been a different world then. The birth of the girls had changed everything.

'That wee lad died last night so I heard,' Ethan told her.

'The one wi smallpox? Oh God,' she sighed, 'God help his family.'

'Ay, last night,' he repeated.

Maggie's face and body stiffened.

'It ain't right,' she said then.

'Never is.'

'A young lad, so young.'

'Teks anyone.'

'So what should we do about the girls?'

He rested his pipe on his thigh and asked, 'What about em?'

'I think we should just keep em here and let em stay off school.'

'And what the hell difference would that mek?'

'I just thought it would be safer.'

'You know it don't work like that. Any disease like smallpox don't just stay in one place, school, home or wherever meks no difference.'

'Don't say that Ethan.'

'Well I am cos it's true.'

'You mek it sound as if whatever anyone does meks no difference.'

'And it doesn't.'

'I'm going inside.'

'Maggie, there's nowt we can do,' he said as he took her arm.

'Well whatever it is I just hope....'

'And that's all we can do, hope,' he interrupted as he released her arm and she went inside the hut.

Ethan continued smoking while he remembered the previous evening when at the end of work instead of going with the rest of the men down to the store huts he had continued along where the new line was to be laid. There were rules about who could be on this finished section of the viaduct but he was not bothered as he had walked out onto the first pillars. A few men had been still tidying up but they had ignored him. He had never set foot on the viaduct before and had been surprised at the height of it as he had looked down below at the stacks of planks and jumbled lifting gear, ropes and trucks and all the rest of what was needed before he had taken in the wider view up and down the dale and over to Whernside and then south to Ingleborough. He had been more than impressed. The viaduct was such a huge structure. He felt a sudden rush of pride at his own small involvement in such a large project. Gingerly he had stepped along the planks to where there was a gap to the next partly constructed pillar. Between them was a sheer drop of nearly a hundred feet. He thought of how much effort it had already taken to build it this far with its high pillars lined with massive pieces of cut stone. He imagined the first trains crossing here up in the sky their steam trailing down between the perfectly straight pillars and then this place in the winter with gales screaming through the arches and blasts of sleet and snow whipping across the rails. But he knew it would withstand it all, knew that it would last for generations. When they were all long gone the Ribblehead viaduct would still be here like a monument to all its navvies and their families, the pride he had felt turning into wonder and awe.

'Dad!' Clare called as she came along between the rows of huts with Fraser a few paces behind her. She seemed pale and a little awkward.

'So where have you and Fraser been?'

'We thought it was going to be just music but it was them religious lot who wanted us to sing and listen to a sermon. I never understood a word of it.'

'We were right and proper fooled,' said Fraser as he came up.

'It was stupid,' Clare added.

'And there was me thinking you'd become one of them Methies and that your mother would never live it down.'

'I like Reverend Smith better. At least he speaks proper and I can tell what he's saying.'

'Well your mother'll be glad to hear it.'

'It was bad,' Fraser added, 'Independents they call themselves but I've no idea what that means.'

'And I'm thirsty,' Clare complained, 'where's me Mam?'

'Inside.'

Fraser stood there looking unsure.

'You do so much for her Fraser and for Beth,' Ethan said after Clare had gone up the steps into the hut, 'Don't think we don't appreciate it. I know I should do more,' he unexpectedly added, 'But what wi you and Bill liking to be wi the girls so much I tek the lazy way out and I know I shouldn't. It's not right.'

'I don't mind.'

'That's the trouble, you don't.'

'They're both great lasses.'

'If you say so.'

'I do,' Fraser said strongly, 'They're lively young ones and interested in everything.'

'Oh I know that. Clare might be a bit on the slow side when compared wi our Beth but they both are right curious about things and you tell em so much and buy em so much. You must have spent a fortune on em over the last months.'

'If it's not on them it'd only go on the cards. I'd rather them have it.'

They had never spoken like this before. It sounded strange to both of them.

'Jonty is wi Arnold at the football.' Ethan remarked.

'They seem to be spending more time together them two.'

'Bill is letting em get on wi it. Can't reckon it, the way he ain't as bothered wi Jonty, not like Bill, not like him at all.'

Fraser looked at him and asked, 'What's Bill doing out every night?'

'No idea,' Ethan answered warily.

'It's a strange kettle o fish. He's not a drinker so maybe he's got himself a lady friend.'

'It's a change alright and yet Jonty seems quite happy wi Arnold.'

'That's because Arnold's on the same level I suppose if you think of it like that.'

Ethan smiled, 'You might be right there.'

Fraser stuck out his lips in thought. He started refilling his pipe. The sun had dropped now behind the further huts putting the two of them in sudden shadow.

Out of the warm dimness the Stantons appeared with Beth holding onto Shirley's hand.

Ethan stood and walked towards them, reached down lifted Beth up in his arms asking, 'And where have you been my lovely lass?'

'We've walked for miles Dad, miles.'

'A bit too far,' Shirley said as her Arthur nodded at Ethan.

He held Beth tightly, sensing this young, firm body in his arms. It was all that mattered, this child of his and Clare, these two precious lives.

'And I'm starving,' Beth complained.

'You're a right good un, have I ever told yer that?'

'No you haven't Dad.'

'Well I'm telling yer now and our Clare, a pair of smashers.'

'Who's the best?'

'There isn't one.'

'There has to be.'

'Not possible, not between you two. I'm telling yer.'

'Hello Beth,' said Fraser but she made no response. Ethan thanked the Stantons before carrying her into the hut, her arms held tightly round his neck.

PART THREE

CHAPTER THIRTY SIX

'You came.'

'So it seems Tom.'

'Lucy, you came.'

'You sound more than a little surprised.'

'No, not surprised, just happy you are here.'

'And what if we are seen?'

'Seen? Oh you mean by the gossip mongers or company informers of whom there are many.'

'Yes, something like that.'

'And tell me, is Mr Richard Stockton an interested friend or more than a friend?'

They were walking along an old drover's road. Lucy stopped playing with the end of the ribbon that tied her bonnet. Her expression was stiff and uncertain as it had been since she had set off with Tom after tea.

'I don't think that's any of your business,' she finally replied in a terse voice.

Tom stared at her inquiringly. He was still in his work clothes, his cap tilted over his face.

'You look beautiful Lucy Ormskill, absolutely beautiful.'

'Oh stop it!' she exclaimed.

'Just to be with you is enough. I would give all me life for just one kiss. I would make you the bride of the revolution so I would.'

'Tom Myres you've been drinking.'

'Not a drop.'

'Just listen to you.'

'I want you to listen to me, desperately want you to listen to me.'

The late summer evening's sky was full of low grey cloud, the silence around them ringing across its distances. Lucy felt as if they were in a void and only the two of them existed, walk further on and they would fall off the edge into nothingness. Often this was the effect living here at Ribblehead had on her. It was so isolated, so cut off from the rest of society, frightening the way she was finding it so hard to cope with. And yet recently Tom was the only one who made her feel real and anywhere near herself. She had fantasised about kissing him, about exploring his body with her hands, rousing him with her fingers. She was terrified of these images and yet excited by this dalliance with him, anything to relieve the boredom she had started to experience the moment she had arrived here in the Dales. There was nothing for her here except for the Dales themselves and their lonely, barren beauty.

'I never know when you're being serious or whether you ever mean what you say. It sounds like a game all the time because you seem to enjoy yourself too much. Is that what this is Tom Myres?'

'Yes,' he answered.

Abruptly she walked off from him so he had to run to catch up. He took hold of her arm, 'Lucy, I'm sorry. You just make me so damned nervous I get carried away wi mesell and sound bloody stupid and yet at the same time I mean everything I say to you. I honestly do. You know that really, don't you?'

'No I don't.'

'But you believe me?'

'I don't think I do.'

'So why are you here?'

'Taking an evening walk.'

'And me, why with me?'

'You are here to make sure I am safe.'

'Oh is that it? I'm just here to......'

'Make sure nobody bothers me.'

'What, like Stockton?'

'Why do you have to keep calling him that?'

'Because that is what he is to me. I suppose you know him just as Richard.'

Her face was still stiffly set, the grey clouds subduing the colour of her skin which had become tanned over the summer months.

The carters' track had deep ruts where the wheels had cut into the earth. It went straight up the next hill and on to Horton. On either side the land rose in huge sweeps of coarse grass up to the high limestone escarpments. A few sheep grazed below them, their filthy fleeces hanging off their backs.

'The summer will soon be over,' Lucy sighed.

'But before that a lot of the men'll be off to the haymaking. The farms around here need em or they'd lose their hay and this year seems to have been a good un.'

'How can they just leave their jobs like that?'

'Not leave, just tek a break. Your Mr Stockton can't stand the idea but can't do owt about it except sack half the work force and he ain't going to do that.'

'So the men just do as they like?'

'For once they do. For the one and only time they do and so they should, why bloody not?'

'You're swearing again and you.....'

'Oh ay, sorry, sorry to use such words.'

He teased and he provoked and she loved every minute with him and yet would not show it.

'One of my pupils has contracted smallpox,' she said.

'I heard that. It's bad news alright.'

'It's terrible.'

'The worst thing that can happen in a place like Ribblehead. Here were folk thinking that being so far away from any town would mean they were less likely to catch anything. They thought they might be safe but they're wrong. Disease catches up wi folk wherever they are.'

'But not just the workers.'

'More than likely though.'

'Only because there are a lot more of them.'

'And they've lived lives that have been such a struggle they have little resistance left.'

'Especially the children.'

'Especially them. So what are you going to do about the school?'

'Keep it going.'

'Even though it might become a breeding house.'

'I know that's possible but Richard, Mr Stockton has talked with the directors who suggest we wait and see. So far it is only the one pupil.'

'Tommy Bleacher's lad.'

'You know him.'

'I've told you Lucy, I know all the men here and their families. It's my business to know them all.'

'Archie's a right rascal, but a clever boy when he wants to be.'

'Just like his father.'

'Smallpox,' she repeated, looking up at the grey clouds.

'You have to be careful too Lucy, and yet I don't know what that means when it comes to owt like this.'

'There's nothing anyone can do except keep things normal I suppose. We are still so ignorant when it comes to diseases.'

'And a lot of other things besides. They call this the great civilisation but we're still in the caves when it comes to real human progress.'

'Yes,' she said, 'it seems that way sometimes.'

'Goodness!' Tom exclaimed, lightening the tone, 'You've just agreed with something I've said.'

'Please Tom,' she sighed, 'You mustn't jest all the time.'

'Sorry,' he interrupted.

'I should think so. The last time Archie Bleacher was at school he was in a terrible fight. He's always one to use his fists if things don't suit.'

He took her hand but she made no move to respond.

He turned her towards him. She looked at him without expression, her eyes dull in the grey light.

'Lucy,' he said quietly.

At that she pulled away and abruptly started walking again leaving him standing there. This time he did not follow her. He stood in the middle of the track watching her as she stepped carefully over the rough stones, her figure surrounded by so much empty, desolate land.

She finally stopped and turned. She had walked further than she realised. Tom had not moved. He seemed small, a tiny figure in all this vastness and he was waiting for her. He was that confident she would go back to him.

'You think it's that easy?' she asked as she finally reached him.

He said nothing for a few moments, his face more serious and doubtful in its expression.

'I don't think anything's easy,' he eventually answered.

'So what is it you want?'

'The same as you.'

'But you have no idea what that is.'

'Yes I do.'

'So tell me.'

'That would be me being too smart I reckon.'

‘Not if I want you to,’ Lucy said in a strangely dull voice.

She played again with the end of her bonnet’s ribbon, one foot crossed over the other so her body was at an angle to him. Tom stood with legs slightly apart, his arms by his side as he continued to watch her.

Her breathing slowed. She was lost in thought as Tom turned to see along the track a shepherd with his dogs and a flock of sheep approaching. Lucy was suddenly startled when she heard their approach.

‘Do you know him?’ she asked anxiously.

Tom shook his head, ‘No, so stop worrying.’

‘He could….’

‘Lucy, it’ll be alright,’ he interrupted.

They stepped up against the wall to let the sheep jostle past.

‘Na then,’ the shepherd muttered, ‘Nice evening.’

‘It is,’ said Tom as Lucy looked away.

The two collies worried either side of the flock, one of them chasing a sheep that suddenly darted off across the open stretch of grass by the wall. Quickly it was rounded back up as the shepherd whistled his instructions.

Tom and Lucy watched and waited until they were all much further along the drover’s road.

‘I should be getting back,’ she told him.

He turned, ‘Should you?’

‘I have….have….things to prepare.’

‘Before you do I want you to promise me something.’

She frowned, ‘Promise what?’

‘That you’ll let me hold your hand right now.’

She tried to stop herself smiling, ‘Oh I’m not sure about that.’

‘Yes you are,’ he countered as he took her hand that was warm to his touch.

Lucy hesitated, narrowing her eyes slightly as she looked straight at him.

Tom stepped forward and kissed her. She made no response, her mouth stiff and unyielding.

‘I’m going,’ she told him when she had pulled away.

‘Lucy I….’

'I'll go the rest of the way by myself,' she added stiffly.

'No,' he said back.

'Just leave me please.'

He let her go, watching as she walked quickly along the track before disappearing over the brow of the hill.

CHAPTER THIRTY SEVEN

Jane sat trying to read a novel. She loved reading. Every week she exchanged books chosen by Lucy and brought down from Batty Green's library. The volumes on James' bookshelves in his bedrooms were mainly religious tracts, Wesley's sermons which she had read and Bunyan's Pilgrim Progress. The rest were the works of various Dissenters which she found tedious and uninteresting. It was fiction and history she enjoyed the most and would read for hours each day. It was such a disappointment that Lizzie could not read but she had set her mind on teaching her. They had celebrated Lizzie's seventeenth birthday three weeks before by having a tea together. Jane had bought a coloured scarf from the Batty Green market as a present but it did not seem to be enough. Lizzie had hardly looked at it. Only later did Jane discover why when Lizzie started mentioning her dresses. It was obvious that what the young maid really wanted was one of them. Jane found the idea uncomfortable, especially when it seemed Lizzie presumed she would readily agree to such an idea. When she refused the girl became moody and began to make pointed remarks about their relationship, about how easily people could find out what was going on in the missionary's house. This time Jane realised these threats were more serious. This was no idle chatter. It was her red dress that became the centre of their arguments.

'Me Mam said she can fix it so it fits us,' Lizzie told her.

In her worried frame of mind Jane for the first time had begun to think about ways of escaping from this relationship. The only possibility was to try and find a post as a governess somewhere, something up till now she had avoided. The idea of spending years trying to teach and look after another family's children was both miserable and daunting, but there was nothing else she could do.

It was she who now always asked whether they should go to bed, her needs still overriding everything else.

'Could do,' Lizzie would respond in a dull, empty tone.

'Don't you want to?' Jane had to ask.

'Happen later Miss Jane, happen later.'

It had become a taunting game that the girl was playing and she was playing it well.

'Why do you make me suffer like this?' Jane had asked her.

'Don't be daft. I'm not doing owt. We'll go to bed if you want but not just now.'

'Why, why not now?'

Lizzie had stared at her and said, 'I can suit mesell can't I?'

'Not when it comes to telling lies.'

'Oh ay, listen to you, just listen to you. What are you doing here but pretending all the time?'

And it was true. Everything in the house was a deceit and James was doing exactly the same. Ever since discovering Lizzie praying with her cousin she had realised how both of them were lost. It all now centred on Lizzie.

It was impossible to sit there in the garden on this warm afternoon and read Trollope. Her mind was too full and confused. The nightmare of each day was beginning to take its toll on her health. She was often tired and aching and at night she found it hard to sleep. She had lost her appetite and would often find herself daydreaming, drifting away from the reality of the situation, an escape that made things only worse.

'You must promise me not to provoke James again,' she said strongly.

'And what if the master asks, what then?'

'Don't try and sound so stupid Lizzie. You just refuse.'

'And what if I don't want to?'

'Don't say such things.'

'It don't do no harm does it?'

'Yes it does, to me and him and you as well. It's wrong Lizzie, especially for James. It will destroy him if you're not careful.'

'Oh come on Miss Jane!' Lizzie had exclaimed, 'That's a load o daft nonsense and you know it. Mr James is a proper missionary who is.....is......'

'What?'

'Bothered.'

'Bothered? My God Lizzie, can't you understand it's a lot more than that? You're tempting him.'

'I'm not doing owt and you're only jealous.'

'I've told you before that's not true.'

'Isn't it?'

'I.....I care for you both and I want us to be able to live together in a better way.'

'You'll just leave here when the right man comes along, course you will, stands to reason a good looking woman like you. I can just see a local farmer coming along and teking thee away. What do you say Miss Jane, you a farmer's wife?'

She had not the strength to respond to that.

'Mind you, I forgot. You don't like men in that way, do yer?'

'No I don't,' she finally managed to say, 'and you know I don't and never will. I never will. That is something that will never change, never.'

'How can yer be sure? One day yer might meet some fella and you'll marry him just like that.'

'No.'

'Could happen.'

'No Lizzie.'

'As for me I reckon I'll get married some time and have some kids, lots o kids. I'd like that.'

'Stop it Lizzie!'

'Nowt but me saying what I want.'

'And I don't believe you.'

'Well if you don't you can give us a kiss instead.'

When James came home Lizzie had gone up to her room, something that she rarely did before bedtime.

'And how was it up at the works today?' Jane asked when he finally sat down, 'Are there any more cases?'

'Yes I'm afraid,' James answered in his low, serious voice, 'Two more, a young girl and a woman of twenty five and now the smallpox is there they won't be the last.'

'It's terrible.'

'It means more work visiting the sick.'

'I was going to ask whether I could come with you to help?'

'I have to do it Jane. It's an essential part of my work, but you don't. It's not safe.'

'I know that, I'm just offering, that's all. I want to help in any way I can.'

'It's too dangerous.'

'As it is for you.'

'Please Jane, let's not argue about this. I'd feel much easier if you stayed away from Ribblehead for the time being.'

She forced herself to accept this and then added glumly, 'I'm presuming you've had tea.'

'Yes thank you. I had some at the Hawthorns.'

'So are the patients being looked after by Doctor Shawcross in the hospital?'

'The pitifully small hospital.'

'At least there is one.'

'Yes,' he said abstractedly and then asked where Lizzie was.

'She's up in her room,' Jane answered.

'Why?'

'Went up earlier on.'

'Is she not well?'

'She seemed alright.'

He stood stiffly, his face held rigid, his hands clasped together.

They remained in silence for a time. Jane could think of nothing to say to him. Now there was always this awkward tension between them.

'Right,' he started, 'I have a sermon to prepare.'

'Yes,' she answered emptily.

'Jane, I was thinking.'

'What?'

He shook his head, 'It doesn't matter.'

'James, you once said everything mattered.'

'Did I?'

'Yes you did.'

'Sorry Jane, I'm tired and still have a lot to do.'

'Yes, of course.'

After he had gone she went out into the garden and walked over to the far wall. Gently she rested her hand on the soft, bright green moss that was covering the top stones. It felt like a natural cushion, giving slightly under the pressure of her hand. Momentarily she closed her eyes and breathed in the still warm air, listening to the sounds of the nearby beck and the call of the crows from the high trees behind the church. At least for these few moments she could be free. It felt as if there on the edge of her mind was all that was possible. Then when she opened her eyes and turned round she noticed James at his bedroom window watching her.

The next morning Lizzie started again.

'You have lots of dresses and some of em you hardly ever wear. You don't wear the red one so why can't I have it, just to borrow if you like cos there's the grand opening of the new hall at Batty Green and I want us to go to it together and it would give me Mam time to let out the dress at the seams like she said she would.'

Lizzie was clearing away the breakfast things while was James upstairs writing and Jane suddenly assaulted by this rush of words.

'I never knew you wanted to go to the opening.'

'You never asked me.'

'Lizzie, how can we go together? It would be too awkward.'

'Why? I don't see why. Anyroads who's to know any different? Hardly anyone up there at the works knows me from Adam or Eve for that matter. You could just tell em I was a relative who was stopping at the mission house for a few days. You can do that Miss Jane. I don't see why not.'

'I see you have it all worked out Lizzie Twistleton.'

The maid smiled and gave a mock curtsy.

'And you have to have my red dress?' Jane asked in exasperation.

'I could pay you for it.'

'And how on earth Lizzie could you do that?'

'Wi as many kisses as you want.'

'You really have got it all planned.'

'What do you say?'

'I say no.'

Jane said it to see her reaction. She wanted to see how far Lizzie would go.

'Suit yersell then,' she muttered and went off in a sulk to the kitchen.

'You either threaten me or promise me things,' Jane said after she had followed her into the stone floored room which was at its brightest on this late summer morning.

'I don't do owt of the sort.'

'Yes you do Lizzie. You know exactly what you do.'

At that the young maid turned, her face tight with anger, the moodiness still in her voice before she asked, 'So I can have it then?'

'You're very persistent.'

'And you should be more kind.'

'I would be if you stopped threatening me.'

'I'm not.'

'Yes you are. You make it obvious what you'll do if you don't get what you want out of me or James for that matter. You think you control us, don't you?'

'I don't think nowt. I'm just the maid here, the paid servant so stop talking such rubbish Miss Jane.'

Jane stepped up to her and touched her face that was gradually relaxing, running her fingers over her smooth skin that was slightly tanned and felt so soft.

'It's the gypsy in me family,' Lizzie had joked about the colour of her skin, 'Me Dad's allays saying that's where me Mam came from, dropped off the back of a gypsy caravan.'

Lizzie held her wrist and took Jane's fingers into her warm mouth.

Jane watched with fascination, her body suddenly full of a surging heat.

'James will be going out soon,' she said.

'Good.'

'Is it Lizzie?'

'Yes Miss Jane. Why do you allays doubt what I say nowadays?'

She let go of her hand.

'Afterwards you could try on the dress.'

'It'll be too small. You're much thinner than me.'

'I love you as you are,' Jane interrupted.

'But I can have it for the opening?'

'Of course you can so long as there are no more threats.'

The Horton and District Brass Band had been invited to play at the grand opening of Batty Green's new hall. James had been asked to sing as well but had refused saying he was too busy. Richard and Mr Armsworth had finally agreed that the opening should go ahead even with the outbreak of smallpox in the settlements realising that if it was not done now it might not be done for months.

The hall would have a temporary stage that could be taken down quickly to allow as much room for dancing. Some chairs were brought from the library and reading room. People had been asked to bring their own or to sit on the floor. Because of the smallpox the hall was only half full. Jane and Lizzie in the bright red dress were seated on the front row with others who had come early. After the show there would be light refreshments laid out at the back on long trestle tables. Mr Armsworth made a short speech welcoming everyone before the brass band started up.

At the finish people mingled together, drinking tea and eating sandwiches. The one person who did recognise Lizzie was Lucy Ormskill who had come in late and had been sitting near the back.

'Jane,' she said as she came up to them, 'I never realised you'd come, and Lizzie,' she added, 'Look at you all dressed up.'

'It's one of my old ones, thought Lizzie might as well have it,' Jane said quickly, unsure as to whether Lucy believed her or not.

'And she looks very fine in it. The red suits your colour Lizzie.'

'Thank you Miss Ormskill,' said Lizzie in a slightly different voice, less broad than usual.

'Pity about the turn out,' Jane mentioned.

Lucy looked around, 'Yes. This outbreak bothers everyone. It's dreadful. Absolutely dreadful and there's nothing anyone can do. Some survive and some don't. So how did you get up here and why is James not with you? I heard he was asked to sing this evening.'

'We came on the coach. And as for James he does not agree with the new hall being used for such light entertainment.'

'Oh dear!' exclaimed Lucy, 'and if it's to become a missionary hall as well then I don't understand why.....'

'It will be used for that sometimes I'm sure,' Jane interrupted, 'as well as for other things, but James wants it solely for religious purposes but I don't think that was ever going to be the case.'

'No I don't see how it could have been.'

Lizzie picked up another sandwich as she watched the rest of the crowd around them.

'So did you like the band Lizzie?'

'It were alright.'

'Just alright?'

'Don't reckon on brass bands that much. Mind yer I would have loved to have heard Master James sing. He'd sing hymns, that's what he'd do, all them hymns he knows.'

'I suppose he would. Anyway, it's over now and we didn't get to hear him.'

Lucy noticed then Richard over the other side of the hall talking with Mr Armwsorth. He signalled for her to join them.

'Excuse me, I'm just going to say hello to Mr Stockton,' she explained, glad to be away.

'I hear he's sweet on her,' Lizzie commented with another sandwich in hand.

'Who is?'

'Mr Stockton, sweet on Miss Ormskill.'

Jane looked across at Lucy with the two men.

'She's never mentioned anything to me.'

'And why should she?'

'Because she's a friend or I thought she was.'

'Friends don't have to tell everything, not that I reckon.'

'So long as you do,' Jane said in a quieter voice, 'So long as you do.'

'But we're lovers aren't we?' Lizzie asked then much to Jane's consternation.

'Stop it,' she muttered strongly, 'and keep your voice down.'

'Well it's true ain't it?'

'Not here Lizzie.'

'Don't see why not.'

'Because people will hear.'

'So what if they do? I'm not bothered.'

'Well I am so stop it or we're leaving right now.'

Lizzie laughed, 'Just look at your face. You've gone all red.'

The rest of the crowd were moving around them going back and forwards to the table for food.

'Come on,' Jane said as she took hold of Lizzie's arm, 'we're going. The coach will be waiting.'

'I don't want to go. I'm enjoying mesell.'

'Now Lizzie.'

Jane turned Lizzie round and manoeuvred her towards the door.

'Evening Miss Herbert,' she heard as she pushed open the door without looking back to see who it was.

'What a fuss,' Lizzie complained as they started down the path, the boards sounding out with their footsteps and those of some of the band who were lugging their instruments down to the waiting carts.

Jane made no reply. She walked quickly, angrily. There was a yellow streak of light along the edge of the valley against which Batty Green and the half constructed viaduct stood out as black shapes, the arches of the high bridge silhouetted against this lemon light.

The first thing Jane did the next morning was to write a note to Lucy inviting her to tea on the following Saturday.

The day was so warm she decided to have it out on the lawn that was surrounded by a weathered limestone wall. Lizzie helped lift the table out of the parlour and brought out the chairs.

'You can have tea with us if you like,' Jane suggested as they started carrying out all that was needed. Somehow she had to stop Lizzie thinking the nonsense she did about her and Lucy.

'You don't really want me to,' Lizzie responded.

Jane wiped her brow with the back of her hand and tried to control her frustration as she said, 'I'm asking because I do want you to have tea with Lucy and me. Why would I mention it otherwise?'

'Alright,' Lizzie said before she went back into the house.

'This is lovely!' Lucy exclaimed when she was shown into the garden later that afternoon, 'Tea outside, and why not? I can't see this weather lasting for much longer.'

'The farmers are desperate it lasts long enough to get the hay in. Now Lucy you sit here. Lizzie is bringing the teapot and she's going to join us this afternoon.'

Lucy tried her best to show no surprise, 'The maid having tea, how nice.'

'Yes,' said Jane weakly, 'I suppose it is. I just thought that.....'

'You've no need to explain anything Jane, why should you? This is your house and you should be able to do what you like.'

'I didn't think you'd mind.'

'Why should I mind? The more we break down class barriers the better and like the saying goes everything should start at home. It's only right that things change on a personal level before anyone can expect greater social changes,' she said, suddenly realising she was beginning to sound more and more like Tom Myres.

'I'm not sure if Lizzie is with us for such grandiose ideas Lucy.'

'You're trying to explain yourself again,' Lucy said lightly trying to alleviate some of the growing embarrassment that her friend was so obviously feeling.

'Am I?'

‘Here,’ said Lizzie as she came in with the pot of tea, ‘Should be well brewed by now.’

‘So you’re joining us for tea Lizzie, how very nice,’ said Lucy.

‘If that’s alright wi you Miss?’

‘And why shouldn’t it be?’

‘Cos most folk would think it weren’t.’

‘Well I don’t. I think it’s a charming idea.’

They sat and waited as Jane poured out the tea. Little was said to begin with while they ate their quarter cut sandwiches. Jane finally broke the silence.

‘I’m hoping to teach Lizzie to read Lucy and I was wondering if you could give some tips on the right approach.’

‘Wasting her time she is Miss Lucy. I’ve told her but she won’t listen. I’ve never had any schooling and I think it’s a bit late to be starting now,’ Lizzie laughed.

‘Nonsense Lizzie, everyone should be able to read and write.’

‘Well me Mam and Dad don’t think that.’

‘You should take such an opportunity with both hands and be glad of it.’

‘If you say so.’

‘I do, most strongly. I am a teacher after all. It is one of my strongest beliefs. Everyone, no matter who, should be able to read and write. There is a whole world they’re missing if they can’t. And yes, in answer to your question Jane I will certainly help in any way I can. I can lend you some of our school books to get Lizzie started.’

‘Such a fuss,’ the maid commented but was obviously pleased with all the attention.

Jane felt sick with tension. She thought she would have been able to manage Lizzie being with them but all she could do was wonder what Lucy really made of it. She hoped beyond everything that it would not raise any suspicions and yet she knew that she had made a terrible mistake. Lucy was too sharp and perceptive not to see what was going on.

When eventually Lizzie started clearing the table and carried the tray into the house Jane could not stop herself asking, ‘I hope you haven’t minded Lizzie being with us. It means nothing other than that I am trying to educate her a little if that makes sense and I just thought it would be a good idea for her to take tea with us as part of her education.’

‘And will she?’ Lucy unexpectedly asked.

‘What?’

‘Learn to become more as you wish her to be.’

'I hope that was not a critical tone I heard in your voice Lucy.'

'No it certainly wasn't. I've told you already Jane several times that anything that helps any woman to improve her life has to be a good thing. I admire what you're doing.'

'You see, I wasn't sure what you would think when you saw us at the concert the other evening.'

'You mean Lizzie all dressed up.'

'Yes.'

'I just thought she looked very handsome. I hardly recognised her.'

Lizzie came back and so the conversation turned again to the weather and on to Lucy describing some of the books she had ordered for Jane from the library.

'It's been lovely, really lovely Lizzie. Thank you so much,' Lucy said later ready to leave, 'and I just hope I haven't missed the coach to Dent.'

'I'll come with you to the road end.'

'No I'll be fine,' Lucy said smiling and taking Jane's hand, 'and I would start with Lizzie's reading as soon as you can before she changes her mind and rejects the whole idea.'

'You think she might?'

'At seventeen anything is possible.'

'Yes,' said Jane hesitantly.

'Right, I must go, and thank you again for a lovely afternoon,' Lucy added before she turned and started along the road.

Jane watched her pass the church and cross the bridge before disappearing from sight up the brow of the short hill that came out onto the turnpike road, wondering what Lucy had really thought about the afternoon.

CHAPTER THIRTY EIGHT

'Where are yer teking us?' Beth asked.

'You'll see.'

'Dad, tell us,' Clare persisted.

'To catch yer tea, that's where we're going,' Ethan answered as the two girls followed him up the narrowing valley beside its stream. The water was peaty brown and had cut deep into the land, the beck's rushing sounds loud and constant.

'It's nowt but another Sunday walk.'

'Yer right.'

'And me legs ache.'

'Mine too,' Beth agreed with her sister.

'Well I'll get doctor Shawcross to have a look at em when we get back,' Ethan challenged her.

'I don't want to see no doctor.'

'Well stop yer moaning then.'

He enjoyed this banter between them. It was a bright afternoon and the girls had changed out of their Sunday best. Sometimes Maggie came on one of these regular family walks but she encouraged Ethan to spend as much time as possible with the girls and today had stayed behind in the hut.

'Me Mam says we haven't to get dirty,' Clare tried.

'Yer can allays have a wash in't beck.'

He stopped and turned to the two of them saying, 'Now you've not to tell anyone about this, do yer hear? It's a secret place we're going to and I want nobody else to know about it so you never tell a soul.'

'Not even me Mum?' Beth asked seriously, her dark eyes wide and eager.

'Not even her. This is just between us three, right?'

'Yes Dad,' the two of them answered almost in unison.

'Good, so stop yer moaning and let's get on. It ain't far now.'

A few sheep watched them trudge by. Maggie that morning had tied their hair in tight bunches with red ribbons for church. The stream was only a few feet wide where Ethan quietly told them to stop. Clare looked doubtfully around, her white features showing less interest than her sister as bright clouds shifted slowly across the afternoon sky. The only the sound was of the fast water and a skylark that was following high above them.

'Now you've not to mek a sound, do you hear?'

'What are you going to do?' Beth asked breathlessly, her hands held forward as though ready for action.

'I'm going tickling.'

'What?'

'You heard, tickling, but fer this to work you have to keep dead quiet or you'll disturb the fish. I just want yer to watch what I do. It's hard to do is this, very hard. There's only a few folk can get it right. It's a special thing to be able to do.'

By now the girls were staring at him wide eyed with the sound of the stream gurgling through the afternoon stillness.

Ethan loved the way they readily accepted his exaggeration. If either of them was doubtful he knew it would be Clare.

'So you watch careful like,' he added as he knelt down by the edge of the stream and slipped his hand into the water where the bank formed a narrow shelf and the water slowed.

The girls did not move until he stood up again telling them, 'We'll try a bit further up. It might tek a few times so you have to be patient and then if this works I'll show yer how to do it.'

'Do what?' Clare asked in a low voice.

'Tickle.'

'Oh Dad, stop it.'

'We're here to tickle some trout.'

'And how do yer do that?'

'That's what I'm going to show you, so come on.'

They walked a little further before again Ethan got down on his knees.

'What about yer trousers?' Beth mentioned standing right behind him.

'Not a word.'

'It's yer best suit.'

'I said you have to be quiet.'

They were held to the movement of his outstretched arm as he carefully slipped his hand into the water saying, 'There now, there now,' and after a few moments suddenly half turned. In an instant a fish was flicked out of the water onto the bank as the girls started shouting and then screaming as the large trout writhed at their feet.

'A good un!' Ethan exclaimed.

'It's alive! It's still alive!' Beth was shouting.

'Course it is yer daft hapoth, but not fer long.'

'What are yer going to do to it?' Clare asked.

'You'll see.'

'Kill it! Kill it!' Beth repeated, 'Kill it Dad.'

Ethan took up the first stone he found and slammed it against the trout's head.

'Oh no!'

'You've done it.'

'That's horrible!' Clare was screaming, her face lined in anguish.

'It's stopped moving,' her sister laughed.

'Just grand fer yer tea Clare,' Ethan joked.

'No.'

'Why not?'

'No,' she said again in a panic.

'Can I have a go?' Beth urged.

'Just slow yersell down. Let's try a few more places first. This might be the only one we catch.'

'How……how did yer do it?'

'I told you, by tickling it nice and gentle like, just stroking it lightly under its belly is why they call tickling. It kind of puts the fish to sleep and then before it can react you have it whipped out of the water and Bob's yer uncle, Sunday tea ready and waiting.'

'Poor thing.'

'You wouldn't be saying that if yer were starving hungry,' he told Clare.

'Well I'm not and even if I were I wouldn't eat it.'

'I would,' her sister announced.

He looked at them, gauging the difference in their expressions. They were different and yet were held together so strongly, one always looking out for the other. Beth was the sharper and Clare stronger, a combination that had always worked for the two of them. Even when Beth was younger she would be the one her sister would rely on. She would wait to see what Beth thought before acting. Their arguments were rare but could be fierce and in them Clare would sometimes lose her temper. Only twice had she ever really got angry and then had regretted it for weeks, hating to see Beth upset and resentful.

The girls followed on hopefully but for the next half an hour there was to be no other fish.

'It's a dud girls I'm afraid,' he finally said, 'they're all hiding from us.'

'Can we go home now?'

He looked at Clare and smiled, 'So long as you carry the trout.'

'I will not!'

'Suit yersell.'

'You said I could have a try,' Beth reminded him.

'Another time lass, it's no good this afternoon, not here anyroads.'

She pulled a disappointed expression then accepted his hand as they started back down the narrow valley with the fish under his other arm and Clare following miserably on behind.

The next morning he was more than usually aware of everyone around the table finishing their breakfast. Beth and Clare were in bed still asleep and Maggie was standing at the stove. Jonty had his mouth full and seemed more agitated this morning. Jock belched loudly before pouring out more tea. With some of his front teeth missing and his hair all over the place he showed signs of his regular hangover. Beside him Fraser sat quietly and self absorbed as usual while Bill at the end of the table found it hard to sit still. He was always complaining about the arthritis in his hips these days.

Ethan's thoughts were concentrated on his wife. They had agreed that Clare and Beth should carry on at the school for the time being but he knew her anxiety about the smallpox was growing day by day and he could do nothing except try and reassure her as much as possible. This enemy was everywhere, was unseen and deadly. It stalked now the rows of huts filled with so many people. It had always been like this. The whole of society lived under its shadow. She knew the threat to the family. There would be nothing for them to live on. All that would be left was the utter misery of the Work House and to avoid that he and Maggie would do anything they could.

'I just wish you would pray with me,' Maggie said often to him.

'So do I, I will if I thought it would mek any difference,' he would answer.

'It's the only thing keeping me going.'

'And us, the four of us.'

'You know that. I mean about us four.'

'I can't trust in someat I don't believe. You're lucky you have your faith. It's at times like this I wish I could feel the same but that would be just a blether on my part, kidding myself and that's no good for you, me nor the children.'

The only time they could talk was when the girls were finally asleep, even though Ethan was as exhausted as ever and had to force himself to stay awake.

'It's such a terrible thing, the smallpox. Remember when there was that outbreak in Nottingham. The government started inoculating people but it was too late. It was pitiful the way folk were still struck down,' Maggie reminded him.

'I remember. There were all sorts of rumours of who'd brought it to the town as if that made any difference. People are allays needing to blame somebody when things go wrong.'

'It was awful.'

'Like every disease that kills folk.'

'Not ours Ethan, not ours, please God not ours,' she repeated.

If he woke up in the night to use the piss pot she would often be lying there wide awake staring up at the ceiling in the half darkness of the late summer night. By that hour he was stupefied with tiredness and did not know what to say. All he could do was stagger back to bed and hold her, put his arms around her and pull her to him and just wish he could do or say more.

'Right, better mek a move,' Bill said as he got up from the breakfast table.

Fraser and Jock glanced at him and then went back to their bread, butter and tea. Ethan had noticed how over the last weeks the two of them seemed even more strained and belligerent when it came to speaking to Bill. Something was going on but Ethan had no idea what and he certainly was not going to ask. Bill was spending a lot of time in the evening visiting different folk he had worked with on other sites while Jonty would be with Arnold in the hut or up at the Reading Room.

'Come on Jonty lad, move yer arse.'

Jonty looked miserably up at Bill and shook his head.

'I said come on and I mean now before that bloody hooter goes.'

'Why don't you leave him be?' asked Jock.

Bill ignored him as he pulled on his jacket, swung his food bag over his shoulder and waited for Jonty to rouse himself.

'Right, me as well,' Ethan said as Maggie came over with his dinner bag.

Fraser and Jock were out of the hut before him. There were groups of men walking down towards the tool sheds. Thankfully it was still light at six o clock. From behind the high moorland at the top of the valley a pale blue sky lit along the horizon. The men were quiet, their boots and clogs rapping along the boards in the warm, late summer air. They queued up to be given their shovel or pickaxe just like they did when it was pay day at the office door. Some headed further down to the far embankment the other side of the viaduct whereas most of them climbed up the path that ran across the tramways to the cutting or like Ethan further on to the tunnel. Over most of the summer he had been working with the rest of his gang inside the tunnel shovelling loose rock blasted from the far end. With the light of his lamp he heaved up the rock to fill up the tramway trucks pulled by the ponies out of the tunnel then tipped down the sides to shore up one of the embankments. The horses plodded along slowly in the hot darkness before emerging into the light. As usual when Ethan started work his mind immediately numbed off. He thought of nothing. He was an empty instrument, an extension of his shovel. It was the only way he could survive the sheer knackering monotony of what he and the rest of the men had to do. In the tunnel everything was cramped and soaking wet. The men were stripped off to the waist, sweating skin glistening in the light from their candles and the few lamps hooked to the wooden supports holding up the roof. All of them hoped that they would continue in the tunnel through the worst of the winter, the only real bonus for this work.

At the end of the day Ethan had agreed to meet Tom in the Railway Inn. They usually met there at least twice a week now that Ethan was increasingly interested in Tom's ideas.

They had just started on their first pints when two navvies, Cockney Smith and Rednecked Foster as they were called came over to their table. The pub was quieter than usual it being early. Most of the men liked to get their dinner before setting out on a drinking session.

'So here's fucking little Red Myres with one of his thickheads and I hear Myres that you're at it again, this time stirring them up who work in the tunnel. Can't leave bugger all alone can thee?'

Foster was a big, filthy faced worker with tattoos down both arms.

'You're well informed,' Tom said back.

'You bet I fucking am.'

'So who tells you all this? It wouldn't be Murray would it?'

Smith's gut stuck out over his belt. He was one of the steam crane operators which meant he never broke sweat all day. His teeth were black and his dust smeared head perfectly bald.

Ethan was frightened. Any threat like this left him cold with tension.

'And you Granger, a married man wi kids, you should know bloody better than having owt to do wi the likes of this filthy shit.'

'We're having a drink,' Ethan managed to respond as the beer turned sour in his guts.

'Just leave us alone,' Tom tried.

'No,' muttered Smith back.

'No, cos we're here to teach you a lesson Myres to keep yer fucking trap shut. All you do is cause trouble so it's either here or outside.'

Ethan's stomach tightened. These two were so big and intimidating. His head began to spin as he gripped hold of the table edge.

In contrast Tom just looked from one to the other, his face without expression. Then he took another mouthful of beer. By now the rest of the pub was silent until Bill Arnold from behind the bar said, 'No bother from you lot. Just tek it outside if thee's being serious.'

'We're fine Bill,' Tom said back.

'Outside,' Foster ordered him.

Tom shook his head and took out his pipe.

'You'd better fuck off Granger before you get what's coming to this pile o shite.'

'Yes Ethan, you go,' Tom agreed.

Momentarily Ethan thought about it. He would have loved to have just walked out of the pub. He was lost to the fear of being in a fight and yet could not move, his whole body stiff and tight as he sat staring at his beer glass.

'I'm.....I'm going nowhere,' he finally managed to say.

'Well you're more fucking thick than I took thee for,' said Foster.

Everything seemed to be tilting sideways as he tried to retain a grip on himself. He could not manoeuvre his way out of the situation and yet he knew he would never retaliate, would just take what was coming to him. Violence only led to more of the same. He had seen it too often. All he wanted was for these two brutes to just turn and walk away, to leave him and Tom in peace and let their evening survive without any injury.

Smith made the first move by leaning over the table in an attempt to grab Tom by the throat.

'No! Fucking leave it!' Bill Arnold was shouting as Tom swung a punch into Smith's mud smeared face.

Ethan sat paralysed until Foster suddenly dragged the table away and fisted him hard sending him crashing to the floor with blood spurting out of his nose. The other two were by then locked together with Arnold rushing over to swing a club at the back of Smith as he tried to kick out at Tom with his hob nailed boots.

'Yer fucking bastard!' Smith screamed as he swivelled round and hit Bill Arnold full in the face sending him crashing over another table as the rest of the drinkers started making for the door.

But Bill was not done. In moments he had dragged himself up and this time his club cracked the back of Smith's head knocking him out cold.

This stopped Foster who spat hard in Tom's face before he barged out of the pub with some of the others.

Ethan laid there on the sawdust his whole head throbbing with pain. Slowly he pulled himself up onto his hands and knees before spewing out everything left in his guts. Around him was blackness and at its centre was this pain splitting his head apart, the blood pouring freely off his chin onto the floor. He hated himself, hated his weakness and fear. Through the aching throb came a rush of resentment and self loathing, here on his hands and knees no better than any beast of the field.

'Come on Ethan,' he heard from somewhere but he could not move.

'Get....get him out of here,' Bill Arnold said breathlessly.

Ethan felt the unsteady arms of Tom trying to lift him up.

'Go on, fuck off out of here,' again Arnold shouted at them.

Outside Ethan fell on his hands and knees again, the blood choking him as it dribbled into his mouth. He was dimly aware of a few others stood watching, waiting. Beside him crouched forward Tom was coughing and spitting out blood and bits of teeth.

The minutes went by as the evening began to darken. New customers walked past without comment.

'Bastards,' Tom finally muttered.

'Why?' Ethan gasped.

'Cos that's the way it is, the way it's allays been, any threat and some bugger gets clobbered.'

'And why......why them two?'

'Oh Foster and Smith'll do owt for a few pounds. It'll be fucking Murray whose set this up.'

'Murray?'

'The second in command. It'll be his idea. I bet fucking Stockton knows nowt about it. This ain't his style. It's bloody Murray who'll be at the bottom o this.'

Eventually Ethan stood up, his legs shaking and his head spinning with the thumping pain at the front of his face that felt as if it had swollen to twice its size. He wanted to be sick but there was nothing left.

Tom was still breathing hard, his features set in anger.

'I'm sorry I didn't put up.....put up much of......'

'There's nowt else you could have done,' Tom interrupted, 'Those two fucking thugs were just ready for it.'

Nothing was said for a few more minutes before Ethan said, 'I'll be going then. Christ knows what the Missus'll say.'

'Does it matter?'

'No it don't,' he said hesitantly.

'Well then.'

'I'll....I'll....'

'You just get yersell home Ethan.'

Ethan walked off, putting one foot unsteadily in front of the next. There were children, workers and women everywhere on this still warm evening. He knew they would be looking at his bloodied face and it bothered him. He knew the gossip would already have started, tales of Ethan Granger fighting in the Railway Inn, the big drums of Ribblehead sounding out across the valley.

He would not go home. He would get away from the settlement and allow the pain to subside and his mind to calm down because at that moment his self disgust was beyond control.

'Now then Ethan!' people called but he made no response.

A few sheep rushed away from him as he passed by the brick factory.

Further on two gangs of kids were having a stone fight with bits of rock flying through the darker air.

The stench from the huts and privies mixed in with the nausea caused by the pain from his nose.

He had been attacked and abused and it felt as though his whole being had been assaulted. He had always avoided violence except for that ridiculous boxing contest that Arnold Wainwright had organised the day of his arrival at Batty Green. Now he felt disgusted. How absolutely ridiculous he had been to ever believe he could fight for a cause, could have considered violence ever being an answer to anything.

He had reached the moorland, walking above the cutting that led to the tunnel. His head was still spinning as grey clouds shifted across the deep blue sky. Finally he found a rock to sit on, lowering his head between his knees and trying to suck in big mouthfuls of air. Tentatively he explored his nose and mouth. He still had his teeth and his nose did not seem to be broken. It was just huge and both nostrils were crusted up with dried blood. He leant forward to rub his hands in the soil at his feet before smearing it over his face, tasting it, smoothing the dirt down his neck and onto his chest. He wanted to become part of the land and of the night, to disappear as the man and become something that was solid and everlasting. Over and over again he covered his hands, face, neck and chest with more of the dirt and then his arms and into his hair. He wanted to merge with his surroundings and become invisible. He sat without moving, sat absolutely motionless except for the shallow rising of his chest with each small breath. With his arms by his side and his head sunk forward he closed his eyes to became as nothing, absolutely nothing, empty of thought, empty of feeling, a still, silent thing sat there like stone on stone.

CHAPTER THIRTY NINE

The mason finished chipping at the block of stone and walked round it running his hand over the surface. Ropes were set underneath and the steam crane started hoisting the slab of rock slowly up near to the top of the viaduct to be placed as another facing stone on the seventh pier. Initially they had drilled deep down through the mud of Batty Moss and then poured in concrete to form the base for each pier. Finally the brick layers gradually built the frame. As it grew this frame would be filled in with rubble from the tunnel. The final process was to face the inner brick structure with worked stone that was brought down from the quarry.

Richard watched the piece of stone swing slowly towards where the men were ready to move it into place. He thought again how the viaduct would come to dominate this area of the Dales. The remote and empty Ribblehead would he hoped become better known because of it, this construction that would dominate the whole area once it was finished.

He was chatting to one of the masons when he leant over the balustrade to see Andrew Murray far below furiously gesticulating at one of them men but because of all the noise could not hear what he was saying. By the time he had climbed down the ladder Andrew had stomped off towards the office.

'What was all that about?' Richard asked breathlessly when he eventually caught up with him.

'Just one of the men,' Andrew answered quickly as though he was in a hurry.

'Well what about him?'

Andrew stopped and turned, his face still stiff with anger as he said, 'I sacked him. I told him to pack his stuff and get off the site before the hooter went this evening.'

Richard felt a wave of disappointment mixed with irritation.

'I want you to come with me to the office.'

'I have something I.....'

'In the office Andrew if you don't mind,' he said firmly.

The moment the office door was shut behind them Richard asked, 'Why? Why did you sack him?'

'Because I found him sat smoking his pipe. The man knew I was there and yet he thought he could just carry on without a damned care in the world.'

'Who was this man?'

'Daniel Flinders.'

'He's one of our best stonemasons.'

'I'm sorry Richard,' Andrew started defiantly, 'I don't care who or what the hell he is. The man thought he could just sit there smoking when he was supposed to be working.'

Richard flicked over a sheet of paper on the long table, his expression more sombre now.

Finally he said, 'The haymaking has started. You are aware of that?'

'Yes I know,' answered Andrew.

'And we're losing men every day. You're aware of that fact as well I suppose.'

'It's beyond belief! They just think they can walk off the job and then in a couple of weeks' time just walk back and carry on.'

'They call it their unpaid holiday, just like last year.'

'That's nonsense and we know it!' exclaimed Andrew.

'We can't afford to be losing men like Daniel Flinders, not now.'

'So you're saying Richard that I have overstepped the mark?'

'I'm saying you were too hasty.'

'But it was my decision, you do agree with that?'

'I suppose I have to, yes.'

'I was in my rights to sack the man?'

'Yes you were.'

'Well then?'

'You should have discussed it with me first.'

'And what exactly would you have done Richard?'

'I would have given him a warning.'

'Bah!' Andrew muttered, 'I knew it. I just knew that's what you're getting at. You're always telling me to take more responsibility for the men and when I do you contradict me.'

'On this occasion I think you've made a mistake Andrew, an unfortunate mistake because naturally I would not think of reinstating him and embarrassing you.'

'And I'm supposed to be grateful for that am I?'

'Damn you man!' Richard exclaimed, his face reddening, 'Why can't you just take a piece of advice? Why can't you do that?'

Andrew made no reply. The longer the silence lasted the angrier Richard became.

'I respect your work,' Andrew finally said, 'You know that. I came here so I could work with you, but that does not mean I have to agree with your attitude towards managing these men.'

'You've made that perfectly clear.'

'I can't Richard.'

'You mean you won't.'

'This is not a matter of choice.'

'Well what the hell is it then?'

'It's what I was brought up to believe.'

'But surely things can change?'

'All that means to me is yielding to the men.'

'It's not a war Andrew. We're not fighting them. We're all supposed to be on the same side, all of us. We're all here to do a job and they work bloody hard.'

'Some of them, when they're sober,' he responded forcefully.

'God almighty!' Richard exclaimed, 'Just listen to yourself!'

'I'm sorry, but that's the way I see it and nothing, absolutely nothing can prove to me that I'm wrong.'

'If it was up to you then there would be no changes at all. The working class should just remain as it's always been, stuck there at the bottom of the pile keeping quiet and accepting their lot?'

'Exactly,' Andrew replied.

'It's moronic Andrew. You're still living in the past. You just don't see it. Progress is inevitable and it's right that it is.'

'No it isn't. It's the only way to keep society intact. Once you start giving more then where the hell will it stop? They'll want it all Richard and it'll be us and our families at the bottom of the pile as you put it. It'll be us the servants of the master class. Well no thanks. I'd rather do anything to make sure that doesn't happen.'

Finally Richard sat down and took off his hat, wiping his brow with his handkerchief. He had never felt so tired at hearing the same old arguments. He did not agree with them. He never had. Society had to be fairer unless it wanted increasing disturbance and riots.

He got up and went over to a side table to pour himself a mug of water before sitting back down again. At that moment he felt like insulting his engineer in any way he could.

'Myres was attacked in the Railway Inn last night,' he said slowly, with an emphasis on each word.

Andrew took a seat but made no response. He dropped his hat onto the table and yawned.

'I just wondered...'

'Wondered what Richard? That I had anything to do with it?'

Richard looked straight at him, 'Yes, something like that.'

'God almighty!' Andrew shouted as he got up and threw his chair backwards, 'What the hell do you take me for?'

'I'm no longer sure what you're capable of. I do know that you detest Tom Myres and always have done, detest what he believes and the power he has over the men. I'm no great defender of a man like Myres. In fact my life would be a damned sight easier if he was not within a thousand miles of Ribblehead. But he's here and at the moment so we have to put up with him and those who follow him. If that changes it will be my decision, mine Andrew. Do you understand?'

'And when will that be?'

'When I say so, that's for me to decide.'

'Do you want me to resign?'

'I want you listen to me

'Myres just wants to stir up as much trouble as he can. That's all he's here for, certainly not to work.'

'So you thought a little warning would be a good idea, rough him up a bit and he might get the message. He'll know it was us. Don't you understand how bad your reputation has become? He'll think you paid some thugs to give him a beating. You have no idea about men like Tom Myres, none at all. Do you honestly think punching him about is going to stop him, is going to change his mind about anything at all? It will only make him more determined. If you did set that up then you're a greater fool than I thought.

Andrew looked as if he was about to say something but then changed his mind, grabbed his hat, rose and stepped over to the office door which he slammed behind him.

Richard slumped back in his chair and stretched out his legs. His head ached and his stomach was cramping. He hated such confrontations, hated to lose his temper, but he was sick of Andrew's pathetic sense of superiority.

Out of the office he walked over to the stables and asked the boy to saddle up one of the company horses. All the ponies had been chosen for strength and were wide and stocky. Riding over the bridge to join the Ingleton road Richard looked incongruous on his wide backed, thick legged horse that lowered its head with every forward step. Once over the beck he tried to forget about his spat with Andrew and allowed his mind to drift as always to Lucy. She dominated his daily thoughts. Once he would never have thought it possible, this growing obsession with a woman, this overwhelming desire for her. He felt embarrassed by his own needs, felt so critical of how he had allowed this to happen. His self reliance of which he had always been proud had been shattered by her and part of him despised her for it, for what she was doing to him just by her being here at Ribblehead.

A light drizzle began to fall from darkening clouds. He hunched forward, tilting his head so the rim of his hat sheltered his face. He was aware of his hands loosely holding the wet leather of the reins, aware of himself in such a torment of feeling that he hardly recognised who he had become. All his inner strength had been burnt away by a love that confused him more each day. He was now careful with his clothes, careful with his morning wash, his shaving and well brushed hair, checking in the mirror to see what impression he might give Lucy if they chanced to meet. On Sundays when he knew he would see her he was even more concerned that he appeared as sharp and fashionable as possible. He thought only to impress, even considering beforehand what topics of conversation might interest her.

At the junction he turned onto the Settle road that gradually led up out of the valley, nodding at the drivers of two carts that trundled past. Whatever the weather bread, milk and other essential provisions were brought up this road everyday. It would not be long before the line between Settle and Ribblehead would be completed and everything would come up by train. Already the new line had reached almost halfway between Horton and the hamlet of Selside. Images of Lucy followed. His mind was drifting until he was considering how weak his position seemed.

Momentarily he stopped the horse at the sight of two crows perched on the roadside wall, their black feathers sheened slightly by the rain, their prominent beaks in perfect line with the shape of their heads. They were motionless, aware of him, their black eyes flickering from side to side in anticipation of any movement he might make.

'Please sair, please sair.'

A voice brought him out of his reverie, a thick Irish voice that sounded desperate and pleading. He looked up at the skeleton thin man and the heavily pregnant woman beside him with two young boys standing close by. All of them were in rags and were filthy. They were barefoot and carrying very little. The woman had obviously been crying and the boys were ashen face and constantly scratching themselves with their grubby hands.

'Please sair,' the man repeated.

Richard turned the horse towards them.

'Is this...is this like the way to Rib.....Ribble....'

'Ribblehead?'

'That'd be it sair. Ribblehead as you say cos that's where we with God's help are headed. We hear there's work so they say and that's....'

He was interrupted by the woman suddenly sobbing and retching at the same time, her matted hair flung over her scabby face.

'Fucking heel,' the man muttered at her, 'Set yersell woman, set yersell or what will the gentleman think then?'

'What's wrong with her?'

‘Nothing sair, nothing that a wee bit o food would not solve in the way of the thing sair.’

‘Yes,’ Richard said then, ‘This is the way to Ribblehead.’

‘Cos we were told plum on like that Ribble...or whatever was the place where jobs were going to be grabbed by them who could make their way to the place we were told by those who should know like if they were right in what they said.’

‘Yes, there might be chance of work up there,’ Richard added, wondering whether anyone in such a miserable state as this man could manage anything like physical labour.

‘Weel God bless yer for saying so.’

‘It’s not guaranteed mind.’

‘Not all sir, not at all, but we’re beholden to youse so we are. We’ve tried the local farms but nothing, none o them wanting.’

‘Well good luck,’ Richard said before setting off his horse.

‘And to you sir, and to you,’ the man called after him.

By the time he had returned along a drovers track and reached the turn off down into Chapel le Dale his stomach was churning and his head hot and spinning. Automatically he jerked on the reins to change direction, the horse turning down the sharp slope and then over the moss covered stone bridge into the small hamlet. At the church gate he dismounted and tied his horse to a small rowan bush growing by the church wall.

Inside it was dark and cool. An old lady was carefully placing two brass candlesticks either end of the altar. She stepped back to inspect them and then turned.

‘Good day sir,’ she said as she came down the narrow aisle.

‘Good day to you too.’

‘I’ve just been cleaning the brasses. I do it every week. It’s my little contribution to the life of the church. We all have to contribute, don’t you think?’

‘Yes, of course,’ Richard answered as she walked past him and shuffled through the open door.

Momentarily he stood there trying to clear his mind. Everything here seemed small and somehow neglected. Then he slid onto the first bench, seated himself, leant forward, clasped his hands together and began to pray for the first time in years, to pray fervently, deeply, almost desperately.

CHAPTER FORTY

Bill was sitting on the front step of the hut smoking his pipe while watching Maggie hanging out the washing. Groups of workers and their families were chatting as they passed by on this late summer evening.

'Bill, will you be at the haymaking?' Maggie asked.

She waited, noticing his pale, tired expression.

He took out the pipe and said, 'Mug's game Maggie.'

'Ethan talks about going.'

'Well more fool him.'

'Oh I don't know,' she sighed, 'I suppose it's someat different.'

'For what? Yer get paid hardly owt. The farmers around here are as gormless as their barn doors and all I'd finish up wi would be worse back trouble than I have already. So no I won't be going.'

His tone was harsh and critical but Maggie was used to it. She knew that behind his aggressive exterior there was a different Bill that was she beginning to understand, a person more concerned and thoughtful than he pretended to be. Nobody would have looked after Jonty the way he had without that inner care.

He watched her continue pegging out the sheets and work shirts, his breathing slow and steady.

'This is a lovely evening,' she finally added.

'Lovely for some perhaps.'

'Oh come on Bill.'

'I suppose there's nowt much else around here to enjoy in this God forsaken place.'

'Listen to yer. You sound in a right down mood.'

'No, not really, just the usual aches and pains, that's all.'

'You should go see the doctor.'

'And what good would that do?'

'He might have someat.'

'Not that I've ever heard of, not fer what's ailing me.'

'What you need is a right hot bath.'

'And where do yer reckon I could have that, middle o the night up on these moors?'

'We could give it a try when the rest of em are out.'

'There's allays someone around, especially the lasses and the last thing they need is to see an old bugger like me teking a bath or you for that matter.'

'Well I'd agree with that,' she laughed.

'So we agree fer once?'

She glanced over at him before saying, 'Give us a go on yer pipe Bill.'

'I will not.'

'Go on Bill, just a puff.'

He smiled and shook his head, 'Maggie Granger yer a right one you are.'

'Have to keep up the spirits Bill or where would we be?'

'In the grave likely.'

'There you go again.'

'I reckon that would be my idea of hell,' he said after blowing out a mouthful of sweet smelling smoke.

'What would?'

'Working here until the end of time, in the factory baking bricks forever. Can yer think on it? My that would be purgatory alright wi Jonty moping on behind as well, having to listen to him over and over again, time wiout end.'

'You don't mean that last bit about Jonty. I don't believe yer.'

'Why not?'

'Cos....cos yer think more of him than that.'

'Course I do,' he answered warmly.

'Now it's your sense of humour that's getting the better of you.'

'Is that what you'd prefer?'

'I would.'

'Well then.'

'Except I'd rather have you on yer feet helping me wi this washing.'

'Oh alright I suppose,' he sighed, if yer say so,' tapping his pipe on the underside of his boot before slowly standing up.

On the other side of Batty Green drink was sold in Jessie Jones's hut all day and most of the night. A few tables and chairs were squeezed into the central space with sawdust on the floor and beer in jugs from the barrel as well as whisky and gin bottles on the shelf by the stove. When the place was full, which it was most evenings, the atmosphere was thick with the fug of pipe smoke, drink and the odour of filthy work clothes. Jessie's two daughters Maisie and Alice offered other services in the two bedrooms while her husband George with his thuggish features ensured there was never any trouble.

Jock and Fraser were waiting for Arnold Wainwright to join them.

'So why? What are we waiting for Jock?'

'Keep your voice down man.'

'Nobody's listening.'

'How the fuck do you know?'

'I'm only asking, why are we……?'

'I heard youse,' Jock interrupted.

'So tell me,' insisted Fraser looking around to see whether any of the other drinkers seemed interested in their conversation.

Jock swallowed a large mouthful of beer, smacked his lips and wiped his mouth with the back of his hand. The mud had dried a light blue over his face and arms. His trousers and shirt were just as filthy and his eyes were moistened with the drink.

'Where the fuck is that shite Wainwright?' he muttered.

Fraser was watching the plump, red faced Maisie taking a navvy he did not know to the knocking room. Momentarily a wave of disgust went through him. He could think of nothing more repulsive than a roll around with fat Maisie. There were certain bodies that were perfect, were almost untouchable, the rest were like farm animals.

'So do we tell Arnold?'

'Do we fuck,' muttered Jock angrily, 'Are you off your fucking heed? Tell him and you're telling the whole fucking place. Darker nights is what we need, darker nights so not every bugger is wandering around the place.'

Fraser's expression remained blank.

He lit a cigarette, 'Jones must have the custom officers in his pocket. This place has never been raided and I should know seeing as there's a card school here near every night, strongest game in the settlements.'

'So you say.'

'I do.'

'Where the fuck is that Arnold?' Jock asked, getting more agitated.

'He says he has news.'

'I don't know if the silly sod meks it up as he goes on.'

'And why should he do that?'

'Because he's an arse, that's why. That's why and him and Jonty get on. They're both as pig thick as each other,'

'I feel sorry for Jonty. It's not his fault he's so backward.'

'Well whose fault is it then?'

'God's. I blame him.'

'What the fuck do you know about God?'

'A damned sight more than you, you heathen bastard,' Fraser answered.

Arnold came in, his face covered in sweat and his shoulders hunched forward as he shoved his way across the crowded room.

'And where the fuck have you been?' Jock asked as Arnold flopped into a chair.

'Don't feel so good today lads, sorry.'

'Why, what's wrong with thee?'

'Bad guts, bad head, bad everything fucking thing,' Arnold muttered.

'So Arnold have a pint, that'll get yer going.'

'No.'

'Or a wee whisky.'

'Not that either.'

'Fucking hell man, what do you want?'

'I'm here aren't I?'

'In body maybe,' Fraser put in.

Arnold pulled his arms to his chest and doubled over, his forehead pressed down on the table.

'I'm sick, sick as a pig,' he moaned.

They waited while he recovered. Jock finished his pint and Fraser his cigarette.

'More?' Jessie asked as she flounced up to them, 'Is it another Jock?'

'Another what?'

'Whatever thee likes,' she answered warily.

'Just a pint Jessie. I don't think thee and me were made for each other.'

'And thank Christ for that is all I can say,' she laughed before going off with his empty glass.

Alice the younger daughter of the family brought it back filled to the frothy brim.

'Me Mam says thee might want someat more.'

'Did she now?' said Jock, 'Well no thanks to that lassie. You can keep it moist and warm for some other sod who misses his Ma.'

'Does that mean youse do or youse don't?'

'Go away Alice,' put in Fraser.

Pulling a face before turning away she muttered, 'Suit yersell.'

'So Arnold lad, what have thee to say for theesell? News is it about that bastard?'

Arnold painfully straightened up. His face was as white as flour mixed with his sweat.

'Tom Flowers was down Ingleton waiting for a load a timber and he says he saw Bill go into the constabulary building and was in there well over half an hour.'

'And when was this?' asked Jock keenly.

'Last Thursday I reckon.'

'Last Thursday,' Fraser repeated.

'So Flowers said.'

Jock ran his fingers round his pint glass. Fraser sat straight against the back of his chair as somebody started playing a mouthorgan over the other side of the noisy room. The drink here was cheaper than at the Railway Inn and Jessie Jones' place seemed to manage to avoid the usual visits of the custom officers who put some of these amateur publicans in jail for a night, not that this ever stopped somebody else setting up another drinking den.

'So who is this Tom Flowers?' Jock asked.

'Works on the scaffolding, allays has.'

'Fuck,' the Scotsman muttered then, 'Bill in the fucking constabulary.'

'We should ask him, ask him what he was doing there.' Fraser suggested, 'Tonight, we should go back to the hut and say we heard he was in the police station and see what he says.'

'He'll say nowt.'

'He can't just say nothing, I know him, not Bill. He'll say something.'

'So what do you two think he was doing there?' Arnold picked up the energy to ask.

'It's obvious,' Jock added.

'Of course it is. That's the whole point. He'll be trapped. There's no way he'll be expecting us to ask him directly especially when he has an audience. He'll say something whatever happens. That's who he is, can't keep his mouth shut, so come on finish your pint and we'll go now.'

Jock looked unsure. Arnold groaned and pulled himself up saying, 'There's nowt else. I only heard this today like. I'm going before I spew all over the shop.'

'Yeh, you bugger off Arnold but if you hear owt else you let us know,' Jock told him.

They watched as he pushed his way to the door.

'Come on man, let's go,' Fraser insisted.

'I'm coming, I'm coming. Shouldn't rush a man wi his drink.'

In the hut Jonty was sitting on the floor with Beth going through a picture book of numbers as the two of them entered.

Bill was at the table with Clare sorting out his loose change asking her the worth of each coin. Ethan was reading a week old Craven Herald while Maggie had just brought in some of the washing. They all turned to see what state Jock was in.

'Two, two,' Beth was saying.

'Two porkies,' Jonty sighed.

'Yes Jonty, yes.'

'It's....it's a three penny bit,' Clare muttered to herself.

'And if it is what's it worth?' asked Bill.

Clare frowned and looked confused.

'Come on lass, what's it worth?'

'Don't know.'

'Yes you do. If it's a three penny piece how many pennies is it worth?'

'You're confusing me uncle Bill.'

'Nay I'm not. It's worth three pennies of course!' he exclaimed.

'Three,' she repeated as she turned the coin over and over in the palm of her hand.

'That's right.'

'So Bill,' Jock started.

He looked up at the Scotsman but made no reply.

Maggie felt the tension immediately.

'I hear thee has been in trouble wi the police.'

Ethan carefully folded his paper.

'Don't look so worried Ethan lad, and how's the nose?' Jock asked, 'It ain't looking so good.'

Ethan could not be bothered to respond.

'Don't know what you're talking about again,' Bill said.

Jock stared, his moist, dark eyes set on him.

'We heard you'd been in the Ingleton police station last week,' Fraser tried.

'Oh you did, you heard from who?'

'Yes we heard, never you mind from who.'

'So what's been happening?' Jock persisted.

'One…….two……..three…….four……..five,' Beth was saying slowly.

'One…….two……two……four……five,' Jonty tried.

Bill picked up a penny piece, 'So Clare, what's this?'

'That's a penny piece. I know that one uncle Bill.'

'Very good lass, very good. And for that you can have it. From now on any you get right you can have.'

'Mam!' exclaimed Clare in excitement, 'Uncle Bill says I can have every coin I guess right.'

'Very generous Bill,' Maggie responded as she wondered if this was the time to get the girls in the bedroom before the trouble got properly under way.

'He can afford it,' said Jock.

'Last Thursday,' Fraser continued, 'You were seen.'

Bill took a deep breath of exasperation before saying, 'Was I now? So what if I was? I can go where I like.'

Jock took a step forward.

'Come on Clare, Beth, bedtime,' Maggie told them, quickly making up her mind that now was the time.

'I'll tek em,' said Ethan, 'Come on you two, bed.'

'But I……' Beth started.

'Now,' interrupted her father.

'What about our supper?' Clare moaned.

'Not tonight,' Maggie said.

'More,' Jonty muttered to Beth.

'You can have some more of the book tomorrow Jonty,' Maggie told him.

'Oh Mam,' Beth complained as she scrambled up and followed Clare and her father into the bedroom.

'Now, whatever it is you've got to say you keep it low like. I don't want any row tonight,' Maggie said firmly, 'Are you listening Jock Tarrant?'

'Why me?' Jock asked, 'Why you asking me?'

'I'm not asking. I'm telling.'

'It's alright Missus,' said Fraser, 'We're just looking for a bit of information from Bill here about what he's been up to because if he's in some sort of trouble we thought we might be able to help.'

'Fuck off!' Bill exclaimed.

'Bill, I'm telling you,' Maggie came back at him.

'Help he says,' Bill continued, 'Like ruddy hell.'

A tense silence followed for a few moments. They could hear Ethan talking to the girls as they got into bed. Bill started smoothing the coins along the surface of the table to let them drop off the edge into his other hand.

'You were at the constabulary,' Jock started.

'What if I was? It's bugger all to do wi you.'

'We're just interested,' Fraser tried as he seated himself at the table pushing Ethan's paper away.

Jock remained standing. Maggie went back to folding the dried clothes, still watching intently as Ethan came back in.

'You lot not sorted yet?' he said wearily ,'because if you ain't I'll be going to bed mesell.'

'There's nowt to sort,' Bill told him.

He looked straight ahead as though trying to make up his mind what to do next. Maggie set the pile of clothes on the stool by the stove and unfastened her apron.

'Load o nonsense if you ask me,' she said then.

'Going to the police is no nonsense Missus,' Fraser said to her.

'You might as well tell em,' she added in exasperation, 'or this'll be going on all night. Either that or the three of you can go and have yer row somewhere else. I'm sick of you three at each other all the time.'

'Just leave em Maggie,' Ethan advised.

'No I won't. We have them two girls next door and I'm sick of them hearing things they shouldn't.'

'All he has to do is tell us,' Jock muttered in a more menacing voice.

'Or fucking thump ye instead,' Bill countered.

'Language!' exclaimed Maggie, 'Not in here! No!'

'Youse could try,' said Jock.

'Or just tell us instead,' put in Fraser, his tone steady and firm, 'Because it's either you were in the Ingleton police station to report a crime or tell tales. Which was it Bill? Tell us which it was'

'Well it weren't no telling tales.'

'Glad to hear it, glad you've finally admit you were there.'

'It's my business.'

'Not if we can help thee,' added Jock sarcastically.

Bill laughed before saying, 'You wouldn't help me if I was the last sod alive so shut it you bloody hypocrite.'

'Big word Bill,' Fraser retorted.

'Not as big as my fist.'

'Ethan,' Maggie cut in, 'Tell em to stop.'

'Waste o time,' he answered.

'For goodness sake!' she said raising her voice.

'They'll have it out so the quicker they do the better for all of us,' Ethan added.

'Get outside and have this nonsense somewhere else, not in here!'

'Well we're here now so we might as well just get on wi it,' Jock said.

'There's more than thee here,' she replied angrily.

'Missus, I couldn't care less. I just.....'

'I was reporting a piece o thieving,' Bill suddenly interrupted.

Fraser sat up straight as he asked, 'What thieving?'

'If you must know I'd been down on one o the works carts to find out what had happened to our next batch o coal for the factory. It should have been there on the Wednesday and seeing as there were no sign of it I went down to Ingleton on the Thursday to find out what were going on. I was at the railway station. I'd left the cart outside and by the time I got back to it some bugger had stolen me jacket and me cap. That's what I was doing wi the constabulary. So what the hell do you think I was going there?'

'And that's it?' Fraser persisted as he glanced up at Jock who was shaking his head.

'That's it,' sighed Bill, 'And now you've spoilt the night the girls were having. You've upset Maggie here and all for what? You should keep yer bloody noses out o other folks' business.'

'And we're supposed to believe that are we?' asked Jock in an even more belligerent tone.

'Yer can believe what the hell yer like. You wouldn't know the truth if it were stuck on the end o thee nose.'

'Just leave it,' Ethan said.

'Yes you two, leave Bill alone. He's told you even though like he said what it's got to do wi you two I don't know. Lucky he's told you owt,' added Maggie still angry.

'I've heard everything now, Bill Asquith reporting a crime. A right proper citizen is our uncle Bill becoming. It must be his age. He's becoming all respectable like in his dotage.'

'Suit yersells,' said Bill, 'But I'd still like to know what it is that worrying you two so bad.'

All this time Jonty had been cross legged on the floor listening and watching with his mouth wide open. Only then did Maggie notice that he had wet himself. She took him up by the arm without a word and took him off to his bedroom as Jock and Fraser left the hut.

'Fucking bastards,' Bill muttered as they closed the hut door behind them.

'They've certainly got it in for you. What have yer done to work em up like that? They're allays at yer?' Ethan asked.

'No bloody idea.'

'No, no bugger else has either.'

'I'll do for em one o these days, I will.'

'Jock I can understand cos he's at every man and his dog especially since yer broke his nose, but why Fraser, what's got into him?'

'Fraser follows, that's what he does.'

'What, follows a thickhead like Jock Tarrant?'

'If it suits him, yes, and at the moment it certainly seems to be suiting him alright. They're never out of each other's pockets, but I'll find out eventually. I'll find out what's got into em.'

'Well the quicker you do the better.'

'Oh it might not be better Ethan lad but it'll certainly be different,' Bill added before going off to see to Jonty.

CHAPTER FORTY ONE

When he set off for the haymaking on the following day Ethan for once felt free from the usual miserable routine. On most farms it had begun the week before but he had been undecided about whether to go or not, but now this morning with a group of other men he was setting out past the viaduct on their way down the valley.

'Ethan, so thee kem then,' said Arnold Wainwright as he caught up with him.

'Thought I'd try it.'

'And where are thee headed?'

'I hear they're still looking for hands at Cragside farm.'

'Bloody hell,' muttered Arnold as he struggled to keep up with Ethan's long strides, 'I tried that last year, tried at Cragside. Them Sugdon brothers are bloody crackers. Mind you, there again, there was their sister. How them three were related to someat like her is a bloody mystery. Floss Sugden, beautiful is the word, but I'd still keep well clear o that place if I were you.'

'I'll try it anyway Arnold.'

'Well more fool you Ethan. Thee won't last more than a day. I'd place a bet on that anytime.'

They trudged along the lowers slopes of Whernside before Arnold cut down into the lower fields leaving Ethan with a few others to continue further up towards Cragside. As they got nearer it became obvious the place was a mess. It consisted of a large barn with slates missing off the roof on one side of the yard with the farmhouse and half derelict out buildings enclosing the rest. The stonework was dark with age and damp. Some of the outer walls were covered in moss and ferns growing in the gaps. Most of the buildings had collapsed roofs with their beams showing and the yard was littered with old, rusted pieces of equipment while a few scrawny pigs were churning up the mud. Rotting wood was leant up against the barn wall and a pile of rubble next to what appeared to be the stable. It stank worse to Ethan than even Batty Green, the stench coming from the cess pit behind the barn and the animal shit covering the ground. He and the other men stopped in the yard and waited. Hens pecked around their feet and a line of sheep with straggly wool hanging off their back ends wandered past. The sun was already well up in a clear blue sky. The locals were saying this had been one of the best summers for a long time. Swarms of lies flickered above pig shit and steam rose from old straw scattered over the yard. The stench was so unbearable three of the men decided they had seen enough and turned round and went off.

'Fucking hell,' one of the men remaining muttered as Ethan flicked the flies away from his face.

'What a bloody mess of a place,' another added.

'It stinks someat rotten so it does,' a third commented in disgust, 'Christ, I ain't sure about this.'

Ethan was always one to stick to a decision no matter what. The sweat was trickling down his face and back when he went with the rest to crouch in the shadow of the barn.

'Where the fuck is everybody?' another of the men wanted to know.

One of them walked over to the farmhouse and rapped on the door. There was no answer.

'No idea, nothing' he said as he came back.

'Maybe they're out int fields already,' Ethan said.

'Didn't see nobody,' Mathew Sennan, the tallest of the men, answered.

Finally a man pulling on his shirt came out of the house. He was bare foot and swayed from side to side as he approached them.

'Tasselled! Tasselled!' he started shouting, 'Fucking hell! Where's me.....where's me......?'

He came to a halt in front of them. His face unshaven, hair matted and snot dribbling out of his huge nose.

'And who the shite are youse?' he asked of the group of men.

'Who the fuck do yer think we are?' one of them called Robert Smart said back angrily.

'Toss heads. Shit grubbers all!' the farmer shouted back, his face suddenly beetroot red as he wiped his nose with the back of his filthy hand, staggering until he fell backwards.

'Christ almighty, will you look at him,' said Ben Welkins, the third of the group

Another man appeared out of the house.

'Tasselled!' the first called out.

'No you're helling not,' said the other as he approached the men.

He was younger but with the same coarse features, his bare feet black with dirt and a torn vest was hanging loosely round a fat body.

Two more of the group of navvies walked off in disgust.

'And where are they fuckers shoving off to?' the younger farmer asked.

Now there were only four left including Ethan.

The third man appearing out of the farmhouse was different. He was wearing boots, a waistcoat and scarf round his neck and walked purposefully across the yard. His rough face was red and fat, his eyebrows black and thick above small, narrow eyes.

'This lump on the floor like is me brother Dave and this here is fat Joseph and I'll be John to you lot if you're here to work and if you ain't you can fuck off right now.'

'Well said.'

John was about to continue but was stopped by this interruption.

'What did thee say?' he asked Mathew Sennan.

'I said you talk a lot o fucking tosh,' the Cornishman answered.

'Oh I does does I?'

By now the drunk Davey was on his knees watching while Joe Sugden stood near his brother in support.

'Right,' John Sugden sighed, 'Right it is.'

'We're here to work,' Sennan added in his strong Cornish accent.

'And what kind o fucking twang will that be?'

'Work and get paid fer it.'

'You'll get paid nowt till I says so.'

'So how much?'

'Never you fucking mind.'

'But I do mind,' Sennan argued.

'Smack the fucker,' Davey said to his brother.

'No I won't Davey boy cos this man here thinks he's one above the rest of us so we'll just see, we'll just bide our time and sees who comes out top of the pile.'

'Don't understand.'

'Nowt different there then so shut yer fuck up Davey lad.'

'Are we working or not?' asked Ben Welkins.

John Sugden spat on the floor but made no other response.

'Cos if we ain't I'm for off.'

'Not so fast lad.'

'This ain't fast. This is too fucking slow.'

'Steady now. It'll be steady, it will. If thee are here for the haymaking then well and good. We have six fields that need doing and the faster the better say I cos this weather can't last forever and we're late as it is.'

Ethan had never seen such brutal, ugly faces in his life. Nobody at Ribblehead, Nottingham or anywhere else in his experience compared with the Sugden brothers. They stank. One was drunk and the other was an imbecile and John pretended to be different but was as gormless as the other two. This was poverty and a numbing dearth of brains. But he was here and he would work as long as he could stand this disgusting set up. He knew he could be earning a lot more working back at the tunnel but this at least was a chance of something different, a kind of freedom, something to get him away from Ribblehead.

Finally they made their way to one of the steep sloped fields situated above the farm. The scythe Ethan was given had a split handle so caused blisters within the first hour. Because of the motion of the cutting he was using muscles he had never needed before, swinging from right to left in as smooth an action as he could manage. In no time the men had their shirts off under the strong sunlight that had them sweating and itchy as they worked slowly through the first field.

Davey in his drunken stupor spent most of the morning sleeping it off in a ditch. Joe decided to walk along the line giving instructions while John spent his time sharpening his scythe without actually using it. This meant the four of them from Ribblehead did all the work, not that this bothered Ethan. He had not expected anything else. To him the farm was in such a state because the brothers seemed to have no idea what they were doing or even seemed to care. The hay was so dry from the weeks of drought that it cut easily, the scythe swishing its blade through the stiff stalks that fell line after line.

Even when they stopped to take a mouthful of water from a jug Joseph would start shouting for them to get back to the work.

'Fucking twat,' Sennan muttered as he picked up his scythe, 'I've a good mind to slit his fucking head off.'

'Good idea,' agreed Ethan as he bent to the work, 'After we've been paid.'

'We should o demanded wages afore we started,' Ben Welkins said.

'It'll be a fucking miracle if this lot know what fucking money is,' Sennan added.

'What you buggers talking about?' Joe called.

'Just stuff!' Sennan shouted back.

'What did you say?'

'I said Mr Gladstone is a fine man.'

'Who?'

'Christ almighty.'

Ethan laughed. Out here in the warm air with views of the whole valley and surrounding hills he was enjoying himself. It was a relief to his body and mind to be doing something different.

'Right I suppose!' John finally ordered, 'Thee'll be having a bite and seeing as you've brought bugger all theesells it'll have to be us to be feeding yer.'

The four of them stopped. Joe came close up to Mathew Sennan and stared at him. He made no response.

'Davey, get theesell to the house and tell Floss!' John called.

The drunk pulled himself out of the ditch, staggered forwards a few steps and then trudged down the field in his filthy bare feet.

'Thee's no good is ter?' Joe muttered at Sennan who plonked himself down and lay back putting his hands behind his head and looking up at the clear sky.

'And thee,' Joe continued as he came up to Ethan, 'what sort o man are thee?'

'The best sort,' Ethan answered, having to turn his head at the stench coming out of Sugden's mouth, a mixture of sour beer and something that had been rotting for a long time.

'Yer jesting me.'

'I am.'

'Don't like it. Brother John this here fella is jesting me.'

'So sort it lad. Don't fucking moan at me. I've enough on me plate.'

The two other men laughed at this. Robert Smart and Ben Welkins were both from Blackburn. They were sitting smoking, their caps lowered to shade their faces from the dipping sun.

'She's coming like!' Davey was muttering as he reappeared.

Behind him Ethan saw who he took to be the sister.

'Coming she is!'

Davey stumbled and then picked himself quickly up as the girl passed him. She was in a dress ripped in several places, some of its faded material hanging down by her bare ankles. But it was her hair that first caught Ethan's attention. It was bright ginger and was thickly plaited and hanging loose over her shoulders. Its colour was dazzling in the sunlight as she came further up the field carrying a large basket. All four of the Ribblehead men were suddenly interested, their bodies poised and focused.

'Bout time,' said John to her as she set the basket down.

'She's in a moody,' her drunken brother announced.

'This here is our Floss. Say hello Floss to these men from the works.'

Her eyes were lowered as she unpacked the food. Ethan scrutinised her brown skin under the layer of filth and her high, prominent cheekbones. She was tall, strong limbed with an incredibly moulded body that he could not stop staring at. Her breasts were loose under the thin dress as her hair flickered red reflections over her face and neck with each movement.

'Says nowt,' Davey half spoke and half belched as he joined them.

The stench from the brothers was almost overwhelming. They smelt as if they had never washed in weeks and their skin and clothes were coated in a mixture of animal shit and piss. If they had not been out in the open air the men would have been suffocated within minutes.

When the basket was empty and the bread, cheese and jugs of watered down beer had been set out Floss walked a few paces away and stood there staring across the valley. Her brothers ignored her but the other four were keenly aware of her presence. It had changed the whole atmosphere of the day. The Sugdens by some sort of miracle had this utterly beautiful girl for a sister who had not uttered a word.

'God bless us,' Sennan had to say, 'Wonders will never cease.'

'What's that?' exclaimed Joe, 'What the fuck are thee going on about?'

'This cheese.'

'What about it?'

'It....it tastes different like.'

'That's good sheep cheese is that.'

'You milk em?'

'No fucking likely. That'd be Floss here's work. You tell em Floss. She meks the cheese don't thee?'

The girl made no response just continued with hands on hips to look over to the distant slopes of Ingleborough.

'Ten minutes,' John told them.

'And more,' Sennan added.

John stumbled over to him shouting, 'What I say! Does to hear? Ten!'

'Steady big man or thee'll blow up.'

'I'll fucking blow you up if thee...'

'I what?'

'Go on.'

'Going nowhere. Me and the rest of the lads like it here Sugden. This'll suit us just fine.'

John leant over him and grabbed him with both hands hoisting him to his feet, 'You fucking even think of speaking to me sister and I'll fucking kick yer brains in.'

'Cornish,' Sennan answered unperturbed until John smacked him in the face sending him crashing onto the ground.

'Get up!' John ordered but Sennan remained with his face in the earth.

'There was....' Ethan started only for the eldest Sudgen to turn on him, 'You can shut it.'

'Fuck this,' said Robert as he tossed his piece of bread away and got to his feet followed by Ben Welkins.

'Now look what thee have done.'

They all turned to the girl.

'Help him up,' she told the other two brothers, 'Help him up.'

Davey and Joe pulled Sennan up until he was standing without their assistance. He had blood dribbling out of his mouth.

She came up to him and lifting the ripped hem of her dress dabbed at his lips.

'Me brother thinks nowt before he does somat daft.'

'It's alright,' said Sennan, watching her as though mesmerised.

'No it ain't. It ain't right at all.'

'Just leave him,' John told her.

'When I'm good and ready and it's you who should leave these men alone John cos the fields won't get done and then what happens in the winter? You tell me that.'

'It'll do,' he said back.

'Do nowt,' she retorted.

She stepped away from Sennan letting the hem of her dress fall. Finally she picked up her basket and started off down the field towards the farm.

Ethan watched her go with a rush of warmth through his whole body. Tension focused on her tall figure as it pushed through the hay coming up to her waist, the light dazzling her deep red hair, light that seemed to him glazed around her.

'Are thee coming?' asked Robert as he trudged past him over to the last line of hay that had been cut.

The Sugden's fields were surrounded by the usual dry stone walls. Ethan had been told by an old navvy all about these walls. The first had been built by the monks of Fountains Abbey which was a good fifty miles away. There was a nearby hill still called Fountains Fell. The limestone walls were over five feet in height, high enough so no sheep could jump over them and had stood for centuries. Because no mortar had been used the Westerly winds blew straight through the narrow gaps between each stone making them less likely to fall down. They were a main feature of the Dales, some going in a straight line over the crest of a hill, others meandering from side to side like a stream of stone flowing down into the valley. They patterned all the hillsides and valley floors looking from distance like a patch work quilt made of dull green shapes divided by grey lines.

Unsurprisingly the Sugdens' walls were in a bad state with large sections having fallen into piles of rubble so long ago they had ferns growing out of them.

By late afternoon the first field had been cut. The brothers eventually joined in the work, Joe complaining at Davey for constantly drinking and John for saying nothing at all. The hay was tied in bundles which were leant against each other to make stacks all over the steeply sloping field. As the sun began to drop behind the first clouds of the day John went for the horse and cart up onto which the bundles of hay were lifted by long handled forks. By now Ethan's back and arms were aching. The blisters had burst on both hands. He was thirsty and hungry and yet still full of the warmth of the day.

'We'll get this lot to't barn,' John Sugden finally announced as he climbed up onto the full cart of hay.

'What about being paid then?' Mathew Sennan asked.

'Bloody hell man,' Joe muttered, 'Aint thee had enough?'

John leant forward off his seat and said, 'And if we pay thee now we won't see any of thee again so I say it's when all the fields are done that thee'll be paid.'

Sennan considered this before looking at the rest of the men who seemed unbothered. Ethan for one would certainly be back the next day and every other day if there was a chance of seeing Floss Sugden again.

'What a fucking clarty lot that is,' Ben remarked later that day as the four men made their way along the path back towards Ribblehead.

'Thick as planks,' agreed Mathew as he lit a cigarette.

'But what about the sister?' Robert Smart asked, 'Christ, how the hell was she born out o the same mother as her fucking brothers? It just can't be.'

'We're all thinking the same,' said Ethan in an easy, relaxed voice, 'We're thinking it must be a bloody mistake somehow.'

'Well the more mistakes like that the better,' added Ben with a grin splitting his features as the four of them started down towards Batty Green.

Ethan pulled off his shirt, partly filled a bucket from the nearly empty water barrel and washed his face, arms and upper body, the water feeling good on his hot skin, drying himself then with his shirt. He was starving hungry but still lingered outside the hut. Children were running past followed by two large pigs which were sniffing around for something to eat on the baked dry earth. Voices were everywhere as darkness began to fall. He took off his boots, left them on the step and finally went inside.

CHAPTER FORTY TWO

Jane was seated in the parlour with James in the armchair across from her. She was sewing while he had been playing the piano and singing some hymns for the first time in weeks and now had his writing board on his knees preparing his next sermon. Over the last months they had hardly been together like this with James so busy especially now with the smallpox taking hold in the settlements. He was out nearly every evening of the week and when they met it was only briefly over meal times, but this evening he was taking time off to prepare his sermons for the outdoor services over the weekend. His mood for once seemed easier, his expression softer and more responsive.

'Is it really what you want to do Jane?' he asked as he glanced up from his writing.

Even though she wanted to believe in his concern she still heard little sincerity or real interest in his voice.

'You know it isn't James so why do you ask?'

'Because I would have hoped by now that you might have decided on your future, not that I'm saying there is any pressure as far as I am concerned, you know that. You are quite welcome to stay here as long as you like. This is as much your home as it is mine.'

She set her sewing down on her lap and sighed. Less and less was she able to believe what her cousin said to her. Now the few occasions when they were together were fraught with mistrust. Jane knew this was because of Lizzie. The girl had managed to destroy any meaningful relationship between them. So far it appeared he had no idea she knew all about his prayer sessions with Lizzie or he had any sense of how involved she and the maid were with each other.

'I have simply no notion what I want to do if you must know and I'm tired of it, tired of the frustration it causes me wondering day after day how my life should change. If I think about the alternatives I am sickened by them. The possibilities for women are still so limited. It's monstrous how much subjection we have to suffer.'

'And why do you think that is?' James inquired, surprising Jane that he dared ask such a question.

'Men are scared, even terrified of the opposite sex because they do not understand us. They are ignorant of the female mind. I would go so far as to say they dislike women so much because they inevitably have to depend on them.'

'Oh dear Jane, you have a very low opinion of us.'

'I think an honest one James.'

'Your views have certainly not softened with time or so it seems.'

'And why should they?'

'I used to think that you would like to go into teaching like Lucy Ormskill. I thought she might have interested you in that direction.'

'I did go to visit her class before the summer holidays. I could never manage what she does, sixty loud, rowdy, disrespectful pupils all clamouring for her attention. It was awful and yet Lucy shows not a sign of wilting. In fact she tells me she enjoys it. Her pupils have shown a lot of improvement she says. But I could not be a teacher. I could not. That is certain.'

'A pity I think, you would make a good teacher Jane.'

'Teaching is a vocation. You have to be born to it and unfortunately I wasn't.'

'No, so it seems,' James said emptily.

He went back to his sermon while Jane sat looking out of the parlour window at the garden that James had carefully tended when he had the time and where she and Lizzie had spent many hours together over the hot summer months. Lizzie had threatened again and again to tell everyone what had been going on and Jane had gradually begun to believe she might carry out her threat.

'Being a governess is a very respectable profession,' he finally offered while leaning down to take up one of the books he had spread at his feet.

'Respectable?'

'Yes, respectable.'

'Which means acceptable, socially acceptable.'

'It means Jane that you could do a lot worse.'

'Well so far I've had two rejections. One family did not reply at all and I am waiting to hear from two more.'

'Are these posts advertised in the Herald?'

'Yes, at least there are plenty of families looking for a governess. The middle classes are finding as many ways as possible at avoiding their children, under the care of a governess until they're five or six and then straight off if they're boys to public school. What a perfect system to keep a family's children at arms' length.'

'You sound cynical and it doesn't suit you at all Jane,' he said in a lighter tone.

'I'm sorry James but that's how I feel about the position that I'm in. I have to do something. I can't just wait for something to happen and I'll never marry so it leaves little else.'

'You're twenty three Jane for goodness sake, plenty of time to....'

'To what?' she interrupted, 'Find a husband or be found by one?'

'To at least consider marriage when you meet someone you like.'

'You make it sound so very reasonable James, so predictable. If it's like that, what about you? Will you ever marry?'

He reddened slightly as she knew he would, a sure sign of his agitation at such a pointed question.

'I'm a missionary doing God's work and that's all I am meant to do,' he answered, forcing a smile that seemed so stiff and false, 'You talk about vocation, well this is mine. You know that. I am dedicated to my role and the idea of marriage will never enter into it.'

'But you're not a Roman Catholic. You're not sworn to celibacy.'

'I should hope not. What a monstrous idea,' he laughed as he put the book back on the floor.

'The spinster and the bachelor then it seems.'

'I don't see why it should be like that for you, but for myself yes, absolutely, and now I must get on or this sermon will never be finished.'

'And there was me promising to give you peace and quiet.'

'No, it's good for us to talk. We see so little of each other as it is, but I still can't understand why you are so adamant about marriage.'

'I just am and that will never change.'

'You sound certain Jane and it's sad to hear it.'

'I am and there's an end to the matter,' she said irritably.

He stared at her for a moment, his features tightening.

Jane so much wanted to ask him where his new riding boots were and his father's watch and chain that he usually kept on his bedside table. When he was away working she would often go into his bedroom and had recently noticed different things missing. Some of his books had gone and a small, oriental chest he had brought with him from Leeds. She wanted to ask him even though she already knew the truth.

'I'll be staying with the Fergusons tomorrow night so don't expect me back until late Thursday. The way things are at the settlements I could spend all my time up there. It's a sad business all this illness and death.'

'Yes,' she answered and then added, 'what would happen to Lizzie if I did get a job as a governess somewhere?'

James appeared uncomfortable as he avoided her look and said, 'Well I suppose I would no longer need a full time maid. I'd get someone to come in a few times a week I suppose.'
'Poor Lizzie.'
'Oh I'm sure she'd manage,' James said quickly, 'and anyway, there is always the uncertainty on how long I will be needed at Ribblehead when the work nears its completion. By then the mission will have other plans for me I should think.'
'There is always change. Nothing can stop it,' Jane said and then added, 'It's frightening sometimes how inevitable it seems.'
'It's the way of the world Jane. We must always remember that. Without change there is no progress, and yet we must hold on to some of the past. Without that we will be lost.'
'I suppose so,' she said with a tone of uncertainty.
After he had set off to the settlements the next morning she was out in the garden hanging the washing while Lizzie was still finishing her breakfast. Pegging up the last of the clothes she left the basket on the lawn and went out of the side gate onto the road and turned left down towards the church. There she stood by the wall looking over at the new section of the cemetery. It had been donated by the local landowner and after being consecrated was already being used because of the increasing amount of burials taking place from Ribblehead. This piece of ground with a low wall on three sides was bordered at one end by the small wood running down to the stream and on the other by the church's established graveyard. It felt such a miserable nondescript addition to the church's grounds without any features whatsoever, just a small area of uneven land, sad, desolate and somehow worthless as though the people there counted for so little. Now she felt scared and bothered. She experienced a sudden loneliness. Here in this awful section of the extended churchyard life ended anonymously. Nothing was marked. There were no head stones only low mounds of earth that would soon sink to the level of the rest of the rough ground.
Quickly, miserably she turned away. The bright morning with its expectations had so swiftly been emptied out. For the next hours she would be haunted by the sense of that depressing burial ground. It was a reminder of her own isolation. Only Lizzie could bring back some warmth to her but she had become a threat. There was no trust left between them anymore. The girl was using her position to squeeze everything she could out of her and James and yet she could not stop needing her, loving her, loving to be with her. Everything felt hopeless and lost and was becoming increasingly desperate as she opened the side gate and entered the garden where Lizzie was waiting for her.
'Terrible this is Miss Jane, a sin, and shocking,' Lizzie said warmly as they lay in bed later that afternoon.

'Yes, terrible.'

'It is. I know it is.'

'And I'm glad.'

'Me too I reckon.'

They kissed then.

Later Jane said almost in a whisper, 'I could lie here forever.'

'Lazy bugger,' Lizzie joked.

'It's you who is the lazy one now Lizzie Twistleton and I'm doing all the work.'

'And that's how it should be,' she laughed.

'I'd do anything for you Lizzie, you know that. I just want you to be happy.'

'Well that's alright then.'

'Anything at all,' Jane repeated.

'So yer can mek the supper later on.'

'Yes, of course. We'll have slices of ham with that bread you like.'

'And then yer can put on some hot water so's I can have a bath.'

'I'd like that, yes I will. I'll light the stove and you shall have buckets and buckets full and I'll slowly, very slowly wash and dry you.'

Even though the curtains were closed the strong afternoon light filled the room with an orange glow spreading its colour over their faces and intertwined limbs.

'You do love me, don't you?' Jane had to ask earnestly.

'I'm not sure now you might be leaving.'

'And who told you that?' she asked in surprise, sitting up in bed.

'Why Master James of course, said you were to be a governess or someat posh like that.'

'I'm not leaving Lizzie. I could never do that, I couldn't,' Jane said, her voice sounding increasingly agitated.

'That's not what he said.'

'Well he's got it wrong.'

'So you'd tell me.'

'I tell you everything, and it's true I have been writing off for such positions but only to keep James from going on at me. He thinks I'm wasting my time here.'

'Cos you're a lady and ladies should be doing proper lady like things and not mouldering here wi the likes o me.'

'He thinks everyone should have a clear aim in life. Just because he's got something to believe in he thinks I should be the same, but I'm not.'

'That's alright then!' Lizzie exclaimed.

Jane loved to feel her breath on her skin. She only wished it could be like it had been at the start of their affair. Now she knew Lizzie was using her love as though it was an object to be bought or sold and she hated what she was doing.

They lay together without speaking for a time. In Jane there was always a low current of tension running though her that her cousin might unexpectedly return.

'You've not worn that red dress recently,' she murmured as she lay with her head on the pillow only a few inches from Lizzie's face.

'Gave it to me sister Alice.'

'Why did you do that?' Jane asked in an irritated, surprised tone.

'Cos she said she liked it and anyroads now you've given me the green and the blue ones I don't have as much of a need of it.'

'I thought it was special. You pleaded for it.'

'Well it was, but not now.'

'You've made that very clear.'

'Alice wanted it and it looks better on her anyroads.'

'I find that hard to believe.'

'Believe what yer like Miss Jane but that's what I think so don't try to mek me believe different.'

'I'm not,' Jane said exasperatedly.

'Cos I've as much right to my own opinions.'

'Lizzie stop it. I was…..'

'I know what you're doing,' she interrupted, her eyes flashing in irritation.

'I don't care what you do with the dresses or anything else I give you. It doesn't matter!' Jane exclaimed, her voice trembling with such sudden emphasis.

'Well stop going on then. You mek us cross when you go on as if I ain't a mind o me own when I have. Just cos I can't read nor write and I come from…..'

Jane pushed her mouth over Lizzie's and held her there until the maid forced her away.

'Stop it!' Lizzie cried as she pushed her back, 'Now look what you've done, you've cut me mouth,' she added licking the blood off her lips.

'Let me,' Jane offered.

'No, I'm alright.'

'You're cross with me.'

'You shouldn't try to bully me like you do.'

'Lizzie I do no such thing. You know that. If anything it's the other way round. You have all the control now and you make that plainly obvious. I just wish it didn't have to be like that,' she said, her voice a confusion of anger and disappointment.

'Control, what control have I got?'

'You know Lizzie. You know exactly what I mean so you don't have to ask as though you've no idea what I'm talking about.'

'So……. tell us.'

'Stop pretending,' Jane said in exasperation, 'Stop always making out you're stupid when you know exactly what's going on.'

'Tell us!' Lizzie demanded, her face tightening as she pushed closer to Jane.

'It's plainly obvious.'

'It ain't to me.'

'Yes it is.'

'Just cos I ask yer for things.'

'And you make it clear just what you'd do if I didn't give them. You make sure I understand the consequences and with you Lizzie there are always consequences. Nothing is free with you is it? Nothing at all.'

'Now you're saying you don't want to give me owt,' Lizzie complained in a suddenly soft, exaggeratedly petty tone.

'But I do, you know I do. I don't care what it is, anything Lizzie, anything at all. '

'Well then, stop going on at me.'

'I want to be able to give you things freely and not………not under such constraint.'

'He touched me,' Lizzie unexpectedly announced.

'Who?' Jane exclaimed in sudden shock.

'Master James. It weren't owt really, just a quick feel.'

'What did he do?'

'We were praying like and then he stopped. I opened me eyes and he was just staring at me and then he let go of me hands and ran his fingers down me cheek, wi both his hands, and then held me titties, not squeezed em or owt, just held em in his hands, just pushing a bit, just a bit. It was funny. It was like he suddenly saw what he was doing and pulled his hands away and said he was sorry and went all red and then started praying again, praying really fast.'

'And when was this?'

'When you was away at the Austwicks last Saturday.'

'But you agreed Lizzie that you would refuse to pray with him, you promised me that,' Jane said urgently.

'He's the master.'

'Oh don't talk such rubbish!' she exclaimed.

'If the master asks then what am I supposed to do?'

'Tell him no Lizzie. It's very simple. You tell him no and that's what you told me you would do the next time he asked. He can't do this Lizzie. He just can't do this!' Jane said, her voice becoming louder and angrier.

'But I don't like upsetting the master. It don't feel right.'

'He touched you. My God, James touched you!'

'It was nowt really.'

'He wants you. You're driving him mad because you threaten everything he stands for, everything he believes. It's disgusting the way he puts himself on trial like this, on his knees beseeching Christ to give him the strength to resist you Lizzie.'

Lizzie laughed, a coarse, loud sound, 'Oh what a load of fancy sounding words.'

'It isn't funny!' Jane cried in frustration, 'It isn't funny at all, not at all!'

'I just feel sorry for him, all serious like and eager and angry at himself. What a state master James gets himself into.'

'Lizzie, stop it! This is just a game to you, a game with me, with James, that's all it is.'

'All I know is that he's asked for us to pray together again and I think I'll do it again cos like I said where's the harm?'

Suddenly Jane sat up and gripped the girl's arms, 'You stop this Lizzie Twistleton! You stop this!' shaking her until Lizzie angrily pulled away.

'Now, now mistress Jane, you're only jealous and who can blame you? Blame yer cousin and his funny ways, imagine a man of the church and a young lass like me, holding me titties and all, but I have to do it, have to do what he asks or what'll he do?'

'He can do……can do nothing,' Jane muttered.

'Oh yes he can. He can throw me out, get rid of me just like that, say he don't need me anymore.'

'He would never do that.'

'Why not?'

'You know why not. You threaten him like you threaten me. He can't do anything. He's trapped and he's only himself to blame as I am. We're the ones responsible here. '

'So what do you want me to do?' Lizzie said and then added, 'You see, it's allays me asking yer. I have to ask yer and I'm fed up doing it, sick of it.'

'You hurt me every time you talk like this. You hurt me Lizzie.'

'Me, thick, stupid Lizzie and you like yer cousin all educated and seen a damn sight more o the world than I ever will. No you can't be bothered by stupid me, you can't.'

Jane's eyes moistened as she sighed and started twisting the bed sheet in her hands, her whole body suddenly stiffening.

'Oh for God's sake,' Lizzie muttered, 'If yer going to be like this the rest o the day then I'm getting up.'

'No!' Jane muttered, 'No, please, please stay with me, please.'

'So yer don't mind about master James then?'

'Don't go, just stay. I.......I don't care what else you do. I've given you all I have. I have no money. You have all my clothes, my books, my jewellery however little there was. I know your family sell them and I don't mind, I don't so long as we can stay together like this. Please Lizzie, say you will, say it.'

'How does yer know on what I do wi yer things? How do yer know that? Who's been mouthing off?'

'I.....I just know that's what you do.'

'And what if it's true?'

'I don't mind what you do with them. It doesn't matter.'

'Well it does to me and it does to the rest o me family. I want em to do well.'

'Of course,' Jane agreed.

'To...to better themselves.'

'Yes, that's what any daughter would want for her family.'

'And it's hard miss Jane, hard being just a farm labourer and me Mam doing bits o sewing for folk and the rest of em having no jobs, having nowt.'

Jane closed her eyes, her fingers pulling now at the bed sheet before she said in an empty voice, 'Nobody has anything really, do they? Nothing at all when you really think about it, nothing.'

'Oh here yer go,' sighed Lizzie before she suddenly got out of the bed and walked naked out of the room with Jane calling after her.

CHAPTER FORTY THREE

It was the third day of the harvesting and Ben Welkins, Robert Smart, Mathew Sennan and Ethan were still working for the Sugden brothers. The only reason they were there was to catch a glimpse of Floss Sugden whenever possible. She was the only reason they put up with the swearing, the shouting and the filthy stench from her brothers who seemed half mad with drink most of the time, always arguing between each other, fisting each other in the face when they were fed up talking. Each day it was only John who was half decently dressed. The other two were always in rags and went around bare foot as if they did not have a penny to scrape between them.

'And there was stupid me thinking farmers were allays well off,' Sennan had said the second evening they were making their way back to the settlements.

'They might have pots o gold stashed away somewhere,' Ben had suggested.

'They stink o someat alright,' put in Robert as they trudged along the valley side under a grey, cloudy sky.

Ethan said little. Floss Sugden was stuck in his mind like a standing stone in the middle of a field. Her image was in every minute of his day. His reaction was so different to anything he had felt before it seemed to belong to a separate reality where his family and his work did not exist. He had only seen her a few times and yet those occasions had filled him with a huge desire to see more and more of this farm lass who seemed the only sane one in the rest of her desperate family. The brothers were thugs and ignorant. Ethan could not understand how they had managed to exist for so long on a farm that was obviously falling down around them. Any haymaking seemed to him a complete waste of time. The Sugdens were going through the motions. They revolted Ethan. They were nothing but beasts like the rest of the animals they ignored and yet there was Floss like a flower growing out of the midden heap. Her body seemed to fill the space around her just as her red hair turned everything golden in the sunlight when she brought their food. A painter Ethan thought would have spent months trying to capture this image of the girl in the field with the tattered dress in her bare feet with a basket over her arm filling the day with light and shape.

That evening they came under the viaduct's scaffolding and met a group of navvies, one of whom was Tom Myres.

He came straight up to Ethan, 'Where've yer been Ethan lad? We've not seen thee for weeks. Come for a pint.'

Ethan stiffened. He had wanted to avoid Myres. There was nothing now for them to talk about. He was finished with politics but felt too embarrassed to tell him.

'Been up at Sudgens' farm.'

'I see you're with the haymaking then.'

'Thought I'd have a change.'

'And why not? Mind you being wi the likes of Sykes and Withers can't be easy.'

'They're alright.'

'So what about this pint then?'

'No, not tonight. I'm knackered and I need someat to eat.'

'Alright, if thee says so, but I'll walk wi thee if yer don't mind.'

'If you want,' Ethan had said reluctantly.

He shouted goodnight to the others and set off with Tom past the offices and work sheds.

'Has to rain sometime,' Tom commented, 'But I suppose you don't want it till all the hay is in.'

'Not till then, no.'

'So have yer been avoiding me?' Tom asked lightly.

'I suppose I have,' Ethan forced himself to say.

They stopped and looked at each other as though it were a direct confrontation, a final reckoning.

'And why would that be Ethan?'

'Cos I'm scared to tell thee right.'

'Scared o what?'

'I thought I could be a..... a revolutionary and manage the violence and all that when it became necessary but I was kidding mesell. I bloody detest violence, detest it. I'd be no bloody good. Ever since that night in the Railway Inn I've had it. Call me a coward or what yer will but I can't stomach any o this punching and kicking for a cause. I can't do it and I won't. At least I know now.'

'I suppose you do,' Tom had said in a serious tone and then waited for Ethan to continue.

But nothing was added. At that point James Tranton with some of his congregation passed by on their way from their open air service.

'Nowt wrong wi being scared Ethan,' Tom had finally commented.

'Of course there bloody is. I'm frightened silly, allays have been and I resent having to tell yer this. You should have just left it Tom, just left me alone wi me own questions. You seem to know what yer doing. I admire your strength but it ain't for me cos I'm not political like that and never will be.'

'And there was me thinking you'd joined us.'

'I thought I had till it kem to the first real action and then I was bloody lost. None of it was me. I'd been punched in the face and I couldn't stop thinking about it. I'd have done anything not to have been in that ruddy situation, scrambling around on the floor like a bloody animal.'

'That's how it is though. To become more civilised we have to be more beastly to begin with or nowt'll change.'

'Don't lecture me Tom. I know it. I've heard it enough. I'm sorry like but I'm done wi it all, so if yer don't mind I'm going home and from now on I'd like to be left alone.'

'It's a shame Ethan.'

'No it isn't, not for me it isn't.'

'And there was me thinking you were a real man.'

'Well now you know I ain't so bugger off.'

'Steady lad.'

'Steady my arse,' Ethan had muttered, 'It must be so bloody good to know and believe in what yer doing wi no doubts, just certainty. Well we ain't all like that.'

'I know that Ethan.'

'Do you, do you really? I don't think the likes of you Tom have any idea what it's like to believe in nowt except yer family and sometimes even they're not enough, not really. So just leave it,' Ethan said before setting off up past the factory and the tramways and their two engines.

On his way to the Sugden farm the following morning he had no regrets what had been said between him and Tom Myres. He was going to see Floss. That was all that mattered. He was going to feel his whole body tugged in need towards her in ways he had never felt before. Maggie and the children were in another world. There was no guilt because what he wanted had nothing to do with their reality back at Batty Green. Here everything was different. Nothing existed but his desire to see and be close to her, as close as possible. He knew it was the same for the other men. All they talked about was what they would do to Floss Sugden if they ever got the chance. It disgusted him and yet deep down he felt exactly the same. He just hated the way men had to openly discuss things in this way. There were no private thoughts with them. Anything to do with women had to be expressed to prove how manly they were. To Ethan it was pathetic and demeaning to be so open, to be so crude and vulgar about something that should be the absolute opposite.

They had been working in the third field when Joe came up and told Ethan he had to go to the barn for the pitch forks.

'Why me?' he asked.

'Cos thee is the ugliest shite here,' Joe had told him, 'so get theesell on.'

He put down his scythe aware of the others watching him. The loose straw crackling under his feet as he crossed the field into the next and on through the gate that led into the farm yard. The pigs were there scuffling through some rubbish by the stable door. Everywhere was silent. He stopped for a minute. The outbuildings with their collapsed roofs and beams stuck up in the air added to the forlorn feeling about the place. The door of the farmhouse was shut and he wondered where Floss was and what she was doing. Momentarily he considered knocking on the house door that was stained and peeling just to see if she would answer. He looked down at his boots which now had the straw from the fields sticking to pig shit. The stench in the yard was unbearable. It made him want to vomit. The day was overcast adding to the miserable sense of the place. It frustrated him to see what must have once been a substantial farm being destroyed in this way. The house had no curtains on its filthy windows, the stonework stained with old damp.

He crossed over to the barn and shoved open one of the huge doors. This was by far the biggest barn he had seen in the Dales. It had been so well built it still seemed in reasonable condition as he stepped inside. Here the smell of the new hay thankfully overcame the rest of the stink outside. The fresh hay was stacked up on the upper level reached by a ladder. On the ground floor there was a confusion of bits and pieces of machinery, a pile of old potato boxes, a mound of empty sacks and other farm instruments leant against the walls. He wandered around looking for the pitch forks, his steps muffled in the heavy silence that made him think of a high roofed chapel with faint shafts of light coming through small gaps in the stone on the upper level and the half open doorway. There was an odd feeling of security here, of warmth where time was in suspension.

'You shouldn't be in here,' came a voice that startled him.

Floss came out of the dimness, 'Does to hear?'

'I'm here for a purpose,' he managed to say.

'Says who?'

'Yer brother said.'

'You're one o them bog diggers. What's thee name navvy man?'

'Ethan.'

'God almighty.'

'Ethan Granger.'

'Even worse!' she laughed.

'Sorry yer think so.'

'Well I do and seeing as this is the Sugden farm I can think what the bloody hell I like. Isn't that right Ethan Granger?'

By now she was standing a few feet away from him. Even here in the dimness of the barn her hair still glowed a deep russet. Moodily she rubbed one of her bare feet backwards and forwards along the ground in front of her, pouting her lips and looking around before she started humming a tune.

He did not know what to say. He was overwhelmed by her presence but had to do something to catch her interest.

'Nowt much to say, have thee?' she asked him then.

'I....I didn't expect......'

'What, didn't expect what? It's my farm ain't it? Allowed to go round the place ain't I?'

'Yes you are.'

'Well then?'

'I'm looking for the pitch forks. Your Joe sent us.'

'Joe, Joe,' she moaned, 'He's me brother.'

'Yes, I know that.'

'Looks after me does our Joe and Davey and big John, look after me they do.'

'You're a lucky girl then.'

'No I ain't. I'm just their sister, that's all. Nowt lucky in it.'

Suddenly his mind was empty as his body filled up with a growing reaction.

'So what are we going to do?' she asked.

'What do yer mean?'

'You know's like Ethan Granger.'

'No I don't know.'

'And I don't believe yer.'

'I have to go and get.....'

'Have to what?'

He made no response to this as she came closer.

'I've nowt on under me skirt.'

'Stop this Floss.'

'Stop what? Ain't done nowt and by the looks of it we ain't going to.'

By now he could smell her, could feel the warmth coming from her body.

She pushed up her hair and then let it fall over her shoulders.

'You want to. I can tell. You want to alright.'

'I......I never said I didn't.'

'Well why ain't you doing it someat about it?'

'Because.....'

'Cos what?'

'Nothing.'

'Cos you'll be married I suppose.'

'Yes I am.'

'So that'll stop yer.'

'I never said that.'

'You've not said owt.'

'I do....do like you,' he finally managed.

'Like is it?'

'You know what I mean.'

'No I don't.'

'It's just......just difficult. I never expected to meet a girl like you here.'

'What, in this miserable dump of a farm?'

'Yes, I suppose so.'

'Well leave it then.'

'I don't want to leave it.'

'Says you.'

'I don't Floss.'

'Have to prove it, won't yer?'

'I....I want you.'

'Maybe I've changed me mind.'

'No,' he said forcefully.

'I can do. I can change me mind when I like,' she said, her eyes dark and staring at him.

'Stop it.'

'Stop what?'

'You know.'

'No I don't.'

She pushed out her lips and then started laughing before suddenly Ethan grabbed her so brutally the two of them finished up on the floor, his hands already under her skirt. Immediately he was gone to it, lost to the fast need for her as she eagerly pulled him closer.

When it was over and they lay there in the filth of the barn for once she was quiet. He could hear her fast breaths, feel the rise and fall of her breasts. Above were the thick beams holding up the next level with dust floating slowly down towards them.

Eventually Floss got to her feet, pulled down her dress and without saying another word walked across the barn and out through the gap between the doors.

Ethan lay there half conscious. Looking up at the thick air of the barn was a grey mist mixed with the smell of the hay. He had to repeat in his mind what happened, had to do it quickly so as not to lose any of it, the feel and smell of her, the frantic exploring of her wonderful body so full and strong and eager for him.

Eventually he dragged himself up, buttoned his trousers and started looking for the pitch forks.

'And where the fuck have thee been?' John demanded to know as he returned to the field.

Davey was drinking from the water jug as Joe stopped to watch Ethan. The other three continued with the scything.

He tossed the pitch forks on the ground saying, 'Looking for these.'

'I said they were in the bloody barn.'

'And that's where I found em.'

'I think thee should do some work now then, do what you're fucking here for.'

The rest of the morning passed slowly. He worked without being conscious of it. Ethan was waiting for Floss to appear with the food basket. When she did all of them stopped work. As before she laid out the bread, cheese and jugs of beer and then walked off out of the field not once looking at him.

'What the fuck's got into her?' her brother John asked.

'She's brooding like a fucking hen,' Joe answered.

'Laying her egg!' Davey shouted out and then started laughing so hard he nearly fell over.

The four navvies sat on the earth eating. Ethan had nothing to say. He just listened to Robert talking about whether he was going back to continue on the railway or head south to try something different.

'I've had it up here in this God forsaken place and the idea of going through another winter is my idea of a bloody nightmare,' he was saying.

Sykes and Welkins said nothing. Ethan knew they both had families here whereas Smart had no such responsibilities. He could do as he liked.

The Sugdens sat by themselves which suited the others. A fresh wind had started up and the air was suddenly colder. For the first time in weeks the weather was changing.

Throughout the rest of the day Ethan was hardly aware of what was going on around him. He focused on the next swing of the scythe's blade and the next as it cut through the dry stalks that fell easily to one side. It was only after they had finished the field, had tied up and stacked the new bundles and then forked them up onto the cart did he realise that the next thing would be pitching the hay up into the barn. The four men sat high up on top of the hay as the cart swung from side to side like a ship at sea. John was on the seat and as the cart came into the yard Joe and Davey headed off to the farmhouse.

'Lazy shits!' John called after them, 'Get yer fucking sells back here!'

They paid him no attention as he stopped the cart at the front of the barn.

The place had been transformed. It was now the special place where his life had begun again, his life of sex, of having sex, proper full timed sex inside a woman who was a wonder to him, was all light and warmth and the colour of hayfields, was all fullness and pouting and provocative the way she walked, looked, tilted her head and her eyes flashed in the afternoon glow. He was beside himself and just wanted to be alone to remember over and over again what had happened in this building only a few hours earlier. The sense of excitement was overlaid now by layers of remorse and guilt. He had failed Maggie, failed the girls and yet here he was already planning how he could meet Floss again.

He remained on the cart forking up the hay through the open door where Sykes and Welkins were spreading it in layers on the upper level. The wind had increased blowing stalks of the hay away over the roofs of the dilapidated farm buildings. The men were in their jackets now it being suddenly so much colder.

That night he lay restlessly beside Maggie as she said to him in a whisper, 'Yer in a funny mood tonight. You said you were hungry and yet ate hardly anything. Then yer said you were tired but stayed up wi Bill and Jonty to I don't know what time and now here you are still awake.'

'Just can't get to sleep,' he answered.

'It must be the haymaking.'

'I suppose so.'

'You're not used to it.'

'I like it though, someat different.'

'But yer said it'd be finished end o this week.'

'Ay, just two fields to do.'

'So you've never said what these Sugden brothers are like,' Maggie said.

Ethan tried to control his breaths as he responded with, 'Three of the most gormless, dirty buggers you're likely to meet. They're wild and rough and God knows how they're still on that farm cos it's going to rack and ruin.'

'And is there just them?'

'Ay, just them,' he had to lie.

'They say the famers in the Dales live in a different world, right old fashioned, so I've heard.'

'And they might be right if the Sugdens are owt to go by, and oh yes, they have a sister who yer never see,' he added, suddenly changing his mind as to what to tell her.

'A sister?'

'Called....called....no I can't remember.'

Just then there was a murmur from Beth, 'Mam, I'm thirsty.'

'Just get to sleep now,' Maggie said softly.

'I'm thirsty Mam and me head hurts.'

Maggie got up and went over to place her hand on Beth's forehead.

'She's burning up,' she told Ethan, 'Get her a mug o water while I sort her bedding, it's soaked through.'

Ethan went into the kitchen to bring back some water. With the long dry summer the water barrel at the side of the hut had been regularly replenished with buckets from the stream.

'I'll sit up wi her,' Maggie said later, 'You try and get some sleep.'

'What's up wi her?' Clare wanted to know as she sat up in bed.

'She's alright, just got a bad head.'

'What time is it?'

'I've no idea, but you try and sleep or you'll be in a right state tomorrow morning.'

'There's nowt wrong,' Beth said to her sister then.

'Nowt wrong,' Clare repeated before settling down again.

'I'll bring in some more water for later on,' Ethan suggested, sensing the worry in Maggie's tone as she sat on the edge of Beth's bed stroking the hair away from her face.

On the last day of the haymaking there was an argument about pay. When John Sugden had offered them three pounds for the week the row had started. Mathew Sykes did most of the talking as they faced up to the three brothers in the middle of the last field.

'You said five when we started,' Sykes said.

'Never said nowt,' John replied savagely.

'You buggers,' Tim Welkins shouted.

'Three,' John repeated.

'That's what it is,' Joe added.

'No, fucking no,' Sykes muttered back, 'We want five for the week and then yer getting it bloody cheap so stop messing us around and pay up.'

'Or what? Or you'll what?' Davey shouted at them, his filthy hair down over his shoulders and his face covered in dirt and spots.

'You'll find yer fucking barn burnt down one night, that's fucking what.'

'You bastard!' Davey exclaimed as he tried to grab Sykes who jumped back making the brother stumble forward until he was on his hands and knees.

'Get up for fuck's sake,' John told him.

'He's threatening us, he is,' Davey continued as he dragged himself to his feet.

'You'd be fucked if yer did owt like that,' said Joe before he spat out a mouthful of phlegm.

'So what's it to be?' Sykes persisted.

'Give us the money,' Robert added.

John's face stiffened as though he was struggling to think it through.

'Don't listen to em John,' Joe said to him.

'Shut up a minute.'

'I'm just saying.'

'Well don't.'

There was a tense silence as the first spots of rain started to fall.

'Bloody hell!' Davey with his drunken drawl called as he turned his face to the thick, grey sky.

'We'll pay thee if......'

'If what?' Sykes interrupted.

'Yer clean out the byre when the hay's done with.'

'Fucking hell.'

'That's it or thee gets nowt so help me God.'

Ethan agreed with the other three to accept the offer so finally they could get to work, rushing to have the field done before everything was soaked.

He waited with tight expectation for Floss to make an appearance. It was after the food was finished and as she was walking away he ran over to her.

'I want to see thee again,' he said to her.

She turned and looked at him as if she had never seen him before.

'You shouldn't be talking to me. Me brothers won't like it.'

'I want to see you again,' he repeated, 'I have to see you again.'

She hesitated for a few moments and then said, 'They go drinking in Ingleton on a Saturday night,' and at that she turned and set off through the gate into the next field.

'What the fuck was that about?' John asked angrily.

'Just thanking yer sister for the food she's brought us every day.'

'If you so fucking look at her again I'll fucking smash yer brains in, does to understand me? You don't talk to her, look at her or owt.'

'I just....'

'I heard just. You just listen to me you Irish sod picker.'

'Jesus,' Robert muttered in response.

'You as fucking well!' John shouted at him.

'Irish bastards,' Joe put in as the four navvies started walking away.

CHAPTER FORTY FOUR

Richard spent all his spare time riding over the hills from one dale to the next. He rode to try and free his mind. He rode to be away from the works as often as he could. The tiredness he was feeling seemed to deepen by the day and it was only when in the saddle that he felt almost himself again. With his long cape and wide brimmed hat pulled firmly down on his head he was out in all weathers. The rain had come and September had turned cold. The wind and lashing rain suited his mood. It provoked him to ride even further, sometimes going up onto the higher hills miles away from Ribblehead where he could ride for hours and not meet a soul except perhaps a shepherd with his dogs. The Dales here were empty, the endless stone walls that criss crossed the landscape giving them form and shape. The land was rough with limestone escarpments and high flat topped hills where little could survive but the hardiest sheep. It suited him to be alone and isolated in such an empty, barren place. The colours were shades of brown, green and the lines of grey stone. All was bare of trees, only stunted hawthorn bushes. When the rain was heavy the hillsides became porous with small streams running out of the steep slopes down towards the becks that flooded any flat land on their banks. This land was like his mood. What he felt and how it looked was the same.

He lived now with constant frustration and depression. His life was buried under an avalanche of resentment and confusion. He had come to despise himself for being so weak. Riding around the Dales was a form of release. This was the land he had always respected, knowing how difficult it had been to plan a way through for the railway. Here England was on its furthest edge. Nothing could grow except coarse grass. Stone and water was as much underground as above with potholes and caves all over the area, some with huge chambers large enough to accommodate a building the size of a cathedral, an underworld below, a labyrinth of tunnels and caverns like an enormously complicated geological brain.

Riding again down to Settle for another meeting with Armsworth at the Golden Lion hotel he was worried. He had no idea what this meeting might be about. Usually a meeting with the directors was planned weeks in advance but not this time. He rode towards the market town full of apprehension and misgivings.

Armsworth was already seated at the table by the time he arrived.

The dining room with its dark crimson wallpaper and its plastered ceiling with blackened beams seemed less welcoming today.

'I haven't started yet Richard lad, so come and join me,' was Armsworth's greeting as Richard walked across the empty dining room.

'So, how are you?'

Richard scrutinised him to see any signs of doubt in his eyes, but Armsworth was his usual healthy, red faced self.

'How am I?' he repeated the question, 'I'm well thank you, however I suppose I'm wondering why we're having this meeting.'

'Oh I see,' sighed Armsworth as the owner of the hotel approached them 'Mrs Moffat, are we to have the pleasure of you serving us?'

The small, rotund Mrs Moffat with a sparkling white apron that mirrored her smile answered, 'You are, seeing as two of my girls are off sick.'

'Nothing serious I hope. There's enough illness in these parts so I hear.'

'No, thank the Lord, nothing too serious Mr Armsworth and this is Mr Stockton if I'm not mistaken.'

'Yes it is, hello,' Richard nodded.

'I thought it was you. So what will you have?'

'For me the usual which'd be soup, chops, potatoes vegetables, gravy with some good cheese to finish.'

'And you Mr Stockton?'

Richard was hungry and yet felt tense enough not to want to eat but thought he had better try.

'Yes, I'll have some of the same except smaller quantities than usual.'

'You see Mrs Moffat, it's Richard's way of saying I eat too much, but when I'm here in your fine establishment I cannot help it,' said Armsworth warmly, 'I'm here so I always take the chance to partake of your fine cooking, the best in the Dales by far.'

'Well thank you for that Mr Armsworth,' Mrs Moffat said smiling, 'And what will you have to drink?'

'A pint for me,' Richard replied.

'And a pint of your best ale for me as well.'

'Right you are. It shouldn't be long.'

'We're in no rush Mrs Moffat, no rush.'

'They waited until she had left before Richard commented, 'Your letter sounded urgent.'

'It wasn't supposed to sound urgent.'

Richard again waited while trying to control his impatience. Recently he had begun to find it increasingly difficult to wait for anything.

'It's just that last week I also received a letter.'

'About what?'

'About you Richard.'

'I see. Can I ask who it was from?'

'From Mr Murray.'

Now he knew what was coming.

'If it was from Murray I wouldn't expect it to be very flattering. We unfortunately have had our disagreements recently.'

'He says he's worried about you Richard.'

Richard could not help but laugh, 'Worried! I don't think so. Critical more like.'

'Says you're tired and have been finding work difficult so much so that you've been taking a lot of time away from Ribblehead, going for long rides he says.'

Momentarily he was so angry he could make no response. He should have guessed. This whole thing was totally predictable. Murray now was willing to go to any ends to cause him trouble.

Armsworth looked awkward, taking deep slow breaths before he glanced up at a party of four entering the dining room and taking the table nearest the fire.

'Murray wants my job,' Richard finally said.

'Well he can't have it. It's as simple as that. But is there anything in what he says because if there is I'm here to help?'

'That's good of you.'

'No it isn't. It's sensible. I'm not having our top man becoming a liability. We're halfway through the project and the last thing me or the rest of the directors for that matter want is our chief engineer failing in his job for any reason. So what's this Murray fella on about Richard?'

'Right,' interrupted Mrs Moffat as she set down their steaming, brim-full bowls of fresh vegetable soup and a basket of bread, 'Mind now cos the soup's scolding hot.'

'Smells grand,' Armsworth commented.

Richard had never known this man any different. He was always the same, friendly, humorous, kind and always interested.

'Murray is not exaggerating everything.'

'And what does that mean?'

'The fact is I have felt more tired than usual. In my free time I take every opportunity to go for a ride but I am not shirking my responsibilities and I am not losing any of my dedication to the work. That could never happen.'

'Glad to hear it.'

'But you should know that.'

'Of course I do lad. It's just I don't expect letters from one of your engineers so critical of you.'

'Murray has gone too far.'

'So it seems, but I'm leaving it up to you Richard what you want to do about it.'

'I'm not sure at the moment what I want to do about Andrew Murray except to say I am disappointed but not surprised. We have begun to differ on just about everything especially how to deal with the workforce.'

'So what's he, one of them bash down the workers sort?'

'Exactly.'

'I'm afraid those days are long gone. We're living in changing times or doesn't your Murray read the papers?'

'Probably not or probably he reads what suits him like most narrow minded people.'

'My Richard, that tone doesn't sound like you. This fella must be bothering you.'

'He wasn't until recently.'

'Well like I said it's up to you what you want to do about it. I must admit I have no respect for somebody who'd go behind another's back like that, writing such a letter.'

'Can I read it?' Richard unexpectedly asked.

'I've left it at the office but even if I hadn't I wouldn't have let you read it. He sent it to me and that's personal, not to be shared.'

Richard fell silent.

The director started on his soup.

Another shower of rain rattled the hotel's front windows.

Mrs Moffat had returned to see to the group of four seated near the fire.

Richard was suddenly conscious of it all. Murray was only of secondary significance. At the moment he had not the energy to be really bothered about any of it except to feel that it was pathetic and dishonest. More than anything he felt thankful that Armsworth still supported him. Without that he knew he would be in a difficult position. He wondered how much Andrew had mentioned in the letter.

'We have to discuss what to do about the school,' he finally mentioned.

'What about it?' Armsworth asked, looking up inquiringly.

'Whether to keep it open or close it temporarily because of the outbreak of smallpox in the settlements.'

'And what's your thinking on the matter?'

'Personally I don't think it will make any real difference. I'd rather leave it up to the parents to decide what they want to do on an individual basis. Everyone is packed tight together in the settlements as it is. Closing the school won't change that.'

'And Miss Ormskill, what does she think?'

'Oh I'm sure she'd prefer to keep the school open.'

'Well then,' Armsworth sighed, 'you do what you think is best.'

The remainder of the meal passed in discussing the progress there had been up at Ribblehead followed by the problems they were having with explosions in the tunnel and finally the haymaking.

'More went than last year unfortunately,' Richard answered the last point, 'the best paid workers in the country and yet they're still willing to jeopardise their jobs to go cutting hay. What sense is there in that?'

'They know we can't sack them all. They know we need them.'

'But why do they do it?'

'Something different, a holiday? Who knows Richard? Railway men are a mystery to me and I've known them for over forty five years.'

On the way back the rain had ceased leaving the road deep in mud. The horse plodded on as Richard loosely held the reins trying to decide on what he should do next. He had a list of concerns that needed dealing with and the more he considered them the more irritated he felt.

As he came down off the road and over the bridge into Batty Green the noise of work was intense coming from the viaduct and the sections being levelled off where the lines would be laid. Smoke was billowing from the brick factory's tall chimneys and spreading under charcoal grey clouds and steam blasting from the engines pulling the trucks up the tramways. The blacksmith was hammering away and there was the repetitive grind of the cranes as they lifted huge blocks of stone. Men were clambering all over the viaduct banging nails into new scaffolding and up on the embankments, their pickaxes clattering into the rocky earth. Women and children were moving around the settlement and delivery carts were coming along the muddy road with their loads of coal, milk and fresh bread and other supplies.

He rode up to the hut on wheels and leant forward to peer through one of its tiny windows. Inside were Simpson and Brougham, two of his junior engineers studying diagrams on the long table. He turned then to ride over to the office. As he stopped outside there was a sudden shower of hailstones rattling over the roofs and quickly whitening the sodden ground. He did not move, sat there on his horse as the shower just as suddenly ceased. He waited until eventually Andrew Murray appeared.

'Richard, I've been looking for you,' Murray started.

Richard looked at him for a few moments, his face half hidden under his hat until he finally said, 'Yes, I've been to Settle to meet Armsworth.'

'Oh, I see. I never knew you had a meeting.'

'I would call it an emergency meeting.'

'No trouble I hope,' Murray said weakly.

'No, not at all. I must thank you for writing a letter to Armsworth expressing your concerns about me.'

'Richard I felt.......'

'Interestingly Mr Armsworth did not share your concerns,' he interrupted.

Murray made no response to this, his face stiffening.

A faint mist filled the space between the long huts as people moved around on their daily business.

'And after all, 'Richard continued, 'Mr Armsworth is one of the directors and has a lot of influence on the company which has sole financial responsibility for the building of the line now that Josiah Forbes has been declared bankrupt. Did you know that had happened Andrew? No, of course you didn't because you are not in any position to know. I was the one informed, two weeks ago I think it was.'

'I didn't mean to undermine you.'

'Of course you didn't. You were concerned about my wellbeing and for that I must thank you. It's only a pity you couldn't have said it directly to my face, but I suppose you were too embarrassed and therefore thought it was wiser to write to one of the company directors. Anyway, as I said, Mr Armsworth gave me his full backing and said I had never looked better,' Richard added as he pulled on the reins to set the horse off in a trot up past the rest of the offices and work shed leaving Murray standing there with the rain soaking his hair and suit.

The children were on a mad scramble out of the school as he approached, shouting, pushing and running in all directions. He waited until the rush was over before he dismounted, tied his horse to the wooden handrail next to the three steps up into the schoolroom.

He stood in the open doorway to watch Lucy at the other end of the long room talking to two of her helpers. He felt for once perfectly calm, almost empty of any emotion.

Finally Lucy looked up and said with some surprise, 'Mr Stockton, this is an unexpected visit.'

'Is it?' he inquired

She frowned as she approached him and said, 'Why yes. Why do you ask in such a way?'

'No reason.'

'Would you like a cup of tea? One of the girls can make you one now we have the stove working again.'

'No thank you,' he answered stiffly.

'Right, Shirley, Angela, you can go now.'

'Don't you want us to finish off collecting in the slates Miss?' the taller of the two asked.

'No, you can finish that tomorrow.'

They waited until the girls had collected their coats, said their goodbyes to their teacher and shut the door behind them.

'They are such a help, such a help,' Lucy repeated as though needing something to say.

Richard took off his hat and then unbuttoned his cape.

'You have been out riding in this awful weather,' she said after having noticed the horse tied up outside.

'On business, down to Settle.'

'I see.'

'I have to do a lot of riding around the place on business. It's becoming more part of my job.'

'But you enjoy it?'

'It's necessary, that's all.'

She looked at him anxiously before going over to her desk.

'I've always wished to have a horse. It must be wonderful to just go off by yourself and ride anywhere you like, except there are so many walls in the Dales. You have to stop to open every gate.'

The words came automatically. Now she was nervous she had to say something. He was standing there looking so severe and serious.

'Is this a social call or are you here for any other reason?' she added.

'Has there to be a particular reason for me to want to see you?'

'No, of course not.'

'But you're right. I am here for a reason.'

'Not an unhappy one I hope.'

'What is unhappy to you Lucy I still am not clear,' he said pointedly.

'Oh dear Richard, that sounds ominous.'

She waited then but instead of him saying more he walked to the end of the room and back again, running his fingers along the top of some of the desks, his expression so absorbed as though he had forgotten she was there.

'We have had a good day anyway,' Lucy tried, becoming worried and irritated at the same time.

'I'm glad to hear it.'

'Progress being shown with some of them at last.'

'Yes,' he answered emptily before picking up his cape and adding, 'I'm sorry Lucy but I've just remembered I am supposed to be at a meeting,' he lied, 'So I will see you on Sunday as we have arranged, alright?'

She tried to stop herself appearing confused as she said, 'Of course Richard, but you've only just arrived.'

'I'll see you on Sunday,' he repeated as he took up his hat and left the room.

Lucy went to the doorway to watch him ride off, the flanks of his horse washed over by the late afternoon's dull light. Returning to her desk she sat wondering what on earth his visit had been for. She would not allow his unexpected behaviour to affect her. She would sit and consider as she did at the end of every school day how things had gone and whether overall the day had been worthwhile. For many reasons this day had been better than most. Gradually she was being drawn closer to her rough and ready pupils. They were beginning to be moulded into something almost recognisably civilised except for the usual culprits who were impossible to change. Her teaching had to be more basic, more repetitive and had to adapt to all the different levels of ability, the hardest challenge of all. Thinking again about Richard, if he wanted to pressurise her as regards their relationship then she was not interested.

After locking the classroom door she set off past the huts of the settlement and another light drizzle began to fall. The stream under the bridge was fuller than it had been for months. Crossing the road she could see the procession of carts making their way up from Ingleton and those empty going in the opposite direction. A few weeks before she had watched with most of Batty Green and the other settlements twenty four horses pulling another steam engine for one of the tramways. She had never seen so many horses harnessed together, huge, thick legged beasts working in tandem slowly pulling along the high wheeled cart.

Closing the gate she started up the steep, rocky path to the Johnston's farm. It was when she was almost half way there she began to realise how much easier this climb felt now than it had once been. She was obviously becoming fitter and stronger. When first arriving at Batty Green the walk up the hill to the farm was hard but now it was so much easier and she was pleased with herself. There was she getting healthier and yet at the same time the settlements were stricken with smallpox that seemed to be spreading. Only yesterday she had heard that Beth Granger had been afflicted, the third pupil in the last two weeks. The doctor had advised her strongly not to visit any of her pupils, something she reluctantly accepted. Her feelings for them did not stop just because they were out of school.

She was about to open the gate into the farmyard when Tom Myres appeared from behind the hay shed, cap in hand and a smile on his face.

'Tom what are you doing here?'

'Wanted to see you,' he answered, 'desperately.'

'Oh listen to you. You always exaggerate,' she said, 'and you shouldn't be here. The Johnstons will see you.'

'Not when I've seen them not half an hour ago get on the coach to Ingleton. The farm hands left before that. There is nobody here and the coach coming back from Ingleton does not arrive until near ten o clock.'

'I wonder why they've both gone.'

'You mean you haven't heard? I thought some of your children would have told you all about it.'

'About what?'

'The elephant.'

'Tom, what are you talking about?'

'A group of entertainers are doing the rounds and they have an elephant in tow, must have been brought up by train. It's not every day there's an elephant visiting the Dales. There have been coaches hired for folk to go and see it. I'm surprised you're not on one Lucy.'

'You're making all of this up.'

He laughed and said, 'I swear I'm not.'

'Elephant indeed!'

'You ask your little savages tomorrow and they'll tell you all about it.'

'I'm surprised with the smallpox here that anyone has gone.'

'Can't stop living altogether, life has to go on.'

'I suppose so,' she said thoughtfully and then added, 'Anyway if you think you're coming in you can think again.'

'Oh come on Lucy. It's raining and I'm cold and there's nobody in the house and there won't be for hours yet.'

'Tom……'

'Oh come on. This is daft. What harm is there in it?'

She wavered for a few moments and then said, 'Well only for a while.'

He smiled then and winked at her.

'You're incorrigible Tom Myres.'

'I'm smitten, that's what I am,' he declared as he followed her across the yard and into the house, saying, 'And if there's tea to be made then I'm yer man. I'm not having any woman doing what I can do for mesell.'

CHAPTER FORTY FIVE

Beth could hardly speak. Her mouth was full of sores and blisters as her temperature began to rise. Maggie was sitting beside her bed bathing her forehead.

'I'm.....m....scared......I'm scared Mam,' Beth forced out.

'It'll be alright love. Just you rest and don't try to talk.'

The young girl's eyes seemed enormous as she stared at her mother as desperately seeking an understanding of what was happening in this strange room full of beds and strangers.

Doctor Shawcross was at the other end of the hut. Things had become so bad that another doctor had been brought in so each had responsibility for one of the wards. They had been lime washed inside before being opened. The place was dark and smelt strongly of carbolic soap. Family members were gathered around each bed, their voices low and sombre. From outside came the sound of another rain storm battering down on the roof.

Maggie took hold of Beth's hot hand. She felt empty and so tired when caring for her daughter. Her child was dying and nothing could stop the miserable process inside her tiny body. According to Mr Oswold the new doctor Beth had only a few days to live. They were all helpless. She would be one of many. The graveyard at Chapel le Dale was already filling up. All of Ribblehead was in a permanent state of mourning for the old and the young, for women, men, children. Smallpox was wiping out one after another and all they could do was wait.

The hospital was regularly being visited by clergy and ministers. James Tranton was there every day as was father O'Leary the Catholic priest come to administer the last rites. The Reverend Smith had been up from St Leonard's at Chapel le Dale and had spoken to Beth and Maggie as well as others of his parish who were suffering, trying to give what comfort he could.

Ethan came each night after work. The previous night he had told her about Fraser taking Clare down to Ingleton to see the elephant.

'It's some sort of circus or someat,' he had said.

Clare was staying with the Robinsons, their next door neighbours.

'Is she alright?' Maggie had asked.

'She wants to come and see Beth.'

'But you told her she can't.'

'Don't mek any difference though. She still wants to come.'

Beyond Maggie's suffering there was always Clare. Her fortitude came from knowing that after all this was over there would be still their eldest child to care for.

'So who's doing the cooking for the men?' she had asked.

'Nobody. We're all fending for ourselves.'

'You cooking?'

'Trying.'

'That'll be right.'

When he arrived each night he came straight from the tunnel, his work clothes clarted in mud.

'No wonder the floor has to be scrubbed here every day,' Maggie commented.

Ethan would stand over the other side of the bed looking down at Beth telling her not to try to speak. Then he would tell her about what he had been doing that day and how Jonty, Bill and Fraser were asking for her and how her sister was getting on. It was the same each night. Beth lay there it seemed intent on every word. Maggie listened as though it was the most important thing she had ever heard. Twice he had brought toys made by Fraser, a small wooden doll one time and a decorated jewellery box on another. Bill had sent her new picture books. Even Jonty had given one of his neckerchiefs. The doctors' orders were that only close family could visit the wards. Under the supervision of a Mr and Mrs Rogers and a new male nurse there were women from the Quakers and Methodists who had volunteered to help with the cleaning and cooking. The Rogers had been brought in to support the doctors and Klem Stewart was a male nurse from Blackburn paid for by the company. The huts were busy and well organised. As much as was possible was being done, a minor miracle in such a remote place as Ribblehead. They were getting more medical attention than they probably would have in the towns and cities of Britain at the time and the Grangers like the other families deeply appreciated what doctor Shawcross and Oswald were doing for their loved ones.

Ethan talked to Beth about when she got better. He described how he would fulfil his promise and take her trout tickling, how they would have a party when she got out of hospital.

Maggie blamed herself for having ever agreed to coming to Ribblehead and for letting Beth and Clare continue at the school where she thought she might have contracted the disease. There were doubts because no one knew how smallpox was passed from one to another. Everyone put it down to fate.

'I'm not good Mam,' Beth managed to say before her mother helped her drink some water.

'Sssh, try and sleep my pet.'

'I...I want to.'

'Well then,' she said softly.

The evening room was lit by a few lamps. The volunteers were still at their work. Earlier they had brought some broth for Beth to try. Maggie could not thank them enough. Concern was everywhere. It resonated around the hut as each family stood beside the bed of their sick relative lost to a helpless waiting.

'I've brought yer the clothes yer asked for,' Ethan said that evening as he came in with the smell of the tunnel's dampness on his filthy trousers and coat.

Maggie took them and set them on the floor by her feet.

'And how is she today then?'

'Nowt much different,' Maggie answered as she continued to bathe Beth's forehead.

In Beth's eyes was sheer terror and confusion. She continued to look at her mother for minutes on end, her dark eyes growing larger as her face shrunk so much the outline of the skull was beginning to be exposed under her snow white skin. Maggie knew what was to follow. She had seen the different stages in some of the other patients. From her daughter's beautiful smooth, pale skin would grow hideous purple hills of poison. These bumps would quickly turn into blisters and then into pustules that would crust over like red, contorted wounds. It was almost unimaginable for Maggie to think of this happening to her daughter. The last stage when the blisters finally fell off would leave disfiguring scars over body and face. She just hoped that none of these blisters formed near Beth's eyes or she would go blind. In the ward at the back there was a stretcher for the dead on two large wheels that would take the sheet covered body out to the shed at the back of the hut where the coffins were stored. This had already happened several times since Beth had been admitted. Maggie tried not to think about anything so final. She had to concentrate on the present with all the emotional and mental strength she had, praying for a miracle to happen like the water into the wine, the raising of Lazarus, the bread and fish for the five thousand, a Christ given miracle to save her daughter.

'Clare's off wi Fraser again. He's teking her up on the tramway to the quarry and back. She likes that. He's teken her before,' said Ethan as he took hold of Beth's hand, leant forward to kiss her on her red hot forehead saying quietly to Maggie, 'She's burning up is the lass.'

'It's the fever.'

'It feels worse than last night.'

'She can't get anything down. Her poor mouth is so blistered up she can only manage a small sip o water once in a while. I'm teking the cold broth they bring her.'

'I should think so. You need someat or thee'll finish up poorly as well.'

Maggie glanced at him, at his mud smeared face and hands and his moistened eyes. Sometimes she hardly recognised him. In this place he was a stranger who just appeared each evening and yet she wanted to respond, wanted to share in his concern and love.

As they sat there the great bulbs of disease were being planted under Beth's skin. The process was going on right now as they spoke. Maggie had seen too much not to realise how things were developing, mysteriously, inexorably. The small pox was gradually destroying her young life and she had no resistance to it. Now she was shrinking into half the girl she had been only a few weeks before. She looked pleadingly at her mother for sustenance, for hope, her eyes deeply set.

'Mam, 'she would mutter and say nothing else.

Often Ethan too had nothing to say. What was happening was too overwhelming for his shattered spirit to express itself. He would be there and that had to be enough. He would remain by his daughter's bedside until midnight before he finally accepted Maggie's command to get himself some sleep.

'Eight to six shift we're on now so I get extra time in bed,' he had told her the night before.

'Ten hours,' Maggie had responded, 'So you'll be getting less of a wage.'

'It was one or t'other and the men wanted the ten hours.'

'More fool them.'

'You speak for yersell woman. It suits us.'

'Of course it does.'

'Bloody hell Maggie, listen to yersell. Once of a day yer would......'

He suddenly stopped himself, his face tightening in frustration before he added, 'Sorry. I shouldn't be talking like this, not here.'

'No you shouldn't.'

'Anyway, if anyone wants to work twelve they can and that's the last thing I've got to say on the matter.'

He looked down at Beth. Not once had she turned to him.

Doctor Shawcross came along to Beth's bed a few minutes later.

'Ethan, Maggie,' he said sombrely.

'Good evening doctor,' said Ethan.

'And how is our Beth tonight?' Shawcross asked as he leant forward to take hold of the girl's wrist to check her pulse.

Beth continued to look at her mother with fear in her eyes.

'She's settled doctor,' Maggie told him.

'Yes,' he said before placing his hand on her forehead as he asked, 'And is she managing to drink anything?'

'Just a few sips o water.'

'Well good for that Beth,' he said to her, 'As much as you can and that'll help greatly.'

The girl glanced at him.

'Bless her,' Shawcross added.

'We hope God will,' Maggie put in.

'Yes, of course. Right I'll be back in a while,' the doctor said before going on to the next bed.

It was nothing more than a gesture but it was enough for the parents to feel as much was being done for their daughter as humanly possible.

The room grew darker. More rain rattled over the roof and against the small windows. Some of the women were changing the jugs of water and straightening the bedding. It was the men without family who had no one at their bedside that the women talked to the most to try and comfort them.

Ethan sat there considering the men he had left back in the hut. He had noticed how rapidly things had changed since there was no Maggie or girls there. It was Jonty who had been the most affected. Bill had found him in the early hour of the morning sat cross legged beside the stove tearing out pages of the number book he and Beth used to read together sobbing and moaning.

'So did you see Clare?' Maggie asked him.

'Ay, just before her and Fraser went off to the market. She seems alright.'

At the mention of Clare with Fraser Maggie felt the usual uncertainty, the usual worry. It was alright in her mind for Bill to take an interest in the girls but not Fraser. She did not trust him and could not understand why Ethan showed no concern with the amount of time he was spending with Clare.

'And have you asked her about school?'

They had decided that for Clare to be moping around the Robinsons' hut all day would not be for the best so had kept her on at the school.

'Oh you know what Clare's like about school, says nowt.'

'She never has liked it.'

'Not like her sister.'

'No, Beth loves school and lovers her teacher Miss Ormskill,' said Maggie, forcing a smile at Beth whose eyes were at last closed.

'She's sleeping.'

'Best thing for her.'

'You should get an early night,' Maggie suggested.

'You must be joking, in that place there's no chance.'

'And why is that?'

'Cos they're at each other every bloody night. There's Jonty away wi the fairies cos o what's happening to our Beth and then there's Fraser and Jock going hell for leather at poor Bill. They hate his guts, hate him they do.'

'And what's that about? What's Jock Tarrant got to do wi anything. I thought he was allays in the pub.'

'Oh he's still drinking alright, more than ever. He somehow packs it in and yet manages his nightly barny wi Bill. What a bloody state them three get into sometimes. How the hell they haven't started knocking lumps out o each other is beyond me. Fierce they are, bloody fierce and I'm having nowt to do wi it. One way or another I'm keeping well out. And there's poor Jonty crying his eyes out most o the time wi snot dribbling off his chin and getting hisell into a right state. It's him I worry about the most. He can't understand what's happening. He keeps asking where you and Beth are and what the hell am I supposed to say that he'd understand so I just have to leave it and that does him no good at all, poor sod.'

'Poor Jonty,' agreed Maggie as she stood up and stretched to ease the ache in her back.

'So I'm staying here until the buggers get to bed or Jock drinks hisell unconscious, one or the other.'

'What a state.'

'So long as thee know that I've nowt to do wi it.'

'Bill won't put up wi that for much longer.'

'He's ready to burst is the man, but he's getting on is Bill, complains all the time about his arthritis and has his glasses on all the time now or says he can't see a thing. It's like his fighting days are over. If them two press him hard enough though he'll have a square go and then God knows how it'll end.'

It had been a long time since she had heard him so animated. She put it down to his worry about their Beth. He was struggling just as much as she was and yet she could not share what she was feeling with him. The connection was the deepest possible, a bond that gathered together all the suffering and dread so that Maggie could absorb it all, could take from her daughter as much as she could.

The ward was settling down into its nightly routine. Ethan would finally leave and Maggie would get on the narrow bed and lie beside her Beth and hold her then, stroke her fevered forehead and damp hair and pray for her, pray with all the intensity she could muster, pray to God that somehow or other her daughter would be spared from that stretcher on wheels.

CHAPTER FORTY SIX

Beth was slipping away, her face and body a hideous mess of crusted scabs. She was so thin and weak. Her life was fading as Maggie and Ethan sat there by her bed unable to do anything but watch their dearest daughter succumb to the disease.

'It shouldn't be long,' doctor Shawcross had stated, 'It can't be long.'

Her parents could not believe how Beth's body had been transformed by this awful disease. Even though Maggie thought she had been prepared to see her own daughter so disgustingly disfigured was more than she could bear. There was hardly any skin left that had not been affected. The smallpox had almost turned her body inside out. She was all angry red lumps, scabs and weeping blisters. She had been unconscious for the last few hours but still thrashed from side to side in the throes of a terrible pain. Her tiny face was soaked in sweat and her breathing so fast that there was hardly a pause between one breath and the next. Her arms, legs and upper body were so covered in bumps that it was hard to see how thin she had become.

Maggie had lost all sense of hours and days. She had been there by her bedside for so long that she had forgotten what life was like outside. When doctor Shawcross had suggested that she went out for some fresh air she had refused even that. Nothing was going to keep her away from being with her Beth through every second.

'She's going Ethan,' she said.

'I know, I know,' he responded emptily.

There was nothing left in either of them. They had been stretched to the limit and now there was only the dull, miserable dread of what was so obviously approaching.

Maggie was trying to resist the memories of her healthy, happy, curious daughter, her baby, the one who everyone loved and who loved everyone in return, who enjoyed everything there was to enjoy, the noisy, inquisitive, happy Beth.

She looked at her little girl, what remained of her and was shocked and disgusted at how much her body could be destroyed in this way. It was the end and she could not believe it. She had prayed endlessly to God to save her and he had failed, had failed her Beth. She held Beth's tiny hand that was so very hot, watching the child shift from side to side, moaning and gasping for breath. Even now she could still hope something would change, that a miracle was still possible through her own force of will. But she knew it was hopeless. Doctor Shawcross had told them it would soon be over. She was almost finished herself, so exhausted from all the days of suffering and the dread of what was to come. Ethan looked pale and lost. She had never seen him so diminished. Between them was their dying daughter and it was an absurdity.

The only thing that kept her going were thoughts about Clare. There was still a daughter that more than ever needed their love and care. She had hardly seen her over the last weeks but she was always there in her considerations. All of her life would be focused on Clare, their eldest and soon only child.

'She's settling,' Ethan suddenly said.

They both watched as Beth's breathing slowed and she became still. Their only focus was on the slight rise and fall of her chest. It was the only thing that mattered, the visual pulse of life still there, the intake and release of each living breath. It became hypnotic. They were both held to it until they were unconscious of their surroundings, of the doctor on his rounds again and the women volunteers bringing in lunch. Nothing existed but the breathing of their Beth. And then as though it was a mistake of their eyes it stopped. Both of them looked harder but there was no motion in that tiny chest. Maggie squeezed her hand hard but there was no response. Ethan stood up and leant forward to put his face close to hers and then straightened.

'She's.......she's gone,' he said.

'No,' answered Maggie.

'Our girl's gone.'

'Please God no.'

'It's over,' he continued.

Maggie looked up at him, her expression one of utter exhaustion.

Neither said or did anything for a few moments. Finally, slowly and gently Ethan picked up Beth in his arms with the sodden sheet swathed around her and started walking up and down the crowded room, squeezing his daughter as though to mould her body back to life, to take the living pulse from himself so she could become whole again. People stopped to watch him holding his daughter's corpse in this way as he walked up and down mindless of everyone else.

Maggie finally followed him out of the ward and out to the back shed. She brought out the smallest coffin she could find into which Ethan carefully placed their Beth, wrapping the sheet around her but leaving her face exposed. He went back into the shed and returned with hammer and nails. Maggie got down on her hands and knees to give her daughter one last kiss before Ethan started nailing down the coffin lid. When it was done they stepped back, holding hands and looked down at the small, simple coffin.

'Bless her,' he said strongly.

'We loved her so much,' Maggie added.

'Allays will.'

'Yes.'

'Our Beth.'

'Our Beth,' she repeated.

'She's gone from us Maggie.'

'To a better place where there is no more suffering.'

He turned to her and said, ‘I’ll let em know at Chapel le Dale. Someone’ll tek a message to the curate.’

‘Yes,’ she agreed as doctor Shawcross came out to speak to them.

Two days later Fraser, Jock, Bill and Ethan were on the cart that was taking Beth’s coffin down to the church. This was to be the thirty fifth funeral at St Leonards since the smallpox epidemic had started. None of the men spoke as the wheels of the cart turned through thick mud over the road. Momentarily Ethan glanced over at Jock still surprised that he had asked to come. Arnold Wainwright had stayed behind with Jonty who was in such a state that it was decided he could not be left alone. Maggie was with Clare at the Robinsons where she had been ever since the afternoon of Beth’s death.

A light drizzle shrouded the hills on either side of the valley, the rain being whipped into the men’s’ faces by a Westerly wind. Simon Tomkins the carter was taking them down to Chapel le Dale. He was one of the men contracted to the company to carry goods up from the Ingleton railhead. Having just come off work the four of them had not had time to get a wash and were seated on the floor of the cart, their hands on top of Beth’s coffin keeping it steady. Ethan could not rid himself of the image of her there in the small wooden box with her face covered in raw scabs and large purple bumps. Only two days before he and Maggie had watched her last breath. There was nothing beyond this. It had finished him and he was now doing everything automatically, shifting from one place to another, one task to the next without thought or consciousness.

The journey seemed to take far too long. By the time they turned off the muddy road the men were soaking wet and stiff. Simon brought his horse to a stop near the church’s lynch gate. Awkwardly the men climbed down out of the back of the cart and lifted the coffin that was so light between the four of them and carried it through the gate, between the headstones of the old cemetery and then lowered it at the edge of the large, untended graveyard, a patch of featureless land. For a few moments none of them moved, the sound of the stream coming from over the wall at the lower end of the graveyard. There it flowed between moss covered stones on its way down to Ingleton.

‘There’s.....there’s no bugger here,’ Bill said then.

‘There’s no grave been dug,’ Ethan added.

‘I’ll go and see what’s happening,’ Fraser put in.

They watched him leave the cemetery, walk up the road a little way to the vicarage where he disappeared through the front garden gate.

Ethan without another word went back to the cart and got out the shovel that Simon always kept with him in case he got bogged down in mud or snow. Returning he chose a place near the side wall of the new patch of consecrated ground and started digging. After a few minutes Fraser came back to tell them that Reverend Smith’s wife had said there was no word of a burial in the church diary but that her husband was expected back soon from Dent where he had been attending one of his parishioners who was grievously ill.

‘What a bloody mess,’ Bill muttered.

Ethan made no comment. Angrily he worked at deepening the grave until he was satisfied. He struggled out of the hole whose earth was now sodden from the ceaseless rain, threw the shovel down and walked over to the church.

The others waited and then flinched at the sudden ringing of the church bell, its sound resounding through the wet afternoon's silence. Ethan continued ringing, pulling on the bell rope over and over again before he appeared through the church door to see the Reverend Smith rushing towards him. His apologies went unanswered. Ethan gave him such a dismissive look as he stopped and joined the others at the grave side and quickly went through the burial service to which none of the men listened. They ignored him as he tried to shake their hands in commiseration, waiting impatiently for him to finally leave.

'I'll wait until you have filled the grave,' he told them.

'You've no need,' Bill interrupted him.

'No, no need,' Fraser agreed.

'In fact Reverend, we'd just like to be by oursells like if yer don't mind,' Bill persisted.

The vicar forced a smile, again apologised for the confusion and walked quickly away, putting up his umbrella as he did so, his cassock flurried in the wind.

Ethan climbed back down into the grave to take hold of the end of Beth's coffin as the other three lowered it towards him. He had to press himself against the side of the hole to get the coffin in the right position before they helped him back out.

For a few moments they stood there at the edge of the grave looking down at the sodden lid of the wooden box that already had bits of soil falling upon it. They had taken off their caps and gripped them tightly between their hands. The rain wet their hair and smeared over their faces. The only sound was of the nearby stream and crows drifting overhead. The men were absorbed in their own thoughts as the wind whined through gaps in the graveyard walls.

As he stood there Ethan saw again Beth's damaged face. He saw his daughter there in the box under four feet of sodden earth. He was there with her under the coffin lid, lying there and looking up, always looking up as the thick soil pressed downwards. It was his Beth but she could not hear him or know that he was there. It was his Beth buried so miserably, so emptily on this wind swept, wet afternoon. He was beside himself with anger and grief before he alone filled in the grave and used the blade to flatten the top soil. There was not a thing in this graveyard for the dead of Ribblehead. That was all the men and their families were worth, a miserable mound of earth and that was all. It disgusted him. His Beth had joined the unknown, those so badly abandoned in death. Nobody in the future looking at this small area of ground would ever know who was there. Ethan felt ashamed and in a rage. Miserably he carried the shovel over his shoulder and joined the others as they trudged along the path, under the arch of the lynch gate where Simon was waiting. The rain steadily increased and the crows made more of their plaintive sounds as they floated on the strengthening wind currents below the afternoon's grey sky.

PART FOUR

CHAPTER FORTY SEVEN

A line of sheep traversed the hillside. Below was the church and the roofs of the small town of Hawes shining in the late September sun. It was the first break from the incessant rain that had been falling for over a week flooding the fields of the valley bottom creating expanses of water like several huge mirrors reflecting the light. The air droned with distant activity as Lucy and Richard sat in his gig looking down over the small Dales town from their position up on the crest of the steep valley.

'They have their sheep,' Lucy was saying, 'and a weekly market and Sunday church or chapel and that's it I suppose, the life of the Dales.'

For the last few trips Richard had reverted back to his stiff reticent self. She knew something was bothering him and had already guessed what it was. It was pathetic how men always displayed their weakness through silence.

'Do you agree Richard?' she persisted.

'I'm sure your experience is much wider than theirs,' he eventually responded.

She looked at his grave expression and wanted to laugh but instead asked, 'And isn't that a good thing? I think it is.'

'You've already answered your own question and don't need my opinion.'

'But I do. I want to hear how you view life up here. Is it enough for you or not?'

'I am still here, of course it must be.'

'But surely that's only because of the work?'

'I enjoy my work. Yes it's important to me. This place is important to me.'

'Is it really Richard, really?'

'I'm sure it means more to me than it does to you Lucy,' he said pointedly.

She was silent for a while before finally saying 'I hear Andrew Murray is leaving.'

'Yes. He's decided to head south and look for something new.'

'So he hasn't got work to go to?'

'No, but it shouldn't be a problem for someone who has such aspirations and such confidence in his own abilities.'

Lucy could hear the judgemental tone in his voice but decided not to pursue it.

An open carriage full of chapel goers was being pulled slowly by two horses up the steep incline towards them. Its passengers smiled and nodded as it passed and Lucy tilted her head in acknowledgment.

'They seem contented enough,' she added.

He still had the reins in his hands as his horse shook its head before lowering it to explore the grass by the side of the road.

Lucy wore her bright green Sunday dress with a matching bonnet. Around her shoulders she held a silk shawl. Her skin was slightly tanned from the long rainless summer, such smooth skin with a glint of amusement in her eyes as she continued to look down over the town.

Richard was still trying to impress her. He was always sharply dressed and generous as well when they went out for tea. She wanted to like him more, even love him a little but his hopeless restraint left her feeling empty and often irritated. She realised that to actually break off any kind of relationship would threaten her position. As the manager at Ribblehead her teaching post depended on him more than anyone else.

'It's a lovely afternoon,' she said blandly, 'such a relief after all the rain.'

'Yes,' he answered, forcing an awkward smile.

He had placed his black hat on the seat next to her like a space that had grown between them over the last weeks, dark, formal and tedious.

'Don't you ever feel burdened by all your responsibilities at the work? I would have thought it was awfully daunting to be in charge of such a huge undertaking.'

'No more than yours Lucy, no more than yours. You have responsibility for all those young lives whereas I just build bridges and dig tunnels.'

'You're being too modest by far.'

'I don't think so. Education is the future.'

'Just as the Settle to Carlisle railway will be, the future I mean.'

'For those who like to travel over some of the bleakest scenery in the country I have no doubt it will be.'

'Beautiful scenery surely,' she said, 'I mean look at this view.'

'But you wouldn't want to spend the rest of your days here?'

She was not prepared for this. His tone was still as ungiving but at least he was talking. He hardly knew anything about her and that was his fault. He never probed or asked her any interesting questions.

'No, you're right. I couldn't live here for any length of time. I like it but not enough to want to settle down here.'

'That's something I find hard to imagine, you settling down anywhere. It's the idea of being settled. I find that difficult to see in you.'

'I wonder what kind of impression I make on you sometimes.'

'Of someone who is still searching Lucy.'

'Isn't everyone doing that Richard?'

'No, not in the way you are.'

'And what way is that?'

He twitched the reins to make the horse turn round.

'Richard, answer me,' she said.

'I think we should be heading back. The evenings draw in so soon now,' he answered as the horse broke into a trot shaking the gig as its wheels bumped over the rocky surface of the road.

Lucy was angry that he had not asked her whether she wished to return. It was so predictable from him, so pathetic that he thought she would be impressed by such sudden decisiveness.

'I thought we might have gone into to Hawes and had some tea!' she had to shout over the noise of the gig.

When he made no response she grabbed his arm making him jerk at the reins until the horse stopped.

'Did you hear what I said?'

'You shouldn't do that when I'm guiding the horse,' he said brusquely.

'I wanted to go into Hawes. I thought that's why we came.'

'Yes, I heard you,' he interrupted.

Becoming suddenly self conscious she tried to calm herself, saying, 'So why have we started back?'

'Because it's getting late.'

'The sun is still well up.'

'And will go down quickly.'

'You're just being awkward.'

'No I'm not. I'm being reasonable.'

'Reasonable to whom? Certainly not me.'

'I'm sorry you feel like that Lucy.'

'You don't sound it.'

'And how then should I sound? I thought I would show you something before we returned.'

'Show me what Richard?'

'Well if we can continue I'll be able to let you see what it is in the next few minutes. Patience Lucy, patience,' he repeated before setting off again.

She sat there hating his condescension until after half a mile or so they turned off the road onto a rough track that ran into a narrow valley with rocky escarpments on both sides.

Further ahead they could see smoke rising it seemed out of the ground. Lucy's feelings changed as her curiosity got the better of her.

When they eventually halted she was looking at a squat mound of rock with a turf roof through which the smoke was coming.

'What is this place?' she asked him.

Richard climbed down from the gig, came round to her side to help her down saying, 'Come and see.'

A rough plank of wood acted as a door. Inside the hovel all was dark except for where light came through gaps in the walls and roof. The floor was of bare earth, the stench unbearable as shadows started to move across her line of vision.

'For God's sake, what is this?' she gasped, holding her shawl up to her mouth.

'It's where people live, where Arthur Smalling, Betty Jane and their three young ones survive. It's a home, a house Lucy,' he told her and then added in a raised voice, 'How are we?'

'Middlin squire, middlin like as we are so,' a deep Yorkshire voice replied as a man came out of the smokey fug.

He was stooped, bare foot, dressed in layers of rags with filthy grey hair over his shoulders.

Lucy, breathing through her mouth, was transfixed by him, by his sunken features, the beard that hung on his chest and the way his hands moved around like thin claws. Then a woman appeared next to him, such a tiny creature, no more than four feet in height with even longer hair and rags trailing behind her as she came closer. Involuntarily Lucy stepped back and gulped in air that made her want to wretch. The stench was of shit and piss, smoke and unwashed bodies, was of something sour like rotten meat mixed in with a pungent smell of damp and decay.

'Brought un fine un,' the woman muttered through blackened teeth.

'This is my friend Lucy Ormskill,' Richard said, 'and where are the children?'

'Ut ont fells I reckon,' the man answered.

'And are they well?'

'As they are liken to be.'

'I've brought you something,' Richard said before he went back out leaving Lucy standing there.

The woman stepped closer and reached out to touch her face but Lucy recoiled backwards.

'Did yer see Arthur? Did yer look at it un?'

'I'm looking at un. Is Mr Richard's friend liken to be. Never brung a woman befur.'

'She here now though.'

Lucy was about to leave when Richard came back with a parcel under his arm saying, 'Just some meat and cheese and sticks of candy for the children. It will give them lots of sugar.'

Greedily the woman grabbed the parcel and disappeared into the dimness. The smoke from the half burnt peat spread over the other three.

'I want to go,' Lucy said strongly.

'Of course,' Richard responded, 'Of course.'

'We're going now Arthur, but I'll be coming up next week as usual.'

'Thankee Mr Richard fur thee kindness un.'

'Not at all, now keep them young ones well.'

'Wilt be doing as yer say the blighters are nowt but hungry a day, nowt but.'

'Goodbye Betty,' Richard added and then took Lucy's arm and escorted her outside where she gulped in mouthfuls of air so deeply she thought she was going to faint. The stench still followed them as she noticed the piles of human excrement littered around the area.

She said nothing as she was helped back into the gig and said nothing as they returned onto the Ribblehead road. Only when they reached the brow of the hill that looked down onto the settlements and half built viaduct did she say, 'I'll walk by myself from the bottom gate thank you.'

Richard made no response for a few moments. She turned to him and added, 'If that's alright with you?'

'If that's what you wish.'

'What I wish is for you to tell me why you took me to such a place.'

'To show you how some people, too many people live up here.'

'You thought that was necessary, did you?'

'Lucy, it's not only in the cities that there is poverty.'

'My God, how naive do you think I am? I know a lot more about poverty than you ever will. It's ridiculous for you to think I'm ignorant of such things.'

'It's just that our radicals or whatever you want to call them never seem to take rural poverty into account anymore. Probably it's because there are a lot fewer of them than there used to be and they don't have a voice.'

'I wonder who you're thinking of exactly?'

'Oh come now Lucy. I hear you know a lot more about them than I do.'

She said nothing to this. Now it was obvious why he had taken her to that miserable hovel. It was obvious and pathetic. It was also him trying to show he cared as much as the next man, but she knew who the next man was and it could no longer be avoided as she finally said, 'I know of one politically minded gentleman who does not consider me as ignorant as you do.'

'Gentleman you say.'

'Of course.'

'Oh dear,' he sighed, 'how disappointed you're going to be.'

Lucy suddenly thought of a phrase she had read in one of George Eliot's novels, irrational vindictiveness. This perfectly summed up the consequences when men were in competition with each other, especially over a woman.

'So who do you think I'm talking about?' she decided to continue.

Richard scoffed at this saying, 'Are we now having to play a guessing game when it's perfectly obvious it's Tom Myres we're talking about? I've been told you've been seen walking out with him on several occasions lately.'

'Even if I have, what's that to you?'

'It has everything to do with me and you know that, everything!' he exclaimed.

'I don't see why, not at all. Surely it's up to me who I see or don't see.'

'Don't be so damned stupid. This is a place over which I have ultimate responsibility.'

'Nobody said you didn't, but there's been no crime committed here Richard although you make it sound like there has.'

'It's not just me you should be considering. There's the people who live in the settlements and send their children to your school. You should have more regard for your behaviour.'

'I am aware of that for goodness sake,' she said, beginning to feel a little anxious.

'It's the principle of the thing and how the parents view it. To them Tom Myres is a navvy just the same as themselves who should not be seen walking out with the teacher of their children. Why in God's name am I having to tell you something as obvious as that?'

'Because it's not how I view it, that's why. There's no reason why I can't meet anyone I like. Nobody should be able to dictate to anyone else who they should befriend.'

'Befriend,' he muttered.

'Yes Richard, befriend. I find it easy for Tom to be a friend, just because you have no time for him.'

'And why do you think that is? This is the 1870s and there are still unwritten rules and conventions we are all required to abide by. This man threatens this whole project, that's why, with his ridiculous ideas. He stirs up the men. He's at it again with those who work in the tunnel. It wouldn't surprise me if the next thing will be the threat of violence. Tom Myres would go that far.'

His face was now a florid red as he gripped hold of the rein and sat stiffly erect beside her. She could feel the incredible tension in him. It was winding up his whole body like an emotional spring.

'Just because he does not think like you,' she tried, now angry and intimidated.

He turned to her, his lips pressed tight together.

A group of workers and their families in their Sunday best walked past on their way down to the settlements. The sun was setting at the far end of the valley covering the land in a deep pink that glowed under the darkening sky. Lucy and Richard waited while the workers set off down the steep incline, their faces shining in the last of the sunlight.

Then he carefully took hold of her arm. This was so unexpected Lucy shuddered a little in response.

'I'm not the tyrant Lucy,' he started in a milder tone, 'who seeks to have all men agree with what I thinks. You know I'm not that. Most reasonable men would not disagree with my ideas. They don't threaten everything like those of Tom Myres. He is dangerous Lucy.'

'So why is he still working for you? Why not dismiss him?'

'Oh don't worry. That's about to happen. I think we've all had enough of Myres stirring up trouble. I've tried to be patient and accept that some of the men might react badly if he was sacked, but I think we've gone beyond that now. Myres is a menace. He threatens the whole project.'

'And that has nothing to do with your feelings for me I assume?'

'Of course it has!' he said strongly, 'I'm not going to pretend it hasn't. I don't want you meeting such a man. It's as simple as that. So I have two good reasons to get rid of him. Why should I delay any longer?'

'Because you'd be hurting me by getting rid of him,' she dared to say.

'Well in that case Lucy I'm sorry for you. Perhaps you should consider your own position.'

'You're just doing what you want to do and yet plainly I'm not allowed to do that in return.'

'You're a professional woman who should act like one and give no cause for gossip or resentment. The company does not pay you to go around with any working man that takes your fancy. For God's sake surely you understand that?'

'I understand that supposedly I am an independent woman and capable of making my own decisions.'

'Nobody is that independent. Society expects certain standards of behaviour. Living with other people necessitates those rules we all have to follow, you included.'

'What if I admire the ideas Tom Myres has?'

'Then you're a bigger fool than I could ever have imagined. They're not ideas. They're words of an ignorant man who wants to smash everything down. They are nothing more than hot air.'

'Oh dear,' said Lucy with a sarcastic tone.

'Nobody wants such dangerous nonsense here at Ribblehead.'

'Except me it seems.'

'No Lucy!' he exclaimed, gripping her arm tighter, 'No!'

He moved nearer to her, his face intent and tight as he pushed his face close to hers.

'You're hurting me.'

'And you're hurting me. I don't....don't understand what you want Lucy. I know what I want. I know what I want right now,' he said pursing his lips before starting to kiss her cheek and neck.

'Let go of my arm Richard!'

'Why can't you.....?'

'I said let me go!' Lucy exclaimed pulling angrily away from him.

'It should.....should be different to this,' he muttered breathlessly.

'Well it isn't.'

'You've never let me near you, never.'

'Stop this Richard before you make a greater fool of yourself,' she said harshly while straightening her bonnet.

'Oh we're all fools!' he muttered sarcastically, 'Fools to ourselves.'

They were silent for a few moments as they both tried to calm down. The sun had disappeared behind thick, grey clouds leaving the land in deep shadow. These were the minutes when day and night were suspended together before one took over the other and darkness descended over the Dale.

'You're being warned,' he said harshly then, his face pale and tight in the fading light, 'We cannot have a company teacher flaunting herself around the place.'

'Well at least that's clear enough.'

'Listen to you. You still think all of this somehow goes beyond you. Well it doesn't. I wanted all of this to be so different. I don't want to be speaking to you like this. Of course I don't. I was hoping that we could look towards a future together. I am more frustrated with the whole thing than you could ever imagine and yet like you said all of this is my responsibility. The company expects me to do the right thing. Whatever my feelings are for you doesn't change that.'

'And what are your feelings for me Richard?' she suddenly asked.

He shook hard at the reins to shift the horse into motion.

'I asked you a question,' she persisted as the gig set off down the hill towards the smoky Batty Green.

'I'll set you down at the bottom gate as you asked,' he finally said and added not another word.

CHAPTER FORTY EIGHT

Ethan and the rest of his gang had been taken off the tunnel to work on emergency repairs to one of the cuttings. Part of it had collapsed after the days of incessant rain and the men were trying to shift the mud from the side of the embankment before they could start shoring it up.

'Fucking useless shit,' Jock, one of the gang, muttered angrily, the rain dripping off his cap as he stretched up from the shovelling.

'Ay,' Ethan agreed, 'Nowt but mud and rain.'

'And us, it's allays us.'

'We'll shift it only fer it to fall back in.'

'So what's the fucking point?' the Scotsman asked.

'There's none, none at all except they get theirselves into a panic.'

By working together the two of them had come to more of an understanding. The only difficulty was the bad feeling Jock showed to Bill Asquith. No one could escape the tension they created when they were in the same room together.

Overhead the sky was black. More than a hundred navvies were working on this section of the cutting. The tramway had been blocked further along the line so the mud and rock had to be hand carted to the end of the cutting over quarter of a mile away before it could be loaded onto the tramway trucks. The men were sodden as they worked, their jackets sticking to their backs, boots and clogs thick with the dark blue mud. Their moleskin trousers were tied just below the knee and caps pulled low over their faces. They shovelled up the mess of wet soil and stone to be wheeled off in a handcart as an empty one returned. Others were carrying in railway sleepers that would be used to shore up the side of the cutting, their breath steaming in the sodden, cold air as they continued through this miserable afternoon. They were finally so exhausted nobody had the energy or wish to speak.

Ethan worked now with a mindless efficiency, his thoughts only of Cragside farm. It was a regular thing every Saturday when the Sugden brothers went off to Ingleton for a night's drinking. He told Maggie that he was in the pub meeting with Tom Myres and his crowd, not that it mattered to her what he did. Since Beth's death she had gone so far into herself that the only one who had any effect on her at all was Clare. Only Clare held her mother to some kind of life. So his lies and excuses made no difference. He could still feel guilt but it was mixed in with his own depression and sense of pointlessness. His relationship with Maggie had become a sullen, silent thing where she went through the motions of the cooking and cleaning and washing for him and the rest of the men. There was no purpose to it other than to pass the time before Clare came back from the work she was doing with one of the Cleverly girls. They had put themselves forward to do some sewing and mending with Mrs Cleverly, who had once been a seamstress. It gave Clare something to do now she was too old for the school and kept her away from her mother's overburdening concern. It had taken all Ethan's strength to manage Beth's death and her funeral. Now he had nothing left. The same old weaknesses were back and with them the frustrations and anxieties that plagued his thoughts. He made work automatic, a grinding determination to get through each day.

He shovelled, he stopped for a breather, he wiped his face with his neckerchief and went back to the work over and over again, the mindless process that kept him going. He was hardly aware of the other men around him, only the occasional look or muttered disgust passed between them. Tom Myres and two others approached his gang when they were on the morning break sat huddled in their coats on their shovels and pickaxes.

'So lads,' Tom started, 'bloody mess of a day.'

Albert Sykes and Andrew Fisher were with him, men who had always been members of his political group .

'You're out o the tunnel to be doing this shit instead, not much of a choice now is it lads?'

'What the fuck do yer want Myres?' Jock asked him before spitting in his general direction.

'There's a true Scotsman for yer, wants to know what's what straight away.'

'We're not interested,' said one of the men sat near Ethan.

'Of course you ain't when you ain't heard what I have to say. Just five minutes lads. That's all I ask.'

'Listen to the man,' added Albert Sykes who was looking from one to the other.

'Ay, give him a chance,' echoed Andrew Fisher who was wearing a ripped bowler hat, half of it hanging down the back of his neck.

'We've bloody listened afore and what good has it done us?' another wanted to know.

Tom waited a minute for the general resentment to settle down.

'I've come to say that thee should not go back into tunnel wiout guarantees for your safety. There's been too many blasted in there losing their life or an eye or whatnot. Guarantees are needed lads or there'll be more fatal injuries. So what do yer say? Stay out until the company, until Stockton agrees cos he will lie and promise and nowt'll be done.'

'Fucking listen to it!' Jock exclaimed.

'That's what I want yer to do,' Tom countered, 'and to think about it lads. If it were up to me I'd have the tunnel entrance blasted down if they can't mek the work in there more safe. Cos it's your lives on the line lads, not Stockton's, not the company directors', but yours.'

'So yer would blow it up would yer?' Ethan asked.

'I would Ethan Granger if I thought it would help the men live a few years longer.'

'And you'd do it?'

'I would.'

'And what happens to our jobs then?'

'They become a lot safer.'

'They wouldn't fucking exist, that's what would happen. We'd be fucking done,' Ethan said angrily.

Tom stared, taking time to consider how to reply to this sudden attack.

'Nay Ethan lad. It's sad, I find it sad like to hear thee talk like that.'

'Like what?'

'Like one who has given up bothering.'

'Oh I've given up bothering with what you have to say Tom Myres.'

'And that's an unfortunate business so it is. I understand thee might shy away from violence but this is you doing nowt. This is just you leaving it all as it is.'

'Agreeing wi you, is that all that you ever want?'

'If yer want to put it that way, yes it is.'

'I don't want to put it any way. I'm done and so is the lot of us, do you hear? So bugger off.'

'Now then Granger, not so fucking fast,' said Fisher.

'Ay tek it easy Ethan,' one of the group added, 'yer not speaking for everyone, you ain't. There's sense in what here Tom says. I don't want me fucking head blown off cos some sod forgets the cap in the hole.'

'Ay,' a few more agreed, 'he talks sense he does.'

Ethan remained silent. He sat there in the pouring rain listening to Myres stirring the men up sufficiently for most of them to finally agree that something had to be done. The idea of blowing the tunnel was too extreme. It would be the last resort.

‘So you’re with me on this?’ Tom asked finally.

‘We’ll think about it,’ Archie Baldwin, a navvy with one of the loudest voices, said strongly, ‘Won’t we lads?’

A general murmur of agreement sounded out as Tom looked at Sykes and Fisher, ‘Right you are then. I reckon a couple o days should be sufficient for thee to think it through. So I’ll say good day and be back with yer on Monday to hear what yer have to say.’

They watched the three of them walk off along the cutting bottom.

‘Fucking chancer,’ Jock said.

‘Just shut it,’ Baldwin told him, ‘Just cos thee can’t be bothered either way.’

They went back to work even more miserable and sullen than ever. Nothing was ever right, their lives shunted from one side to another. One said this and another said that and none of it made any difference. They still had to shovel shit ten hours a day.

Ethan was sick of Myres and his constant campaigns, sick of his arrogance and confidence, talking to the men as if they were sheep which unless they were careful would be sheared naked without them even knowing it had happened. Politics was just another lie. It was always the working man being told what to do. He was always the consequence of other peoples’ cleverness. Ethan was disgusted by the whole thing. Work was work and it would never change because it did not suit those in power to change it. Since history started the working man had managed little to alter his situation and he was not about to start now whatever the likes of Tom Myres might say.

Outside the hut at the end of the shift he pulled off his boots. Jock as usual had gone straight to the pub. Maggie, Clare and the other three were all there in the warm hut when he entered. Jonty laughed at him and then shouted something indecipherable. The hut was cluttered with washing. The stove was full on heating the place, steaming up the windows until they were all in their shirt sleeves. Maggie turned to him, hands on hips and then went back to the cooking.

‘Look Dad, see what I’ve done!’ Clare exclaimed as she shoved a sample of her sewing at him, ‘Mrs Cleverly says I’m getting on grand.’

‘So you are,’ he answered.

The girl looked disappointed with his empty response and went to start setting the table.

‘Lousy day,’ Bill said, ‘Glad I weren’t out in it.’

‘The usual,’ Ethan said back.

‘At least you and Jonty are inside all day, ‘Fraser added as he looked over the top of the Craven Herald.

Jonty laughed again, a loud, guttural noise.

‘Jonty grand!’ he shouted.

'So I hear,' Ethan answered him.

'Jonty grand!'

'Behave yersell,' Bill admonished him, 'and sit theesell down.'

Sheepishly Jonty lowered his head and shuffled to the table.

'Nearly ready,' Maggie announced, 'Put out the bread Clare, there's a girl,' she added warmly, patting her daughter on the backside at which point Clare gave Fraser a quick glance.

Fraser put down his paper and watched her for a moment, his eyes narrowing slightly so no one else would notice such a slight shift in his expression, no one except Clare.

'So how's it been?' Bill asked Ethan.

'Oh we've had Myres round today trying to work up the lads.'

'And what is he on about now?'

'He reckons we should blow the tunnel if it don't become any safer working in there.'

'The man's a bloody fool,' Bill said.

'Trouble is most of the gang I'm working with think someat has to happen, maybe not blowing it but someat.'

'That's cos they've no mind of their own.'

'Not like you Bill, eh?' Fraser put in.

Bill looked at him angrily but made no response except to say, 'My arthritis is giving me gip. That's all I know.'

'Yer need yer glasses to see owt, never mind politics, all a bit beyond yer like,' Fraser persisted.

'Here,' Maggie interrupted as she set down the plates full of cabbage, chops and potatoes and Clare added the bread, jugs of water and beer and a slab of Wenslydale cheese.

'Champion,' sighed Bill, 'That looks grand Maggie.'

'Food!' Jonty exclaimed, stabbing his fork into a chop and lifting the whole of it to his mouth.

'Careful lad,' Ethan admonished him with no effect as Jonty chewed the crispy fat and then the meat, 'Anyroads I'll be going to the Railway tonight to see Myres and his gang of merry men. I'd like to ask him what he was going on about this afternoon.'

The lie came out easily enough. No one seemed bothered, especially Maggie.

After eating he went out to wash himself and put on a fresh shirt and trousers, a clean neckerchief and finally put on the jacket and cap he wore on Sundays.

'I'll be going then,' he said when he came out of the bedroom.

Bill and Fraser were arguing about something in the paper while Jonty was sat on his chair rocking backwards and forwards. Clare was helping Maggie wash the dishes.

'I said I'm off,' he repeated for his wife's benefit.

Maggie glanced over her shoulder at him saying, 'I heard yer the first time.'

'Right then.'

'Tell Myres to fuck off from me,' said Bill.

'Ay, that's you alright,' put in Fraser, 'Your answer to anything political, smack someone in the mouth.'

'Political my arse.'

'But you're too old Bill, too old for any fighting now. Yer should know that.'

'And you say so do yer?'

'I do, I do say that.'

'Well we'll see, that's all,' Bill muttered as Ethan shut the door behind him.

On Saturday evenings Batty Green was at its busiest. The market was drawing to a close with a line of people trudging up the tramway towards Tunnel Huts, it being the driest path to get there, the rest being bogged down in autumn mud. The drinking dens and pubs would be full. Card games would be starting. Folk would be going to the library and reading room or the Institute. There was to be a dance later in the large new hall. A group of women met each Saturday evening at Betty Middleton's to make decorations for the harvest down at St Leonard's. James Tranton was holding one of his last of the season outdoor meetings. The few Quakers of the settlements would be getting together as would those of the Temperance society. A bare knuckle fight was planned for up on the moor and some of the younger ones had just finished a football match on the only flat piece of ground near the stream.

Nobody paid any attention to Ethan as he made his way past the blacksmith who was working late. He went under the scaffolding of the viaduct and started up a path that steepened as it cut across the lower fields towards the slopes of Whernside. His boots were quickly clogged up with mud and his breathing increased with the steepness of the climb. The smoke from all the settlement chimneys followed him for a while as it spread over the lower valley. He clambered over a style in the first wall he reached, the stone feeling wet and cold as he steadied himself. At last he was alone. He enjoyed walking in the dimness as the last of the sunset faded to the West, turning back for a moment to see all the lights from the market and the sight of the lamps on the carts heading back along the Ingleton road.

It took him over half an hour to arrive above Cragside. A light was shining from a front window. Expectation was growing in him, a warmth that gradually flooded his body in readiness for seeing Floss. Images of her rushed through his mind as he waited, leaning on a gate, watching for the light to go out, a sign that the brothers had already left for their drinking session in Ingleton. The Saturday before he had arrived early enough to watch them climb onto their cart and head off out of the farm yard, across the stream and follow the track across the wide valley bottom until it turned onto the main road. The Sugdens disgusted and scared him. The last thing he wanted was to ever meet them on one of these Saturday liaisons with their sister. He knew they would kill him. In the week of the haymaking they had warned him and the other men plenty of times to not even look at their sister. They were capable of anything when they were drunk or angry enough. Coming to see Floss was a risk and yet it was desperately essential. Just once a week was not enough. He had pleaded with her to let him meet her in the middle of the week but she had refused.

'Can't you go for a walk or someat?' he had asked her on several occasions.

'Don't be daft!' Floss had laughed, 'Who ever heard of anyone going fer a walk? Silly that is. Silly to think on it even. I do enough walking in't day and me brothers would think me stupid for mentioning it.'

'People do go for walks.'

'Not me I don't. It wouldn't be right Ethan. They wouldn't have it so that's an end to it,' Floss had concluded.

For the rest of the week he was increasingly frustrated with his need for her. She filled his mind and his body at night until he grew so restless it took him hours to get to sleep. By the end of the week he was so shattered and on edge that he could hardly wait for this time with her. His guilt was overwhelmed by his physical desire. He was completely lost to it. Even though he knew it could lead to nothing but some hopeless conclusion he had to be with her, touch her, smell her, feel her, have her. Nothing compared with what she offered him. He was utterly fulfilled by her in ways he had never experienced before. She gave herself completely in the most naturally eager way possible. She was as desperate for it as he was. The moment they met they could not stop themselves. And when it was over it was only to wait until he was ready again, having her two or three times until she forced him to leave before the brothers returned.

'They'll do for thee Ethan if they ever catch yer here wi me. Yer knows that,' Floss had often warned him.

But when he was with her he did not care. Sex overcame everything else, an overwhelming rush of all emotions, of being almost unconscious to it.

'Bugger em,' he would say to her.

'No, it'd be bugger you, they'd cut thee throat and not care a fuck.'

'I know. So I know that. So I want to see you whatever happens, so that's it.'

'I want yer as well, as bad so I do,' she would say and that would answer everything for him.

The light in the front window went out and on again and he started down the top field. Maggie, Clare and Batty Green were in another world. Here he was free to fulfil himself. Beth's death had finally confirmed for him that his life would never change. He was in the prison of his own circumstances, made by him, suffered by him and now resolved forever. His hopes had been stupidly unrealistic. Nobody looking at him would ever guess that here was a man who once had hoped for a different life, one of books and culture. It had been a joke played out in his own futile imagination and he had believed it until he had lifted down his daughter's coffin and covered it with soil. Only then had he felt his own coffin lid being nailed down as well. He was a navvy. He had always been a navvy. That would and could never change. The only thing left him was to walk down this field and have the woman he wanted.

In minutes he was on top of her as they lay in the straw. The barn was cold, dark and smelt of the hay and old cow shit. She wore nothing under her thick, winter dress. He ran his hands quickly up her firm, long thighs that were smooth and warm to his touch.

'Bloody hell,' she muttered when he finally rolled off her.

Ethan lay there gasping for breath, his chest heaving up and down, his eyes closed as he trembled to the sudden emptiness and sense of fulfilment.

'Bloody hell Ethan Granger,' Floss repeated as she sat up.

'Are you alright?'

'As right as I ever will be I reckon,' she laughed.

'Well that's good then.'

'It's funny,' she said, 'We do the haymaking so's we can lay on it.'

'Just for us.'

'I like the smell, reminds me of you and what yer put into me, smells the same it does.'

'Come here,' he laughed before pulling her down into another kiss.

'Yer a greedy bugger I know that much.'

'For you I am.'

'Oh ay, I bet you say.....'

'No I don't,' he interrupted her.

'You don't know what I was going to say.'

'Yes I do, and I've never said words like that before.'

'Not even to yer wife?'

'Not.....not even to her.'

'Poor her then.'

'I don't want to talk about her.'

'Neither do I.'

'Well then.'

'So yer like me?' she asked, strands of her ginger hair down over her shadowed face.

'You know I do, don't you? You know Floss.'

'Suppose so.'

'Or it wouldn't be like this.'

'Like what?'

'So good.'

'In a barn like the rest of the animals.'

'But we aren't animals.'

'Could have fooled me.'

'Cos it means someat.'

'Maybe the cows and sheep think the same.'

'Oh ay!' he laughed.

'And what would you know? You're no farmer.'

'I know enough.'

'Says you.'

'Enough to know that this is someat we have to appreciate.'

'Don't know what that means.'

'It means we have to take care of every moment.'

'And how the hell do yer do that?'

'Just feel how good it is.'

'Words mean nowt.'

'No, you're right. In the end they don't.'

'So stop talking so much.'

'I like talking to you.'

'But I don't like listening. Never was any good at that.'

'So what do yer like Floss?'

'You know.'

'Do I?'

'Well if yer don't by now yer more stupid than I reckon.'

'I'm not stupid.'

'Says who?'

'I do.'

'Think a lot about yersell, don't yer?'

'Not really.'

'Sounds like yer do.'

'So I'll shut up then.'

'Good.'

He reached up to stroke her hair that shone red from a shaft of moonlight coming through a hole in the wall.

'You're beautiful Floss Sugden.'

'Give us another kiss then. I'd rather have that than you talking.'

'And another and another,' he murmured happily.

Eventually Floss told him he had to go before her brothers got back rotten with drink and looking for a fight.

'I'm as hoping they'll all be gone wi the drink and the buggers'll leave me alone,' she suddenly added.

He had never heard this from her before.

He was pulling on his jacket and standing above her when he asked, 'What's that supposed to mean?'

'Nowt,' she answered sharply.

'Floss, what did you say then?'

'Said nowt, nowt,' she muttered angrily.

Again he asked her but she refused to answer. They climbed down the ladder from the storage level of the barn. Floss crossed the yard with him. They kissed at the first gate, he fondling her breasts under her coat before he said, 'You sure you didn't mean anything bad about you and your brothers?'

'Didn't mean owt. You get yersell gone.'

'I'm going, and I'll see you next Saturday.'

'You will.'

'Are you sure?'

'Sure I am.'

'I'm glad.'

'Well you bugger off now Ethan Granger,' she said before turning and running back across the yard.

He watched her shadowed figure rush into the house before he heard the sound of cart wheels not far away. Quickly he set off up the field without looking back. It was only when he was at the top wall of the Sugdens' third field that he stopped and turned and looked down at Cragside. There was no light on at the front of the house. All he could see was the dim outline of the barn and the broken roofs of the out sheds and byre as a moon appeared momentarily between fast moving clouds.

CHAPTER FORTY NINE

The note had come late the previous evening but Lucy decided to ignore it and continued with her school day as usual. Three weeks had passed since she had last seen Richard. One of the workers brought the second note just as the children were leaving the classroom later that afternoon. The note was short requesting her to come to his office at 5.00pm. This time she decided to go.

When she entered Richard's office there was a stranger seated at the table next to him.

'This is Mr Brompton, the company accountant. We've just finished looking at the monthly figures and I've asked him to stay for this interview if that is acceptable to you Miss Ormskill,' he said before asking her to sit down.

'I don't see why not,' she answered, already agitated by him using her surname.

There was a moment's pause as he settled himself at the other side of the table next to the accountant.

The man's face looked severe with his thick eyebrows and long sideburns. There would be no sympathy from him Lucy had already decided.

'What am I being interviewed for Richard?'

She emphasised the sound of his name as he avoided her look.

'I think Mr Stockton would be more appropriate in the circumstances,' he added awkwardly.

'And what are the circumstances that bring me here?'

'We have to discuss your position as the incumbent teacher.'

'Discuss what?'

Brompton was glowering at her, his long, pale features set in an expression that was cold and remote.

'The fact that your being in such a post is no longer tenable.'

She could not believe that he would dare confront her like this, especially in front of another company employee. She could not decide whether he was gambling on her remaining reticent about their relationship or whether he felt so betrayed by her that he was willing to argue it through whatever the consequences. In these few seconds she was aware of the sounds of the work going on outside the hut, the banging and hammering, the release of steam from the cranes on the viaduct and the engines on the tramways. Outside was the largest engineering project in the country and one of the most audacious and here she was with two men, one who wanted now to destroy her livelihood while the other looked on with a stiffly formal expression.

'No longer tenable you say,' she said then, 'Why may I ask?'

Richard would not look directly at her. His confidence was obviously failing him. His voice was too loud and brusque. At least he was finding this as difficult as she was.

'I'm afraid your post is to be advertised and your services are no longer required.'

She could never accept this. It was so pathetic. His jealousy had made him lose all respect for her and now he was expecting her to just acquiesce and leave her position, one that she had come to enjoy. It was this obvious show of power that infuriated her. She had always known that without Richard's support her position in the settlements would be tenuous, but for him to treat her so brutally, so miserably was something she had not sufficiently calculated. His jealousy was now overriding everything else. She had wanted his love and respect as a guarantee, a security. She had enjoyed leading him along, but in the end Richard Stockton had failed to interest her.

After looking at him and waiting for him to continue she finally asked, 'I ask again, why?'

Brompton coughed and glanced at Richard who remained looking down at the table.

'I asked why Mr Stockton? I would like an explanation as I'm sure Mr Brompton would. After all he knows nothing about this situation unless you have discussed our relationship already.'

'No I haven't,' he answered abruptly.

'Well then, for his sake as well as mine tell me why I am to be dismissed in this way right in the middle of the autumn term.'

'This is not my decision.'

'Well whose is it then?'

'The board.'

'Who met where and when?'

He was not prepared for this question. He frowned and turned over a sheet of paper to take a little time with his answer.

'They met in Leeds.'

'I thought so,' Lucy said strongly.

'Has that significance?'

'Yes, I think it does, as in my recollection, which is usually very accurate, none of the directors have ever visited the school and therefore have never seen me teach.'

'This decision has nothing Miss Ormskill to do with your teaching which I know is of a very high standard and that you are popular with your pupils.'

This response confused her a little until she continued with, 'So what has this decision to do with?'

'It is based on my recommendation.'

Now she knew he was gambling everything on her remaining silent.

'Why?' she repeated the question.

'Because I thought it was best.'

'Best for whom?'

'For the community.'

She willed him to raise his head and look at her. She wanted to see how far he was willing to go. Instead she said, 'And I think it would be best if Mr Brompton was not in this room.'

'He stays here,' Richard responded immediately.

Brompton himself was at last beginning to redden slightly as he took out a handkerchief and coughed exaggeratedly into it.

'I could step outside if necessary,' he finally managed.

'No David. I wish you to stay here,' Richard told him.

'As you like,' Brompton said while carefully stuffing the handkerchief back in his jacket pocket.

'It's because I think your reasons for my dismissal are personal and not professional that I think we should be alone to discuss this. We surely don't want to embarrass Mr Brampton.'

'It's got nothing to do with the personal.'

'Well if it isn't I'd like to know on what basis I am to lose my position. Have I failed somehow in the management of the school? What have I done wrong? Surely I am entitled to know the reasons for my dismissal.'

He looked straight at her, his eyes unwavering as he said, 'I'm afraid it is to do with your role in this community.'

'My role being exactly what?' she asked him.

Richard pursed his lips and gave a slight nod as though he had expected this question until she added, 'Such as our Sunday outings together and our becoming more intimate over the last months. Are they part of my social role Richard?'

Again the pointed use of his Christian name unsettled him.

'I'm not talking about that.'

'Of course you aren't, how silly of me,' she derided.

'I'm talking about other peoples' perception of you, of how the general community views their teacher, the teacher of their children. You know exactly what I mean Miss Ormskill.'

'I certainly do not.'

'I should have thought it clear enough.'

'Well it isn't, not to me, not to someone who cannot imagine what I have supposedly done to upset this community.'

'You might disparage the people of the settlements but it is they to whom you are beholden. It is to them that you are responsible.'

'I respect every person living here at Ribblehead and you know I do because you know me Mr Stockton, you know me well enough, more than well enough to know that I have no condescension towards anyone. You don't become a teacher and look down on other people just because you have a profession. Teaching is a vocation, a job of caring and sympathising as well as educating. How dare you suggest I have anything but the highest regard for the pupils I teach and their parents?'

'You do not show such regard in your actions Miss Ormskill as it seems you haven't in the past. I have only recently learnt some of the reasons you were asked to resign your post in Burnley. It seems whatever you might say that you did not respect the feelings of your scholars and their families there either. The decision has already been taken. We are not here to argue the case, only to inform you of what has already occurred. As I have told you, your position is being advertised. There is nothing more to discuss.'

'Maybe Mr Brompton might be interested in such things as our relationship and not as much about my past, maybe everyone in the settlements who I supposedly have upset so badly might like to hear about it all. There is another side to this affair. There is always another side. You think that being a woman I can be pushed aside just because I am not the person you want me to be, just because I will not do what you ask of me. My dismissal is nothing but personal vindictiveness. You should be ashamed of yourself Richard Stockton.'

Again he looked directly at her asking, 'Have you finished?'

'No I have not,' she answered sharply, more worried now he knew about what had happened to her in Burnley.

'Nothing you say makes any difference to my decision. You have had a member of our workforce, a known agitator, to escort you on certain isolated walks and in my opinion and that of the company that is totally unacceptable behaviour. You were warned Miss Ormskill and yet you chose to ignore such warnings.'

Desperately she was trying to control herself. She could not believe how blatantly hypocritical he was being, but she would not back down, not until she had said everything she needed to say. She hated how he was behaving, hated having this other man there as a support.

'So now you are telling me who I should see or not see. Nobody mentioned this at my interview as a requirement for this post. Nobody said you are not allowed to be seen with any of the workforce. But Mr Brampton I assure you that is not the issue that Mr Stockton is so concerned about. It is about one man, a man here at Ribblehead. His name is Tom Myres and the chief engineer here detests him for numerous reasons, one being that Mr Myres has always shown an interest in my well being ever since I arrived at Ribblehead. He is a gentleman. He is interesting and well spoken. Just because Mr Stockton does not agree with his politics then as far as he is concerned I am not to associate with such a person. It's ridiculous. It is spiteful and pathetically immature and yet because of his position and how favourably he is thought of by his employers Mr Stockton has the power to do exactly what he wishes. I have nothing but my integrity to challenge this power. Ribblehead is his fiefdom. His word here is the law by which everyone must abide and there was I thinking that he was a civilised man. How foolish I have been, how blind.'

'I think that's enough,' Richard said.

'Of course you do.'

'I just hope for the sake of your pupils that you will remain at your post until someone can take your place.'

'My God!' Lucy exclaimed, 'How dare you ask me to do such a thing and use the children in that way? It's disgusting and immoral. I cannot believe you would use them so cynically. And Mr Brompton, why is he really here? Do you honestly think I would leave here and start making things up about what was said in this room? If he is your insurance that the truth will be told then I hope more than anything that he will tell everything that has been said here. I hope he has the courage to do that. Have you? Have you Mr Brompton?' she asked him directly.

The accountant's features reddened perceptively. He glanced at Richard before saying, 'I am here in an objective capacity Miss Ormskill. Mr Stockton asked me to remain here after our previous discussion had ended without any word as to why or wherefore. I can assure you that I would not say anything untoward or exaggerate in any way what has been said here. As far as I am concerned my position has always been one of discretion and will remain so in this situation as in every other. I'm sure Mr Stockton and the company are doing what's best even if that does not suit your own requirements madam.'

She was about to say something back at him but stopped herself. Exhausted from a day's teaching she wanted to be out of this room with as much of her pride intact as possible. She would no longer argue against Richard Stockton's will.

She rose suddenly, surprising them. Involuntarily David Brompton stood up as well, leaving Richard turning over a sheet of paper in an attempt to appear uninterested.

'Good day gentlemen,' she said easily and turned to leave.

'We hope to have your position filled in the next two weeks,' Richard responded.

His pride necessitated that he had the last word. Men were so predictable. Sometimes she wondered why she ever bothered with any of them.

Shutting the office door behind her she took in a deep breath of Ribblehead's smoke filled air and started angrily towards the bridge over the Little Beck, her mind a turmoil of resentment and anxiety. Suddenly everything was dissolving around her leaving her suspended in a feeling of emptiness, of total uncertainty as to her future, a state which was familiar but which she hated. She climbed the path up to the Johnstons using long strides, her anger being her source of energy as she reached the top of the hill and entered the farm yard.

CHAPTER FIFTY

'There is only one way to the Lord and that is through repentance, to accept we are all sinners but to know that our salvation lies within the power of our God. The Lord Jesus Christ came to earth as one of us to show that we can be redeemed through repentance, through true contrition of the heart. The Lord Jesus shows us the path we must follow to be pure in spirit and strong in our faith. It is this faith that will save you, a strong, unbreakable faith that will resolve all confusion, all weakness and finally bathe you in the light of our Lord. It is not he but you who must take responsibility for your own salvation. It is you who must reject all base thoughts and actions. Our bodies are weak but our spirit must be strong. We must be resolved through praise of the Lord to follow his way to true righteousness. We are his servants. We live to worship in his name. We come to Christ as our redeemer. We are in an everlasting struggle against all sinfulness. There will be temptations. Our pride and greed will taunt us into succumbing. Nothing is necessary other than the love of God. Nothing is more important than to give of ourselves completely to him. Have faith. Have strength. Defeat all that the devil requires of us. We are the warriors of our Lord and we will fight the good fight and in so doing will discover the glory of our saviour Jesus Christ, amen.'

James stood there with his eyes closed for a few moments. The hall was full, all of them still focused on him. He knew within another minute they would become restless, but at the end of his sermons he always gave his congregation a short time for reflection. His breathing was deep and slow as he experienced the satisfaction of a successful sermon, something he never took for granted. Even now he still waited with anxious anticipation to see how many would turn up to hear him speak. To see the hall so full indicated how well his mission was progressing.

'Fine sermon Mr Tranton,' a young man from his congregation said as he was standing at the door shaking hands with each one of them as they started to leave.

'I hope to see you on Wednesday John,' he replied, always taking the opportunity to remind his congregation of the next service.

They were all his, his Methodists, some nodding to him, others with eyes lowered, children, women and the men here after their dinner, people from all over the country, Scotland, Cornwall, London, the Midlands. They were his true believers who never missed one of his services. They were the reason he was here, the only thing that kept his spirit strong. As they shuffled towards the door he knew all their faces and all their names. These people before the new hall had been built had stood out in all kinds of weather to hear him preach. He admired their resolution, their willingness to be guided by him.

When they had all finally departed he returned to the front of the hall to pick up his Bible and notes for his sermon. He looked back over the lines of empty benches at the main door that had been left open. There was nothing else in the hall, no piano to accompany their hymn singing, no trappings at all to distract from his words. As he had stated in his sermon, simplicity was the way to a pure realisation. Nothing should ever distract from the word.

Riding back along the dark valley road his mind shifted away from the service to what had occurred on the previous week. Lizzie's father and one of her brothers had come to the house with a pony pulling an old rusted cart that creaked at every turn of its wheels. They had come to take the piano and his bureau. These were the last things in the house that had been his and now like everything else they were gone. Nobody except Jane and Lizzie had ever been in his room before and these two filthy, ragged farmers had trampled their muddy boots over his floorboards before dragging out his bureau down the narrow staircase and out onto the cart to be taken away he was sure to the auction at Settle. Lizzie had ensured that everything had been taken and he could do nothing to stop her. He was powerless. He had crossed the line of acceptability and now was paying for his sins. She had used him so cleverly that he had not a penny or book or any other object to his name. His fear of her had left him totally under her control, a girl of seventeen dominating his life. He wondered whether her family had started any rumours. Still as far as he had heard there was nothing up at the settlements to trouble him. If Lizzie's family had said anything it had not reached Ribblehead. He had employed her to ensure that there would be no scandalous gossip about him living alone in the same house with his cousin and here he was now living in fear and trepidation at what Lizzie might do. She could destroy him and more importantly his mission. She could smash down all trust and belief. It was something he could not contemplate. He was losing everything to her and yet he was doing all he could to resist her effect. Lizzie had squeezed him dry and now that there was nothing more to give he was more fearful that she might, out of sheer malice, tell people what had been happening in his house at Chapel le Dale, about Mr Tranton on his hands and knees in front of an seventeen year old girl urging himself not to give into his desperate need.

The sky was clear as he rode homewards. The ruts in the road were full of rain water silvered in the light of a full moon. On his left was the perfect outline of Ingleborough against a deep blue background. A slight wind rustled the branches of the few hawthorn bushes over the other side of the wall. From the isolated farms of the valley came the faint glow of their lamps. In the silvered darkness the tiny population of the Dale was preparing for the night. Life here was in such isolation, echoing the same loneliness he was feeling as he hunched forward against the cold wishing for something to free him from his torment. He was trapped by his own sin. He was held and being tortured by his own lustfulness. Lizzie was driving him to madness. All she had to do was exist in this world and he was lost. It was more than he had ever experienced. Nothing compared with these last months when he had been so drastically challenged. It was up to him with the support of prayer to overcome this terrible failing, to be strong enough to fight back against all temptation. He was being tested. His faith was being confronted, he who had to find a way to God's grace, to will himself to succeed.

Jane was sitting in the parlour in front of a blazing fire when he arrived at the house.

'Lizzie thought it was so cold a fire was needed,' she said to him the moment he entered the room to pre-empt any caustic remarks about heating and costs.

He was so lost in his own troubles that it had not struck him how Jane too was also being affected by their young maid, how she too had lost everything she owned and was beginning to look increasingly thin and haunted.

'Lizzie thought,' he repeated as he came to stand with his back to the flames, 'Did she?'

Jane did not wish to speak with him. He disgusted her as much as she disgusted herself. There was little feeling left between them. All she saw in front of her was a hypocrite. Her cousin was so full of deceit. Still he was continuing to pretend when she knew how much he had humbled himself, just as much as she had humbled herself. She detested being anywhere near him. Often she just wanted to strike out at him but did not have the strength or energy. She had been emptied out of all determination.

'The hall was full tonight,' he went on as though nothing was wrong.

'Was it?' she asked emptily.

'And where is Lizzie?'

'I don't know, in the kitchen probably.'

He failed to notice her grubby dress, the same dress she had been wearing for weeks, did not notice her white face and tired eyes, the thinness of her arms and how she never looked at him.

All that he sensed was her reticence, her nervous manner as she kept glancing towards the door.

'Is there any supper do you think?'

'If there is it'll be left for you…..'

'In the kitchen, yes?'

'Yes, it will be there as usual.'

'Are you well Jane?' he asked after a few moments silence.

'Well?' she repeated, 'What is well? I'm afraid I don't know and don't really care what it is. But I'm sure James you're about to tell me.'

Her remark was cold and sarcastic. It stopped him short. Instead of replying he rubbed his hands together and widened his stance in front of the fire. The atmosphere around her was so miserable and withdrawn that he had no idea how to affect it or even whether he wanted to.

'Lizzie is well,' she unexpectedly added.

'I'm glad to hear it.'

'Of course you are.'

Again there was that tone of voice. He was beginning to feel uncomfortable and increasingly resentful.

'So what have you been doing this evening?' he forced himself to say.

It took a strange length of time for her to consider her answer to this question.

'I've been reading.'

'Anything of interest?'

'No, not really.'

'That's a shame.'

'Words often fail I think.'

'I hope not too often or my future prospects would be bleak.'

His irony had no effect whatsoever. Jane and Lizzie had everything planned. Now they were ready and all he had to do was go to the kitchen, but still he remained there looking inquiringly at her.

'There will be something for you James in the kitchen. I know there is because I prepared it myself, just a little ham, some cheese and the bread you like from Settle.'

'I thought you said you weren't sure whether there was anything.'

'Well I am sure.'

'You seem a little confused this evening Jane.'

'Lizzie will serve it for you if you ask her,' she said impatiently.

'I'm sure I can manage myself.'

But still he did not move. Jane was becoming impatient. Lizzie could not wait forever out there in the freezing kitchen.

'I heard something this evening that might interest you,' James continued.

He felt compelled now to gain her full attention. He hated to be ignored in this way, to be talked to in such a sharp tone.

She shook her head and said, 'It takes a lot to interest me at the moment and I'm sure what you have to say will fail so I am warning you James before you speak. What is it you have heard? Pray tell me if you have to.'

'No, you're right, I don't have to at all. Anyway the news I'm afraid will only trouble you I believe.'

'Oh for goodness sake,' she exclaimed irritably, 'What is it?'

'It seems Miss Ormskill has been dismissed from her post. I know you think of her as a friend but it's unfortunate if what I've been told is true.'

'It can't be true, not Lucy.'

'I'm afraid it is.'

'Why? Why should she be dismissed?'

'That I do not know.'

'But she's such a good teacher and has being doing so much good work at Ribblehead and she's only been in post for a short time. It doesn't make any sense,' she said in frustration.

'Jane that is all I know. I'm sure in the next few days more will come out as to the reasons why she has been dismissed, but that's the news and I knew it would distress you.'

'And you were right. It does distress me. I have few enough friends as it is without losing one so unexpectedly. It's......it's dreadful. I....I must see her at once. I'll write a note inviting Lucy down here telling her to come as soon as she can. If it is true that she has lost her job then she will need all the support possible.'

'Said as a true friend I might add.'

'I'm not sure James whether your opinion has any significance at the moment. Why don't you go and have your supper?'

'You treat me harshly this evening and I have no idea why. Maybe you really are not well,' he said strongly as he unclasped his hands and waited for her to respond or at least look at him. When she did neither he angrily did as she had suggested. He turned and abruptly made his way to the kitchen.

The coldness of the room was the first thing he noticed, that and the shadows from the lamp flickering over the ceiling. Only then did he notice the dimly lit figure of Lizzie stood at the sink with her back to him.

'Oh there you are,' he started as she turned to face him.

She was naked from the waist up. In those few first seconds his eyes took in her glistening hair from which water was dribbling down over her fully rounded breasts and their dark crimson nipples, took in her bare arms and her shadowed features. In one sudden violent movement she flicked back her hair away from her face, the excess water causing a silvered spray of light in an arc above her head.

James was transfixed by her, especially how she was drying her breasts to make them seem even fuller and more obvious.

'I'm washing me hair,' she told him.

'Get dressed! Pull your dress up!' he exclaimed as he stepped back, 'Stop showing yourself like that.'

'Like what?'

'You know like what.'

'I'm just washing me hair Master James, nowt wrong wi that, surely there ain't.'

'Do as I say.'

'Now yer can't be telling me what to do, yer knows that, so stop yer carry on wile I dry mesell, unless thee'd like to do it,' Lizzie said slowly and boldly.

James turned abruptly and walked quickly along the hallway, past the parlour door and up the stairs. In his bedroom he picked up his Bible, opened it, closed it and slammed it down. His face was rigid with anger as he quickly returned down the stairs, opened the front door and went across to the stables. He lit a lamp and quietened Bess before taking off his jacket and shirt. His breath was clouding across the lamp light as he took down the rope with the knotted end from a hook on the stable wall. Then on his knees with all the strength he had he started flogging himself over his shoulders and across his back, the knotted end opening up old wounds and bruising the few areas untouched from previous beatings. Over and over he hit himself, making a grunting noise as the self inflicted pain became more unbearable. He would punish himself for all his sinfulness, his desires, his passions and lust. He would through suffering obliterate Lizzie's image. Eventually the rope began to cut into his skin. Blood started dribbling down his back from the deepening cuts.

Finally he could take no more, collapsing onto the frozen stable floor, his whole body throbbing around the centre points of pain, of the deepening agony that he had beaten into himself. His mind was blank, his feelings reduced to nothing but this suffering as he squeezed his hands together in an attempt to relieve some of the torture. He had to silence the torment of his thoughts and drive away all the echoes of his sinfulness. Only then could he be at peace. Only then could he face himself.

He lay there until he became so cold he had to move. Painfully he struggled to his feet. To put his shirt back on was an agony of material making contact with his bloodied skin. Thoughtlessly he replaced the rope on its hook and then in pain bent to pick up his jacket. Before leaving he managed to pat Bess on the head and settle her down, the horse looking at him with huge bewildered eyes.

Outside the moonlight was still shining on the slates of the roof of the house. The windows of the house were in darkness. Without realising it he was carrying the lamp limply by his side. He lifted it, its beams revealing the thin twisted branches of a gorse bush that had been left to grow by the side of the building. These thin, contorted shapes were as his pain, were the patterns inflicted over his back and the top of his arms. The bush was a symbol of his suffering. Its branches could make the crown of thorns for Christ's crucifixion. He stood there staring at the bush and it frightened him, began to haunt him as though slender fingers were twisted in agony, as though strands of hair were held in terrified shock and pain.

Finally, painfully he lowered the lamp and started back to the front door. He could hardly walk. He was totally emptied out. The devil was in the bush and somehow he had to cut his way through its contorted branches until he could find his faith and his freedom again.

CHAPTER FIFTY ONE

Lucy was looking her fashionable best. The purple ribbons to tie her bonnet hung down over the front of her stylish dark blue winter coat she had bought in Burnley two years before. She looked at Tom and felt such warmth for him. He was the only one on whom she could depend. She was lost and the future was frighteningly empty. But at least she was here with him on this late afternoon walk up on the Dent road. There was no longer any necessity to hide away their relationship. Now they could be seen together wherever they liked.

'But you promise me Tom,' she was saying in her most intimate voice, the one that would draw any man closer to her, 'the last thing I want is for you to end up in the same situation I find myself in.'

'Nay, it's gone way beyond that,' Tom said, holding her arm as they walked slowly along the empty road.

She looked to the side at the huge sweep of light brown land covered in dead heather and sedge grass with clumps of rusted bracken flattened by the autumn storms. The cold air was nipping her face and for once she felt her troubles were only secondary to his.

'It's strange, right from the beginning I've never felt that my job was secure here.'

'It's the nature of owt to do wi building railways.'

'Yes, I suppose so. I came to Ribblehead needing a change.'

'And yer certainly got that.'

'And a lot more Tom, a lot more than I ever imagined.'

'Because it seems to me you're the kind of beautiful woman who would mek things happen wherever you were.'

'I hope that is meant as a compliment.'

'Nowt else I assure yer.'

'I came here with no preconceptions.'

'That's a big word teacher,' Tom interrupted.

'I had no idea what I was coming to. What was described at my interview in Leeds certainly had little to do with the reality that is Ribblehead.'

'Wilder, rougher?'

'That and a lot more,' she answered.

'Wilder and rougher and wi more of a stench.'

'And then yesterday I thought how in a few years time there will be nobody here at all. The work will be finished and the settlements will have been abandoned. It's creates a strange feeling to think of such a thing. The viaduct will be here and the tunnel, but nothing else. Passengers will look down from the viaduct and see only open moorland and never imagine that once there were over a thousand people who lived and worked here. They will see nothing of all the lives spent and lost in this place. I find that such a sad idea. After all the noise and business there will only be silence. I'm sorry if I sound awfully maudlin. Any situation is temporary in this way. It's happening to me now and soon it will happen to everybody else, including you Tom.'

'I'm used to it.'

'Well I'm not,' she replied before noticing smoke trailing up into the sky coming from the other side of a low hill. She remembered the hovel Richard had taken her to and wondered if it was coming from there.

'I'm going to stay with my sister for a while and then I really don't know. If Richard Stockton does not give me a reference I'll be unemployable.'

'He's a jealous man Lucy whose been scorned by you so I wouldn't rely on him.'

'I just don't know what he's likely to do.'

'It won't be good, I'll tell yer that much.'

'I hate the idea of not being able to teach. I have to make my own way somehow and that's all I know.'

He squeezed her arm as a cart and its driver passed by with two farmers sat in the back on white painted chairs smoking their pipes, nodding as they went by closely followed on foot by what looked like a travelling salesman with large bags strapped to his back.

'This is the Dent road I've been told about,' the man said in a strong Lancashire accent.

'Well you've been told right.' Tom answered.

'It would take me how long does't reckon?'

'Wi yer carrying that lot over an hour if not more. Depends if yer is heading fer the town or what.'

'I am. Have customers there, regular ones. That's what I like best, regular customers, dependable like. Meks everything a lot easier. Anyway, I'm much obliged to you and to your lady friend who's already brightened up my day. Now if all me customers were as pretty as she my job would be right champion so it would,' the salesman joked before walking unsteadily away.

'I'll be leaving as well Lucy,' Tom added in an empty voice.

She turned to see his bearded face and dark eyes.

'Stockton's been told about me speech up at the tunnel entrance. Just what he's been waiting fer. It won't be long before the constables come calling. That's who he'll use, making it more official. He'll have me in the jail if he can.'

'He won't do that Tom, surely?'

'Don't talk daft, of course he will. That's just what he'll do. But I've promised yer that I'll leave the bugger alone and I'll stick to it. I don't want him to have the satisfaction of seeing me angry enough to smack him in the face except that's what he deserves. His sort depend on folk remaining civilised like. He's relying on it, that I'll leave him alone knowing that if I do owt else it'll only be the worse fer me.'

Lucy leant towards him to kiss him firmly as he placed his hands on her back to pull her closer to him.

'My Miss Ormskill, kissing on the public highway, whatever next?' he tried to joke as they stepped away from each other.

They walked on for a few minutes in silence. A wind was stirring, cutting across the moor bringing colder air from the East. In the distance came the call of crows flying towards the Dale from where smoke could be seen rising into the light blue sky.

Lucy had never felt closer to him and yet within days they would be forced apart, another episode of her life ending so badly.

'Come with me,' she suddenly said, 'Come away with me Tom.'

He stopped and stared at her inquiringly, 'And where would we go?'

'Does that matter?'

He paused, his eyes intent on her uncertain features.

'There's nothing to stop us,' she added.

'You don't really want that Lucy.'

'I do, I do or I wouldn't have said it,' she said strongly.

'Me and you,' he mentioned, 'Me and you, the teacher and the navvy.'

'You've just said yourself you're going to have to leave Ribblehead.'

She felt him hesitant and troubled as he continued to look at her.

'What is it Tom?'

'How I leave is what's important.'

'What's stopping us taking the next train from Ingleton and going anywhere we like?'

The cold wind flurried between them, strands of Lucy's hair escaping from under her bonnet. Tom had his scarf tightly wrapped around his neck, his hands in his pockets trying to keep them warm.

'I'm not skulking away like a rat in the night,' he said as he glanced away at a sudden movement in the rough grass at the side of the road.

'You don't want to be with me,' she said sharply.

'I do.'

'Well I could leave and you could follow on, what's wrong with that?'

'There's more than just us to consider.'

Her face crumpled in a miserable frown before she exclaimed, 'Oh it doesn't matter! I should never have said anything!'

Quickly she turned and started walking away.

'Of course it bloody does!' he shouted after her.

'Well prove it!' she called back without stopping.

He rushed up and grabbed her arm, spun her round before kissing her, his lips forced hard against hers as her head bent back from the pressure until her bonnet slipped off with only the ribbons holding it round her neck.

When he released her he said loudly, angrily, 'You couldn't live wi me. You're lost at the moment and don't know what's best. I'd be just another man until yer found someone else.'

She slapped him across the face, the sound of it loud in the silent afternoon.

'How dare you say such a thing?'

'I'll say what I bloody like,' he answered, his cheek reddening.

Lucy rearranged her bonnet. She was confused, almost desperate as she tried to control her breathing.

'You ought to slow down and think things through Lucy. You're going too fast for either of us,' he said in a stern voice.

'I....I thought you would want to be with me.'

'And you're not wrong.'

'Well then?'

‘It’s just not that easy. I wished it were. I do. I wished I could just pack me bags and go wi yer.’

‘So what’s stopping you?’

‘There’s more to consider than just us.’

‘You want to be arrested by the constables. That’s what you want, to be a martyr for the cause, you and your damned politics.’

‘Ay, you say that when it doesn’t suit.’

‘No it doesn’t suit.’

‘I’m not the answer Lucy. I could never be that for you. Christ, I’m even surprised you asked. I care for you, I do,’ he said as he tried to touch her face only for her to jerk away from him.

‘Don’t touch me!’

‘And I want to be wi yer, but……’

‘But not enough,’ she interrupted.

‘No, maybe not enough, not enough for you anyway.’

‘You just don’t want to look bad in front of the men and that’s more important than anything else.’

‘In this situation, yes it is. I’m sorry, but that’s the way things are.’

‘How disappointing,’ she said sarcastically.

‘The teacher and the navvy,’ he repeated as they began walking again.

‘I thought you wanted to get rid of social distinctions, you always said so.’

‘And I do.’

‘Well why can’t you start with us Tom? Why not do something that would make a difference?’

‘You’re only saying that to suit yersell. If we went off together it wouldn’t change a thing.’

She tried to calm herself, tried to find a new resolution that would leave her feeling stronger.

‘You’re right,’ she eventually said.

At that he took her arm, ‘I have to see this through, otherwise what the hell’s the point?’

‘And I have to catch the afternoon coach. I promised to see Jane Herbert,’ she said as though thinking aloud.

‘There’s plenty of time.’

‘That’s one thing I haven’t got, not now.’

‘I promise you one thing,’ he continued, ‘We’ll be seeing each other again whatever happens.’

She glanced at him as she quickened her pace, 'You don't know that.'

'I'm telling you.'

'I don't see how it matters.'

Again he stopped her and turned her to him, 'Lucy.....Lucy.'

'It's alright Tom. I've said I agree with you. It wouldn't work us going away together. It was a foolish idea.'

'What would the men think, me mouthing off, getting em all stirred up and then just buggering off leaving em to it? I can't do that.'

Weakly she smiled at him, stretching up to touch where she had slapped him.

'You'll never give up will you Tom Myres?'

'Not if I can help it. I could never be the answer Lucy to what you want and you know that,' he interrupted.

'It doesn't matter.'

'It does to me. It allays will to me.'

'I have to go,' she reminded him.

'And I'll walk with you the rest of the way.'

'No, I'd rather go by myself if you don't mind.'

'And what if I do mind?'

Again she smiled, 'Leave it Tom, please, just leave it.'

'That's one thing I'm not good at.'

'For me,' she insisted.

'But I care fer you more than you realise.'

'Let's just accept what's been said and leave it at that.'

He frowned, his eyes absorbing her, 'You don't mek it easy.'

'Nothing in life is easy, not for people like us it seems.'

'That's cos we want someat different.'

'It might be.'

'The world doesn't like being challenged, never has. People get set in their ways and that's how they want things to stay but neither me nor you do. We want change and we have to fight for it.'

'So long as we agree now that we don't have to fight each other. Goodbye Tom,' she concluded, 'Please look after yourself.'

He stood there as she walked away before he suddenly shouted after her, 'You tek care as well Miss Ormskill and I'll be seeing you again!'

Lucy made no response, disappearing round a steep bend in the road as Tom stuffed his hands back in his pockets and started to make his way over the rough grass and up the next hillside.

CHAPTER FIFTY TWO

The moment she opened the door Lucy knew something was badly wrong. First was the fact it was Jane and not Lizzie who was standing there and secondly her friend's appearance had changed so drastically since she last had seen her. She looked ill and grubby, far too thin wearing the same shabby dress.

'Come in Lucy, did you catch the afternoon coach alright?' Jane asked in a distant, empty voice.

'I did, and I'm glad to be here,' Lucy said as she followed her down the hall into the parlour.

'Miss Lucy,' Lizzie said as they entered, 'Very nice to see yer.'

She was seated beside the fire and was wearing a bright winter's dress and had her hair in a fashionable style that made her look older.

Lucy did not know how to respond, the maid of the house sat there appearing as though she was now the mistress.

'Lizzie,' she finally managed, 'I....I did not....'

'Did not what?' the young maid asked quickly.

'Expect to see you sitting there.'

'I live here yer know.'

'Yes, I do know that Lizzie.'

'And Miss Jane was just going to bring in the tea, weren't yer Miss Jane?'

Lucy watched Jane's pale, drawn expression and the way she meekly turned to the kitchen.

'Sit down Miss Lucy and tell us what's happening about that job of yours.'

But Lucy did not sit down.

'If you don't mind, I would prefer to talk to your mistress alone.'

'And why would yer want to do that?'

'I don't think that's any of your business.'

'And what if I think different like?'

'I don't really care what you think Lizzie. I would just like to be with Jane by myself.'

'To talk about what?'

'Lizzie, stop this!' Lucy finally exclaimed.

'I'm stopping nowt and don't yer come in here telling me what to do. Things have changed since you were last here so you just listen to what I have to say.'

Lucy immediately turned and walked out of the room to look for Jane in the kitchen.

'What on earth is happening?' she asked her when she came down the kitchen steps.

Jane had the tea tray in her hands.

'Answer me Jane, what on earth is going on?'

'You tell her Miss Jane,' Lizzie said from the top of the steps, 'Tell her how we're sharing things now, sharing everything like.'

'I wasn't talking to you,' Lucy tried, purposively standing with her back to her.

'Please Lucy, let us just go and have some tea in the parlour,' Jane said in a weak, troubled voice.

'Not until you tell me what is happening here. You look ill. You look as if you have not even washed yourself recently if you don't mind me being so bluntly frank.'

'Oh we don't mind being frank whatever that means.'

Lucy ignored this remark of Lizzie's and continued by saying, 'Put down the tray Jane. In the circumstances I do not want any tea, thank you.'

'Everything is fine, just fine Lucy.'

'No it isn't and why you have to say such a thing I do not know.'

'Maybe cos she means it. Here give it to me,' Lizzie said as she took hold of the tray.

Jane's eyes moistened as she added, 'It is just that things are different now since you last visited.'

Lucy was so bemused she had no idea what to say. Eventually they returned to the warm parlour where Lizzie set down the tea things. The three of them sat in silence. Lizzie poured the tea and helped herself to a slice of cake.

'Miss Jane med it,' she finally mentioned, 'and not bad, and why shouldn't it be, seeing as I taught her like?'

Jane looked down inspecting her hands clasped tightly together. Lucy tried to calm herself, seeking to understand what was going on. It was something strange and very disturbing. The roles had been completely reversed and now Lizzie seemed in charge. Lucy wondered how James Tranton fitted into this unlikely scheme. She quickly looked around the room noticing how bare it was in contrast to her other visits. There was no piano and no bureau. She thought one of the rugs had gone and the mantelpiece was now empty of all its ornaments. Two hard backed chairs that had been set in either corner of the room were also missing. Her anger began to rise again. She was disgusted and genuinely worried about her friend at the same time. Something absurd and peculiar had happened in this house and had happened in such a short time. Other than the maid oddly sharing tea with them on her last visit none of this had been apparent. The situation seemed already utterly perverse.

'I'd like you to leave us alone now Lizzie,' she started.

The young girl scoffed, bits of cake flying out of her mouth as she muttered, 'Like hell as like.'

'I want to speak to Jane alone.'

'But maybe she don't.'

Lucy looked at her friend questioningly but all Jane managed was to turn her head to the blazing fire.

'Jane?' Lucy tried.

'Yer see Miss Lucy. She wants me here, don't yer Miss Jane? Tell her, tell her you want me to stay.'

'My God!' Lucy exclaimed as she suddenly stood up, 'I've had quite enough of this. Will you just go, now?' she added loudly.

For the first time Lizzie appeared unsure, her mouth tightening and her eyes darting around the room.

'Please Lucy, it's alright,' Jane put in feebly.

'No it isn't Jane. It's not alright at all. Now get out! Lizzie leave this room now!'

The maid slowly set down the remainder of her cake and rubbed her hands down the front of her dress. Lucy thought she seemed plumper which made her appear even more vulgar and rough. She waited as Lizzie was obviously trying to make her mind up about what to do next.

'Seeing as yer se keen about getting me away I'll leave yer for a few minutes to get a pot of fresh tea, only a few minutes mind cos I don't want yer upsetting Miss Jane here.'

Lucy stood waiting for her to go.

'So a few minutes like.'

'Just go.'

'No thank you then,' Lizzie said, 'You're a rude woman so yer are Miss Lucy. Here am I doing yer a favour but yer thinks different and yer come in this house and try to tek over like so think theesell lucky I'm going anyway cos I've as much right to stay if I want, and more wi all I've done for this bloody miserable dump of a place. Anyway Miss Jane'll tell us everything that has been spoken when yer has gone. Won't yer Miss Jane?'

She went out of the parlour, slamming the door behind her.

Lucy felt relief as she sank back into her chair before leaning forward to take Jane's hands in hers.

'What is happening here Jane? Why is Lizzie acting like this? It's ridiculous letting her carry on like that. She's the maid for goodness sake and yet there she is wearing one of your dresses, all made up and acting as though she was the mistress of the house. Jane tell me please, what is going on?'

Her friend gave a weak smile and answered, 'I'm sure you're exaggerating Lucy. I thought....thought you'd like the idea of us women sharing more together, being more equal if you like.'

'Equal!' Lucy exclaimed, 'I don't call it equal when it's you answering the door, you making the tea while she just sits there lording it over you. That to me Jane is everything upside down. James employed her as a maid not as your companion.'

'It all started when I began teaching her to read and write and she helped me to learn how to bake and things. It just went on from there.'

'And I don't believe a word of it. You seem to have handed over everything to her and she has just taken it all. Where is all your furniture and why are you looking so unkempt and ill? Jane, please tell me.'

Jane said nothing, her pale features lined with uncertainty.

Lucy gripped her hands even tighter, wanting her friend to absorb some of her anger and frustration.

'And James, what does he think about all this? Surely he's aware of the situation.'

'He sees nothing wrong.'

'Well he must be blind or he's hardly ever here, one or the other. I'm determined to speak to him, to tell him what a state his cousin is in and ask why he's doing nothing about it. This has to stop.'

'I hear you've lost your job,' Jane said, ignoring Lucy's comments as if she had not heard her.

'That is irrelevant at the moment.'

Jane finally looked at her with her large, moistened eyes, 'How can you say that when it means you will be leaving here?'

'That's why I wanted to see you but I certainly did not expect this. I know we have not seen as much of each other as I would have liked over the summer months but this must have happened only over the last weeks. Why is Lizzie doing this and why Jane are you allowing it?'

'Please Lucy, stop asking so many questions. They're making my head hurt.'

'I am only concerned Jane, that's all,' she said, trying to soften her tone.

'I can assure you there is nothing to be concerned about.'

'I can't accept that Jane.'

'Please, you must.'

'Why, why must I?'

'For my sake.'

Lucy released her hands and stood up again. Going over to the window she looked out onto the bare garden. Suddenly Lizzie barged back in.

'Right, I'm back. I think yer have had enough time nattering between theeselves. I know Miss Lucy you kem to talk about losing yer job like and we're upset fer yer.'

'Are you?' Lucy asked angrily.

'But we don't want Miss Jane to get tired now do we?'

'How considerate you are, quite the good friend. So Jane, you have nothing more you want to say about.....about this situation?'

Jane nervously took out a handkerchief from the sleeve of her dress and blew her nose.

'Right, if there isn't then I don't see any point staying here any longer,' Lucy continued strongly as she gave Lizzie a furious look.

The maid smiled back at her.

'Yer can see yersell out.'

'I will.'

'And as we won't be seeing yer again I hope that everything goes better than it has done fer yer up there at Ribblehead.'

Lucy had never slammed a door shut as hard as she did when she left their house. She was far too early for the return coach to Ribblehead but was so upset she strode angrily past St Leonard's church and the vicarage, over the beck and up onto the road and started walking in the cold darkness, walking as hard as she could.

That evening after asking and searching around the settlements she finally met James Tranton coming out of the one of the hospital huts.

'Mr Tranton, I'm Lucy Ormskill, a friend of your cousin's,' she started as she struggled along the muddy boards towards him.

James stopped, took off his hat and stared at her before replying, 'Yes, of course.'

'She offered her gloved hand which he held for a moment, 'We've never met but I've been wanting to have a few words.'

'I'm sorry, but I.....'

'I need to speak with you Mr Tranton,' Lucy said strongly as a tinker went by rattling under all the pots and pans he was selling followed by a group of men who had been working late on the viaduct.

'Well, if you don't mind walking along with me, I have several visits yet to make,' James informed her.

'I wanted to talk to you about your cousin Jane. I'm extremely worried about her.'

'Worried, and why should you be worried Miss Ormskill?'

'Because I care about Jane and I think things are in a perilous state for her, extremely so. I don't think you understand how serious the situation is.'

'And what is this so called situation?' James asked sternly.

'In your own house.'

'I know what's going on in my own house.'

'Jane is not well and your maid......'

'I can assure you Miss Ormskill,' he said, striding out and making it difficult for Lucy to keep up with him, 'That I am aware of what goes on in my house and am perfectly capable with dealing with it. My cousin is my responsibility so long as she lives there.'

'She is living in degrading circumstances Mr Tranton.'

'Nonsense.'

'Surely you must see what's going on?'

Suddenly he stopped, the dank, cold air and stench of humans and animals around them, 'There is nothing as you put it going on. So if you will excuse me Miss Ormskill I have a lot to do this evening and I.....'

'You can't just leave it like that. Your maid Lizzie is....'

'I think I've made myself very clear.'

'You can't.....'

'Now let me wish you a pleasant evening', he said before abruptly setting off again leaving Lucy stood there as icy rain began to fall, smearing her bewildered, angry expression.

Two days later she was standing on the platform of Ingleton station, which in such weather had taken her over an hour to reach, with her travel bags either side of her. There were a few others waiting for the Leeds train and more travellers on the opposite platform waiting for the one going north. She was still worrying about Jane. Her situation was almost too strange to contemplate, too insidious the way things had changed. She could only assume Lizzie had something over her friend and that for some reason James Tranton was not accepting or taking it seriously enough. But now she was leaving and there was nothing more she could do.

Batty Green's new teacher was a Mr Bartley from Nelson who had taught abroad and in several Northern towns. He had come to the school to introduce himself to her and to inquire about the work she had been doing with the children. Her pupils had given her two wonderful gifts. The older girls had each knitted a section of a long, colourful winter scarf and the boys had somehow managed to discover her shoe size and had all chipped in together to buy a pair of green, leather boots from Silkin's shoe stall at the market. Lucy was deeply touched by their presents. She had not known what to expect leaving like this in the middle of the autumn term.

It was then she saw Tom come onto the opposite platform escorted by two constables. The shock made her draw breath as the group of three stopped opposite her. Tom smiled and nodded. All she could think of as a response was to raise her gloved hand a little in acknowledgement. So Tom had got what he wanted after all and was to be taken away on the same day at almost exactly the same time she was to catch her train. It seemed too much of a coincidence. Surely Richard had not arranged this to happen. She could not believe he could be so vindictive and yet here they were facing each other across the tracks.

Instinctively she left her bags, carefully stepped down off the platform, lifted up her coat and dress as she crossed the two sets of rails and climbed up onto the other platform.

'So this was your promise to see me again,' she said as she stopped in front of Tom.

'Seems so,' he answered easily.

'And you really have martyred yourself.'

'Step away from the prisoner Miss,' one of the constables told her.

Ignoring him she slowly took off her right glove to gently touch Tom's cheek before she leant forward to kiss him lightly on the mouth.

'I said step away,' the constable said strongly as she kissed him again before turning round and retracing her steps back across the tracks and up onto the other platform, standing there with a defiant look in her eyes until her train appeared in a throng of movement and thick steam blowing everywhere.

CHAPTER FIFTY THREE

She was lost. Jane was lying beside Lizzie as still as she could so as not to wake her. There was no escape. Desire had destroyed her. All the applications for a post as a governess had been unsuccessful. This was the deepest emptiness into which she had fallen and now there was only the bleakest of times, of endless days where she dreaded everything and hoped for nothing. The body beside her which she had once craved for was now like a huge stone set over the entrance to her prison. It dominated her, those huge breasts and buttocks and thighs all washed and perfumed now, all smooth and well fed.

The curtains were still open so she could see the snow falling in the moonlight. The fire that had been lit in the bedroom was now only dull embers but still gave off a little warmth. Jane looked to the fire and then back to the huge flakes of snow, the heat and the cold, the one to melt in the other, the contrast between the warmth of life and the dread of the endless winter crusted over the hills and moorlands. She dare not move. She must not move. Lizzie was snoring lightly beside her, her hip mounded like the slope of a hillside under the blankets. Jane felt each flake of snow as herself, falling and melting, falling and melting to be absorbed over and over again until she no longer existed.

She lay now night after night without sleep, her mind in a torment of regret and dread. The prison was the winter, was the darkness, was this house's isolation. The snow was falling. All she could do was watch its white lines cutting through the moonlight. Was God still here, still in this house? Would James ever find him again? Something had to change, but she was helpless and so scared that James would eventually succumb to his own passion. For her now there was no God, no otherness, only the tattered remains of herself like an old piece of cloth that nobody wanted. She did not want to be who she was. It disgusted her to be like this. She was exhausted, ill with so little sleep, without any care for herself. Nothing mattered now except that somehow James might survive. She was hoping he would not return, that he would stay the night at Ribblehead because of the weather. But within a few minutes she heard the dull clomp of his Bess's hoofs as he took her round to the stables. Thankfully Lizzie slept on.

Carefully Jane got out of bed and stood there listening. It seemed to take James so long to unsaddle the horse and feed her. Eventually she heard the front door open. She waited for him to take off his hat and coat and then go off to the kitchen which he always did to look for something to eat. She glanced over at Lizzie but her breathing was still slow as her body rose and fell with each breath. Jane put her hands up to her face and held them there until at last she heard James mounting the stairs.

For a few seconds she waited before crossing the small room in her bare feet, going out onto the landing where she gently knocked on his door.

Almost immediately he opened it, his face ashen white and his hair wet, 'Jane, what's wrong?'

She pushed past him into the room.

'Close the door,' she whispered, 'Close the door James.'

'What's the matter?'

'Not so loud,' she insisted, 'you must not wake her.'

He came over to her, his dark eyes reflecting the candle he had lit.

'Jane, are you well? You're shivering. What are you trying to say? You should be in bed asleep by now.'

'We have to stop her,' she said.

'Stop who?'

'Please James. I have so despised you. We must stop her James. You must stop her. Forgive me. You have to forgive me for hating you so badly. My God I am so sorry,' Jane gasped as he helped her to sit on the edge of the bed.

'Jane, you're not making any sense. You must try and…….'

'I am so sorry,' she interrupted.

Anxiously he sat beside her, taking her hand, 'You are troubled in spirit and you need to rest Jane.'

'She's taken everything and I understand now why, I do.'

'How can I help you? How can I take away some of your fears?' he asked concernedly, smoothing down her hair as she leant slightly towards him.

'She is the devil's kind and I …..I am too weak to….'

Jane started shivering violently before suddenly standing up.

James still held onto her hand, 'Please Jane, sit back down and calm yourself.'

'I know how you must have suffered.'

'Sit down Jane.'

'You must not let her James. You must not. You must have strength. You must have the strength for both of us.'

'Let me get you a glass of water,' he tried before she jerked round.

'Make this house a place of God again. Only you can do that James, only you.'

He stood up and gently helped her to sit back on the edge of the bed, his face tight with worry.

'Nothing is happening Jane. I am here and I want you to try and calm yourself, just a little and then a little more. I am here and everything is alright.'

'You're not listening. I know. I know everything James but you know so little, so little. She wants you James. I tried.....I really tried but I couldn't stop myself but you.....you have to be stronger.'

His face stiffened, his body tightening slightly.

For a few moments he was speechless. Slowly he put in hand on the top of Jane's hand as though he was blessing her. She started to sob as quietly as she could as he stood there in front of her.

'Jane, Jane,' he repeated in a low voice.

'I'm sorry,' she muttered, 'We have to stop her,' she repeated in a voice that was even more anxious.

He lowered his hand and went over to the window where his bureau had once been. His face was empty, rigid, almost stern as he stood there watching the falling snow.

'Winter comes and with it such bleak thoughts,' he said as though to himself.

'You are not hearing me.'

'I hear you Jane, but not I'm afraid in the way you wish.'

'You have to understand.'

'No, I have to sympathise. I have to share your pain. I have to absorb your suffering and pray that you too might find salvation in the Lord. Come, kneel beside me and we can pray together.'

At that Jane stood up, her whole body shaking with frustration.

'She is the devil's child now,' she muttered.

'You exaggerate. You're not seeing things clearly at the moment. You're not well and I blame myself for ignoring you so much over the last months. It's my fault you're in such a state. I've told you before Jane, you are my responsibility and I've been failing in my duty to you.'

'It's to yourself you have to look James. It's you who are playing with the devil's kind and you....you think your faith is indestructible but it isn't.'

'Let us pray together.'

'No!' she suddenly exclaimed, her eyes wild with fear, 'That's the game she wants to play. You think you can save her but you can't. Don't pray with her James, never again. You must promise, promise me James. Keep away from her.'

'Lizzie is beginning to believe now. She too is part of my mission. I can't refuse to help her just because she lives here. Surely it's more important that I try.'

'Please James.'

'I have to try Jane.'

'She.....she is stronger than you....she will......'

'You must stop this now. You're making yourself worse.'

'There is no worse.'

'And you're shivering.'

'You're not listening to me. You don't want to hear what I'm saying.'

'Of course I do. Pray with me Jane. I know it will help.'

Slowly, emptily, with tears coursing down her cheeks, she got up, walked out of the room and stood there in her nightdress in the darkness of the landing. There was no hope for her because there was no hope for him. He was so lost he had had no idea what she had been trying to say to him. Standing there she had never felt so alone, so completely alone.

When she went back into her bedroom Lizzie was sitting there in bed waiting for her.

'So where have yer been Miss Jane, talking to the master? Yer been saying things about me?'

Jane could not move. Her limbs were frozen stiff and her heart was beating so fast she felt giddy with it.

'Tell me!' Lizzie suddenly began shouting.

'I've....I've said nothing Lizzie. Why should I?'

'Cos you're against me now. I can tell and you're trying to get the master the same. Well, we'll see about that,' Lizzie said as she climbed out of bed.

Jane forced herself to stare down at the floor.

'What's wrong, can't look at me anymore?'

'No.'

'Come on Miss Jane, look at me.'

'Leave me alone.'

'Yer know yer want to.'

'Leave me alone Lizzie.'

'I'm not doing owt. Well if yer ain't interested we'll see what Master James has to say.'

'No!' Jane exclaimed as she moved towards her.

'Or what?'

'You keep away from him.'

'I said or what?'

'You've done enough in this house. Lizzie you know you have. There's nothing left for you to take, nothing so why do you have to persist?'

'Fine words but sod you,' Lizzie muttered as she barged past her and made for the door.

'No Lizzie!' Jane tried as she made to grab her arm.

'Bugger off!' the young maid shouted back, pulling away and forcing open the door.

Jane remained where she was. After a few minutes she could hear their voices from the other room. She noticed the fire was now ashen grey while the snow continued to fall outside. She was a flake melting in the heat over and over again until she was finally absorbed and was as nothing. She was alone in a world that no longer had any place for her, a world that made no sense anymore. She could hear James' voice coming from his bedroom. It sounded so urgent, almost pleading.

Carefully, quietly she went back out again onto the landing.

'James,' she whispered outside his door, 'please James, don't, don't do this for me, for you, please James. '

She went down the stairs and outside into the thickly falling snow. Automatically she trudged in her bare feet past the church and over the bridge to where the road used to begin. The snow had fallen so heavily over the last hours it was impossible to see where the edge of the road was as she stumbled out onto its smoothness and fell to her knees. She was shivering so hard as she scooped up the first handfuls of snow to wash herself with it, to rub and clean and wash, her hands trembling with the intensity of their action. In the pale light of the moon through the clouds her skin was turning blue, her limbs shaking with the cold as she continued to smear the snow all over her again and again, moaning and shivering, breathing fast and hard, now down on her hands and knees exhausted with the frenzied effort to be clean, cleaner than clean, washed clear and white and numb with the cold.

Unseen but slowly coming towards her were four carts attempting to make their way down to Ingleton before the road blocked up altogether. They had set off hours before from Ribblehead, agreeing to go together for safety's sake. Jane could not see the dull light from their lamps as the snow lashed at an angle across the Dale. Her head was down, her sodden hair trailing in the snow, coughing and moaning and shivering more than ever.

CHAPTER FIFTY FOUR

The weather had suddenly changed and the snow of the last two days had melted within hours. The streets of Batty Green were a mess of deep mud, the beck a raging torrent of brown meltwater already flooding some of the huts at Sebastopol and Salt Lake. Around Batty Moss was more dangerous than ever, a huge, deep swamp in which several sheep had been lost over night. Dogs were roaming around in packs and the carts bringing the daily supply of milk and coal struggled to reach Ribblehead while some of the other wagons were still stuck further down the Ingleton road and the fresh bread and vegetables brought up from Settle would take all day to arrive. Streams and waterfalls never seen before were pouring down the slopes of Whernside and Ingleborough as the the Dale had become a huge lake widening by the hour. One of the huts in Jericho had subsided, its structure tilted at an angle as it slowly sank into the water and the cutting up by the tunnel was being rapidly filled with sliding mud and rock.

More rain was falling out of a low, black sky as the last of the workers made their way along the streets at the end of the shift, their boots clogged with the thick, blue mud, their clothes drenched as they struggled to keep upright. They had been beaten down today, fighting against the elements, forcing themselves to work when no work was possible. They were hungry, drenched and very cold. Their minds were numbed off by the hopeless effort of the last ten exhausting hours. All they were interested in was getting out of their sodden clothes and having something warm shovelled into their stomachs as fast as they could. It seemed that there had been nothing but snow and rain for weeks, nothing but trying to survive in this barren place that made men bitter and empty.

Bill and Jonty were first to arrive back.

'Bloody hell,' Bill muttered as he came into the middle room.

'Boots off!' Maggie told him, 'and you as well Jonty.'

'Oh come on Missus,' Bill complained.

'Never mind that,' Maggie snapped, 'you just get them filthy boots off. There's enough mess in here as it is wiout anymore.'

They did as she asked. Jonty fell on his backside, moaning as he tried to pull off one of his sodden boots whose laces had got so wet they had tightened into an impossible knot.

'Here,' said Clare who had just arrived home herself, 'let me help. Jonty what have yer done wi this?' she asked of the knot.

The young man was still loudly moaning, his thick red lips wide apart showing his yellowed teeth.

Meanwhile Bill was pulling off his coat, jacket, scarf, waistcoat, shirt and trousers leaving him only in his soaking long johns.

'Give that lot to me and get into someat dry,' Maggie continued.

But all Bill could manage was to bend forward to rub his knees, 'Christ but they're bad today. All this wet and cold and me joints are giving me gip. Look at me hands Missus.'

Maggie stopped to inspect the large arthritic bumps on each of his knuckles.

'And me hips are killing me so they are.'

'I don't know Bill, you're about ready fer the knacker's yard if you ask me.'

'And today I'd agree with thee woman.'

'Go on, get yersell into someat dry.'

'Off! Off!' Jonty was shouting at Clare managing to pull off his boot without untying the knot.

'And you can do the same, get that lot off and then get theesell into someat dry, 'Maggie ordered.

'Dry,' Jonty repeated.

'Yes, now go!'

'Go on Jonty,' Clare added.

Sheepishly he started taking off his clothes as well and then followed Bill into the bedroom.

'What a sight,' said Maggie.

'They look so daft wi just their underwear on,' Clare agreed, giggling, 'especially Jonty's thin legs and his knobbly knees, what a sight.'

Within half an hour Ethan, Fraser and Jock had all done the same, boots off at the door, wet work clothes left in a pile on the floor before Maggie started to hang them across the room until the whole place was hanging with wet, steaming clothes that stank of the mud and rain.

The men's' faces were all red and fresh from the heat of the stove. Little was said as they ate their dinner, their tired faces intent only on the next mouthful. After they had finished they were off out again, Jock to the Railway Inn and Fraser to another game of three card brag.

When finally Maggie and Clare had eaten their dinner and the washing up had been done Maggie went into her bedroom and came out with a brown woolly hat she had knitted.

'Here, what does to think o this Jonty lad?'

She held out the hat to him and he looked at it quizzically.

'Go on, it's fer you. Put it on.'

'Try it on Jonty,' added Bill who was sitting at the table smiling and smoking his pipe.

Ethan was seated at the other end reading the local paper, uninterested in what was going on around him.

'Fer me?' asked Jonty, reddening with all of this sudden attention.

Suddenly he grabbed at the hat and plonked it on his head of thick hair.

'No, pull it down,' laughed Clare as she dragged down the hat over his huge ears sticking out at ninety degrees.

The rest of them had to laugh good heartedly as he stood there holding his arms stiffly by his side, a look of bewilderment on his weathered face.

'Fer me?' he asked again.

'Yes Jonty, fer you,' Maggie answered.

He suddenly turned and went into his bedroom, coming back seconds later with his work cap pulled tight on top of the woolly hat.

'Would yer look at that!' exclaimed Bill, 'that'll keep yer head warm.'

'Warm,' Jonty repeated.

He was so pleased with his new hat that he kept it on for the rest of the night with his cap balanced on top.

'Mucky weather,' Ethan said to Bill after Clare had settled Jonty down to helping her with one of the jigsaws.

Maggie was sitting sewing near the stove too tired to bother with any more talking.

'Ay, for thee more than me on a filthy day like this,' Bill answered, 'So what yer been on?'

'Trying and trying is the only word to stop that beck that runs int' cutting, the one supposed eventually to go along the new bridge. Couldn't do it, not wi amount o water coming down, bloody hopeless.'

'Well we've doing nowt wi waiting to get boilers fired up. Someat weren't right so we've been bodging rest o the time.'

Ethan watched him smoking his pipe, his cheeks sucked inwards at each pull.

'Early dark as well don't help,' he said then.

'I hear they've got rid o that Tom Myres, teken off wi constables he was,' Bill informed him.

'Ay, so I heard, had to happen sometime. He was allays mouthing off, med sense some o the time and was plain daft the rest,' Ethan answered.

'They reckon it was cos o Miss Ormskill, the teacher. He was keen on her was Stockton but seemingly she had teken a liking to Tom Myres so that didn't go down well. Had her shipped out same day.'

'Rule is don't cross the bosses.'

'Rule is leave the boss's woman alone,' Bill added.

'It's a shame,' Maggie finally had to say, 'She was a right good teacher. Our Beth thought the world o her.'

Bill looked at her with sympathy and added, 'Ay, she were allays talking about her.'

'Every day she kem home she was full of her she was, couldn't stop talking about her teacher, Miss Ormskill had done this, Miss Ormskill had done that.'

'Not like our Clare then.'

'Oh Clare,' Maggie shrugged, 'Never liked it. Wasn't for her was learning.'

'She's med a grand rag rug,' Bill commented of the one on the floor in front of the stove that she had made.

'That's more like it for our Clare. Give her a needle and thread and she's happy.'

'That's me,' Clare finally put in, 'I were listening. I can hear yer know.'

'Nowt critical,' laughed Bill.

'Yes Jonty!' Clare suddenly explained, 'He's right good at these jigsaws Uncle Bill, better than me.'

Bill rose out of his chair to come and watch, playfully pressing down on Jonty's shoulders as he stood behind him.

'Give up!' Jonty complained loudly.

'Yer a right good un Jonty lad, a right good un,' Bill said strongly, 'what wi yer new hat and all.'

Jonty exaggeratedly nodded and lowered his head closer to the table with the pressure from Bill's hands.

'Leave him alone Uncle Bill,' Clare admonished.

'I'm only joshing.'

'Joshing,' muttered Jonty.

'And he's good at these here jigsaws like he is at the draughts.'

'So I keep hearing,' Ethan said.

'He'll be up at the Institute tomorrow night wi Arnold beating ever bugger there is.'

Bill returned to his pipe and Ethan continued reading his Craven Herald. Water dripped from the sodden clothing everywhere as the rain continued to rattle against the small window.

Later the knock on the door was the local farmer apologising for coming with the milk so late as he ladled it out of his churn into the two jugs that Clare was holding steadily with Maggie stood beside her.

'Never seen weather like it. There's sheep been washed away down the beck, carts up to their axles, fallen rock blocking the road above Selside. I'll reckon up wi thee next week Missus if that's alright wi you cos I'm pressed fer time. Ay, it's a bad un alright,' the farmer commented before hurriedly wishing her good night as he hunched up on his small cart and tried to get his horse moving through the river of mud.

'About time,' Maggie said, 'I thought he was never coming. Put them jugs in the cupboard will you Clare?' she asked.

'So I noticed Fraser and Jock left yer alone tonight fer a change,' Ethan said to Bill.

'The buggers can do what they like as far as I'm concerned, but I'll do fer em one o these days.'

'You ought to be careful I reckon. I wouldn't trust either o em, especially Tarrant. He must have some past wi the drunken states he gets hisell into and his awful temper. Yer can't tell me he's managed to keep clear o the constables all these years.'

'That's what they think,' Bill mentioned, 'think that I've been trying me best to get someat on em when I couldn't care less what they've done, but that's what they're always going on about. Some sod has filled their heads wi nonsense about me trying to rake up their past.'

'Well they've teken it serious enough. I'd just watch em. That Tarrant is a violent bugger.'

'Oh I'm not bothered about that little sod, not at all.'

'Come see Bill,' Jonty interrupted.

'He's finished it by himself. I did nowt, honest,' Clare announced.

'Well done lad,' said Bill to Jonty who was beaming with satisfaction.

'Now lass ask him some o yer questions, yer know, the ones yer were asking him a couple o nights ago and see if he remembers.'

'Do yer think he will?'

'How do I know? That's why I'm asking yer to see if he does.'

Jonty was obviously trying to understand what they were saying about him, his face furrowed in concentration until he looked at Clare and gave her one of his big, thick lipped smiles nobody could resist, especially Clare, 'And what are yer smiling at?'

'Smiling,' said Jonty.

'What fer?'

'Did....did the jiggy saw.'

'Yer did.'

'Jonty did it.'

'And when's Arnold coming?' Clare asked her first testing question, seeing if Jonty could remember.

'Ay, that's it,' said Bill, 'see if he can tell yer.'

Jonty now had his lips stuck out while thinking, 'Arnold.'

'Yes Arnold,' Clare reminded him.

Maggie set down her sewing waiting to see what Jonty could manage.

'He's coming fer me.'

'Yes, but when?'

'At night time.'

'Which night?'

'Soon.'

'How soon?'

'Coming.....coming next day,' Jonty said happily.

'That's right. He's coming tomorrow, tomorrow Jonty, the next day is tomorrow.'

'To....tomo......tomorrow.'

'Good. Now, next question, what is the name of our queen?'

Jonty stuck up his hands and widened his fingers as though in mock surprise, 'Victoria!' he shouted as loud as he could at which everyone laughed.

'By God Jonty lad, you're nowt but an entertainment,' said Bill.

'At least he remembers,' added Maggie.

'One more,' Clare started, 'Jonty.'

'Yes,' he answered, looking at her nervously now, his moist, reddened eyes larger it seemed than ever.

'Tell me as many names of the other places here at Ribblehead as yer can, yer know, places where folk live like this is Batty Green, yer know that, so's what's names o the others?'

'The walls of Jericho!' Jonty immediately cried out.

'That's one.'

'Them....them Tunnel Huts where Dodgie lives.'

'Who the hell is Dodgie?' Ethan interrupted.

'Just one o the fellas who work wi us,' Bill told him.

'Good Jonty, yer've got two, what about another? What's like Jericho cos it starts wi a J, a J sound?'

'J....J......I know.....I know,' he repeated, 'but can't say it, too big, word too big.'

'Well just try.'

'Jruslem.'

'Say it again.'

'Jerusslem.'

'Nearly.'

'Oh tell him Clare,' said her mother.

'Jerusalem.'

'I said it.'

'Yer did.'

'I said it Bill.'

'Yer doing good lad, so yer are.'

'If yer can manage one more we'll stop,' said his teacher.

'One more?'

'Just one.'

'What's one oer t'other side o the bridge?' Bill tried to help, 'the one wi some o its huts flooded out. Yer know, we heard that this morning. Tammy Hansen told us. Where does Tammy live?'

Jonty was now kneading his hands together in excitement, his shoulders hunched forward as more spit dribbled onto the table.

'Come on lad, where's he live?'

'Don't know,' Jonty finally declared.

'Yes yer do.'

'Don't know Bill. Don't know nowt.'

'Seb.....'

'Seb....'

'Go on, finish it off.'

'Don't know. Don't!' Jonty said loudly, his bottom lip hanging loose as he became more upset.

'Alright, it doesn't matter,' Clare quickly intervened, 'Yer've done good Jonty. Yer have. No more questions.'

'No more?'

'No.'

'Yer stopped?'

'I've stopped.'

'And I did....I did good?'

'Yer did grand Jonty,' Maggie put in, 'Now come and help me mek a pot o tea, yer must be thirsty after all them questions and jig saws and what have yer.'

'He's such a lovely lad,' Maggie said to Ethan that night as they lay beside each other in bed.

'Jonty yer mean?'

'Ay, and our Clare dotes on him.'

'She does that alright.'

'God knows what's going to happen to him if Bill has to ever pack up work.'

'Well wi the way he's sounding it can't be long. Bill's knackered. He says so and he looks it. Summer's done him no good at all and if the winter goes on like this then it could finish him.'

'Thank God when Bill packs up here wherever he goes he says he's teking Jonty wi him, down to his sister's Bill reckons.'

'He'll have to manage by hisell sometime or other.'

'Let's hope long enough in the future for owt like that,' said Maggie.

'Do yer think that's why Bill has let Arnold in on him a bit cos once of a day he'd let nobody near him, Bill wouldn't.'

'Could be, never thought of it in that way.'

'Just seems a bit of a coincidence that Arnold has made his appearance oer the last months just when Bill is on the slide.'

'I just love that lad to bits. I just wish I could stop allays worrying about him, that's all.'

Ethan turned on his side to her, 'You worry about owt and nowt Maggie Granger.'

'I suppose I do,' she said softly.

'No suppose about it.'

'I just try and think of him, of Jonty wi a Mum and Dad somewhere and I can't. I can't imagine it. It's like Bill says, he just appeared out o the mist on the top road to Dent and that was it, but I'd still love to know where he kem from.'

'And he'll never be able to tell us.'

'No, I can't ever see that happening, not unless there's a miracle and there won't be.'

Finally she went to sleep. Some nights now she slept in Beth's bed. Ethan would lie there listening to her quiet sobs, hoping that they did not wake Clare. It was the strangest confusion, to be thinking of Floss Sugden all the time and yet feeling he loved his wife as much as ever. He was being drained by it. The rain was clattering hard on the roof as he thought of Floss, saw her so clearly in his imagination as if she was there beside him, close enough to touch, to kiss, to have over and over again.

CHAPTER FIFTY FIVE

'Alright lad?' asked Arnold Wainwright, forcing a smile.

Jonty looked up surprised. He had forgotten this was the evening that Arnold came for him with his round face and thin hair and his miserable looking clothes. Arnold was a friend, not as much as Bill was, but still a friend who looked after him when they were out of the hut and took him up to the Institute to play draughts. This was the highlight of Jonty's week and already he was up and putting on his coat.

'Has it stopped raining?' Bill asked Arnold who stood waiting at the door knowing that Maggie did not like muddy boots being traipsed all over the floor.

'And why do you want to know?' Jock interrupted, 'not going courting is thee?'

Bill ignored the remark, 'Now yer behave yersell.'

'I behave.'

'And listen to what Arnold says.'

'Arnold's my friend.'

'That's right,' agreed Arnold warmly as he glanced at Jock and then at Fraser sat at the table.

On went Jonty's cap on top of his new woolly hat.

'He's slept in it last night,' Bill said, 'Won't tek it off

Jonty liked the cold air. It pricked him all over his face like tiny fingers trying to tickle him. Lamp light shone out of the windows in pools of orange over the dark mud. He smelt the smoke and the stench of the privies overflowing with all the rain. Arnold had to stride out to keep up with him. He was excited because he was going to play the draughts. He loved the warm wood smell of the Institute and the pipe tobacco and the slight odour from the newspapers left on the shelf near the stove. It was stacked with peat that had the smell of the warm moorland.

'You alright?'

'Alright Arnold,' he answered with his broad, high pitched voice.

He could see the lines of the scaffolding against the lighter sky, shapes criss crossed, up or flat with others at an angle holding the rest together. The two chimneys of the brick factory stuck up like two big fingers. He worked there. He worked there with Bill. He thought about Bill back in the hut smoking his pipe like he did every night filling the room with its sweet, dark odour. Jonty loved to breathe it in with deep gulps and pretend he was smoking.

'No drinking and no smoking Jonty lad,' he had told him, 'If I'm teking responsibility fer yer then them are the rules. I might have a pipe of a night mesell but that don't mean yer have to be as daft as me, does it?'

Twice he almost fell over in the thick mud. It made his legs all soft and out of control and Arnold was just as bad beside him. He greeted everyone they passed, two lads taking a few sheep along the road, men off to the pub, a girl looking for her geese, some on their way to a service in the big hall and others joining them going to the Institute.

Near the end of their road a coal cart had tipped on its side and the horse with it, the beast lying in the thick mud kicking out its legs in a hopeless attempt to get back up. Coal was piled against the front of one of the huts as the coalman was trying to pull up his horse. Arnold and Jonty with a few others went to help. The horse's eyes were huge and frightened with panicky breaths sounding out of its nostrils. Folk came out of their huts with lamps. Finally they had the horse on its feet and a group including Jonty and Arnold managed to push the cart back on its wheels while a mob of children were either running off with armfuls of coal or helping throw it back onto the cart.

'Look at us now,' Arnold said as they finally walked away, 'A right bloody mess.'

Jonty inspected his filthy hands and the front of his working coat clarted with mud.

'Mud stinks,' he announced.

'I'm sick o it,' Arnold added.

The Institute was the only place in the settlements to avoid women, drink and religion. Here the drive to forget the working day was less intense. It was a space for reading and recreation, a game of cards so long as there was no gambling and the usual a game of dominoes or draughts.

Jonty loved its warm, smoky atmosphere. The men had quickly come to accept his weekly visits, especially when he started beating all comers at draughts and dominoes. Arnold would never play. His role was to stand just behind Jonty and watch his every move and make sure that any arguments were speedily curtailed. The last thing he wanted was for Jonty to go back to his hut all upset about something.

To Jonty the game of draughts was shapes made by moving white on black or black on white. The patterns he had to make to win were obvious. His mind saw them so clearly. It was the same with dominoes. His memory could hold all the different combinations of dots. He might not be able to count them but he could readily remember all the possible ways the black dots could come together. Nobody understood how someone like him could just keep on winning. Hardly ever was he beaten. They could not see how objects and dots made such recognisable and pleasing patterns. Without knowing the word he loved the symmetry they often made. His physical world was made up of patterns, lines and spaces that no one else could perceive. Jonty had a mind that worked so clearly, so sharply when it came to creating new shapes.

'Well damn it, he's done it again!' someone exclaimed as Jonty happily slammed down his last domino leaving his three opponents bewildered as usual.

'Good one Jonty lad,' Arnold said, patting him on the shoulders.

'Won again Arnold.'

'You did that alright.'

'Play again?'

'If yer like and then I'll tell yer what we'll do, we'll go for a quick drink at the Railway to celebrate, what do yer say?'

Jonty looked confused. Instead of sorting the doms he got up and turned to Arnold saying, 'Not allowed to drink. Bill said so.'

'I know he did, but just once won't do any harm. Anyroads I'm thirsty so we can just pop in on the way back.'

'I'll.....I'll get in trouble Arnold.'

'No, yer won't. If it'll be anybody's fault it'll be mine so yer don't have to worry about that. In fact yer don't have to worry about owt.'

Jonty's mouth gaped open as he tried to make sense of what had been said. He looked around at the groups of men at the different tables and those smoking and chatting by the stove, smelt the peat and the tang from the newspapers as well as the stench of mud and hammered stone that everyone brought in with them.

'Bill'll be cross,' he finally muttered.

'Oh hell Jonty lad!' Arnold exclaimed as he took his arm and led him away from the group of players, 'Yer can't allays be thinking about what he'll have to say. Sometime or other yer'll have to mek decisions fer yersell. It's just a quick drink I'm talking about. And anyway I'll be cross if yer don't come wi us.'

'Don't be angry Arnold.'

'Well I will be.'

'You're....you're my friend Arnold.'

'And sometimes one friend should do what the other friend says.'

Again Jonty looked uncertain.

'I mean it Jonty. I'll be cross if yer don't come.'

Jonty became more agitated as he swung his arms about and shouted too loudly, 'It's not fair!'

'Keep it down for God's sake. Right I'm going. Yer've won enough tonight.'

'But.....but....'Jonty tried.

'But nowt. Get yer coat on and we're going off to't Railway or yer can mek yer own way back and then Bill'll be bloody mad at both of us.'

'Arnold.'

'Come on.'

'I.....I.....'

'Get yer coat on.'

Jonty had kept his woolly hat and cap on throughout the evening.

'Yer not going Jonty lad?' asked Toby Andrews, another one who had never managed to beat him.

'We're going,' Arnold announced.

'But yer've just got here.'

'He's won enough.'

'And we want a chance to....'

'To what?' Arnold interrupted, 'What, get beat again?'

Outside Jonty started shivering. His body was suddenly freezing cold with a combination of worry and excitement. He was going to do something he knew he should not and wanted to do it and yet was frightened about Bill's reaction. This was new. This was something that made his belly hurt. He did not want to make his friend Arnold angry with him. He had never had a drink but he had heard all about it. Every other worker drank or so it seemed so why not him? Why should Uncle Bill always be telling him what to do. Maybe Arnold was right and he should do something for himself. But it was wrong to go against what Bill had told him he should not do. Now in his head were all these voices and they were making him dizzy with all their words. He did not know what to do and he did not like this feeling at all. It made him feel very cold and sick at the same time.

'Alright lad?' Arnold finally asked as they passed through the settlement.

'No,' he muttered back.

‘Why, what’s wrong wi yer?’

‘Me head hurts.’

‘Well stop bothering so much and a good drink’ll settle that problem. That’s what yer need Jonty lad, a quick pint to settle yer down.’

‘I feel sick.’

‘Well go ahead, spew yer guts out if that’ll mek yer feel any better.’

‘I want to go home.’

‘No yer don’t.’

‘I want to go home Arnold’

‘After I’ve had me drink. You don’t have to drink owt. Yer can just stand there and watch me. How many times have you been in the Railway?’

‘Never been Arnold.’

‘Well it’s about time yer paid the place a visit. There might be some fiddle music on. You’d like that.’

Jonty made no response as he tried to keep his balance in the ankle deep mud.

‘And don’t yer go getting in one o yer sulks.’

‘I’ll come then,’ he finally announced.

‘I know yer will. I said yer going so I’m glad yer agree cos I don’t want to argue and get angry at yer Jonty lad.’

‘No Arnold.’

‘And yer played well tonight at the Institute.’

‘Thank you Arnold.’

‘So come on, give us one o yer big grins.’

At that Jonty forced an anxious smile as they approached the pub.

The overwhelming impact of noise, heat and colour smashed into his senses as they entered. He had to step back with the force of the place’s impact. It was so different with bodies shifting in strangely uncoordinated ways. Their voices thundered over each other. Lights dazzled and glinted from faces to glasses to the shiny bar top to the lamps and the open fire blazing away. The smells and the heat were glued together like a deep coloured syrup all melting and flowing slowly around his brain. It was so wonderful it made him giddy.

To most drinkers the Railway Inn was a dull, miserably basic place of entertainment with its dark grey slabbed floor and its low smoke blackened roof, but to Jonty it was full of life and voices and smells he had never experienced before.

Then it was too much. Arnold had to grab him by the arm as he made for the door.

'And where are yer going?'

'Going,' said Jonty.

'Not until I say so lad. Calm yersell down and I'll get us both a pint and then yer'll feel better.'

He watched with fascination the golden beer being poured out by a man he had never seen before, a large, fat man wearing an apron and a bowler hat.

'Now Arnold, whose this then yer've dragged in?'

'It's Jonty, Bill Asquith's lad,' said another.

'It is,' said Arnold.

'And where's Bill then. I've never seen them two apart.'

'Jonty's wi me tonight.'

'Well God help him. Don't listen to a bloody word he says lad.'

Their voices were loud and made Jonty nervous again. The room was full of them all talking at once it seemed as they shifted slowly from one crowded space to another.

Finally Arnold found them a seat beside one of the pub's filthy windows.

'Right, sup this down yer,' he said to Jonty who stared at his full glass.

'Drink.'

'That's right, yer drink it, like this,' advised Arnold before he swallowed half his pint.

Carefully Jonty lifted the glass to his lips and took a sip.

'Nay lad, get a good mouthful down yer.'

'A lot?'

'Ay, a lot.'

'Drink it?'

'Like me.'

So Jonty drank, swallowed, drank some more and then quickly put the glass down.

He waited to see what might happen. To begin with all he could taste was the sweetish beer until its warmth started to flood his brain and then his stomach.

'Alright?' asked Arnold.

'Alright.'

'Well go on then, get the rest o it down yer.'

The rest went down a lot quicker and its effect was more powerful as Jonty felt everything melting inside his head and a dull, heavy sensation fill his legs.

Now he was on his way as Arnold had hoped. The second and third pints went down just as quickly. Around him everything began to blur into a mess of sounds and movement and colours. A fiddle started up.

'And where are yer going?' he asked as Jonty suddenly sprung up.

'Dancing!' he exclaimed.

'Get yersell sat down, yer big pillock.'

'Dancing.'

'No, yer sit yersell down.'

Disappointed Jonty slumped back on his shaky seat as somehow another pint of beer was there in front of him. Then Arnold somehow disappeared and suddenly Jock was there standing by the table telling him it was whisky in the glass he had put in front of him. For such a small amount it was amazing to Jonty how it blew more heat through him and had his mind begin to gently spin around. His mouth felt full of something soft and by now his legs were so heavy he could hardly move them. But more than anything he could not stop laughing and trying to sing as the fiddle screeched out another tune and Jock sat close beside him as others came up and shouted things he could not understand with his head on fire and his heart so happy.

'Well be going then,' said the voice.

Jonty squinted to see where it came from.

'Are you right Jonty boy cos we're going?'

Jock was there staring at him and asking him a question.

'Going?'

'Ay, but don't worry there'll be plenty more drink where we're going.'

'Jock,' Jonty mumbled, 'Where's.....where's Arnold.'

'That's me boyo, don't thee be bothered wi the likes of Arnold. You're wi me now.'

'Feel sick, dizzy, dizzy and sick.'

'Well let's get yer out in the fresh air then.'

Jock's hands were under his arms and then he was leaning on him as all the men filling the pub seemed to move aside to let them pass. Jonty waved and smiled but nobody waved or smiled back.

Outside the cold air smacked him in the face and knocked him over. He was somehow on his knees and was vomiting up a foamy spurt of beer and whisky and it felt good to be sick, good to let it all out except the smell of it was sour and it was filled with bits of his dinner which he did not like to look at.

Eventually it was over and he managed to stand upright although his legs and arms felt as weak as jelly that wobbled every time he tried to put one foot in front of the other.

'Thank the fuck that's over with,' said Jock.

Again Jonty was taken by the arm and he was glad of it, glad of everything as the night seemed to fill him with a new, happier solution.

'Jock's wi us.'

'Damned fucking right I am.'

'Going home.'

'Not on yer life boyo. Gracie Archers is where we're headed who lives behind the walls of Jericho that tonight fer thee laddie will be tumbling down.'

'Jericho,' Jonty muttered, 'and Jus.....Jruslam.'

It was another room but smaller and more crowded. It had the same smells of the drink but this time mixed in with other much sweeter odours. Here there were women who stared at Jonty and he became anxious again and then upset and wanted to leave until Jock pushed a glass of whisky in his hand and told him to drink it down.

'So who's this big lump of a thing?' asked one of the women.

Jonty looked at her bare shoulders and half exposed breasts and the way she had her skirt hitched up so he could see some of her legs. He winced as she pushed up his chin to get a better view of him.

'Fuck Jock, is he all there like?'

'This Gracie is Jonty the man and he's here to lose something he doesn't know he has.'

'Does he know owt?'

'Does he fuck, but since when did that matter? Here's five large coins and you mek sure that the boy here gets what he's here for even though he hasn't a clue, not a fucking clue.'

She leant close, her lips touching the lobe of his ear as she whispered, 'So Jonty, let's see what yer made of.'

Jonty violently pushed her away so that she went crashing into the group behind her.

'What the fuck!' Jock exclaimed as he grabbed Jonty by the coat collar, 'Yer don't do that Jonty. Yer don't fucking do that. Gracie was only trying to be friendly yer stupid bugger,' he added before slapping him lightly across the face.

And then he was gone. Jonty had another drink and looked for Jock who was no longer there. In his place was a younger woman with long black hair. She had a red dress unbuttoned at the front and had somehow managed to straddle across him so her breasts were pushed up against his chest. Jonty could smell the thick, sweet smell coming from her as his head flowed along lines of golden honey and then her mouth was pressed against his and the two of them were being sealed together and he thought he was going to stop breathing under the pressure of her lips.

His mind was slowly filling with a rich darkness. At one moment he thought he saw Jock in the corner of the room laying on the floor with a woman half on top of him. But a wave of people blocked out such a sight as he was kissed again and drank whisky again until he and the full room had merged together as it lifted up and down and then turned from left to right and back again all in time to the noise of voices that seemed to be singing.

There was the sharp explosion of a bottle being smashed. A table was overturned. A woman screamed and ugly shouts were heard from the men. So many people squashed together as the room shifted about when he wanted it to be still and the stench of flesh, drink and the women's smell like from a huge bag of sweets increased until he was holding back the sick in his throat. He wanted Bill. He wanted to be home in his bed. Now he was very alone and he felt it and he started crying and for once no one paid him any attention. The world spun its top inside his head that was burning and melting until it was as if he could taste his own brains.

He was muttering to himself as he watched the bare arse of some man pump up and down through the gap in a filthy curtain strung across another corner of the room. He was not sure whether it was Jock's, but Jock was somewhere else and Arnold had gone. His body was pouring down towards the floor and his hands and feet were newly furnaced bricks. This was desperate, so desperate and he was scared and upset and he wanted out of this horrible place as another woman with a painted face approached him.

He staggered up and pushed her aside because he wanted to be home now, warm in bed at home and getting no rows from Bill. Amazingly he was on his feet forcing himself through the cliffs of people, falling cliffs of clothes and faces and hair. People were shouting at him but he did not care. One of the men hit him hard on the back of the head but he kept on pushing his way through until he was out of the door, falling down the steps to roll in the mud and start whimpering at feeling so bad about everything that had happened and how his head was bulging in and out like the bellows at the blacksmith's.

'Bill!' he suddenly shouted, 'Bill!,' as he started in a direction, any direction so long as it was away from all those horrible people.

The mud was hands pulling at him. Over and over he fell and was up to fall again to pull himself up, smelling the mud smeared over his face as the tears created tracks down it. He was crying because he was scared and lonely and upset and the drink was still the fire inside his head that made his body wobble from side to side and do things he did not want it to do. Momentarily he imagined he was on the Dent road in thick mist barefooted and frozen cold as Bill emerged out of the greyness and took his arm and led him to where he wanted to be.

'Bill, sorry Bill, sorry,' he muttered as he staggered between huts he did not recognise, black boxes on either side of him.

There were no lines, no definite shapes, no patterns that he could see. All was blobs of light, pools of smells and colour that merged into each other. The world had dissolved and he with it. And now he was away from the settlement and was wandering over a hillside that was all mud and sliding and falling. He wanted to stop. He wanted to lie down and sleep now. The mud was exhausting him, dark glue sticking to his boots and stinking of privies and cut peat. The sky was twisting above him. He spun around with his arms out wide and his head following the motion that was all shadows and broken rings of movement.

Eventually he could go on no longer. The night pressed him down on all sides. The whisky was sour in his throat and the beer was juggling around in his belly as he stepped on something hard, metal hard. He stopped and at last saw lines, two dully silvered lines going up the hillside and disappearing up there into the blackness. Here it was dry. Here there was no mud. Here he could lie down, curl up, hold his knees tight and with his woolly hat softening the side of his head against the metal rail of the tramway fall asleep away from all the horrors of what had happened to him when he wanted nothing more to happen except to close his eyes and let his head flicker about until it finally settled and he could stop crying and slow his breaths and let himself fall into this thicker mud, this thicker glue of deep sleep.

CHAPTER FIFTY SIX

Bill had his head in his hands. Ethan, Fraser and Maggie were standing in front of his seated figure. It seemed they had all said what there was to say and now were exhausted from the effort. It was four o clock in the morning and the room was freezing cold as Clare came from her bedroom with a shawl around her nightdress.

'It's terrible,' she said, something she had already repeated several times.

'I'll mek some tea,' Maggie mentioned emptily.

'He has to be somewhere,' Ethan said.

'We've looked,' Bill started with an effort, his voice broken and frustrated, 'looked oer all over the shop and nowt.'

'Except he was seen in the Railway with Arnold earlier on,' Fraser put in.

'I'll fucking kill that bastard when I get me hands on him.'

For once Maggie ignored the language in front of her daughter.

'We've been to Arnold's. We've been to all of his so called mates and nothing. Nobody knows where he is'

Ethan was only repeating what had already been said.

'And I bet, I bet that bloody Jock Tarrant has someat to do wi this. He was allays bragging he'd get Jonty to the pub. And I warned him. I told him not to bother hisell or it'd be me he'd have to deal wi. That bastard Tarrant. You just see. Arnold Wainwright could hold nowt against Tarrant. He'd do owt he were told.'

'You can't be sure of that,' Fraser said.

Bill suddenly sat up, 'For all I know Henderson you're in this as well seeing thee and Tarrant have been bloody close these last weeks.'

'Don't talk such stupid nonsense.'

'I wouldn't put it past yer.'

'You can think what you like. I'm here to help find Jonty and that's it.'

'Yes,' sighed Maggie, 'that's what we have to do.'

'But how, where else is there to look?' Bill asked miserably.

'He'll be somewhere,' Ethan tried, 'sleeping it off.'

'He's never had a drink in his life so far as I know. Jonty would never manage any drink, never.'

'Where is he Mam?' Clare asked in a trembling voice.

'I wish we knew love, I do.'

'Arnold was supposed to be looking after him.'

'Supposed to be,' her mother echoed.

'Fucking Wainwright, if owt's happened to my Jonty I'll rip the bastard apart.'

'Now Bill,' Maggie chided, 'we don't know that fer sure.'

'Except he was seen wi him in the Railway. What does that tell yer?'

'He.....he might have just popped in fer a minute and teken Jonty wi him so as not to leave him outside by hisell.'

At this explanation nothing was said for a few minutes. Maggie finally managed to get Clare to go and try and get some sleep before brewing another pot of tea. Afterwards the men went back out leaving Maggie there in case Jonty should return to the hut.

By the time the first tinges of light were on the horizon above Ingleborough Bill with the others had again searched around all the settlements starting with Batty Green, onto Salt Lake, Sebastopol,

Belgravia, Jericho, Jerusalem and finally up to Tunnel Huts. They had asked everyone they came across whether they had seen his Jonty but without success.

When the men started coming out of their huts on their way to work Bill thought of going down to the beck bridge to wait for the first supply carts from Ingleton to inquire from the drivers if any of them had seen anything of Jonty. He met Fraser and Ethan coming back down to Batty Green and told them to ask the men on their way to work while he went to the bridge. As he waited there with the beck in full spate another shower of sleet swept up the Dale. He pulled down his cap and hunched his shoulders while looking along the Ingleton road for the first cart to appear. Now the sounds of work were starting up, the engines up the tramways blowing off steam, the sound of metal hammering metal coming from the blacksmith's as the first rattle of the cranes on the viaduct began. Hundreds of men were traipsing to the embankments and the cuttings as the sleet lashed down and the beck roared with the volume of water rushing under the bridge.

Then he noticed a figure appear a hundred yards away or so at the edge of the stream and step into the forcing waters. The man waded out until the peat stained water was up to his chest only for him to stagger and turn back releasing one of the bags off his shoulder that quickly floated away.

Bill immediately recognised who it was. In the vague dawn light he started running along the sodden, muddy side of the stream, his limbs stiff and painful, his breaths hurting his chest. It was his anger that forced him on now that Arnold had seen him and had jumped back into the water.

'You bastard!' Bill was already shouting before he reached him.

Arnold in desperation was trying to push his way forward as the brown water splashed up to his chest and almost sent him spinning.

Bill had his coat off and had jumped in bellowing, 'Where is he? Where is he?'

'I don't know!' Arnold shouted back while trying to steady himself against the force of the beck.

'Where's my Jonty yer fucking bastard?'

Arnold was halfway across where the water was at its deepest when Bill lunged forward to grab him by his coat that was swirling around his waist.

'Bill I don't know where he is!' Arnold screamed as he was hit on the shoulder, the two of them struggling as the water crashed around them.

Bill swung another blow that fisted this time straight into Arnold's sodden face and sent him almost under. Only by grabbing hold of Bill's arm did he manage to pull himself up gasping for breath with more water rushing at him.

'Tell me!'

'I don't.....'

'Fucking tell me!'

Arnold tried to pull away to reach the other side only to stumble and this time disappear under the brown rushing flood. Bill stretched out to grab him, pulling him up to hit him again and again, the blood from Arnold's face swirling away in the frothy rush.

He made one last attempt to break free only for Bill to bend his arm and swing it hard into the other's mashed up features. Momentarily they were clinging onto each other as both began to weaken. They were still midstream, their bodies locked together as they stumbled and turned with the beck rushing over their heads. Both were desperate to breathe, gasping for air as Arnold's terrified eyes made one last silent plea for this to stop before he was hit again, his head jerking back so fast the bone snapped in his neck. He went down. Bill hit him again before releasing his limp body and watch it flow quickly away, Arnold's coat bulging up with air as it turned over, a dark mound of clothes floating down the valley until it disappeared from view.

Later a sodden Bill was walking back past the work huts when Ethan approached, his face set in a miserably drawn expression.

Bill looked up and knew straightaway.

'They've found him,' Ethan said.

'Where?'

'He'd been laid out on the tramway. The first load went straight oer him.'

Bill staggered a little and then settled himself, rocking backwards and forwards and then standing straight as he looked at Ethan.

'It's bad Bill,' Ethan continued.

'How bad?'

'Flattened him Bill, nearly cut his head off. Yer would hardly recognise him.'

'And who found him?'

'The driver, he felt it, stopped the engine and got out to see.'

'Jesus Christ,' Bill muttered and then added, 'I want to see him. I want to see my Jonty and what they've done to him.'

'I don't think that's....'

'I know what yer think Ethan.'

'Just leave it Bill. Leave it. Have a better memory of the lad, not that, not that mess.'

'Mess is it?'

By then others had joined them but Bill would have none of their consolations as he walked away with his sodden coat over his arm and water splashing out of his boots.

Later that day Maggie managed to talk Clare into going down to Alice's to do some sewing, telling her, 'Yer doing no good here moping about.'

'Will Bill be alright?' Clare asked as she had put on her coat.

'No love, I'm afraid he won't, not in a long time, if ever.'

'Poor Jonty,' the girl muttered with more tears in her eyes.

'You just go now. Yer Dad and Fraser are seeing to everything and we'll leave Bill in his bed, alright?'

When she had left Maggie knocked gently on the door and went into Bill's bedroom. His was the second bed from the wall next to where Jonty had slept.

'Do yer want owt Bill? Is there owt I can get yer?'

She knew he was awake but sensed that he wanted to give no answer.

'Well if yer do I'm just next door. Yer try and sleep if yer can.'

'He's gone Missus,' he unexpectedly said then in a low, empty voice.

'I know Bill.'

'Jonty lad has gone.'

'It's...it's worse than terrible Bill so it is, worse than owt.'

'I loved that lad.'

'We all did Bill,' she said concernedly.

'He meant the lot to me. I should never....never have left him with that bastard Wainwright, never. I was responsible for him, me, nobody else and look what happened.'

'Yer can't blame yersell Bill.'

'Of course I can and I do and that's that, that's all there is now, nowt else.'

'That's not being fair on yersell. Yer did everything for Jonty. Yer were allays there fer him.'

'Not last night I weren't.'

'Yer won't to know.'

'Well I should a done.'

'How could yer know what was going to happen?'

'I should have never let him out o me sight, never.'

'Yer had to trust Arnold. We all did.'

'I know it's not just him. I know there's somebody else involved.'

'Yer meaning Jock?'

'I mean him.'

'And why would....?'

'Because the bastard has it in fer me, allays has, ever since he got here that little shite has been wanting to get one on me, to do us down.'

'But yer don't know that for sure.'

'Yes I do.'

'Bill yer can't be certain, yer.....'

'I know it woman,' Bill interrupted, 'Just leave it at that.'

Maggie made no response. The light was dim in the room and still Bill had not moved, lying there on his back staring up at the low ceiling.

'Are yer sure yer don't want owt?' she finally asked again.

'No. Just leave us now.'

'Right, like I said, I'll be just next door and Ethan should be back soon.'

Arnold's smashed up face entered Bill's mind and would not leave until finally the image of his body and bloated clothes were washed away down the beck.

'No lad,' he sighed to himself as next Jonty appeared in his mind.

His whole body was wracked with pain now especially his arms and legs. His elbows and knees were throbbing and his bursting head felt as though it was on fire. His right hand had swollen to twice its size and he was sure it was broken.

'No lad,' he repeated as Jonty looked at him with his huge watery eyes.

Bill knew there was more. He was resolved, a resolution that ended in a dull hollowness inside him. He was too old, everlastingly old. Jonty had been his meaning, his reason and now he was fucked, fucked to death. He was waiting because it was still not over. Outside were all the noises of the work as the light began to dim and another winter's day was almost finished. But he understood more was to come for him. It would end one way or another as it always did. He felt tired and old and yet ready, prepared to take everything a little further to where eventually it would be settled. There was no fear only resignation like a low ache inside him, a pain like the echo of death, Jonty's death, Jonty all smashed and bloodied so bad that he was almost unrecognisable. The boy had been his life and now he was gone. So he lay there waiting, knowing that some sort of message would come. It was inevitable, as certain as the aching exhaustion in his body and his hand thumping pain and his mind lost to a terrible numbness. He was fucked and by the end of this day others would be fucked as well if he had anything to do with it.

Jonty was trying to say something but for once he did not want to listen. Arnold's battered face rolled over in the brown, surging waters before it went under again. They were both lost then in the darkness that was coming outside and inside him, a terrible darkness.

When Maggie left Bill she walked back into the middle room to find Clare standing there.

'I don't want to go anywhere,' she sobbed, 'I want to stay here wi you.'

'Come here yer daft happorth,' her mother said as she took her in her arms.

'I want to be here wi you Mam.'

'It's alright, you get yer coat off and stay here wi me.'

Maggie watched her. She was growing so fast. Already she was taller than her or Ethan, her body fuller and her face older.

'Have yer been in to see Bill?'

'I have.'

'And how is he?'

'As expected I suppose. He blames hisell fer what happened to Jonty.'

'But it weren't his fault.'

'Corse it weren't but he don't see it like that at the moment. Maybe he will in time.'

Ethan returned just before she set the table for dinner. He went in to have a few words with Bill.

'Does he want owt to eat?' Maggie asked him when he came back out.

'I shouldn't think so.'

'He's had nowt since last night.'

'I'd just leave it,' said Ethan.

'And is everything arranged for Jonty?'

'Funeral'll be on Thursday.'

'Right,' sighed Maggie.

'Can I go?' Clare suddenly inquired as she set out the plates.

Maggie looked at Ethan who said, 'I don't see why not if that's what yer want.'

'I do Dad. I do want to go.'

'Where's Fraser?' Maggie asked.

'No idea. I haven't seen him since earlier on,' Ethan answered.

'I'll try and keep his dinner warm fer him.'

Just then there was a knock on the door and a young lad was standing there.

'I'm looking for a fella called Bill Asquith,' he said boldly.

'And who wants him?'

'I've got a message fer him.'

'Well you tell me and I'll pass it on.'

'Can't do that,' said the youth, his cap tilted far down over his face.

'How come?'

'Have to give the message to Bill Asquith himsell.'

'Yer can bugger off then,' said Ethan only to be interrupted by Bill in his shirt and trousers who had suddenly come up behind him.

'Just leave this wi me,' he told him.

'Are yer sure Bill?'

'I'm sure. I'll talk to the lad.'

Light snow squalls were falling out of fast shifting clouds as Bill made his way up the path with a large bag slung over one shoulder. Up his sleeve was the short shafted hammer he used for smashing up spoilt bricks that with other rubble was used to fill in the viaduct's pillars. The path was one that went over the tops down into Dentdale passing close by the entrance to Blea Moor tunnel. His destination was a small hut at the top of the tramway a few hundred yards from the Tunnel Huts settlement. It was just light enough for him to make out the next few steps he had to take up the rough path that was thick with boggy mud in places.

Anger had taken over. Now he wanted to smash his way back to Jonty. He was using his last reserves of energy as he approached the hut where he could see the faint light from a lamp shining through the tiny window. He stopped and waited, the snow flurrying around him. Momentarily he turned to look back down towards the lights of Batty Green and those illuminating part of the viaduct's scaffolding and the station being constructed at its far end. The only sounds were of the wind and a dog barking from the direction of Tunnel Huts. It was past ten o clock and everything else was quiet.

A shadowed figure appeared from the hut as Bill let his bag fall to the ground.

'I want to talk.'

Bill made no response to Jock's voice.

'I want us to talk this through Bill.'

Another figure appeared and came towards him.

'Henderson,' Bill muttered, 'I knew you'd fucking be in on this somehow.'

'We want to talk Bill.'

'About what?'

'You know,' Jock added as he waited for Fraser to join him.

'Yer killed my Jonty, what is there to fucking talk about?'

'We didn't kill the stupid fucker. How were we supposed to know he used a bloody tramway rail fer a pillow?'

'Yer got him drunk wi that Arnold fucking Wainwright.'

'We took him fer a drink. Why not? The lad needed a break.'

'I've no time for this,' Bill said strongly.

'So why are yer here then?'

'I'm here to fucking smash both of yer fucking faces in, that's why, yer fucking bastards, just like I did to that bloody shit Arnold Wainwright.'

'Easy now,' Fraser tried.

'Easy my arse. I've no idea what the hell you two think yer doing. What, we just talk it through like and that's alright, that's the finish of it? Yer must be fucking mad.'

'Why don't yer just shut up fer once?' Jock retorted.

Bill did not move. His body was aching, his swollen fist thumping pain, but none of that mattered. He was here with Jonty beside him and the two of them would see this through.

For a few seconds the three of them stood there waiting for one of them to make the next move.

'You just never listen Bill, do you?' Fraser started, 'You always think you're right, always.'

'That's cos he's so fucking big headed he can't see his cock fer his feet. But yer fucked Bill, yer past it, way past it. Yer fighting days are over so why don't yer just calm yersell down and listen to what we have to say.'

'Fuck off!' Bill exclaimed.

'No, we won't,' said Jock in a more threatening voice.

More snow flickered between them, their coats beginning to flap in the wind. In the moments before it happened Bill knew what was coming. He was already twisting his body as Jock stepped forward and lunged at him with a knife. Bill's movement had been fast and drastic enough so the knife only cut through his coat sleeve. Jock had jerked so hard with the knife he lost his footing giving Bill the opportunity to swing the hammer with all his strength, sinking it deep into the side of the Scotsman's head, splitting it open like a broken egg shell, blood and brain tissue spewing down his chin as he collapsed to the ground.

'That'll do you yer fucker,' Billy muttered breathlessly.

Fraser too shocked to move stared down at the body giving Bill enough time to grab his arm and fist him in the face.

'No Bill! No!' Fraser started screaming.

'Go on, look at him, look at him!' Bill demanded as he shoved Fraser forward, 'Nowt much now is he?'

'I had nothing to do with it Bill.'

'So what the fuck are yer doing here then?'

'I...I came because....'

'Cos what?'

'I had nothing to do with Jonty's death Bill. I didn't.'

Bill turned him towards him, his hand squeezing his arm causing Fraser to wince in pain before Bill hit him again.

'You're a fucking bastard Henderson!'

'Nothing at all Bill. I didn't,' Fraser mumbled as the blood poured out of his nose, snowflakes sticking to it for a few seconds before melting, 'You have......have to believe me.'

'I've never, never believed a word you've ever said so I'm sure as hell not going to start now.'

He pushed Fraser away before telling him to get down on his knees.

'What are you going to do?'

'Do you as well.'

'No Bill!'

'Why shouldn't I?'

'Because you've done for Arnold and now Jock. They're the ones, not me.'

Bill said nothing to this as he gulped in the cold air. Momentarily the wind flurried more snow across the moor, its sounds whistling through the frozen heather. His breaths were deep and hard. He was having to fight back the sudden exhaustion that was coursing through his body, aware of Fraser lowering his forehead onto the ground as he started whimpering, his back jerking with the sobs.

'What a miserable shit you are Henderson.'

'What are you going to do Bill? Tell me,' Fraser muttered with his head still lowered.

There was nothing said then as he continued to sob, the cold darkness all around them as the snow swept across the moors. Slowly Fraser struggled up onto his hands and knees.

'I'm begging you. I'm begging you,' he repeated.

'And I wonder what Jonty would say to that?'

'He'd say you'd done enough.'

'Would he now?'

'He'd say with Arnold and Jock you've......you've done enough and that......that you have to stop now.'

'Seeing as you didn't care a shit about Jonty what the fuck do you know what he'd be thinking?'

'Please Bill.'

'You never bothered wi the lad, never.'

'That's not true.'

At that Bill kicked out, his boot thudding into Fraser's ribs sending him sprawling. He took another step and kicked him again, Fraser moaning with the blow.

'I'm........I'm begging Bill, please.......please,' he started muttering.

'So what was supposed to happen now?'

'Please Bill.'

'Go on, tell me. What were yer going to do wi me body, what just leave us here?'

'No.'

'Well show me.'

'I can't.'

'Yes you can. Get up.'

'I....I can't.'

'Get up yer fucker,' Bill shouted as he grabbed him by the hair.

Fraser tried to resist until he was dragged to his feet, trying to steady himself, his coat covered in dirt and snow, his hair flopping over his filthy face. Still he had his head lowered.

Bill waited, his whole body on edge.

'It was all Jock's idea,' Fraser finally said.

'What was?'

'He had it all planned.'

'But he needed you, didn't he? Couldn't have done it by hisell, so don't tell me it had nowt to do wi you. Do yer hear?'

'No......no he couldn't have done it without me.'

'So show me.'

Miserably Fraser turned and Bill followed him up the slope, past the hut, stumbling over the frozen clumps of grass to where they could look down into the shadowed swallow hole.

'Down there,' Fraser said emptily.

'So that's it, is it?' Bill responded.

'We were going to push.......push you under the rocks. There's a gap and we.....'

'You knew fuck all about Jonty.'

'I never wanted any of this. I didn't.'

The two of them stood there for a few moments. Here the wind was stronger, the snow stinging against their faces. When they turned they could see nothing of Batty Green and its lights down below. All of it was shrouded in the flurried night that continued its incessant sounds as they returned to where Jock was lying, the hammer still embedded in the side of his skull.

'You get his legs and I'll tek him under the shoulders.'

'I can't Bill.'

'You fucking will do or you'll be joining the bastard, de yer hear?'

'I feel.....feel sick.'

'I couldn't care a damn what yer feel!' Bill exclaimed before he started slapping him across the face, Fraser's head jerking from side to side. 'Now pick the bugger up.'

Eventually with Fraser holding his ankles and Bill his shoulders they half carried, half dragged Jock's body away from the hut and up the short slope to the swallow hole. There Fraser started removing some of the rocks covering the dark narrow fissure. Bill pulled out the hammer and threw it down the hole before with an effort they turned the body upside down and started lowering it down into the jagged gap in the rocks, first the mutilated head and then the rest. As his feet disappeared one of Jock's boots was pulled off. Bill picked it up and tossed it down with the rest.

'Go and get his cap and whatever he had in the hut,' he told Fraser.

'He didn't....didn't......'

'Just fucking go and do it.'

It was a few minutes before Fraser returned. Never once had Bill doubted that he would not return. He took the cap and Jock's knack sap and stuffed it down between the rocks and then watched as Fraser covered the hole.

'So that was me, was it, down there?'

Fraser stood beside him made no response.

They remained there for a while, Bill staring down at the pile of rocks, his whole body aching and exhausted. Finally he grabbed Fraser by the arm and dragged him back down to the hut, turned him round and fisted him hard in the face again.

'Are yer listening? Are yer?'

Fraser hunched away from the next expected blow.

'Cos you're out of here. Right now yer get yer stuff, yer say nowt and you bugger off from Ribblehead and you never set foot in the place again, never. Do you understand or should I fucking beat it into you?'

Fraser jerked up at this, 'I heard Bill. I heard.'

'You piss off!'

'You're....you're tricking me.'

'Listen, you would be down there with Tarrant already if I wanted it.'

Fraser hesitated, the blood drying from his nose.

'Why would you let.....?'

'Cos that's what I'm saying so don't mek me change me mind,' Bill interrupted.

'You mean it?

'Just bugger off.'

'When should I......?'

'Today! Now!'

'Today?'

'That's what I said and you never set foot in the place again, never, cos if I ever hear you have I'll be back here and beat yer to fucking pulp.'

'Yes Bill.'

'So fuck off!'

Fraser, his arms shaking and his face twisted in pain, looked at Bill for the first time that night.

'I can go?'

'You can.'

'Now? Do you mean it?'

'I said, bugger off.'

'I.......I didn't want any of this Bill. I didn't.'

'Just piss off. Piss off. You mek me sick just looking at yer. Fuck off Henderson.'

Bill stood for a time watching Fraser's dark figure stumble down the path before disappearing in a flurry of snow. It was then he noticed Jock's knife. He picked it up, took out a piece of rag from his coat pocket and wrapped the knife in it before putting it in his bag. At his feet was the mess of blood and brain tissue from the Scotsman's head that Bill with the sole of his boot rubbed into the dirt and snow. Quickly he turned his cap round so the peak was at the back and tied his scarf over his mouth and nose and set off across the moor in a Westerly direction, his body bending against the growing force of the wind.

After half a mile or so he had to stop, his whole body aching with exhaustion. His head was on fire and thumping pain as he sunk forward putting his hands on his knees, the snow stinging his eyes

'Come on Jonty lad,' he started muttering, 'we can mek it wi God's help. Come on Jonty,' his voice drowned out by the noise of the wind.

For a time he had no energy to continue. His fists were swollen and his throat was burning up.

'Come on Jonty lad, come on Jonty lad,' he forced out over and over again before he finally started forward, stumbling over the rough grass and heather as he gradually merged into the darkness.

CHAPTER FIFTY SEVEN

A few weeks later Ethan was thinking about the days he would walk across the lower slopes of Whernside and wait above the Sugdens' farm hoping that there might be some chance of seeing her. Only twice had she managed to get away in the middle of the week. Floss would lie with him behind huge rocks well hidden from the farm. All he wanted was to be with her, touch her, smell her, have her and hold her. If anything this obsession for her had deepened. It made him ashamed of his weakness, his inability to control his desires. Always he had tried to become strong enough so that his need never got out of hand, never began to dominate. But again he had failed. He had always been weak, never becoming who he wanted to be and here he was crawling around in the winter darkness with his tongue hanging out all for the sake of a young farm girl.

'Did yer hear about the carry on down at Chapel le Dale?' Maggie was asking him, 'Ethan are yer listening?'

He looked up hoping that guilt was not written on his face.

'They say that Mr Tranton's cousin, that lass who's been staying wi him was found on the Ingleton road in her nightdress. If she hadn't been found by some carters trying to mek their way home she would have froze to death. Jane Herbert she's called and she was in a right old state so they say. The carters managed to get her down to the doctor in Ingleton just in time. They reckon another ten minutes or so and she would have been dead wi the cold, frozen to death.'

The sudden image of this woman suddenly burst through into Ethan's consciousness.

'What were she doing?' Clare asked.

'Yer shouldn't be talking about such things wi our Clare here,' Ethan admonished his wife.

'Yer might not have noticed Ethan Granger but your daughter is growing up into a fine young woman who should be learning about the ways o the world.'

'Says who?'

'Says me.'

'Anyway I told her she could go wi Fraser tonight to see the dancing. She's been going on at me fer weeks.'

'Oh I see. I thought I told you young lady that.....'

'Just this once Mam. Me Dad said it were alright.'

'She'll be fine, Fraser'll look after her,' Ethan added.

'That's just what I'm afraid of.'

'And what's that supposed to mean?'

'It's just cos she doesn't like him. She never has,' put in Clare.

'It's nowt about liking him or not, I just don't trust him,' Maggie said.

'So what's wrong wi him?'

'Oh there's no good talking to you about it cos yer blind to most o what goes on around here.'

'Oh here we go again,' Ethan muttered in irritation.

'It's true,' Maggie said defiantly, 'You're never here so how would you know?'

'It doesn't matter,' their daughter put in, 'if there's going to be another row it don't matter. I'll stay at home.'

'No, you get yersell to the dancing wi Fraser if it's only fer an hour or so to see what it's like.'

'Yer can both suit yersells,' Maggie finished angrily before going to the stove.

Clare looked at her father and pulled a face to which he just shrugged his shoulders.

She was right, there were more arguments now than there ever had been. Whatever he did it was never right. Every day there was some disagreement or other. So much had gone wrong so quickly. The day after Jonty's death Arnold Wainwright's body had been found in the beck two miles down the Dale caught on the branch of an overhanging bush. Arnold's face had been smashed in so badly it was said he had not only a broken nose but most of his teeth had been ripped from their gums and his left cheek bone splintered. That same night Bill and Jock Tarrant had both gone missing while Fraser had returned to the hut with his face badly bruised saying that Bill had attacked him up by the tramway. Rumour had it that Bill had done for Arnold and was now on the run from the constables while Jock had left the settlement earlier, scared that Bill would catch up with him having blamed him for Jonty's death. The Grangers had been questioned by the constables and Fraser interviewed several times, twice in the hut and twice down at the Ingleton police station. All he told them was that Bill Asquith had attacked him accusing him of being involved in Jonty's death. Another rumour was that Mr Stockton had asked for a detective from Leeds to come and help with the investigation. Ethan knew the pressure was on all of them. Maggie was suffering more than most, especially now both Jonty and Bill had gone. Evening dinner was a strangely empty, quiet affair with no Jonty, Bill or Jock. Often Fraser went straight from his work on the tramway to some card game which just left the family at the table. Ethan knew Maggie missed Beth more than ever. She was the one who had always done most of the talking, chatting away about school or what had been going on in the settlements. Beth had been the source of such life and now she like the rest was gone leaving the three of them to try and rediscover each other which none of them was finding easy. At least Clare had her work and had made new friends, but Ethan and Maggie had only each other and that had become increasingly strained now that all he could think about was Floss Sugden.

'I miss him Mam,' Clare said one evening, 'and Bill. I miss em both real bad. Jonty……Jonty was so funny….so…..'

'I know love,' Maggie replied.

It was Bill who she longed to see walk through the door and sit down for his dinner. Bill had been her friend, the one who had supported her and now like her Beth he was gone. Then Jonty, Clare grieved over him every night, sobbing for her sister and now Jonty. It was all too much, far too much, the loss of so many people in such a short time with no explanations only the usual gossip. She could not step foot out of the hut without being asked about it all over and over again until she was sick of it, sick of the rumours and malicious stories going the round of the settlements.

'Bill wouldn't have done what folk say he has,' Clare continued in a distraught voice looking miserably at her sewing.

'Folk say too much.'

'They say he killed Arnold.'

'They can say what the hell they like. No one knows owt, not the constables or anyone else so they mek it up as they go on.'

'Bill……Bill just blamed hisell fer what happened to Jonty.'

'He did, we all know that,' Maggie agreed.

'And he were wrong to do that.'

'I don't think he could help hisell. He was too upset to see sense and I can't blame him fer that.'

'Can't blame Bill fer owt, nor Jonty. I just wish Mam.....wish they were here right now.'

Maggie went over and pulled Clare gently into her arms.

'I can't say owt that'll mek any difference.'

'I know Mam.'

'They're gone and that's all there is to it.'

'And our Beth,' Clare sobbed.

'Ay, her as well.'

'But why Mam? What's happening? Why us? Why's all this happening to us?'

'I wished I knew, I really do, but I don't and nobody else does either only God and he's not saying much at the moment,' Maggie answered miserably.

On top of everything else Ribblehead settled into one of the worst winters there had been for many a year, punishment, according to the locals, for the grand summer the Dales had experienced. For several days in a row the weather was so bad no work was done on the viaduct or in the cuttings. Snow was blasted up the Dale from the West by raging gales so bad the scaffolding on the viaduct was ripped away, planks flying about as though they had been turned into small sticks. When the men did manage to get to work it was a process of trying to survive the cold and gales. Richard finally accepted that progress was going to be severely compromised for the next weeks. He had gone to Leeds on several occasions for progress meetings. The directors who had invested substantial amounts of their own money into the construction of the Settle - Carlisle railway line were far from happy. The pressure was on everybody. Some days the children could not make it from the outer settlements to the school. Often the Ingleton road was blocked which meant supplies regularly ran short. It seemed absurd that anyone could have planned building a railway line across such God forsaken country. The valley and the hills were frozen into a huge spread of ice and packed snow, but it was the wind that cut through every last shred of confidence and resilience.

'It has to stop sometime,' Maggie would say, 'or where's the milk and the coal and the bread coming from? We could all starve from cold and hunger.'

'Everyone's in the same boat,' Ethan would answer.

'As if that meks any difference.'

'Nowt to you these days does that.'

'Cos things aren't right. You don't just lose Beth and then Jonty, Bill and even Jock Tarrant without thinking someat is badly wrong,' Maggie said.

‘Wrong wi me yer mean.’

‘No I don’t. Don’t be so stupid Ethan.’

‘Sounds like it.’

‘Sounds nothing,’ she would say back angrily.

But this was now Saturday tea time and Ethan’s expectations were building. All he could think about was somehow getting through the next few hours before setting off.

Ignoring Fraser sitting across from him at the dinner table he announced, ‘I’m going fer a drink tonight.’

‘You should try Davie Mack’s,’ Fraser told him, ‘they reckon he’s cutting the price of beer to get more customers.’

‘I thought the customs men had nobbled him.’

‘So they had, but this is a different place he’s set up.’

‘I thought you were a Railway man.’

‘Not bothered either way,’ Fraser said indifferently, ‘so long as it’s cheap and not the watered down rubbish that some try to sell.’

‘Oh there’s plenty o rubbish in Batty Green.’

‘The constables were up to see me this afternoon,’ Fraser announced.

‘What, in this weather? Why this time?’

‘Yes, desperate they were to see me.’

‘And what were they wanting now?’

‘The usual questions about when I had last seen Jonty, whether I’d seen Jock that night and so on. I’ve told them over and over again what Asquith did to me. Christ I would have thought it was still damned obvious what he did with me face looking like God knows what. They say the bruising won’t go down for weeks and me ribs are still bad so I don’t know how much dancing I’ll be doing tonight the state I’m in,’ he said in a dull, flat voice,‘ The constables are trying to catch us out for some reason. But I tell them the same story every time so I just hope they’ve had enough because I have. I’m getting sick of being pestered by them all the time.’

They all looked at his still swollen cheeks covered in dark blue bruises and his lips thicker than usual hiding his missing teeth. Fraser was gambling that Bill Asquith would never return to Ribblehead. He had unfinished business that he refused to abandon no matter what Asquith had threatened him with.

‘That’s cos they’ve got nowt better to do,’ Maggie finally said as she dished Clare a plateful of food.

‘I don’t want as much as that,’ the girl complained.

'You eat what yer given girl.'

'But I....'

'Eat it,' her mother said strongly.

'It's not fair.'

'Cheer up,' Fraser tried, 'we're going to the dancing now your father says it's alright.'

While saying this he looked purposefully at Maggie as though challenging her to disagree.

'I'm saying nowt.'

Later Ethan asked Fraser, 'So they've no idea where Bill or Jock have got to?'

'Seems not.'

'I reckon Bill will have gone down south and as for Jock, God knows. He could be anywhere.'

'Why down south?'

'Because I'm sure that's where his sister lives, somewhere near Winchester I think.'

'Isn't that a bit obvious? I don't think he'd do that,' Fraser stated.

'Depends on how serious the police are taking this.'

'Well as far as I'm concerned they're taking it seriously alright or they would have left us alone by now.'

'They've asked me the same questions so yer not the only one Fraser, but you were close to Jock like, closer than anyone else. So yer've no idea where he might a gone, not that it bothers me one way or another what that crazy bloody Scotsman does except if anybody did fer Jonty it'll be him. Arnold was just doing what he was told to do. He wouldn't stand up to the likes of Jock Tarrant, not a chance I reckon.'

Fraser's swollen eyes were steady but watchful as he lifted his mug of tea.

'What do yer think?' Clare interrupted as she came out of her bedroom in a dress she had made herself.

'Yer look champion,' said her father.

Fraser inspected her while smiling and then said, 'You look like a proper lady miss Clare, you look lovely.'

Maggie turned from the stove asking, 'And where did yer get the dress from?'

'I med it mesell wi the help o Alice.'

'Very nice.'

'Do yer think so Mam?'

'I said so didn't I?'

'And it's alright me wearing it fer the dancing?'

'Yer better ask yer father. He's the one said yer could go.'

Clare twirled round and said, 'Dad, is it alright?'

'Course it is.'

'Grand!' she exclaimed, 'I'll tek it off until we're ready to be going.'

'Whatever yer like Clare.'

'Yes, whatever I like,' she repeated happily.

Later Maggie turned to Ethan who was cleaning his boots over old sheets of newspaper and said, 'What's happening Ethan?'

He looked up at her, 'What do yer mean?'

Now that there were only the two of them together with Fraser and Clare at the dancing Maggie's mood had changed. Her mouth had softened from its tight expression as she came over, wiping her hands on her apron and sat with him at the table.

'I just miss her,' she said then.

'I know, so do I Maggie.'

'Just miss her to bits and instead of getting easier it's getting harder.'

'It won't get any easier for a long time,' Ethan told her in a sympathetic tone.

'And all this other carry on. It meks me worried about you.'

'Me?'

'Yes, what wi Jonty going like that and then it seems Bill, what he did to Arnold and that Tarrant disappearing. I can't get any of it out o me head and it meks me bothered about you. They were all from this hut and now they're gone and why? What does it all mean?'

'Steady,' he said, 'I know it's bad, bloody awful and it doesn't mek any sense, you're right, but how in God's name could it? That's two dead and two just buggered off and like I was saying to Fraser it doesn't fit together, none of it.'

'And how are we to know he weren't involved?'

'Fraser? No. Why should he be?'

'Cos he was as thick as thieves with that Tarrant.'

'Fraser's here. If he'd owt to do wi it he would have buggered off as well.'

'But he's cleverer than the rest, sly like and cunning.'

'Not that I've noticed. Anyroads it's like our Clare said, you just don't like him.'

'And why should a man of his age want to be teking just a slip of a lass to the dancing?'

'Bill was the same in that way. Yer know they both doted on our Beth and Clare. I don't see nowt wrong wi that. It's you and your suspicions about everybody. I supposed yer got some about me,' he said.

'I might have at that.'

'Oh ay, such as?'

'Like I said I'm more worried about yer than owt else. The last thing we need is someat happening to you.'

'Nowt's going to happen to me,' he scoffed.

'I bet that's what Arnold Wainwright thought and look what happened to him and if you're not bothered well just let me be cos that won't change.'

CHAPTER FIFTY EIGHT

He was trudging through the deep, frosted snow. The winter sky was clear with an almost full moon ghosting over the land, over the huge white sweep of valley and hillside. Ethan was the only thing in motion on this bitterly cold night, his boots breaking through the icy crust at each step making his progress slower than usual. His fast breaths clouded in front of him as he shifted from side to side over the steepening slope of Whernside. Already he could see the farm further along the valley like dark cubes surrounded by a white expanse.

Finally he reached the huge boulders where he always waited for the signal from Floss that the brothers had gone off on their Saturday night drinking spree. He was apprehensive that this time the weather might be too bad for them to get down to Ingleton. Back up the valley he could see the smoke and the dim lights from the settlements and the huge man made embankments of snow covered earth on either side of the viaduct. Momentarily he thought of Maggie and her sudden rush of concerns that afternoon. He had no answer for her. All he knew was that life had drastically changed.

Down in the valley bottom he could see nothing moving along the Ingleton road. Cragside farm was locked into a frozen stillness with no animals to be seen. He had to stamp his feet on the bone hard ground to try and keep them warm. The huge boulders were covered in ice that glistened in the moonlight like chunks of some glacier that had been ripped away. Behind him he could see the dull, white edge of the top of Whernside. And still he waited. The longer this lasted the more he thought about how desperate his need for Floss had become. Nowadays they had to dig down into the hay to find some that was still dry enough to lie on. In the summer and autumn they had laid there naked but now they had to do it with their clothes on which made the whole thing for him less exciting. Their sex had become a function. He felt Floss was not as eager as she had been. The sense of urgency from her had slowed and she had become more irritable. They had little to talk about. She was eighteen and knew nothing but the life of the farm. He was not really interested in anything else about her. All he wanted from her was what she could give him physically. That was enough, better than anything he had ever had before. And yet he hated himself for being on such a level, for being like one of the beasts on the farm.

Finally down below the three brothers appeared out of the farm house making their way over to the shed. He watched as John led the horse out while the other two brought out the cart. It took them a few minutes before it was hitched up. Davey ran back to the house for something, reappearing a minute later. Slowly then they made their way across the narrow bridge over the beck. It seemed to take them so long to reach the main road, the horse slipping and the cart sliding on the icy surface. Only when he saw the lamp taken away from the front window of the house did Ethan start making his way down.

Floss was waiting for him in the yard.

'Never thought they were going,' she said as he came towards her.

Now they never kissed unless it was part of their love making.

'And I thought me feet were going to become bloody blocks o ice,' he said to her as they turned towards the barn.

She was wearing her thick coat, winter boots, a scarf round her neck and another tied under her chin. The moment he was near her his body became anxious, became tight and expectant.

They walked in silence over the crusted snow.

'Where's all the animals?' he asked as he helped her drag open one of the barn doors.

'Sheep are still up top. I told em but they wouldn't listen. They'll be crawled up against a wall somewhere smothered to death by now. Nowt but stupid not to get em down. I said to John before the snow got bad but he couldn't be bothered to move his arse, lazy shit that he is.'

'Sounds daft to me.'

'Ay, daft.'

Shafts of moonlight from holes in the roof cut across the dim space of the barn's interior. Automatically they climbed the ladder up to the hay.

'It's bloody freezing,' Floss complained through chattering teeth.

'It's not that bad.'

'It damned well is.'

'Aren't yer going to tek yer coat off and yer scarves?' he asked, waiting to see what kind of mood she was in, whether she was going to be easy tonight or not.

'No I'm not!' she exclaimed.

'Oh come on Floss, at least yer coat and scarves.'

'Me scarves maybe, but that's all.'

'Christ,' he muttered in disappointment.

'The quicker we do it the better so come on,' she said as they both started pulling at the frozen hay to find something drier underneath.

She lay down, hoisted up her coat and dress and opened her legs.

'Just for you Ethan Granger I'm wearing nowt down here so……'

'So,' he interrupted, 'I'm…..I'm…..'

'Yer what?'

'Not ready.'

'Bloody hell! This ain't like you,' she added. 'Going off us then?'

'Don't be daft.'

'Once of a time yer were on top o me before I could get me breath.'

'That was when it was a damned sight warmer.'

'Shouldn't mek no difference.'

'Well tonight it does so come here,' he said as he dragged her down and got on top of her.

'About bloody time.'

'Come on Floss. Yer know yer like it.'

He pulled at her coat, trying to untie the rope that she used as a belt. Failing at that he pushed his hands under her clothes to feel her thighs, searching further and quicker, needing desperately to touch her skin, to feel the warmth of it as at last he pressed himself deeper into her.

When it was over he rolled away. Floss straightaway pulled down her skirt and coat and sat up.

Suddenly there was a voice from down below.

'Has he finished?'

'Ay, he's done,' Floss answered.

'Get yersell down here Ethan Granger.'

It was John's voice and Ethan felt immediately sick.

'What have yer done Floss?' he asked in desperation.

'I'm fed up, that's all,' she answered.

'Come on yer dirty bastard, get yersell down here or we'll have to come up and get yer.'

'You told em,' Ethan muttered at her.

'So what?'

'So you've fucking killed me, that's what.'

'Yer better get yersell down,' Floss told him, 'and I don't care what I've done, so there.'

The three brothers were stood near the foot of the ladder as he came down. His whole body was tight with fear, his head thumping in a panic of dread.

Immediately Davey hit him across the face shouting, 'Yer filthy bastard!'

'So,' John started, 'yer think yer can just come here and fuck our sister do yer? And you were warned. You were warned Granger long back, but yer didn't listen did yer? You didn't and cos o that you're going to pay yer bastard.'

By now Ethan was trembling and about to cry as he muttered, 'Christ...please......'

'Shut yer fuck up!' Joe went at him.

'What doe's to say sister?' John asked her.

Floss shrugged her shoulders and answered, 'Not bothered what yer do.'

'Why don't we show him where yer true feelings are? What doe's to reckon Floss lass?'

'If yer want,' she said emptily.

'Right then. Yer see Granger yer've no idea what goes on here. Floss loves us as family, course she does and we love her mightily.'

'It's my turn,' said Davey.

'Is it hell,' answered Joe.

'John were yesterday so today it's my go.'

'Fuck off!'

'You fuck off.' Davey put in.

'Hurry up,' Floss interrupted, 'it's freezing cold here.'

She laid herself down on a pile of sacks and hoisted up her coat and dress while Davey had his trousers down before lying on top of her.

'Yer watch yer bastard!' John said, grabbing Ethan as he tried to turn away.

Davey's actions were slow and Floss's moans loud and urgent.

Ethan felt sick at this hideous show that had been put on for his benefit. It was disgusting. Everything about Floss Sugden was destroyed. He hated her and her brothers and the filthy, sickening world they lived in. This was a nightmare. He knew then he was going to die here as Davey pulled up his trousers and Floss sorted her clothes.

'That's how it's done,' John said then, 'don't yer think our lass?'

'It's alright, better than him anyroads,' she added, nodding towards Ethan.

'Right lads, now he's had his little lesson let's get the bastard stripped.'

'No!' Ethan screamed as the two brothers started wrestling with him to drag off his jacket and trousers.

'Be still yer stupid fucker!' Davey gasped.

'Leave....leave me alone,' Ethan cried out as they dragged him across the floor pulling off the rest of his clothes until finally he was naked. They grabbed him by the arms, stood him up and pulled him back to where John and Floss were standing.

'Yer've no idea how bad we feel about this here carry on lad. We're fucking going to do yer. We only wished our sister here,' he said suddenly slapping Floss so hard she fell to the ground, 'had told us a lot earlier about what yer were doing to her.'

'Yer had no need to do that,' moaned Floss as she got to her feet, holding her face, blood trickling out of her mouth.

'No need!' John bellowed at her, 'and yer tupping wi a fucking navvy and yer say no need. Fuck that lass. Yer can fuck that right out o yer stupid little head. So shut it and let's get done with this piece o shit. Tek him out lads.'

Ethan was so terrified he had wet himself, everything rushing away into darkness and the sickening effect of sheer dread. He was lost.

Davey and Joe dragged him out of the barn and across the snow packed yard, Floss smirking and rubbing her face as she followed them. They dragged him round the back of the sheds.

'What yer going to do wi him?' Floss finally asked as they stopped at the edge of the farm's cess pool.

'What the fuck do yer think?'

'I don't think owt, remember. That's what yer reckon, so why are yer asking me?'

'Cheeky bitch.'

'Cheeky nowt.'

'Well just fucking watch then and let the lads get on wi it. This bastard is going to get washed in shit like the shit he is. Throw the fucker in!' John shouted.

'Don't.....don't do this,' said Ethan, gasping for breath in a last desperate attempt to survive.

'Shut the fuck up!' the eldest brother shouted back at him.

The other two forced him forward where he slipped and went down crashing through the ice into the dark filth. When he tried to clamber out Davey fisted him in the face sending him sprawling back into the cess pool. Again Ethan tried and again he was hit so hard this time he went completely under.

The rest watched as it went on with Ethan's attempts becoming less and less effective until finally instead of trying to crawl his way out the last blow from Joe knocked him unconscious. His body floated on top where the ice had been broken, his arms outstretched, his legs dipped under the black water.

'That'll do fer that fucking shite,' said John.

'Serves him right,' added Floss.

'Ay, and it should be thee in there as well wi all yer carry on.'

Davey and Joe started laughing and shouting as Ethan's body turned slightly in a freshening wind and the light of the moon reflected off the surface ice around the edge of the pool of dark, stinking animal shit.

CHAPTER FIFTY NINE

A sheep dog found Ethan's body down near the beck the next morning. He had been tied naked to a hawthorn bush, his skin frozen a light blue, his grey tongue lolling out and the lobes of his ears a deep purple like the rest of his smashed in face, crucified on the sharp thorns with his legs outstretched and tied wide apart. When they had finally cut him down his back, buttocks and the back of his legs were covered in tiny pinpricks where each spike had penetrated.

Maggie and Clare never went to the funeral. Maggie knew she would never be able to cope with it and she did not want her daughter going. What she had been told about his death made no sense to her. It was only over the next days that the gossip eventually reached her telling all about Ethan's weekly trips to the Sugden farm. To begin with she did not believe the rumours. Folk liked to imagine the worst. It made them feel better about themselves and their own miserable lives. Once again the constables were up at the hut asking her all about her Ethan, what he did on Saturday nights, when she had last seen him, what kind of mood he had been in that night. She found it a lot more difficult when the constables started asking Clare the same sort of questions. She saw no reason why her daughter had to be dragged into all of it.

A few days later she heard they had been to the Sugden farm but that with lack of evidence no charges could be brought against anyone. Maggie was told the name of the sister involved, this Floss Sugden that everyone in Batty Green talked about, but she was too overwhelmed to feel anything. She had lost everybody, except for Clare there was nothing left for her only her loneliness and anger.

'It's not true what they're saying, is it Mam?' Clare asked one evening.

'Who's saying what?'

'Yer know, folk, about me Dad.'

'What about him?'

'Come on Mam, yer know.'

'Well if I do it's a load of nonsense. They have to mek up someat to blether about.'

'So me Dad.....me Dad never....'

'No,' she said firmly, 'Yer Dad was a good man and he so loved you and our Beth. Folk talk rubbish and I don't want you paying any heed to it, do yer hear?'

'I hear Mam, but it ain't easy, especially when folk want to know why the constables have been here so many times.'

'They're just doing all they can to find out what happened to yer Dad. That's their job. It doesn't mean we're in trouble, or yer Dad. It just means they want to find out how he died, just like they're doing with Jonty and Arnold Wainwright.'

'It's....it's terrible,' Clare had said with tears in her large, dark eyes.

'Of course it is.'

'Me Dad and the others and they're all dead now and it feels.....feels like it can't have happened.'

Maggie took hold of both her hands, pressing them hard as she said, 'We have to stick close now, stick as close as we can.'

'And what are we going to do?'

'What if I asked you the same question? You're old enough now to have an opinion.'

'Am I? It don't feel like it,' Clare had said in desperation.

'Of course yer are or I wouldn't be asking.'

'I just want me Dad back and our Beth and the others. I just want to go back to how it was when we were all here together. I.....I don't want owt else.'

Maggie made no response. She hated everything that had happened so deeply and yet still had no idea what to do about it.

'Fraser says if he moved in wi another family then we would have to leave.'

'Oh he did, did he?'

'So he's staying wi us so that don't happen.'

'How generous of him,' said Maggie as sarcastically as she could.

'He's only trying to help Mam, and if yer don't like him so much why did yer let us go to the dancing again last Saturday.'

'Because I thought yer could do wi someat to tek yer mind off things.'

'Well it didn't work.'

'Of course it didn't.'

Clare looked at her mother with doubt in her expression.

'I want yer to be alright Mam, and yer can't be,' she said and then asked anxiously, 'So are we leaving Batty Green?'

Maggie waited to answer, her breathing slower as she considered what to do.

'Cos I don't mind Mam so long as it's what yer want to do. We kem here cos of me Dad and he's not wi us anymore so it don't matter staying on here except I've got me sewing wi Alice and I suppose Fraser still pays for his board and lodging.'

'He does.'

'Well then, we have some money still coming in.'

'And I have what I've saved.'

'So we should be alright,' Clare said hopefully.

'How can we ever be that?'

'But yer know what I mean.'

'I suppose so, but whatever happens it won't be easy, not after all that's happened. I loved yer father whatever he did and I still miss him.'

'Oh Mam don't. You'll only.....'

'I know,' Maggie interrupted, 'And I suppose,' she sighed, 'I'd better get the dinner on even if it is only for the three of us now.'

Later that night she lay in bed unable to sleep. Often over the last weeks Clare had come in with her but tonight she was in her own bed and had thankfully fallen asleep straightaway. Maggie accepted now that Ethan had been seeing the farm girl and that he had been killed because of it. Fraser had described the Sugden brothers or what he had heard about them as animals, so primitive they lived on the same level as their cows and sheep. She was so angry with Ethan. She knew he had hated the work he had been forced to do to keep the family going, hated the kind of man it had made him. She tried to think about the good times, their Sunday walks, the family together and happy for once. Ethan had been at his best then, had managed to forget all his frustrations and had just been there for them. It was unbearable that he was gone. He had failed her, failed Beth and Clare. That was the worst, to think that he had been carrying on with that farm girl at the same time Beth had been dying. It was impossible that he could do such a thing.

The snow and ice had melted and now the land was again a quagmire of floods and mud when next morning she trudged past some of the huts and under the viaduct works before heading along a boggy path. Here streams appeared gurgling out of the ground every few yards. This land of limestone was a sieve. Waterfalls crashed down over the scarp sides of Whernside under a low, grey sky.

She stopped in a field that looked down on the Sugden's farm. It was a filthy looking place with pieces of rusted machinery everywhere, a pile of rubble in one corner of the yard. Two of the out sheds had collapsed roofs and the barn was surrounded by water. A few hens were scratting about and cows with their ribs showing were grazing on the edge of a flooded field. It was cold and drizzly but Maggie waited. She had not planned to come here. It was only after she had finally managed to get Clare to go to Alice's that she had made the decision to come. From where she was standing she could see all the carts going up and down the main valley road with Ingleborough sloped up behind, could see the beck full with brown rushing water and the smoke from the settlements drifting under low, dark clouds and hear the muffled noise of all the work going on. This morning none of it seemed real. It had lost its purpose. People were dead, her husband had been murdered and death had destroyed all sense, all reason. She was feeling empty, bitter and more alone than ever. She was functioning automatically, reacting mindlessly. She did not care anymore because it seemed whatever she did made no difference to this blighted, unbearable life. Things might improve for a time but it was all a lie because eventually everything would be smashed back down again. This time she did not want to start afresh. She wanted nothing more of any of it.

A young woman came out of the house carrying two buckets. Her coat was filthy and the loose soles of her boots dragged over the surface of the stone yard. Maggie could see her ginger matted hair and the ambling way she walked, could see her dirty face and sullen expression. For a moment the woman stopped, put down her buckets and looked up towards her. Neither of them moved or made any gesture. They just stared at each other across this quiet space before the woman picked up her buckets and disappeared into one of the out sheds. Maggie turned and started back. Even this idea had been a waste of time. So she had seen this Floss Sugden and all this had done was make the whole thing about Ethan even more depressing. He must have been desperate to do it with such a rough, slovenly looking woman. She might have been young but that was all. It was pathetic and disgusting that he had reached such a state. She was so angry that he could have failed his family in this way, angry and frustrated.

With these thoughts repeatedly going around in her mind she returned to Batty Green. It was strange to be in the hut by herself. Time passed slowly. She could always pop next door and have a blether with Shirley but she did not feel in the mood for drinking tea and suffering her neighbour's questions. So she did some washing, some sewing, started on the dinner, went out for more coal, more water, walked down to the few stalls to buy a few things and then waited for Clare to return.

That night Fraser came back earlier than usual so the three of them sat down to an early dinner. Maggie had suspected that there was something on his mind, something he wanted to say to her. He seemed more irritable than usual, more on edge. He kept glancing at Clare and she could not understand what was bothering him until finally he said, 'I was just thinking.'

'Steady Fraser,' Maggie immediately responded in her sarcastic way which she often did with him, 'Yer not used to thinking, remember.'

'Oh ay Missus, the usual from you,' he said back just a little too strongly, 'I was thinking that now there's just the three of us.'

Maggie went cold suddenly knowing what was coming. Her stomach sank as her brain stoked up a fast furnace of anger, sheer bloody anger.

'What about it?' she asked already knowing the answer.

'Well seeing as we're still using two bedrooms I........'

'Yer think we should have more lodgers,' she interrupted.

He frowned and clattered down his knife and fork saying, 'You're not listening.'

'Mam, let Fraser say what he wants to say,' Clare put in.

Her mother gave her a disgusted look which only confused Clare even more.

'Please let me finish.'

'Go on then, finish what yer have to say.'

'Well I was thinking me and Clare could share. Instead of her with you she could.....'

'Be wi you?'

'Yes. She's a good girl.'

'Fraser, don't,' Clare suddenly started pleading, 'don't say nowt else.'

'A good girl,' he continued, 'accommodating, generous and I just thought that seeing as me and her get on....get on so well together....we could.........'

'Yer can stop right there!' Maggie exclaimed as she stood up so quickly she knocked over her chair, her fists tightened, her arms beginning to shake.

'I was only saying.'

'Mum, leave it,' Clare gasped, as though she too now knew what was coming, 'he don't....Fraser don't....'

'I know exactly what Fraser means and what he wants,' she said back, 'I've known all along and there was your father thinking there was nowt wrong when this disgusting thing of a man was plotting his filthy ways. Disgusting! You're disgusting, do yer hear? You're sick in the head so you keep away from my daughter! You keep right away from her!'

'I want her to be with me,' he said more forcefully.

His face exploded in surprise and bewilderment as Maggie hit him as hard as she could sending him stumbling over his chair.

'Get yer things, now Clare!'

The girl stood there not knowing what to do.

'I said start packing yer things, right now Clare, now!' Maggie was shouting at her, 'get to the bedroom and ….'

'There's no fucking need fer that,' Fraser interrupted as he steadied himself.

'Go on!' repeated Maggie to her daughter.

'I was just….'

Clare!'

'Mam I….'

'Get yer things packed cos we're going and we're going now and I'm not going to tell yer again. Get out of my way!' she shouted as Fraser tried to stop them, 'or I'll bloody do the same as Bill did to yer, you disgusting animal! Get out of the way!'

He lifted his hand only for Clare to scream at him, 'Fraser no! No! Leave me Mam alone!'

'Fucking hell,' he muttered, 'what a fucking pair you two are.'

Before he could say anything else they were in the bedroom with the door slammed shut behind them.

'Where are we going Mam?' Clare asked in desperation as a short time later they were going over the Beck bridge and up onto the road in the drizzle and cold wind.

They were carrying all the bags they could manage and Maggie was walking so hard that her daughter was struggling to keep up with her.

'Home,' she said loudly.

'What do yer mean?'

'Nottingham. We're going back to where we belong, that's where.'

'But we….we can't just leave like this.'

'Yes we can Clare and we are.'

'Fraser meant nowt by it.'

'I don't want that man's named mentioned to me ever again, do yer hear?' Maggie shouted as she stopped and violently swung round to Clare who stepped back quickly, 'do yer hear me?'

They continued having to walk along the sodden grass verge next to the wall to avoid the mud filled road.

'We ain't said goodbye to Alice and Sissy or Shirley or the other lasses,' Clare bravely started her complaints.

'We've no time fer that now. We're going and that's that.'

With their shawls tightly covering their heads they were bent into the icy westerly wind. The bottoms of their coats and boots were already clogged with mud as they struggled with the heavy bags strapped to their backs and hanging over each shoulder. Clare stumbled and almost fell, her thin, pale features distraught and shocked. She had never seen her mother so angry, so furious.

They were the only figures this late afternoon walking the road as the light dimmed and the clouds lowered.

'This ain't right,' Clare tried again but her mother made no answer.

Gradually she slowed letting Maggie go on ahead, the rain whipping up the Dale against them until the girl was a long way behind before her mother stopped and called, 'Come on Clare!'

Her daughter stopped, pulled the bag off her shoulder and dropped the other one she was carrying. In frustration Maggie had to come back to her.

'What yer doing Clare?'

'I don't want to go Mam.'

'Well yer are.'

'Please, no Mam.'

'We're not staying in this place a minute longer. We're leaving Ribblehead and we're getting the train to Nottingham and that's that. It's my decision and yer going to have to put up wi it so pick up them bags and let's get going before we get soaked.'

Clare looked at her with an utterly desperate expression, the rain dripping off the edge of her shawl.

'I need yer with me Clare. We have to stick together, I told yer that. And I'm not letting a daughter of mine think she can shack up wi that disgusting sod of a man, not on my life, so you'd better get that in yer head.'

'I'm just fed up.'

'I know.'

'Leaving just like that, wi no word or owt.'

'It has to be like this.'

'Don't see why.'

They turned quickly at the rattle of a cart approaching from behind.

'What's up you two, gone far enough have yer?' the carter called as he pulled his two horses to a halt.

'Just making our way to Ingleton station,' Maggie told him.

'Well climb on up then the pair o yer.'

'Are yer sure?'

'Corse I'm sure. I'm not having two ladies trudging along in this weather when they could be on me cart and down in Ingleton in no time.'

Maggie swung her bags up onto the seat and then clambered up after them.

'Come on,' she said then to Clare who did not move. 'Clare yer have to come. Yer can't leave yer Mam like this, yer just can't. I'm asking, I'm begging yer to come wi us.'

The carter listened but said nothing as they both waited to see what the girl would do.

Finally she said strongly, 'It ain't fair,' and then threw her bags up and joined her mother.

'No it certainly ain't fair lass on a day like this,' added the driver

The horses trudged on down the road. Maggie tried to take Clare's hand but she pulled it away. When they came to the turn off to Chapel le Dale Maggie suddenly asked the driver to stop.

'Nay, this ain't Ingleton unless it's changed a lot over the last few hours.'

'I want us to stop here,' Maggie repeated as she climbed over Clare and onto the ground.

Puzzled and uncertain the girl followed her dragging down all their bags.

'Are yer sure like?'

'Thank yer for the ride,' Maggie answered.

'Well it's another couple o miles to the town if that's where yer finally going,' the driver informed them before jerking the reins of his horses to set them in motion.

'Why have we got off here?' Clare asked sullenly as she walked after her mother over the moss covered bridge, past the vicarage and into the church yard. Clare waited near the gate as her mother started looking around.

'There's nowt here,' she announced when she came back.

'There won't be,' Clare explained, 'it's just a plot o land the navvies and their families have been given. Fraser....I mean Bill told us.'

They walked to the edge of the church yard to where there was the rough stretch of ground, the low walls on three sides. The ground had some freshly dug humps of soil where the most recent graves had been dug and a few wooden makeshift crosses put up.

'One of them'll be me Dad's' said Clare as they set their bags down, 'and our Beth will be somewhere.'

'God almighty,' Maggie sighed, 'just this.'

'Except Bill said the names and age and reasons for em dying are in the church register wherever that is.'

'The church register,' Maggie repeated in an empty voice.

She did not know what to expect, but not this, just this rough piece of ground where so many from Ribblehead were buried. It was disgusting. It was tragic and beyond words that people were here with so little to show who or where they had been buried.

'It's shameful,' she said, 'There's......there's nothing.'

She then realised it would be the same for everything else that was at Ribblehead. Like these graves, all of it would disappear. There would be a railway line, a viaduct and a tunnel but not a thing left to show how many people had lived and died building them. Here lay her husband and her daughter and yet there was nothing to mark their graves, just a stretch of coarse grass and a few mounds of earth.

Darkness had fallen when they finally walked out of the church yard, the two of them walking together now, across the bridge over the raging beck and up onto the road.

CHAPTER SIXTY

The author thought the reader might like to know what happened to the main characters in this historical novel.

The first train crossed the Ribblehead viaduct in August 1875.

A passenger can travel over the viaduct nowadays and look down on either side and see not a sign that settlements with a population of over fifteen hundred people once lived and worked there. There is nothing but rough grass, moorland and sheep.

Maggie and her daughter Clare set up a successful washing and sewing business in a back street of Nottingham and thrived thereafter.

Jane Herbert became a governess and years later retired to live alone in a small flat in Scarborough.

Her cousin James Tranton died of malaria while working as a missionary in Central Africa.

Lizzie Twistelton married a local farm labourer and had five children, three who survived into adulthood.

Lucy Ormskill met and married a wealthy cloth manufacturer and lived with him in a large mansion in its own grounds in Cheshire. They had two sons who both became well established lawyers.

Richard Stockton continued his successful career as an engineer working in the Rocky Mountains of both the United States and Canada. He never married.

Tom Myres also emigrated to the United States where he was involved in industrial riots in Chicago before moving West.

Bill Asquith died of pneumonia in a Rochdale boarding house three weeks after leaving Batty Green.

Fraser Henderson was hanged in Strangeways for the murder of a thirteen year old girl.

None of those who survived ever visited Ribblehead again.